THE OUTRAGEOUS
FORTUNE OF
ABEL MORGAN

THE OUTRAGEOUS
FORTUNE OF
ABEL MORGAN

CYNTHIA JEFFERIES

Allison & Busby Limited
11 Wardour Mews
London W1F 8AN
allisonandbusby.com

First published in Great Britain by Allison & Busby in 2018.
This paperback edition published by Allison & Busby in 2019.

A CIP catalogue record for this book is available from
the British Library.

10 9 8 7 6 5 4 3 2 1

ISBN 978-0-7490-2334-8

Typeset in 10.5/15.5 pt Adobe Garamond Pro by

For my children,
Gavin Landless, Rebecca Henderson and Sebastian Goffe
In memory of my good friend Caroline Van Oss

CHRISTOPHER MORGAN

1

It was deep night when the coach reached Dario. Time was lost to him but, somehow, he must have packed his belongings and put himself on it, for he had been carried along for many hours. The coachman roused him with a growl and he realised he was the only remaining passenger. The unmatched pair of horses fidgeted as the coachman untied Christopher's box and let it drop onto the road. Christopher clambered out. Steam from the sweating horses rose up into the cold night air like mist from a sullen lake in the moonlight. Christopher reached back into the coach for his leather travelling bag. Almost before he had taken it and closed the door, the coachman whipped up the horses. Startled by their lightened load, they set off at a canter, kicking up the road grit. Christopher bent his head against the cloud of dust that engulfed him, holding the edge of his cloak over his mouth. By the time he lifted his head, the coach had gone and the only living thing was a fox, sniffing at a midden before leaping onto a low wall and disappearing under some gorse.

The Rumfustian Inn seemed smaller and older than when he had bought it. The great grey stones of its walls seemed to grow out of the ground, and the low roof undulated under its thatch. In the centre of the building was a broad, heavy door, with a small window to either side. Smoke came from a chimney, and the windows were dimly lit. There was sound, too: the rumble of voices and occasional laughter. Christopher shrank from the idea of company, but he must have a bed to rest his aching bones. And he could be relieved that someone was awake at this hour to give him entry. He closed his eyes for a moment but, open or closed, the same terrible memory was still being played in his head.

Time must have passed. He was chilled now, shivering in his long cloak and dust-grimed hat. He stooped to pick up his bag and left the box in the road.

It was a few short steps to the great oak door. It felt fissured under his hand, like the face of an old man, but the latch lifted cleanly and the door swung wide with hardly a sound. As he stepped in, the lintel knocked his hat askew so that he saw only a portion of the room. It was warm, even hot, with a great fire burning high in the hearth. Christopher had not been so close to such a generous fire since before his exile. Even the King had been forced to be parsimonious with fuel, relying as they all did on the generosity of others. To have a hot fire so late in the night must mean a great store of wood, or perhaps a festival of some sort.

The room was crowded. Surely, almost every man in the village must be here. All were making merry and, at first, the silently opened door attracted no attention. But, as the draught touched the nearest drinkers, they twitched with the sudden chill, turned and saw Christopher hesitating in the doorway. Soon, all were staring at him with eyes that looked alarmed, even hostile, and every voice became silenced.

Christopher knew that strangers were often viewed with suspicion in the countryside, especially so late into the night when few honest travellers were abroad. He might be the new owner of the inn, but he was certainly not expected. Mr Gazely, who had sold him the Rumfustian, had agreed to stay and look after it until such time as Christopher could safely bring his young wife across the country to take up residence. But Christopher looked for him without success. He put his bag carefully down and righted his hat before closing the door behind him. As he turned back to face the room, his eyes met those of a middle-aged man staring at him. The man looked pale and frightened, as if Christopher might be a ghost. This was the servant, William, who, along with his wife, Christopher had bought with the inn to brew and serve beer, cook and generally do his bidding. As Christopher attempted to form his mouth into a smile of greeting, William looked ever more like a dog expecting a whipping. Christopher attempted to speak, but the obstruction in his throat, which had been there as long as his latest sorrow, strangled most of his words. He had wanted to form a reassuring question, but it sounded more like a demand.

'Mr Gazely?'

The name prompted a murmur from the assembled company, and the switching of attention away from Christopher towards the hapless William. However, it wasn't William who replied, but a man Christopher had not so far noticed. He sat at a table near the fire, along with an elderly man and several lads who looked so alike they must be of the same family. While most of the other drinkers held tankards, he had a glass of some spirit. A small gold hoop in his ear sparked in the firelight.

'Gone, sir,' was his remark to Christopher. 'This forenoon.'

One of the lads at his table laughed, but the man silenced him with a look.

Before the man could add more, William found his tongue, pushing his way between several drinkers to come close to where Christopher stood.

'Mr Morgan, sir!'

Everyone redirected their attention to the servant. He blushed deeply but ploughed doggedly on.

'I'm sorry, sir, not to have recognised you at once, but . . . we weren't expecting you so soon . . .' He glanced at the man at the table and then quickly away. 'I do apologise, sir, but I'm sure all of Dario would want to welcome the new owner of the Rumfustian Inn.'

The silence was so solid it could have been sliced.

'I want no ceremony, William,' said Christopher, finding his voice, 'just a bed prepared, for I am very weary. I am sorry to arrive so late and without notice. Did Mr Gazely give word as to when he will return?'

William shook his head and the man at the table cut neatly in. 'He will not return, sir. In this inn, we are as you see us, rudderless and in need of a captain – but no doubt a bed can be found.' He raised his glass to Christopher and took a nip of the liquor. 'SALLY!'

His sudden shout made Christopher jump. He couldn't recall the man, but he seemed to have no difficulty in acting the host. Perhaps he had been a friend of Mr Gazely.

A young girl, no more than a child, presented herself to the man at the table, but he pointed her towards Christopher and busied himself with enjoying his drink.

'I will show you to your room, sir,' she said to Christopher.

'Thank you.' Christopher retrieved his bag and followed. The drinkers moved aside to let him past, but none met his eyes or spoke. Christopher wondered if there was some form of greeting he should give them. 'Perhaps you could ensure everyone gets a drink as a welcome from me?' He looked at William. Although the man nodded, Christopher had the uncomfortable feeling that it had not been the right thing to say. A quickly stifled guffaw came from the other side of the room. Christopher looked to see who had laughed, but it was impossible to tell. As he turned back to William, the movement slightly opened the front of his cloak. William, being so close, was the only person who could have seen what lay beneath. With terror on his face, he stepped back into a table. A bottle upon it juddered and almost fell. Neither man spoke, but Christopher pulled his cloak across his body once more.

'My box,' he said quietly. 'It is in the road. Please bring it to my room.'

He followed Sally's flickering figure. At the stairs, she held her candle up to light his way. It was a generous, well-made staircase, but over the years the green oak had settled eccentrically into its foundation, and Christopher had to tread carefully on the sloping timbers. Along a groaning passage and around a corner . . . Sally seemed to have forgotten him, but the shadows on the wall showed him that she had stopped, and he reached her without mishap. She was entering a room. He hesitated but, seeing her light another candle and then kneel to a laid fire, he surmised that the room must be his.

The infant fire soon caught from her candle. She piled some fragments of peat onto the twigs and then sat back on her heels to await the fire's progress. She hesitated after adding some sticks, but Christopher was impatient.

'I can tend the fire. Go . . . Stay!'

She had stood up and now looked curiously at him, seeming unafraid of her new master.

'Bring me some beer.'

She reached the door.

'And perhaps some bread?'

He wasn't sure if she had heard the last muttered order, but he couldn't bring himself to call her back again. He took off his cloak and hung it from a nail on the door. Then, after depositing a bundle on the bed, he removed his hat, scattering grit all around. It crunched underfoot as he tossed the hat onto a small table and seated himself in a chair at the hearth. He busied himself with the fire, adding more wood and nudging it with his boot until it fell together in a burning heap. Staring at the fire, he fell into an exhausted stupor while figures danced in the flames, unendingly replaying the tragedy in his head.

The woman might have knocked, but he didn't hear her. The first he noticed was her sturdy figure standing near his elbow, staring with fearful concentration at the region of his stomach. In her hands she held a pewter mug and plate, both dinted. When he moved his head to look at her, she jumped as if a devil had landed on her back. Beer slopped from the mug and she almost lost the contents of the plate, some bread and a piece of yellow cheese. He hadn't met her before. She was of middle age and with a face, if it had not been so alarmed, that would have been warm and friendly. It was the face of a servant who looked comfortable with her place and used to knowing more than was required of her.

Christopher found himself flattening the fabric of his shirt to his chest in response to her staring. 'Is something amiss?'

'No, sir.' She sounded more puzzled than convinced as she moved to the table, where she laid down her burden. 'You asked Sally for beer, sir, and I thought to bring you something to eat, in case you were hungry.' They stared at each other for a moment, each elsewhere in their thoughts. Being a servant, she recovered herself first. 'I'm Jane, sir, William's wife . . .' She was trying to keep her eyes on him, but he could see that they kept darting away, examining the room and especially his belongings.

'Is William attending to my box?'

She looked away from his cloak, hanging as it was like a dark, empty shroud. 'Yes, indeed . . .'

'Then please tell him to bring it up.' It sounded as if the revellers were ending their evening. Through the cracks in the boards there came from below much noisy scraping of stools, tramping of feet and unmistakable farewells. 'I don't want it carried off and lost to me.'

'It's secure, sir. Harold Pierce, the roadman, and William brought it in. It sits in the passage, safe enough for now.'

Two steps took her towards the door and past the bed. She glanced at the bundle and gave a gasp. 'Oh, God save us!' A pause. And then, 'Is it dead?'

'Yes.' He didn't look at it or her.

After a few moments, she was once more at his side. He ignored her and concentrated on the flames, although he was aware of her agitated presence.

'Sir. Sir!' Her voice was unsteady. As he continued to ignore her, she ventured to touch his sleeve. 'It lives, sir! Its heart is beating. But it is very weak. It needs nourishment and . . .'

'I gave it beer . . . but it will die.' His voice, too, was dying.

She was impatient with him. 'But while it breathes, surely . . . You cannot mean to let it die with no attempt to save it?'

It was those last five words that forced him to turn to her. He didn't realise his tears were visible. He thought they were inside his head, as his grief was. Only, through his blurred eyes, he saw her expression alter from urgency to pity. And he could not speak. She said some words.

'Do I have your permission . . . ?'

The nod was hardly perceptible, but she saw it. First, she bundled out of the room like a whirlwind, leaving all behind. It was quiet now, below. Then came her voice and her husband's. She sounding like a scold, he floating up angry and then conciliatory. Eventually, the great door banged and her footsteps were audible, tramping up the stairs and along to his room. She was breathing heavily as she entered, sounding as if she had just run a race.

She brought life and energy and urgency with her, but stopped it up as she reached his side, as if this was hallowed ground. He was twisted away from her in his chair, staring again at the fire, as if all he wished for were there.

'May I . . . pick it up?'

He turned to her, then, and his voice came as a rising sob.

'What use is there in that? It will still die . . .' And without warning he collapsed against her, as a tree might fall against another in the wood, leaning his head against her ribs, clutching her skirts with fingers like twigs.

For a few seconds she was struck dumb, then she began to talk quietly in a soft, soothing voice.

'It's all right. It'll come right, it will. So, calm yourself. And William is sorry but he caught just a glimpse when your cloak

14

opened, and he thought it was a devil creature, God save us . . . hush now . . . an imp, like the paintings in the old church down the way, foolish man that he is . . . There's one with a devil coming from a man's belly, Lord bless us, and it frightened him so as a child, when he'd gone there for a dare . . . nightmares he's had for many years, but he's sorry . . .' She kept her voice low and calm, paying no more attention to his sobs. Her words wove a little repair into his tattered mind, meaning being less important to him than her gentle tone. 'If he'd known, he wouldn't for the world . . . it was just . . . he wasn't expecting . . . you a gentleman and all . . . he'd never imagined a gentleman with such a thing . . . and no woman to care for it. We knew you were bringing your wife once she had birthed . . . so did she die, then? I know it feels like the world has ended but all will come right in the end. Be still now. William's gone . . . to ask the blacksmith's wife if she'll come down and see to it, so, you know all will be well. Her babe isn't more than three months and she has plenty of milk . . . so don't you fret . . . it's all well now . . .'

She tried to move away then, but he only held on more tightly, his body shaking as he wept. She began hesitantly to touch his tangled hair and his back, stroking both gently and constantly, while all the time continuing her quiet talk. Slowly, his grip loosened as he became calmer. Now there were voices again in the room below, William and a woman, querulous, complaining, being hushed. Jane spoke again in the same calm, gentle voice. 'That's her now,' she said. 'She will do her best for it, put it to the breast, and she can stay here tonight if you wish it, stay close, keep it warm and safe, warm and safe . . .'

With that, she gave his hair a last caress and dared to put her arm around him, holding him reassuringly close. When she released him this time, he let her go. She went to the bed and picked up the motionless form of the infant, still talking to Christopher in the same way. 'Now it's wrapped in two shirts, I see . . . we'll leave the one here. I told William to be sure Margaret brought an extra shawl, and I can make clouts. I have old linen here. I can use that for swaddling, and it'll sleep with her in the bed and be warm that way.'

Christopher watched her through his hair and she showed she was aware of his gaze, bringing the bundle for him to see. When he showed signs of wanting to take it from her, she resisted, softly but firmly. 'Now, they'll be in the next room and not far at all. What you must do is pray for it, as we all shall, and then sleep, for it's up to God now and Margaret to do her best . . . but its heart beats still, for all it's so quiet. I'll be back in a moment to make the fire safe and put you to bed, so don't you fret.'

He was still in the chair when she returned without the infant. He made no protest when she knelt and removed his shoes and stockings. He stood like a child for her to remove his jacket and britches. She led him to the bed in his shirt, not asking if he had a nightshirt with him. Pulling back the covers, she helped him in and tucked him up. He turned away from her and lay on his side in the cold bed, while she attended to the fire and blew out the candle. Once she had left, he sat up and felt for the shirt he had used to swaddle the baby. Dragging it under the cover with him, he wrapped his arms around it and huddled with its scent to his face, waiting for sleep.

2

His dreams buffeted him as if he were standing on a steeply shelving beach facing an ocean of losses, all rolled into one unrelenting wave. It was as if he were attempting to wade while wearing his boots and heavy jacket. The grief sucked at his unconscious body, pulling him hopelessly under. It rolled him in its breakers and tossed him onto sliding shingle where he sought and failed to keep his feet. It soaked him through, filling him up with its cold misery until he leaked from his eyes, even in his sleep, bitter salt tears. If he could die, he would be at peace, but grief refused to consume him. His heart still pumped and his lungs still breathed, in spite of him drowning.

When Christopher woke he felt queasy, as if the sea still washed within him. At first, he did not know where he was. When he remembered, he discovered that having crawled exhausted into bed, he now found it impossible to rise. It was not that his legs were weak, but his resolve had quite left him. Far from this place being a new beginning, he felt it was the place where his life was about to end. He did not want to be told of the moment when his infant child ceased to breathe. He had already accepted that inevitability. Thinking of the babe made images of his dead wife caper horribly in his head. The yells of the blacksmith's lusty infant made his loss the harder to bear and the only way he could gain some relief was to force his mind to recall incidences of his earlier life. And so, while the business of the inn carried on much as it had for close on two hundred years, its new owner lay upstairs, fighting to find a reason to live.

Cocooned in his nest, he thought of his long-dead mother. Her face was mostly remembered in a portrait that had hung in the great hall at home, a moated manor, slighted during the war, burnt and now little more than a heap of building stone. Her scent could be conjured, and the particular rustle of her dress. Christopher had a clear memory of sitting, splay-legged, hidden under her skirts, feeling entirely at peace. It must have been long before he was breeched. That important day he could clearly remember. The suit of adult clothes arriving from London, being dressed in them and proudly going to show his father. He remembered wearing the miniature sword, which his father had owned before him, on the occasion of *his* being dressed for the first time as a man. How he had cried when it became clear the next day that the sword was not his to play with, but only to be worn on special occasions. Injustice had burnt within him for a week, but then the freedom of breeches instead of tangling dresses was so delightful that the sword was soon forgotten, especially as play swords aplenty were to be had in the nearest hedgerow.

He slept a little more, to be woken by the girl, Sally, drawing the curtains. He could not bear the light and so she drew them over again, left meat and drink on his table and went to her other chores.

Urgency made him rise to use the pot. He drank a little but could not eat. Sliding once more into the warmth of his bed, he kept his mind on the past, frightened as he was for his sanity if he allowed the present to intrude. His father had provided him with both sword and pistol at the beginning of the war, before they buried the plate, his mother's jewels and as much money as they could spare. Plate, jewels and most of the money had been found and taken by others. The remaining cache of coins he had was now mostly spent, and the pistol and sword he had thrown away on that dreadful day when Worcester was lost.

He had long since ceased thinking there was anything honourable about the act of fighting. It was a grunting, sweating, close quarters meeting of men he would prefer to argue with than kill. Had he killed? It was difficult to tell. He had caused wounds, yes, and had a line of puckered skin along one arm as his own evidence of engagement. How many of those wounds he had inflicted had proved fatal? The ball from his pistol that had lodged in that man's face? He had gone down with a scream and had been trampled over in the narrow street by his own men. Everyone had been afraid of losing their footing on the slick cobbles of Worcester. Christopher remembered that. He remembered having, during the war, a prolonged and heightened state of fear, leavened by ennui while waiting to engage. During the rout, when he fled, along with others, hiding wherever they could, fear consumed him. He had got across the Channel, at last, for the price of a month's hard graft harvesting turnips, as well as all the money he had. Once safe from the militia, in France, it took him some time to find out where he should go, with rumours of his king being killed, arrested, or in hiding. He had been just one of that ragtag of disheartened, traumatised young men in exile, trying to find their way to their nation.

Christopher turned onto his back and stared at the darkness. He had always tried to view his escape to France as lucky, even though it was a prelude to years of wandering the continent as a pauper. Should he thank God that he still had his head upon his neck or that he hadn't been pressed into the New Model Army and sent to rot in Ireland? He didn't pretend to understand the convoluted behaviour of God, striking one down, sparing another, allowing so much suffering of the godly, and innocent children. But that was dangerous ground.

It had been a lucky chance that had brought word to his ears that Charles had landed just down the coast from where he was attempting to keep his body and soul as one. Yes, he could admit that as luck. And so, too, the luck that had made raw the prince's feet while in disguise, though not so very lucky for the prince. Lucky, though, that Christopher should arrive in time to offer Charles his own shoes, having – yes, by good fortune for them both – similar sized overlarge feet. And lucky that his height made him memorable. Such ridiculous serendipity made Christopher despair at the unevenness of life. But it had made him a junior member of this dishevelled court and, for a while, a friend of the king-in-waiting. It was not true friendship, not the friendship of equals – he had always known that – but Charles had been grateful and said so. Christopher even got his shoes back, once Charles's mother had ordered her son a new pair made. In fact, Christopher had them still, much patched, or at least he thought he did . . . if he had stuffed them into his box, which had been brought up and lay untouched under the window.

He turned over again and looked at the dark shape of his box. He should get up, unpack a few necessaries and go down to take mastery of his realm. He willed his body up, but it refused. What was the use? Everything he loved had gone and he, a gentleman, had come now to this, owner of nothing but an ancient, slipshod building at the edge of a nondescript village that would oblige him to be in trade for the rest of his days. How had he got himself into this apology for a life? He could have taken himself to the newly restored court in London, asked for favour as one who had shared the King's years of wandering. But those thoughts were taking him dangerously close to memories of meeting his wife and what came after. He shied away from that. He should get up, be a man, deflect himself from dismal thoughts. He did rise then and crossed the creaking boards to the window. He looked out onto the high road. Few people were about. It was another dry day, but no sun shone.

He put his hand on his box but could not bring himself to unstrap it. He was too weary, too weary to live.

The next time he woke the day had gone and it was evening again. Light seeped up through gaps between the boards on his floor and he gazed at them, these shafts of light from a separate world. No doubt there was a good fire in the huge hearth and candles on the tables, as before. It was quiet though, nothing like the hubbub when he'd arrived. He wondered if the inn made as good a profit as Mr Gazely had assured him. The crowd busy drinking on the night he arrived had certainly given that impression, but tonight it sounded as if William was selling little ale. It had been quiet during the day too. Perhaps Jane had impressed upon each customer the importance of quiet as a form of respect for his circumstances or maybe this day of the week . . . and which it was he couldn't recall . . . was usually quiet. It struck him that his Oxford education would be of little use to him now. How many of these people could read or write their native language, let alone Latin and Greek? There were several volumes of poetry in his box. With whom would he enjoy and discuss these pleasures now?

He looked away from the light in the cracks on the floor, and away from the meat and drink that he had not touched. Although he had slept for many hours he was still exhausted and slept again, yet his dreams as always were full of terror. When he woke once more it was still dark, but a thin sliver of grey light slid from the window where he had not completely closed the curtain. All at once, he felt he could not bear another minute on his back. Before his mind could object, he had lowered his feet to the floor and staggered up on legs that felt foolish with inaction. It was cold. He pulled the curtains wide to let as much dawn or dusk light in as possible. He could see that there was no fuel ready in the hearth. He lit a candle and stood it on the table to aid the examination of his box. He smelt rancid to himself, but there was no water in the bowl with which to wash. He dragged off his shirt and replaced it with the one he had used to swaddle the baby. Then he wrapped his cloak around himself and took a sip of the beer. In a moment he had drained the tankard. He had not realised he was so thirsty.

To prevent himself from seeking the warmth of his bed yet again, he began to walk to keep warm. It was only a few paces from the table to the door to the hearth, and hence to the window, but it did him good. Sharp grit from the floor bit into the soft places on his feet and made him feel more alive. As soon as he felt able to tackle his box, he knelt in front of it and undid the straps. It was packed full of a miscellany of possessions. The box had not been fully unpacked after the journey from Holland to Norfolk with his wife. The top layer was a jumbled mess of linen, books, a small box with his remaining money inside and his journal. There was also, to his relief, his second suit, much worn but serviceable enough. He took it out, along with some clean linen, and laid everything on the bed. It was getting lighter. Soon, surely, the servants would be up and he would command some hot water be brought and soap if they had it. Then, clean, refreshed and dressed, he would feel better able to make the journey downstairs. He wouldn't allow himself to think any further than that.

3

It was the child, Sally, who came again, to take away yesterday's food and ask if he wanted more. For a moment she didn't notice him where he sat, wrapped in his cloak and coverlet and hunched in his chair. When she did, she stared at him before speaking.

'Did you want me to lay the fire, sir?'

'No. I want hot water in that bowl. And soap.'

'The kitchen fire is not hot enough yet, sir.'

He looked at her. 'Then, with as much haste as you can muster. I do not wish to wash in cold water.'

'No, sir.'

The water when it eventually came was steaming. It gave his body pleasure, as did the donning of clean garments. He told himself that all would be well, as the anchorite Julian of Norwich had it, but she had believed in God's goodness. He no longer trusted in God, or anything else. It seemed he could not even rely on himself. He must go down and confront the day, but the courage he had used to slash at his enemy's head in battle did not seem to be of any great use against grief. It was not that he thought himself special. Many others had lived these past years with just as great or greater disasters than he had suffered. So why could he not be a man and face his life as it was? He had all his limbs and both his eyes. He had a roof of sorts over his head and servants to do his bidding. He had, he hoped, the means of putting food in his belly by mastering the trick of being the owner of an inn. William and Jane must know what they were about. He could manage servants. He could, he thought, inspire loyalty and so make them want to serve him well. He was not afraid of account books. But he was afraid of his heart. He was afraid that it was dying and, in so doing, taking his will for life away from him and replacing it with a will for self-destruction. In the face of that unholy desire, even a man such as he, with little faith remaining, feared hell.

A sudden shaft of early spring sunlight slanted into the room, making the grey ash in the hearth seem for a moment lit by pale yellow flame. The simple arrival of the sun transformed the room. In the dark it had seemed a place of refuge; now it looked to him tawdry, grimed and a mess. The bed was unmade, the floor was gritty underfoot and the table was strewn with crumbs, dust and a bowl of dirty water. Discarded clothes lay tumbled on the floor. As for the chair, it had held his shaking body as he disgraced himself by weeping into the skirts of a servant. It all shamed him, but if he could just bring himself to leave the room he could, surely, begin to find himself again.

The trick of it was to act, not to think. His legs had got him out of bed, his hands had washed and dressed him. Now his hand would open the door and guide his body along the corridor, down the stairs and into his world as it was today and would be henceforth. It faltered, that hand, but he willed it with all his strength, and he found that he was indeed walking along a corridor lined with dark panelling, pierced halfway along its length on one side by a window and on the other by two doors. He had no memory of walking it before, but once he stepped upon the stairs it was better. He recalled them, with their wayward slant. He trod them slowly, getting their feel beneath his feet and their sound into his head, while his hand slid easily down the bannister worn smooth by countless hands before him. Once down in the stone-flagged passage, he looked about him. To his left was a closed door and to his right one stood open, one he remembered. It led him into the room he had first entered from the road.

The room smelt of stale beer, woodsmoke and unwashed bodies – though none were in evidence. It looked abandoned. Sun was struggling in at the grimy windows, but where he was standing all was gloom and shadow. The great door was shut, the tables empty and several mugs stood about, as if their owners had left in a hurry.

It struck Christopher that his first view of the inn, when he had met Mr Gazely and been impressed at the jolly nature of the place, had been mistaken. Then he had not noticed the grime. Now it offended him. How could he have thought to bring his wife and babe to such a place? The good oak settles had not been polished for years, perhaps never. How clean and ordered in comparison had been the home in Holland of his wife's parents. After his years of homeless wandering, their comfortable and attractive home had soothed his heart. He had wanted to provide the same for his young family, but this was not it. No matter. He had no family. If this was what the village men demanded of their inn, then who was he to argue? But he could at least make sure his own quarters were kept sweet, swept and polished, and his linen washed. He left the room and went in search of his servants. Rather than call for them he would surprise them in their quarters. That was the way to discover how things really were.

Next on his right was the small parlour where he and Mr Gazely had conducted their business. When he opened the opposite door, he discovered steps leading down into a cellar. He closed that door and made his way along the passage, towards the kitchen. He stood for a moment in the doorway, taking in the scene. A small fire was burning in the hearth with a pot above it, and at the large table Jane was busy making pastry. Sally was scrubbing turnips in a bowl on the floor. It was a scene of quiet industry and Christopher was almost disappointed. There was nothing here to complain of and, besides, the smell of the broth bubbling away over the fire had given him a sudden appetite. Perhaps it was lack of direction, rather than laziness, that allowed the inn to be less cared for than it should be. As he was making up his mind to demand some broth, William came in from the outside door, carrying a basket of logs. He was the first to see Christopher and made haste to put down his load to better greet the master. Christopher didn't miss the swift glances exchanged between his servants. It was natural for them to be discomfited at him arriving unannounced in their domain. He wanted to set down his rules for the household as speedily as possible, but his recent loss made him feel vulnerable. He needed to be liked. The compassion shown to him by Jane had shamed him, but her welcoming smile, dutiful but genuine, made him trust her and he found it easiest to speak first to her.

'Are you making a pie, Jane?'

'I am, sir.'

'I look forward to tasting it.'

She looked embarrassed. 'I can make another . . .'

'She only means that the pie she is making is . . . ordered . . . for . . . a customer.' William appeared as unhappy as his wife, but Sally, looking up from her scrubbing, showed no such trouble on her face.

'He does like his pies, does Daniel Johnson. Best not cross him on that!'

Christopher smiled at her. 'I would not wish a good customer to go without. By all means, Jane, make another. But while I am waiting I find I am very hungry. Would I be robbing this Mr Johnson if I had some of that broth?'

Jane went at once to the fire and ladled a little of the broth into a bowl. 'I can bring it to you in the parlour, sir.'

'But there is no fire in the parlour.' Christopher found he preferred the company of his servants to his own. 'I will have it here.'

He made to sit on a nearby stool, but William wouldn't have it. 'I will fetch you a chair from the parlour, sir.'

He bustled away down the passage and returned with a chair the twin of the one in Christopher's room. He set it to one side of the hearth, close enough but not too close to the heat of the fire. Christopher sat, feeling somehow chastised, but the broth and a heel of bread soaked in it did as much good to the inside of his body as the wash and fresh clothing had done for the outside. He realised, as he enjoyed the fire, that this was the first time since he was a child that he'd had a proper home, and the first time ever he had one to call his own. The thought, and the knowledge that he had no one to share it with, sent a pricking behind his eyes that threatened to overwhelm him, so he shifted in his chair and set his empty bowl on the hearth. It was removed and replaced almost immediately with a mug of beer.

'William?'

'Yes, sir?'

'I will need to speak to you about the running of the inn: the brewing of the beer, the purchase of spirits, the renting of rooms . . . I freely acknowledge I have much to learn. I intend to be fully involved with the inn and I have certain standards I wish to impose. This room seems clean enough, but as for the rest . . . they are not. I wish the furniture to be polished and the floors swept.' He looked at Jane. 'If you need to engage someone to help you then that must be done.' She nodded. 'But today I want my room cleaned properly, my linen washed as soon as may be and my suit brushed.'

'We will all do our best for you, sir.' She looked troubled and hesitant, as if speaking was painful. 'Do you not wish to know about your son?'

He did not. And he did not want it called his son, as if it were a real dead person instead of an unbaptised corpse. Thinking of it brought his wife to his mind, and grief and guilt and horror. All of a sudden, he couldn't breathe and his heart felt squeezed as if by an iron fist.

He got up abruptly. 'I will inspect the brewhouse.'

He abandoned his beer and made his way to the kitchen door. Once outside, instead of crossing to the outbuilding, he made his way to an overgrown orchard at the back of the inn and took a deep breath of cold air. The memories came, unbidden.

She had been alone when he arrived back at the rented house. She was lying in their bed, quite dead, with the infant in her arms. He had thought it dead too. They both looked so peaceful there, her face white like ivory above his tiny features, but there was a smell of blood and death, pain and horror. He had paced about, upstairs and down, distraught, not knowing what to do, or, if knowing, not able. He remembered writing a note to the owner of the house, asking for his wife to be laid to rest and leaving money for it. He couldn't remember how long he had spent there. He must have lingered overnight, but had he slept at all? He did remember going once more to the bed in the morning light. He had tried to pray for their souls as he looked again on those dead faces. And it had been then that the infant had moved.

He did not want it to live. It had killed his wife. More, he did not want to leave it there, to disturb her sleep. And perhaps, too, there had been jealousy. Why did it lie next to her heart, enfolded by her love, when he was now and for ever denied it? So, he took it from her cold arms, hardly knowing what he did.

What was she now other than flesh rotting? He could no longer believe in the mercy of God, or that they would meet again in paradise. And where did her body lie? He had paid for a coffin and prayers, but would the money have been used for that? He had abandoned her in life and he had abandoned her in death.

He would never know where she lay. The babe should be with her, baptised and buried with its mother, not abandoned in some unhallowed, unmarked hole. He had done everything wrong and so now did not spare himself. His was all the blame. No. He did not want to hear of his son.

A thrush sang out of sight and a blackbird rummaged for the few remaining morsels of last year's rotting fruit. A tiny blackened apple still hung upon the tree and, suddenly, the smell of earth and decay was too much to bear. Christopher abandoned the orchard and made his way past the side of the inn and onto the road, with no plan other than to escape his thoughts. To his left, the village ended. The road wound up a slight incline until it disappeared around a rocky outcrop in the distance, heading, he thought, for the coast. Golden gorse flowers lit up the verges. To his right, houses lined both sides of the road. It was fitting, surely, he thought, to discover a little about the village.

There were few people about. Most, he supposed, must be at work, either in the fields or at their various trades. A heap of withies lay ready for stripping. Chickens scratched and pigs grunted in the cottage gardens. In the middle distance he could see a mill on the river and beyond it some meadows. Nearby he could hear a smith ringing his efforts on the anvil. The church was small but with a fine tower. He hesitated there, wondering if he could bring himself to go in and pray for the souls of his wife and son, when a cart drawn by a sorrel mare came out of a side alley in front of him. He recognised the driver almost as soon as the driver recognised him.

'Mr Morgan!' The man halted the cart and looked down at Christopher. 'Daniel Johnson. We met in your inn last night.'

He had the same easy smile he had worn in the inn, when advising Christopher about Mr Gazely's departure.

'You're looking lost,' he said. 'Is our new captain adrift?'

'No, I would not say that. I decided to walk out to see a little more of Dario.'

Daniel laughed. 'It will not take you long, but why not climb up and let me show you what there is?' He reached down his hand and Christopher took it. In a moment, he was sitting beside the man with the gold hoop in his ear, a person who was quite obviously not a gentleman but seemed a helpful sort. Christopher found himself engaged in much useful conversation as Daniel drove him briefly around the village and through the water meadow before depositing him back at the inn. He showed him the farm, which gave employment to most of the village, and the other inn, which he said was a poor apology for an ale house, and nothing compared to the Rumfustian.

'You will have a good living here,' he said, before Christopher got down. 'I know because I supply your inn with good French brandy and wines, and many other things unobtainable in the village. I am just sorry that Mr Gazely saw fit to fleece you on his exit from the inn.'

Christopher looked at him in surprise. 'What do you mean?'

Daniel smiled like a cat and the gold hoop in his ear flashed in the thin sunlight.

'Only that having sold you the inn along with all its contents he proceeded to instruct William to give away all the drink after he had gone.' He looked at Christopher as if to challenge him. 'It is just as well that you arrived when you did, or all the alcohol you had paid for would have gone.'

Christopher frowned. 'I suppose Jane brews regularly, but I will check with William to discover what else we need. Thank you for telling me. I . . . know I have a lot to learn.'

'Rest easy, sir. Your servants are mostly honest sorts, and I will make sure you lack nothing for your business. There is a useful passage directly into your cellar, so you need not concern yourself with any inconvenience. What you need will be delivered there, I guarantee it. My family have been friends of the Rumfustian Inn for many years and I will make sure you have all the advice you might need.'

'I am grateful,' said Christopher, 'to have you to advise me.' The man was too forward and perhaps not altogether trustworthy, but Christopher knew he would need advice and he could not expect to get all he needed from servants. Daniel was certainly friendly, and Christopher was in need of friends. What was more, this Daniel Johnson was a distraction from the horrible drama that still played in his head.

His father would be appalled at how low his son had fallen, but the times were different. Christopher did not wish to be a courtier, even if he had felt that he would have been welcome at court. Nor did he want these people to call him 'Sir Christopher'. It would be better to have friends than to insist on his correct title. His circumstances did not warrant it. This was where he had landed, and here is where he would stay. He would learn. And he would start now, with Daniel Johnson's help.

He entered the inn with new-found energy, calling for William as if a storm was about to remove the thatch. William came running, his expression even more anxious than usual.

'I mean to learn everything about this inn, William, and I mean you to tell me all I need to know. Where are the spirits kept? Is our supply depleted? What day does Jane brew? And I wish to see the account books.'

From despairing inertia to frantic action, Christopher filled the long day exploring his assets, demanding explanations from his servants and haranguing William for carrying out absent Mr Gazely's last order, for all to drink freely without charge.

'Mr Gazely was absent, sir, but Daniel Johnson was not!'

Christopher stared at his servant. William's attempt to excuse himself angered him. 'Mr Johnson was not your master, William. Once Mr Gazely had gone, I was, though absent. Any other man's instructions meant nothing.' Seeing William's wretched expression, Christopher felt even more annoyed. Either the man was stupid or deliberately trying to appear so. 'Daniel Johnson was pleased to tell me what good servants you and Jane are. Don't repay his kindness by trying to make him responsible.'

Christopher saw various emotions pass like shadows over William's face. Anger and injustice, swiftly followed by hopelessness as he subsided, as a servant must. Christopher was not much interested in what had passed before he had arrived. He was, in any case, unlikely to get to the truth. William didn't seem the sort to volunteer information. He seemed, more than anything, cowed, but Christopher was fairly certain that he had not given the man a reason to fear him. Had Daniel? Well, if he had, it was in the past, now William's new master had arrived.

There were more important things to consider. Christopher had lost the list of the inn's possessions given to him by Gazely, so he created another. Turning his journal over, he dated the top of the last page and began. From room to room, he scribbled what it held, from feather pillows to leather chairs, gridirons to pewter ware. Firkins, bottles, hops, barley, cheese, flour – right down to the last broken stool in the cellar and the last egg in the kitchen.

In the evening, well pleased with his labours, he felt ready to meet his customers. Few men were drinking. Most of the tables were empty, but he was happy to see Daniel Johnson at the table by the fire, eating the food Jane apparently prepared for him every day. Christopher poured a little brandy into two of the English glasses the inn possessed and took them over. A day ago, he would have shrunk from conversation. Now, he was alight with the achievements of his day.

'You were right about the lack of spirits and wines,' he told Daniel. 'I have been about my business all the day and am beginning to know it.'

Daniel paused in his chewing, smiled slightly and inclined his head in acknowledgement.

'If you are still interested in supplying what I need I would be grateful for what is on this list.' Christopher laid a piece of paper, torn from an account book, on the table and Daniel glanced at it.

'I daresay you would be grateful to have these things sooner rather than later.'

Christopher nodded enthusiastically. 'Indeed, I would!'

'It will add a little to the cost for me to make a special trip to Chineborough, but I would be happy to oblige you. I can have most of what you want by tomorrow and will stow all in the cellar as I always do . . . if that would suit?'

'I am most obliged, and much heartened by your kindness to me.'

Daniel pushed his empty platter away from him and picked up his glass. 'I am always ready to help a friend.' He raised his glass and Christopher did the same, surprised at feeling so cheerful. All that had gone before was dust and he would mourn the loss for ever, but he had a new home, new servants and now a new friend. Suddenly, life felt a little less empty.

4

The accounts, such as they were, itemised payments for the usual necessities but were less informative as to how the inn derived its income. Occasional lump sums did nothing to explain to Christopher if beer made more profit than food and if spirits indeed paid for themselves. Very infrequently, travellers had stayed overnight, and these events did appear in the accounts. Everything else was a mystery.

He could tell that both William and Jane viewed keeping records with dismay. William treated writing with great suspicion, or perhaps he was embarrassed at his lack of skill. Jane told her master that she was used to spending less than the kitchen and brewhouse earned, but Christopher was not to be deflected.

'It is my will that you do this,' he said to them both. 'How can I balance my income and expenditure if I don't know the facts of my situation?'

'It is not just the inn that needs an accounting,' said Jane.

'What do you mean?'

She looked at him with the greatest amount of frustration that a servant might allow herself to show. 'Why, there's Mistress Smith given suck to your son and no hint of coin to recompense her.'

Christopher felt himself rightly rebuked. 'I have been trying to keep the tragedy from my mind. She must of course be paid what is due to her. Perhaps you could ask her and settle up with her on my behalf.'

Jane was not satisfied. 'But you must decide what is to be done, sir. Margaret was happy to help as a good Christian soul, but she wishes to know if you want her to keep the infant until he is weaned, or if you will engage a wet nurse for him from elsewhere.'

Christopher stared at her. A roaring filled his ears.

'He lives, sir.'

It was like the roaring of a chimney fire, ready to burn down a house.

'Sir? He lives, sir.'

It was a raging summer storm, lashing a full leafed wood.

'I tried to tell you several times how he did, but you didn't wish to hear it. He almost died that first night, but she says he is feeding well now, and gains strength every day.'

'He lives?'

'Yes, sir.'

Christopher stared blankly at her for a moment longer and then abruptly left the room. He felt nothing as he went upstairs and wrote two words in his journal. *He lives.* He looked at the words and, as their meaning rose from the page and up into his mind, he began to tremble. For a few moments longer he sat with his hand poised over the page, but he could think of no more words to write and, besides, his hand was shaking too much. Unable to sit still, he hurried back downstairs and out into the orchard. If he had a horse, he would ride until he was spent. He had to do something physical to quieten the churning in his stomach. He couldn't think clearly. He couldn't decide what he wanted to do or what he should do, so he took a billhook and began slashing at some of the brambles and nettles. When he eventually had to stop to catch his breath he had cut a swathe through the most tangled area. A bramble thorn had raked his cheek and he wiped at the trickle of blood with the back of his hand, smearing it down one side of his face.

He felt no better; in fact, he was even more agitated. He hated to know that the infant lived while his young wife had died. And yet he had pulled it from her dead arms. To save it? New doubts assailed him along with the old. Had *she* even been dead? Had he been too hasty in abandoning her? Where before he had known certainty, suddenly there were doubts. He was certain of nothing any more, except that he was losing his mind.

Christopher flung the billhook into the mess of tangled brambles. He tried to calm himself. His wife was dead. Her lack of breath, stiff limbs and cold skin had proved it. It was the living he must consider. Her infant lived, for the moment at least, and that changed everything. Why had he tried to save it if he had not wanted it? It was not the infant's fault that his mother had died. Christopher remembered how his father had tried to comfort him when his mother had died of a fever, with him no more than a child. He had felt then that somehow he must be to blame. He had never spoken of it to anyone, but even now, at his most vulnerable, the childish thought was still there. Surely, he wouldn't want the babe to suffer such useless guilt? His role now must be to put aside his own grief and be a comfort to his son. His son.

He called for Jane as he hurried back into the inn. 'I will see my son now,' he told her as they met in the kitchen. 'Where is he?'

'At the smithy, sir, where Margaret cares for him along with her own baby.'

'Then send for her. No. I cannot wait. I know where the smithy is. And . . . I will take coin for her. You see, Jane. I do not forget my obligations.'

Every yard was too long and at the same time too short. His head was in turmoil. He should write to the infant's grandparents in Holland. He had not yet written to tell them of their daughter's death. Perhaps he should send the babe to them? But then he would not be a father to his son. He would engage a wet nurse and have her and the child at the inn. He would teach him to read and write, and would send him to Oxford to study, as he had done.

By the time he arrived at the smithy, his son was grown and betrothed, a dutiful son to his father and a comfort to his old age.

Christopher arrived breathlessly, with blood on his face and twigs in his hair, to find that his son had shrunk back to a helpless infant, lying in a box. As he bent over his son, a yellow blackthorn leaf dropped from his hair and landed on the covering. Christopher reached down to pick it up and the infant opened his bright black eyes. He had held this infant for many hours on the journey to the inn, but somehow it felt as if he was seeing him now for the first time. He had not thought it before, but the babe was so like his dead wife it made Christopher wince. It was too much to bear. He couldn't do it. He would send him to his grandparents across the sea. But he could no more do that than strap feathers to his arms and fly. He was imprisoned by love, love of his wife that wouldn't let him lose the only part of her that remained. There was his living son: a tiny Lazarus, a second chance.

He walked back to the inn. For the first time since he'd discovered his wife dead, a different scene played on his stage. His life would not be the babe's. The infant would, if it continued to live, build its own version of a life, and he must see to it that it had everything it needed to thrive. Seeing his infant son had opened some kind of understanding in his own head. For the first time, he identified what he was: a man alone and lonely. Perhaps loneliness was his natural state. Perhaps he was always destined to lose those he loved and see them only in his dreams. At that thought, a kind of desperate panic took hold of him and he almost turned back to the smithy, to take the babe, in spite of its need for milk. He stood in the road, forcing himself to be calm. He was not going to make another mistake. He was going to care for his son as a son had never been cared for. He would watch over him from the moment the sun arose until it set at night. Jane would help and William would run the inn, and he would ask that helpful man, Daniel Johnson, to keep it supplied and tell him if William needed guidance. His son was all. Nothing else mattered. His first and only duty was to his son. Then a pitiful thought struck him. His son must be even more lonely than him, too young as he was for friends and with no mother to comfort him. What frightening pictures of abandonment and isolation were playing in his infant mind? It was not to be borne. However difficult, he would learn to love his son. This would be his purpose and his reason to live. His son was a gift from the God he had almost ceased to know. In gratitude he would call him Abel. God's breath.

Loving Abel was not difficult. Christopher very soon found life unimaginable without him. Setting himself to be a mother as well as father to the child, he rejoiced at his first smile, encouraged his first steps and soothed him from his nightmares. Not having been familiar with babies, he soon became an expert. He would have liked to discuss the bringing up of children with his friend, but Daniel Johnson was not interested in such things. He had a wife, though never spoke of her, and a number of children who he could neither name nor seemed to care about. Finding him reluctant, Christopher turned to Jane. She had no living child of her own and was a servant, but she had a down-to-earth approach and a willingness to share it, which Christopher found pleasing. In the winter, family life revolved around the kitchen, where Abel could toddle after Sally, and where it was always warm and fragrant. In the summer, Christopher and Abel could often be found outside. Christopher had a wish to make a garden, but his efforts were irregular and his expertise fragmentary. The weeds he so laboriously cleared with his son one month grew back stronger and wilder than ever the next, but the exercise amused them both. In season, the tangled currants, gooseberries, plums and apples that had been planted long before still fruited, giving them a feeling of achievement when they delivered them, triumphant, to the kitchen.

Time passed. Christopher could almost forget he was master of an inn, for it effortlessly provided his small but adequate income while he lived his domestic idyll. William served, Jane cooked and Daniel supplied its needs, while Christopher enjoyed his child. In this way, life went peacefully on until Abel was four years old. He and his milk brother, Charlie, the son of Coleman the blacksmith, had a close friendship and often played together. On this particular day in October, Abel was without his friend. Instead, he was in the kitchen, eating the curls of apple peel Jane was letting fall from her knife. Unusually, Christopher was at his desk, struggling with the accounts. For some time, income had been falling and all day long Christopher had been trying to discover what was wrong. He had just begun to realise that over the past months Daniel appeared to have been paid twice over for the goods he had delivered. The usual amount was recorded, but double that had been paid out. The realisation was more than uncomfortable for Christopher. His conscience troubled him. He should have kept a tighter rein on the business. Now he would have to ask questions of William, who paid Daniel from the cash box, and Daniel, who knew where the cash box was and could have easily helped himself, should he have wanted to.

As he closed the book at last with a sigh, he heard Abel's footsteps, running swiftly along the landing. He smiled with anticipation at the explosion of enthusiasm his young son always brought with him. Sure enough, the force of Abel's push sent the door crashing against the wall and Christopher prepared himself to remonstrate gently with the boy. But the horror on Abel's face didn't invite a telling-off.

'Father! Come quick! Sally is dying!'

For a moment Christopher thought it was a game, but then he realised that whatever the truth of the situation, young Abel was completely sure the girl was at her end.

'It's not as you think,' he said, holding his arm out ready to embrace the boy. To his surprise, Abel refused to be comforted.

'She is,' he insisted. 'You must come and save her! Jane says she can't do it in the kitchen and William has gone to lay some straw down for her to die in the stable.'

The boy was in tears. Christopher got up and went to him. He would have picked him up, but Abel grabbed his hand and tugged at him.

'I don't want her to die, Father. Don't let Jane send her to the stable to die.'

'Don't be silly. No one would do that. I'm coming. But take it steady or you'll fall on the stairs.'

As they reached the passage that led to the kitchen, a scream split the air and Abel tugged his father's hand even harder. *Something* was wrong, but by the time they reached the kitchen all was quiet and Christopher was hard put to see what was amiss. Jane was standing over Sally, as if to scold her, and Sally was bent double, holding on to the table for support. Of William there was no sign.

'What is going on here?' Christopher felt awkward. It was not his business if Jane was beating the girl for some wrong, though it was a little out of her usual behaviour. Jane turned to face him with something close to despair on her face.

'She's sorry for the trouble, sir. But it's too late. It's all too late now.'

Christopher saw blood on the girl's skirt and felt doubly awkward. 'What has she done wrong, Jane? Don't beat her any more. It upset Abel.' Sally let out the beginnings of a scream, which turned into a deep groan as she gritted her teeth and lowered her head to the table.

'Don't let her die, Father!'

Jane pulled Sally's pallet from a corner and threw it down by the girl. 'Too late to move her, sir. Take the boy away. This is no place for children – or men. Go! Leave us!'

Jane had never spoken to him like that before. The urgency spat out of her like the sting of a hornet. He backed away, suddenly aware of the truth. Abel was crying and so he picked him up and carried him, kicking and protesting, from the room and out into the garden.

'It's all right,' he comforted Abel, though he didn't feel it would be all right at all. Sally was only a servant, but Abel was very fond of her and Christopher wanted to spare his son any sorrow. If she died, he would be inconsolable. He walked up and down with Abel in his arms, muttering comforting words to him while feeling more and more angry. Sally was no more than a child and by no means given to flirting with the customers. Some lad in the village had obviously forced himself on her. Well, Christopher would make him pay for his pleasure. He would make the scoundrel marry her, and look after her and the child – if they lived.

Abel grew quiet, but Christopher's guts were churning. Of course, girls got pregnant all the time, and Sally had no mother to advise her, but surely Jane had talked to her about the ways of men? And she was his servant! How dare any man take her! No wonder they had been hiding the girl's condition. They would know that if discovered he would put her out of her job. Indeed, how could she do her work with a babe to care for? It was not possible. Besides, the inn wasn't profitable enough to take in some lout's brat. But even as he fumed and inwardly cursed, Christopher knew himself. He could never throw the child out. After all, he was sure she was an orphan and would die in a ditch without work and a roof over her head. It was not just Abel who was fond of her. He had seen the way she had played with his son as a tiny babe and watched over him as he toddled precariously in the kitchen. She was part of the household. She was not family, but like Jane and William, her place was here, except that some man had ruined her. It was man's job to fight, and woman's to breed and die. He would not be a woman for all the world. They had by far the hardest part.

Abel had become heavy in his arms. He realised his son had fallen asleep on his shoulder, having exhausted himself. Christopher sat on a stump and waited. It seemed a long time but couldn't have been more than an hour when Jane came to find him. Abel had woken up and the two were tossing stones at a discarded old cast iron pot that was used to hold scraps for the chickens.

'Well?'

Jane looked at him as if ready for a scolding. 'It's over,' she said. 'The babe is very small and weak. I doubt it'll live.'

'Where are they?'

'Still in the kitchen, sir. William has made a bed in the stable, if you will allow her to be there until she recovers . . .'

'If the infant is weak it will need care. I will not be blamed for hastening its demise. Let them stay for now in the kitchen if you can manage with them there. Abel? We should go in. It's getting late. You may say hello to Sally, but you must be a quiet boy and not run about.' Abel looked confused. 'Sally is very tired,' Christopher added, and Abel seemed satisfied with that.

Later, when Abel was in bed and William was attending to customers in the inn, Christopher went to speak to Sally. Jane was just about to give her a posset but set it back on the table when their master arrived.

After a few hours' rest the girl looked remarkably healthy. The contrast with his poor dead wife was extraordinary and he felt a huge wave of sorrow for what might have been. Then he looked at the infant, lying in its child-mother's arms. He could only see its tiny face. It looked sallow and slack, as if living was too much effort. He remembered how Abel's face had looked like pale pink marble, while this infant had about it the look of old parchment.

'Give her the bowl, Jane. I can speak to her while she eats her food. Now, Sally.' He pulled a stool from under the table and sat close to his servant. 'Tell me: who is the father of this infant?'

Sally stared into her bowl. 'I cannot tell.' Her voice was so quiet it was hardly more than a whisper.

Christopher was shocked. 'I thought you were a good girl, Sally. In fact, I was sure of it.'

'He says I'm wicked. He says it's my fault. I'm bad, sir. He says I am.' Tears dropped from her eyes into the bowl.

'Who does?'

'I can't tell, sir. I mustn't!'

'Whatever this lad has told you, Sally, is wrong. But we can put things right. Do you love him?'

43

'No!'

Christopher leant towards the girl, feeling sad. 'Did he force you then? Don't be afraid.'

She nodded.

'Then he is the wicked one, not you. Tell me who he is, Sally. You are my servant and I can protect you. He should be made to marry you, but if you do not love him I will not insist upon it.'

She shook her head. Her sobbing woke the babe, who gave a high, thin wail.

'I can only help if you tell me his name.'

The only reply was more weeping. Christopher was ready to give up, but then Jane spoke. 'Child, you must listen to the master and answer him truthfully.'

'Jane is right,' he said. 'Just say his name once.'

'He says bad things will happen to me if I tell.'

Christopher's temper was rising at this fruitless conversation.

'I tell you, Sally, bad things certainly will happen if you do *not* tell me.'

She glanced at him with her wet, frightened face. Then she looked away again. She mumbled a name to the floor.

'Johnson.'

Christopher strained to decipher it.

'One of the Johnsons?'

She nodded.

'They are a large family, Sally. You must say a Christian name too.'

The girl stared at the door with frightened eyes, as if she expected to see the person standing there.

'Daniel,' she said, holding the babe like a manikin, her voice a little more than a whisper, full of bitterness as well as terror. 'It's Daniel, sir, who's used me so these past three years.'

Christopher threw himself back in his chair. 'Sally! It's wicked to falsely accuse any man.'

She looked at him now, wretched and hopeless. 'You don't believe me. He's your friend. You'll turn me out. I knew you would.' She made no sound of weeping now, but tears continued to fall from her eyes, dripping onto the oblivious infant's head like a miserable baptism.

Christopher wanted to disregard what the child had said, but the truth seeped into him as if her tears had fallen on his own head. Sally had no reason to lie. It would bring her no advantage. He wanted to tell her that Daniel was no friend of his, but he had given his servants that impression for years. He had shown Daniel friendship because he was weakened by sadness and it had also been convenient to do so. But he had always known Daniel wasn't the best of men. Best? He regarded Sally with horror. The orphan child was in his care. He had thought her safe, sleeping in the kitchen. He could hardly dare to ask her but ask he must. He made his voice gentle and kindly.

'Tell me, Sally. Where did he do these things to you?'

'Here, sir. At night, when the inn was quiet and all in bed.'

A horrible realisation dawned over Christopher. He got to his feet and went to the cellar door. The key used to hang on a nail by the door, but it was not there, nor in the keyhole. He lifted the latch and the door opened easily, revealing the steep steps down into the dark. He closed it, feeling a chill creep over his body. How long had it been like this? Four years and he had noticed nothing amiss? They might as well have not bothered to lock any door at night if this route in was left unsecured.

He hurried back to the kitchen and asked Jane, 'Where is the key to the cellar door?'

'I don't know, sir. I have no reason to need it. William used to have care of it.' She glanced at Sally, who had lain down and was now a shapeless huddle under a blanket. 'I think Daniel Johnson has looked after such things for a good while now because he delivers much into the inn that way, as you must know.'

Her unspoken accusation angered Christopher, but though he felt himself tremble with fury, he knew the barb to be just. 'Will Sally be fit enough to mount the stairs by nightfall?'

Jane nodded.

'Then tonight she must be taken up to the attic with you and William. She cannot sleep in the kitchen any more.'

Christopher didn't wait for a reply. Instead, he went out through the back door and round the side of the inn until he reached the road. He couldn't bear the feelings that tortured him. It was not simply the plight of that poor girl, due in part because of his neglect of duty. The smell of those birthing fluids had taken him right back to the moment when he had found his young wife dead and abandoned. He had tried so hard to put those memories behind him. He had hoped that by loving their son more than life itself he had at least partly atoned for having been absent, but here were his guts twisting again and his heart snapping in his breast. Was he doomed always to make decisions that ended with hurt to others? Was he so inadequate a person that he couldn't even take care of his own servants?

In his agony of self-hatred, he longed for his dead mother to be there to encourage him with her love. But he had no family to advise him. No friend, nor wife – no one to comfort him. There was no one to ease his burden. He must do it himself. He must somehow be his own support and carry on, although he would rather lie down and die.

Four years ago, he had been in this very place, looking at the lighted windows of the inn with despair, certain the babe in his arms was dying. And yet, four years on, he had a strong, happy, growing son. He must not allow himself to despair again. It took too long to overcome it. He did not have time to wallow in self-pity. He must act now, if he were to create any sort of security for his family. And to do that he must go and see Coleman the blacksmith.

After the inn was closed, Christopher held a lantern while John Coleman fitted a new lock to the cellar door and two large bolts, top and bottom. William had, as usual, locked the outer doors, but before he finally went to bed, Christopher checked them again.

The next day, Christopher woke up feeling rather as he had done before the battle of Worcester. It was almost certain there would be a skirmish against Daniel Johnson, and overnight Christopher's anger at the man had given way to fear. He knew very well that the opinion in the village was that the Johnson tribe was not a family to be crossed. No one used the word 'smuggler' about them, but it was common knowledge that this was their trade. Daniel had always been perfectly civil to Christopher, yet how would he react when he discovered he was to be denied not only access to the girl but also free passage to the inn, from where, perhaps, he moved goods secretly in and out of the village, as well as helping himself to Christopher's money? Before he went downstairs, Christopher rummaged in his old travelling box and unearthed his pistol. He had won it in a game of cards in Holland and had never fired it. He feared it might blow up in his hand if he did. But it was a weapon of sorts and Daniel would not know it was more for courage than combat.

He chose a time when the inn was quiet. As Daniel was finishing the meal that Jane provided for him every day, Christopher approached him.

'I have something to say to you, Daniel.'

'Oh yes?' As always, half a smile hung around his mouth. Christopher was trembling, but the insolent smile helped him rediscover his anger.

'You are to leave my servant Sally alone from now on.'

Daniel laughed. 'That slut! She should learn to run faster.'

'You had her in her own home, where she should be safe!'

The smile was still there. 'Indeed, she has been failed by her master.'

Christopher wanted to take the pistol from his belt and fire it into Daniel's insolent face. With an effort he kept his voice matter-of-fact and his expression cold.

'You will leave her alone from now on and you will pay for the food you have in this inn. You will be paid no more than is your due for the goods you bring and you will no longer intimidate my servants. If you ignore my wishes I shall terminate all my trade with you.'

Daniel pushed away his empty pewter plate and stood up, still loosely holding the small knife he had used to cut his meat in his hand. He was still smiling.

'You well know your purchases from me are irregular and a hanging offence,' he told Christopher. 'And if you think you can threaten me, take note that I can do far worse to you. We are in partnership, you and I. Do you only now know it? William will continue to pay me what I tell him and, as for that girl, she is no good to me now. I don't like them when their bellies grow.' One by one, he picked up from the table the plate, glass and bottle of brandy. He hurled them all without warning into the fireplace. The sound and sudden violence shocked Christopher into silence. After a moment, Daniel pushed insolently past him to the door. Christopher could feel the point of the blade, dragging across the fabric of his shirt. He looked down. There was no blood and the linen was not damaged, but his flesh could still feel the scraping of it.

The next time he saw Daniel was at church. Both men attended, as the law demanded, but what little faith Christopher had salvaged from his past was of no use to him. God would not help him in his struggle to free himself of the Johnson clan. Sometimes during the long sermon, he glanced at his nemesis. Was the pious expression on Daniel's face as false as his smile? Christopher didn't relish being sent to hell, but he wished Daniel's death far more fiercely than he had any man's during the war. He wished him to burn in a pit, to be dangled screaming from red-hot hooks in his flesh, to be hanged, drawn and quartered – that terrible punishment reserved for far more terrible crimes than Daniel's simple ruination of Christopher's peace of mind and a spoilt maid.

There were some small actions he could take. He hid the cash box in his room, doling out money to William for specific items. He made sure he was there when William was obliged to explain to Daniel that he no longer held the purse strings. Christopher expected retaliation and bought a better pistol in Chineborough in order to face it, but arms were not needed. Instead of violence, Daniel countered by providing inferior goods and fewer of them for the halved amount of money. Christopher didn't challenge him, preferring to have won a small victory of sorts, rather than invite violence on himself or his servants.

No more was said about the meals Jane provided. She continued to provide them, and Daniel continued to eat them for free. Christopher could see that this was the best way to protect Jane and William from harassment, but Sally was another matter. Daniel had injured her both physically and in her head by getting her with child. What was more, it was clear to them all that her infant was dying. It refused to feed and faded from the first, in spite of all Jane could do to drip milk into its tiny mouth. It was an ugly thing and should never have been made, but it broke Christopher's heart to think of it being buried in a ditch or even in the garden.

'We will have the babe baptised,' he said to Jane. 'It may give Sally some comfort to know her daughter will be buried in the churchyard.'

Jane shook her head. 'I don't know, sir. She says she hates it because it is Daniel's.'

'And yet she holds it so tenderly, as if she wills it to live. Her heart and her reason are at odds.'

The stones of the inn seemed to sigh with relief when the infant finally breathed her last and was laid to rest in the churchyard.

'It's as well,' Jane said on their return from the burial, when Sally was in her room in the attic. 'No child born of incest could thrive.' She noticed Christopher's expression. 'Did you not know, sir? They say Sally is one of Daniel's bastards.'

Christopher struggled to convey his feelings. Finding his command of language inadequate and his emotions violent, he resorted to a question. 'Did the priest know?'

Jane shrugged. 'Nothing can be proved, sir. The priest would know that.'

The following Sunday, he sat once more in church and observed his adversary again. What if he were to speak out now and denounce the man for getting his own daughter with child?

But too many men were entangled, willingly or not, with the smugglers to side with him over a servant girl. Maybe even the priest was in his grasp? No. No one would take Sally's part. They would think it dangerous to anger the Johnsons so unnecessarily.

During the prayers that gave Christopher no solace, he continued to think about Daniel. Indeed, he thought of nothing else. It occurred to him that it was not so much the evil the man did, bad though that was. It was more his attitude to his crimes that Christopher found so hard to fathom. Many men, being imperfect, did bad deeds, but most suffered remorse or guilt. Some tried to redress the evil by doing good in other ways, yet Daniel seemed to feel nothing but pleasure. Did he not understand the suffering he caused? Christopher came to the conclusion that it wasn't that he didn't understand, he did it because he *did* understand, and it gave him pleasure to cause others pain. It struck Christopher with horror that perhaps Daniel had targeted his servant simply because it amused him to see how angry, appalled and impotent Christopher would be when he discovered it.

One unresolved issue still remained between Daniel and Christopher. It was Daniel's use of the tunnel and the inn's cellar. Daniel and his family, on occasion, brought barrels and boxes out from the cellar, through the inn and on to Christopher knew not where. Daniel did not encourage questioning, and Christopher had, over the years, tried to persuade himself that it was not his business. But by ignoring the activity on his premises, which must surely be illicit, Christopher had put himself outside the law. He could hope that the steps he had taken might stop the smuggling, but his greatest fear was of Daniel. When Daniel found the door locked against him, he would surely demand the key. If he was denied, what would he do? As one of Christopher's dark moods threatened to descend upon him, he struggled all his waking hours with this question.

The answer happened halfway through that week.

One evening, when the last customers were beginning to leave, William and Christopher were startled at a banging coming from the cellar door. Christopher put his fingers to his lips and they both listened in silence. After a few minutes, the noise stopped. They could hear muffled conversation and footsteps retreating back down into the cellar.

'Don't be afraid, William,' whispered Christopher, trying to sound confident. 'Whoever it was has gone now. I will speak to Daniel tomorrow. All will be well.'

In the morning, Daniel Johnson appeared at the kitchen door, the great front door being still locked. Christopher was quick enough to bar his entry and leant with affected nonchalance against the door post, trying not to look afraid. Daniel had on his most ferocious smile and was obviously ready for a fight. Christopher forestalled him with a rush of words.

'The very man!' he said, as if there was no enmity between them. 'I have been meaning to speak to you for the past few days.'

Daniel was visibly thrown off balance by Christopher's manner, but he was not about to be mollified.

'What's this about the cellar door being blocked?' he said. 'You are not the only man to have customers in this inn. I *will* have access or—'

Christopher interrupted with a laugh. 'The very subject I have been meaning to raise. Of *course* you will.' He took from his pocket a key to the new lock. 'I have a key for you! Here.'

Daniel took it and was beginning a growl of a reply when Christopher spoke again.

'You will have free access until seven every night. Unfortunately, my son has begun to sleepwalk and I am feared he may fall down the cellar steps if the door is left undone during the night. Good day.'

He slammed the door without warning in Daniel's face and threw the bolt across. Ignoring what sounded like a hefty kick at the door, he hurried along the passage and up to his room where he sat quietly in his chair until his hands stopped shaking and his heart stopped its pounding. He listened, but the man seemed to have gone.

A loving God, if such He were, would doubtless forgive Christopher's small lie about his son, who at four years old slept soundly every night. And it was surely a small matter to allow Daniel free rein of the inn during the day if Christopher and his household could sleep easy at night. He did not hope to curtail the smuggling. After all, it was the way of things here. A few unpaid taxes and the occasional broken head were part of life. But Christopher hoped, by denying passage during the night, he could argue, if necessary, that he had done his best to keep his inn lawful. If only Daniel would accept this partial denial of access. Christopher's greatest fear was that he would not.

As the days passed Christopher slipped into one of his darkest moods, even while he struggled to stay vigilant against whatever Daniel might do next. After a few days he was unable to get out of bed. He slept long but badly, and his dreams were full of anguish. His only pleasure was to have his son in his arms as he read to him or told him stories of his early life. But Abel did not want to spend all his days in his father's room, lighted only by a candle even on the sunniest days. With Sally instructed to mind them, he and Charlie played outside and in, their voices floating up to Christopher where he lay dozing uneasily or brooding through the long hours.

By the time he managed to conquer himself and rise from his bed, nearly two weeks had passed. He found that the world still turned and the inn still functioned, although it was perhaps a little less popular than before. Daniel seemed to have accepted the small restraint put upon him. The inn was still supplied with spirits, though of an even more inferior quality. The smugglers' barrels continued to appear in the cellar from the tunnel and out into the village. Christopher asked no questions of Daniel. In fact, neither spoke to the other or acknowledged the other's existence, even when they met in the Rumfustian. In this way, days turned into weeks and weeks became months and then years. Because of the evil Daniel had done to Sally, Christopher could not forgive. But it seemed he could forget. At least, it eventually appeared on the surface that he and Daniel were, if not firm friends, at least on nodding terms. Life went on as it always had. Christopher, as ever, was the doting father and Abel continued a happy and contented boy, greatly loving his father. He grew like a weed and at eight years old it was obvious he was going to have his father's rangy form. Abel was the embodiment of all that was good in Christopher's life. Yet it was Abel who unwittingly brought his father the fuse that, once lit, would burn out of control and change their lives for ever.

5

Abel's education was becoming a concern. The picture book Christopher had found him in Chineborough was helping with his son's Latin, but he wished he had a book of philosophy. Abel was quick-witted and would have benefitted from a better mind than his father's. He should go to Oxford, but there was not enough money to engage a tutor for him. Christopher did his best to impress upon the boy that he was a gentleman and that one day, when his father died, he would become Sir Abel Morgan. The boy wasn't much interested in that. He saw that his father did not use his title, so why should it count for him? He hadn't even wanted to learn to ride until his father coaxed him. In spite of that, he turned out to be a good rider, even though a pony would have suited him much better than the rangy old horse Christopher had bought a while ago. Unfortunately, there was no spare money for ponies to be grown out of. Seeing him perched so high, Christopher had been too concerned about Abel taking a tumble to allow him any more than to trot sedately up and down the village street, but he knew he shouldn't cosset him too much. It was selfish to keep him too much by him, although Abel didn't seem to resent his life. He was fond of hanging his arm about his father's neck and teasing him, while Christopher did his best to teach his son the rudiments of mathematics, a subject he had always found trying.

Abel showed every sign of being the better mathematician and was a good and enthusiastic reader too. Even without the education he deserved, he could have made his way in the world. He was bright, lively and good, with his young life before him. They were beginning to read and discuss the poetry his father loved. Christopher would have been all contentment if their lives could have stayed this way for ever, but he knew it wouldn't do. He must try, and soon, to help his son to a better life, if he could only discover how to do it. As always, lack of money was the problem.

Not many broadsheets found their way to the village, but on this day a traveller had stopped to break his fast. When he resumed his journey, he left the sheet behind. Abel knew how much his father liked to read the news and so he took it to him.

'Look, Father! Here is a broadsheet for you.'

Christopher was in the garden. He had built a bench in a sunny spot and planted roses nearby. He was drawing a plan of how he would like to develop the garden but patted the seat and smiled at his son.

'Sit with me, Abel. Tell me what you have read.'

Abel scrambled onto it and leant against his father.

'A big crowd at a beheading in London last month and the King has built a new ship.'

Christopher raised his eyebrows. 'All by himself?'

Abel nudged Christopher. 'Of course not. He must have thousands of men to build a ship for him!'

'Well, a lot, most certainly. You're right. Is it all London news? What of Bristol? Does nothing happen there?'

Abel turned the broadsheet over and eyed the smaller articles. After a few seconds, he grinned triumphantly at his father. 'A gentleman of the road was hanged in Bristol. He was a desperate murderer and his name was Abraham Harvey.' He laughed. 'It says he bowed to the ladies and kissed their hands when they gave him their jewels!' He looked at his father for his response but got none. 'Father? Did you hear me?'

Christopher looked at his son.

'I heard you, Abel. I'm sorry. I knew someone of that name during the war. He was, I think, a good man.'

'How funny! This highwayman must be a different person with the same name as your friend.'

'Perhaps.'

For a few moments they sat together in silence. Then Abel slid off the bench and put the broadsheet next to his father.

'I'm going to see if Sally has any leavings of pastry for me. Do you want some, Father, if she does?'

Christopher spoke gently to his son. 'I think I'll wait for the cooking to be done. I don't have a taste for raw pastry like you, Abel.'

'Very well.'

Christopher sat on after Abel had gone. He closed his eyes and lifted his face to the sun. It was warm, but his heart felt as if it had been splashed with cold water. He was sure the soldier he had known and the highwayman were one and the same. Abraham and he had met at a war-ravaged farmhouse while foraging. They had both become separated from their regiments and, with night coming on, decided to stay there overnight. The house had been burnt, but the stable remained, with straw enough to be comfortable. There they had slept with their horses, hoping to stay safe until morning. Lying in the straw, with their horses breathing calmly, surrounded by the accoutrements of war, they had exchanged histories. Abraham had spoken of the enmity between himself and his older brother, who was fighting on the other side along with their father. It had made sad telling. Abraham had been bitter about his family falling-out and at first Christopher had felt that he must hate them. But then, as Abraham fell silent and they tried to sleep, he thought over the story again. It was the silences between Abraham's words that had said the most. Christopher realised that Abraham's fear of the battle to come was not so much of dying, they all feared that, but of meeting the people he loved at the point of a sword.

In spite of his sad history, they had spent such a sweet night, wrapped together in something that had felt very much like love. It had been hard to part in the morning, but part they must. Although Christopher had never seen Abraham again, he could not believe him dead. There had always been a place for him in his heart. In the chaos of battle, it was hardly surprising that they had not met, and after that the whole army was scattered. But now this. He read the piece again. What had happened to bring him so low? To be hanged as a common criminal was a terrible thing. Had his family survived to continue to ostracise him? Had he been forced into stealing to put food in his mouth? Surely no family of good name would allow such a humiliating end to one of their own, unless they were powerless to prevent it? He said a prayer for Abraham's soul, wishing things could have been different for them both.

Christopher fell to thinking of his own circumstances. What would he have done if all the buried silver had gone? If he had not had enough to buy the inn, what then? Would he have gone back across the sea to his parents-in-law, hoping to be taken into trade? He had indeed written to them, eventually, telling them of their daughter's death. They had invited him to visit, but he had not gone. He did not have money to spare for sea voyages, and besides, it made him too melancholy to think of these things. He feared melancholy. He knew that dwelling on sad times could send him into a spiral of despair, and he strove always to avoid that, for his son's sake.

To distract himself, he picked up the broadsheet and began to read other news. A small item caught his eye. A wreck, on the Dorset coast, off Chineborough Point. All hands lost and all passengers drowned – poor souls – including two women. The ship had been carrying French brandy, spices and silk. A gang of wreckers was blamed for luring the ship onto rocks at a cove a few miles to the west of the town. In lurid detail, the broadsheet described how the gang had brutally clubbed to death the survivors and how all but two of the bloodthirsty wreckers had escaped with much of the booty. The two had been hanged and their names were William and Thomas Johnson.

Christopher stared at the names. There could be no mistake. He had met them, coming out of his cellar with Daniel, about six months ago. They were two of Daniel's cousins and had drunk regularly at the inn.

He got up and went into the kitchen.

'Where is the ginger spice Daniel brought last week?'

Jane looked at him in surprise. 'It's here, sir, in this box, where I always keep it, when we have any.'

Christopher took the box and opened it. He threw the contents onto the fire and replaced the box on the table, ignoring Jane's consternation. He went upstairs and into his room. He took a new silk waistcoat from his chest and bundled it under his arm. Entering his son's room, he took a sky-blue robe he'd had made from the same bolt of silk that Daniel had sold him. It had been a birthday present from him to Abel because his son so liked the old scarlet one Christopher had. Without hesitating, he carried the clothes downstairs. Even on a summer's day there was a small fire to keep away the damp and Daniel was, as usual, sitting next to it. Christopher went up to Daniel Johnson and shook the clothes in his face. His voice trembled with passion.

'You are no longer welcome in this inn, nor are any of your evil gang. Get out.'

He tossed the silk into the fire, turned and left without waiting for a response.

He went along the passage, through the kitchen, without a word to anyone, and out of the back door. He saddled old Troubadour and swiftly mounted. He set a fast pace, heading along the Chineborough road. When he got to the turn that gave a view of the sea and the town far below, the horse was blowing. He pulled up and allowed him to crop the short grass. Christopher leant on the pommel and looked out to sea. It was calm, and as blue as the sky overhead. Butterflies danced over the gorse and several buzzards mewed, drifting in wide circles above him. There was a honey scent in the air and many bees went about their business. A warm breath of wind like a loving caress ruffled his hair. Peace was everywhere, except in his head and in his heart.

There had been too much death in his life. He was repulsed at the very thought of having encouraged murder by being willing to buy the fruits of such an evil trade. He could not allow his fear of Daniel Johnson and his gang to compromise his morality. He had done that for far too long. How could he possibly hope to bring Abel up to be a good and honest man if his own example was so poor?

The warmth of his horse beneath him, the chink of the harness and crunch as Troubadour cropped the grass were comfortable, simple sounds. He had asked for nothing more than to raise his son as well as he could, but life was not simple and never had been. Christopher thought of all the inhabitants of the village where he lived. One way or another they were mostly in Daniel's pocket. By intimidation or manipulation, they kept their heads down and looked away. How was he any better than they? He, too, had looked away and told himself that a little smuggling was mostly harmless.

He dismounted and looped the reins through his arm. A small vessel had left the port and was heading out to sea with sails set to catch the breeze. Would the poor souls on board be lured onto rocks and bludgeoned by men like the Johnsons?

But doing the right thing would come at a cost. Who would care for Abel if Daniel bludgeoned *him* to death? Surely his son should be his first consideration? What if Daniel drove them out of their home? How would he care for his son then? Would he be driven to highway robbery and be hanged like Abraham Harvey?

Even though his father had been dead for many years, Christopher still found himself on occasion asking himself what his parent would have said. On this question there could be no doubt. His father would have told him that he already *was* as guilty as that highwayman. He might be an innkeeper now, but he had been born a gentleman. Why had he allowed himself to be guilty by association with an evil gang? He couldn't compare himself to the poor fellows who scraped a living in the village. What education did they have? What experience of life? Had they taken arms freely in defence of what they believed in, as Christopher and his father had done during the war? Had his father not died for his beliefs? Indeed, he had, and the result had been the razing of his property and the confiscation of his fortune. Was he, Christopher, prepared to die for what he felt was right? Surely to die for high ideals was something he could not afford, not with Abel to consider. And yet, he had no doubt that he was risking his life by so abruptly opposing Daniel.

The arguments raged in Christopher's mind like two warring brothers. Neither point of view could convince him. They both had something in their favour and something against. And then a third option struck him so hard he felt winded: why not simply leave the inn, as Mr Gazely had? Surely, he could sell it? He would need to, to be able to make a new life elsewhere. In his sudden excitement he began to walk about, causing Troubadour to leave off his grazing, but in a few moments he became despondent again, and the horse took the opportunity to resume his meal. Selling would have been a good idea if he had thought of it before, giving himself time to find a buyer and a new place to live. But he had rushed to condemn Daniel, allowing outrage to guide his behaviour. Without money to support them, he had no way of leaving abruptly. Maybe, given time, he could achieve that, but it was hard to save anything from the income the inn provided. What was more, any wise buyer would insist on seeing the accounts. How much of an asset did he own when the profit was so small? What was certain was that he was not ready to falsify the accounts as perhaps Mr Gazely had done. Christopher had not been born sly, so he would have to do the best he could with the character he had been given.

Thoughtfully, he remounted and sat for a few more minutes, gazing out to sea. The small vessel he had seen had passed beyond his view and was hidden by a headland. The sea was as clear and empty as on the day God had made it. Christopher willed his head to a similar peacefulness and slowly turned his mount towards home.

On his return to Dario, he passed the inn without stopping, and went on to the blacksmith's shop. There he spoke for a while to Coleman before riding quietly home. At the inn, he unsaddled and absently groomed his horse, as if in a dream. He left him in his stable, well fed and watered. Upstairs, he took his old red robe and put it on Abel's bed. Much later, when Abel had been mollified about the loss of his blue one and put to bed, Christopher went into the cellar and emptied onto the earth floor all but one of the bottles of inferior brandy Daniel had supplied him with. He took the last up to his bedroom and drank it down like medicine.

The following day he struggled out of bed with an army of blacksmiths pounding their anvils in his head. His dark melancholia was deep within him, but he managed to rise and take up his pistol. He also unearthed from his box the small-sword he had acquired in London when giddy with new ownership of the inn and eager to impress his young wife. He had not had occasion to wear a sword since the war, and it felt strange to have it by his side. Fighting the pain behind his eyes, he went downstairs. Abel was in his favourite place, in the kitchen with Sally and Jane. Christopher released him from his lessons that day and told him to go and play with Charlie at the forge.

Christopher spent the morning waiting for his nemesis. While he waited, he spent some time in the garden, reacquainting himself with the feel of the sword in his hand. Some skills are not easily forgotten and his came back quickly. He also took care to prime the pistol. Having never fired it, he did so, aiming at the trunk of the old apple tree. It was pleasing to see how far the ball was driven into the wood.

Back in the inn, he went upstairs to his room, the better to watch the road for Daniel. He was certain he would come and come he did, flanked by one of his lads, a young boy well on his way to following in his father's footsteps. The great door lay wide open in the summer sun and they entered at their ease.

Christopher primed his pistol again and had it ready. He descended the stairs and entered the room where the few customers were. Usually, Jane would enter with Daniel's usual unpaid-for meal, but Christopher had pre-empted her. Approaching Daniel and his son, he extended his arm, pointing the pistol at Daniel's heart. The son leapt to his feet, overturning the stool he had been sitting on. He was already backing away towards the open door, but Daniel held his ground.

'This is no way to treat a customer.' He said it lightly, but the smile that was usually on his face had vanished and his skin was pale.

'You are not welcome here,' Christopher told him as before. 'Nor will you ever be. From this day our association is ended. Get out.'

Daniel rose slowly from his stool. 'Why?'

'I will have no goods here from wrecking. Nor will I have murderers under my roof.' He raised the pistol until it was pointing directly at Daniel's face. 'Get out.'

Daniel spread his hands wide, as if to plead his innocence, but the pistol still threatened him. Slowly, he got up and backed away.

When at the door he paused. His smile reappeared, but it was a twisted parody of humour with fury darkening his face, in spite of his upturned mouth. 'You will have reason to regret this,' he said. 'There will be many prepared to swear they saw you regularly sell illegal goods in this inn. Do you think you can take me down while saving yourself?'

'I have no interest in seeing you arrested,' said Christopher. 'Though justice would be served that way. I simply want you out. Out of my life. Out of my inn. For ever.'

The pistol was primed and it was cocked. Christopher said no more, but took a step towards his adversary, holding his aim steady. Daniel crossed the threshold into the sunshine. Before joining his son, who was hovering a little way along the road, he spat, his spittle landing just inside the door. Then he turned his back on the gun and walked away.

Christopher closed the great door with exaggerated care and uncocked his pistol. The several customers who had witnessed the exchange avoided his eye as he crossed the room and went back into the passage. There he met Jane, carrying Daniel's meal.

'You won't need to cook for him any more,' he said, taking the platter gently from her.

'God save us, sir. Is he dead?'

'No, Jane. He lives, but he is dead to us.' Jane looked as frightened as he had ever seen her.

Christopher took the plate into the garden. He sat on his bench and regarded the aromatic pie while his clamouring heart slowly regained its accustomed rhythm. The pie was delicious, but it tasted like ash in his mouth. It took him a long time to force it down. Several times he thought he could not do it. When at last it was finished he sat for a few minutes and then walked to the ditch at the end of the garden. For a moment he regarded the moorland ahead of him, and then he vomited until he was empty.

The darkness in his head screamed at him to get to his bed and bury himself in its solitude, but he did not. For the rest of the day he waited in silence for Daniel to return with others to kill him, but no one came. As the sun finally set, not one customer had stepped over the dried, invisible spittle on the threshold.

With the dark came Coleman's cart, carrying Abel, sitting beside the blacksmith. Christopher sent him to Jane and on to bed while he and Coleman unloaded the cart. They worked for hours, Christopher helping the blacksmith and his assistant when he could be useful. Bars went over every shuttered window, new bolts were put on the doors and, in the cellar, Coleman put a large padlock on the gate to the tunnel. In addition, he set hoops of iron into the stonework on either side into which they slid a great wooden bar. At last it was done, and Christopher paid him what he could, promising to pay all as soon as may be.

'Are you sure you are safe enough from them?' Christopher asked Coleman. 'Doing this work for me?'

'The village needs a blacksmith,' said Coleman. 'And I work for all. The Johnsons need a blacksmith as much as any. Daniel's argument is not with me.'

That night, and for many nights afterwards, Christopher sat up with his pistol cocked, ready to defend his life. One night, very late, he heard noises that could only mean that the gate in the cellar was being attacked. He feared they would use gunpowder, but they did not, and after a while the pounding stopped and they went away. Perhaps they were afraid of bringing the tunnel down upon their heads. After that, there were no attempts on his inn or his life. Daniel kept away, and so did the rest of the village.

6

That year brought a wonderful summer of warm days and soft nights, but Christopher was hollow-eyed and gaunt. It had cost him dear to resist his dark mood. Having not spared himself during the early days, as time went on his exhaustion felt terminal. It was a full month before he could begin to believe that Daniel would not lay siege to the inn and murder them in their beds. Only then did he allow himself to sleep his way slowly back to health. While Abel gambolled his way happily through the dust of August and on to the fruits of September, Christopher walked like a ghost through the inn and sat like an old man on his bench, allowing his bones to receive the sun's healing warmth.

It was only later in the year, when wood must be bought and Coleman had still not been paid, that the precariousness of their living became undeniable. Christopher had hoped that if Daniel did not slit his throat one dark night, the business of the inn would continue and be more honest and comfortable without the influence of the Johnson gang. But Daniel did not have a forgiving nature, nor did he respond as Christopher had expected.

Christopher could see that while Daniel burnt with humiliation at having been denied the inn, with his convenient smuggling route barred to him, life would be difficult. But he had expected an explosion of anger and violence. That had not come. Daniel was cunning as well as lazy. Why would he cause himself trouble and effort if he could with ease get back at Christopher? His influence in the village was considerable, and no one was going to set themselves against Daniel for the sake of having a drink at the Rumfustian Inn.

On one occasion, when he and William were closing the inn for the night, having yet again sold very little, Christopher was in a despairing mood. To his surprise, William, who made a habit of saying little, spoke up.

'Don't you fret, sir,' he said. 'Young Abel is as happy as the day is long. Look to him and maybe contentment will follow.'

'You are right,' said Christopher in some surprise. 'And I do look to Abel, who is so precious to me. But I worry about you and Jane, who have so much less than you deserve.'

William smiled at his master, allowing a little of his lugubrious humour to show. 'Jane and I are used to cabbage,' he said. 'You are not, and yet you are becoming skilled at growing and eating it.'

Jane had indeed praised him earlier for the few leaves he had managed to save from the pigeons, although in truth the cabbage had been a poor thing, with very little heart. He returned William's smile and felt an unaccustomed spark of fellowship. William had irritated him so much when he had first bought the inn. It had taken him a long time to realise that the man wasn't simply mulish but caught between Daniel's intimidation and his master's naivety. William was only a servant, but Christopher was happy to find a kind of companionship with this man, whose worth he had originally doubted.

The villagers were not all against Christopher. On the contrary, when the Johnsons were out of earshot, some men would cross the street to tell Christopher how much they admired his bravery. Yet admiration wasn't an income. There was enough passing trade to prevent starvation; however, by the following year, Christopher Morgan and his household were all but destitute.

Occasionally, when in a manic frame of mind, Christopher would come up with some scheme or other to bring the inn back into profit. These schemes always took more from the dwindling store of coin in his box and never brought the rewards he hoped for. It seemed everything he tried was useless. Sometimes, when he borrowed back his red silk gown while Abel was sleeping he regretted the burning of his son's sky-blue robe. But then he remembered how so much of the fabric had been stained by salt. Then he thought of the poor drowned lost souls and couldn't be sorry.

There were happy moments. Sally fell in love with a shy boy in the village who worked on the farm, and soon she had a babe to love, which she often brought to the inn, to delight them all. She brought food, too, when she could. Griddle bread sometimes and once a piece of fat bacon, proudly offered.

Jane and William stayed on at the inn. They had no other home and Christopher relied upon them. William foraged for wood, bartered for oats for the horse Christopher stubbornly refused to sell and worked in the garden with his master. Jane did what she could with the little they had. Sometimes, when his dark moods were upon him, Christopher would wrestle again with what he had done. Every time he came back to the same conclusion: he might regret not being mercurial, but he had, in the end, acted honestly. And mostly, somewhat to his surprise, they were content. If it sometimes pained him that their stockings were full of holes and his son often preferred to go barefoot, Abel's excellent health and good humour were a cause of joy to his father. They often went hungry, but they never starved and, if Daniel had thought he would drive Christopher Morgan from his inn through penury, he was disappointed. Over time, the two men softened their enmity, at least a little. Christopher found himself able eventually to at least acknowledge Daniel when they met in church or in the village. It took Daniel longer, but even he, after several years, was able to give his adversary a curt good day. Life was not easy, but it was peaceful, and the days slid past as if nothing would ever change. But it is in the nature of things to change.

7

One day Daniel came to Christopher with a proposal. He came with that crooked half-smile on his face that Christopher knew so well, that and his voice that coaxed, wheedled and then cursed. He spoke about Troubadour, what a fine horse he was, and how good it would it be if Daniel and Christopher should work together on a new project he had devised.

Troubadour was not a fine horse. He wasn't as sprightly as once he had been and he was not exactly handsome. Daniel's proposal had made Christopher smile, and that had angered Daniel. But what a foolish thing, to think that he, Christopher

Morgan, would consider riding to the turnpike to lurk there and stop passing coaches so that Daniel's gang could relieve the passengers of their purses.

'I am aware of your argument,' said Christopher. 'I know very well that several disaffected cavaliers have turned to this type of thieving. I know, too, that some of the broadsheets like to make it out to be a gentlemanly sort of robbery. They choose to see romance in such behaviour.' He scowled into Daniel's taunting, smiling face. 'I do not and am not interested in your . . . proposal.'

However poor Daniel might have made him, Christopher was not inclined to risk a hanging this way. Moreover, if he had been so inclined, he would have chosen to work alone, not become a member of Daniel's evil gang. He surprised himself at finding it so easy to say no to Daniel. Perhaps poverty had given him less to lose, or perhaps he had just become less frightened of the man. Having defied him once, he found it was not so difficult to deny him again.

He still sometimes dreamt of sending young Abel to study at Oxford, but knew it was only a dream. He would soon have to apprentice him in Chineborough, if he could find a way of affording it. He would need a trade of some sort, one where he could use his excellent brain and fair hand, but not yet. There was time enough. Let his son be carefree for a little longer.

On this day, as he worked in his garden to turn over the cold spring soil ready for planting, he was not thinking of their poverty and was almost entirely content. His stockings were out at the toe. He had hardly a coin to his name, but the look on Abel's face when he was told he could ride Troubadour alone to the tinker's camp on an errand for Jane was worth any fortune. He had seen his young self reflected in his son's expression. Such excitement was followed immediately by an attempt to look purposeful, in case his father might think him too frivolous to be trusted with Jane's broken pots. He could remember himself behaving in that way, his determination to behave as a man, though still being a boy. And he realised now, though hadn't before, that part of a parent's role was to act as though his son was the man he pretended to be. It made him smile as he thought of it. Abel was ready for more freedom and had been for some time. He was growing up.

'Go on then,' he had said, as if he felt no parental anxiety. 'Take it steady for old Troubadour's sake. A good rider spares his horse. But make sure you are home before dark, won't you?'

It was a little early for sowing, but Christopher Morgan had saved many seeds from last year's crops and was anxious to get his vegetables growing as quickly as possible. He smiled over the screws of paper that Abel had so diligently labelled for him last autumn: onion, leek, bean, cabbage. Each done in a much fairer hand than the hen-scratching his father indulged in.

Christopher picked up the packets of beans and put them down again. They were pretty, these trailing beans from the Americas, and he would be prepared to try eating them this year because looking at the flowers wouldn't fill their bellies. But he should resist planting them in the garden now because they would suffer if there were a frost. When he last had tried a hot bed to cheat the cold, the beans had grown like weeds, but the slugs had eaten every one. This year, he would start them off on a windowsill and plant them out when their stalks were tougher. Perhaps that would deter the slugs. English beans didn't mind the frost and slugs were not so fond of them. He could plant some to complement the ones he had sown last autumn.

Christopher liked his garden. Growing vegetables made him feel useful and it was soothing to rake and plant, rubbing the damp loam through his fingers. Some days he could almost forget that he had ever been anything other than a gardener, though, not having been taught, he had made many mistakes and relied on William for most of his good results, especially in the early days.

Soon, he had two rows of English beans and a scant row of onions planted. He picked up his rake and carried it back to the stable where he left it next to Troubadour's stall.

'Young Abel must be with Tinker Black by now,' he remarked to Jane, going in at the kitchen door.

Jane gave her usual glower at his muddy boots, but also as usual said nothing about them. 'I hope Tinker notices the crack at the handle of the large pot. I forgot to point it out to Abel.'

'I am sure he'll notice,' said Christopher, kicking off his boots and a copious amount of mud at the same time. He wandered up the passageway in his threadbare stockings in search of his buckled shoes. Eventually he found them by the fireplace where he'd left them to dry out the day before. It had been wet for several days and the inn felt clammy and chill. There was a small fire, but it looked a poor affair in the huge, elaborately carved fireplace. The wood was damp and a sulky fire always caused a certain amount of smoke to trickle away from the chimney and into the room.

Christopher held onto the mantelshelf to steady his balance while putting on his shoes. While straightening a stocking he felt his heel go through it. He sighed. Abel needed stockings too. His son's toes were quite cramped in the ones he had. No wonder the lad preferred to go barefoot, although, since he'd found some old boots, abandoned in the inn, he'd been keener to be shod. The old boots were excellent for riding too.

He pushed his other foot into its shoe and went upstairs. Usually he wrote in his journal at night, but occasionally he had the desire to put something down straight away. It was the sight of his little son looking so grown-up that prompted his desire to write. Christopher wanted to commit his thinking to paper while it was still fresh and new in his head. The book he was using for his journal was one he had written in for many years. It was bound in purple Morocco leather and was darkened with the daily handling it had been given. The brass clasp was dulled with use, but there were still plenty of pages ready to take his pen. Often his entries were perfunctory when he named little more than the day. For the year of Abel's birth there was almost nothing, but sometimes, as now, the mood took him, and he wrote with a will, losing himself in his prose.

Some while later he stretched and got up. He felt hungry and realised that it was mid afternoon. He put his journal away and cleaned his nib. Abel would be back soon. He should hurry downstairs to be sure to welcome his son home. Jane might have made Abel some titbit as a reward for going on her errand, though there would be precious little in the larder to make him much of a treat.

He was disappointed when Abel didn't arrive in the next hour. The spring days were still short, and it wouldn't be very long before dusk. Anxiously, he went out onto the high road and stood for a few minutes looking for his horse and his son. The road remained empty.

'I will walk up to meet him,' he said to Jane, who was busy cooking. 'Or . . .' He looked troubled. 'Will he maybe dislike that? I don't want to appear the anxious parent.' For a few seconds he stood irresolute and then he turned abruptly. 'I *will* go.'

He strode away from the inn, aiming to get to the bend in the road from where he felt sure he would see his son coming proudly home. But when he was but a few yards along the way, the fine drizzle turned to rain. Christopher wondered if he should return to fetch his cloak and hat, but he didn't want the bother of it. Instead, he quickened his pace. He imagined his hand on his son's knee as they went home in fine companionship. He would ask how Troubadour had behaved, wonder what the sea had looked like on this grey day and praise the boy for tying the pots back onto the saddle so well.

At the bend, he squinted into the rain that was falling ever faster. There was a horse! At this distance he couldn't tell if it was Troubadour, but it must be. Quite why in this weather Abel was allowing him to graze on the verge was beyond him but it was probably so that the horse wouldn't need so much feed when back at the stable. Christopher was both proud and saddened at that thought. That his son should know it necessary to save money pained him.

He couldn't see Abel, who must be standing the other side of his mount, holding the reins. What a good son he was to be so mindful of his horse's needs on this dreary day. Even so, he should come home now. With the clouds so low, it was getting darker by the moment and he had been told to be home before dark.

It was too far to hail the lad so, feeling rather peeved now he knew his son was safe, Christopher set off to close the distance between them. Abel was generally a healthy boy, but what if he caught a chill because of the rain? It was thoughtless of him to stay out so long.

Suddenly the rain became a downpour. The stony road fast became a twin stream, with rainwater filling the ruts. Water dripped from Christopher's hair onto his nose and trickled uncomfortably down his neck. Then, as suddenly as it had started the rain stopped and pale sunshine edged a low cloud. Christopher shook his head like a dog and looked up. He had made good progress and maybe the horse had wandered in his direction too. But he was angry with Abel now and worried about his health. Feeling that he was close enough he hailed his son.

'Abel! ABEL!'

At once the horse lifted his head and began to trot towards him, but a clanking of pots rose up and the animal slowed abruptly to a walk. Of Abel Morgan there was no sign.

Christopher felt a blade of fear slip between his ribs. Mindless of his footing, he splashed and slid his way at a run towards the horse. Troubadour came to greet him, nickering happily to see his master, but Christopher was in no mood to praise him. He grabbed the dangling reins and swung himself up into the saddle, fitting his feet awkwardly into the shortened stirrups.

'What have you done with him?' he demanded of the horse. 'Did you get loose and wander off while he was waiting for the pots to be mended? Did you leave him to walk all the way home? But no!' He looked at the unrepaired pots still tied with his knots to the saddle. Something had happened before Abel even reached Tinker Black. Had Troubadour been stung by a wasp so early in the year? Impossible. Even so, the horse must have shied, and young Abel must have fallen. If he had not been injured he surely would have been home by now. It was not so *very* far to walk.

Christopher turned the horse and kicked him on. The pots set off such a clanging that Troubadour threatened to bolt so he pulled the horse up, undid the knots and tossed the pots away.

The old horse trotted on willingly enough, splashing through the muddy ruts. The light was fading fast and almost every rock and bush looked to Christopher as if it were his son. But at length he reached the camp and saw to his dismay that the tinker was gone. Had Abel even met him? Should he go on in case his son lay a few yards further?

Christopher was distraught. If Abel lay undiscovered for long he might succumb to the cold. And if he wasn't found soon, light would be needed to search. In vain he rode on, casting his gaze from side to side, still hoping to see his young son walking unharmed towards him.

Eventually it was too dark to see anything. There was no moon, and the rain was coming on again. Christopher's voice was hoarse with calling and his skin was clammy. The cold was seeping into his bones, but he did not heed it. In sudden despair he set Troubadour to gallop back the way they had come. In a mad dash they hurtled, sliding in the mud, to the inn, where Christopher threw himself from his mount and entered, calling for William and Jane. His teeth chattered and eyes were as wild as they had been a dozen years before when he had first arrived as the new owner of the inn.

'My son,' he cried, his voice breaking with pain and passion. 'My son is lost on the road! Make haste to light the lanterns and fetch help. My son. My poor son!'

8

William was first to arrive in answer to his master's call. 'Is Abel hurt?'

'I don't know!' said Christopher. 'I can't find him.'

Jane came too, her face white. 'Where was the horse?'

'On the road, not far away. I've ridden up to Tinker's camp and beyond. But the pots aren't even mended. And there's no sign of Abel or Tinker.' Christopher's voice was shaking. 'It got dark, so I came back for the lantern.'

Jane laid her hand on her husband's arm. 'If you run to tell Coleman, God willing, he'll raise a team of men to help search. I'll set a new candle in the lantern, sir.' She looked at his sodden jacket and dripping hair. 'And perhaps you could put on some dry clothes and your cloak and hat, sir?'

Christopher shook his head. 'There's no time.'

'And yet, if you take a fever you will not be able to help him. And besides,' she hurried, seeing his impatience, 'Abel will need to be wrapped warm when you find him.'

Christopher nodded. 'You are right, Jane. Make haste to fetch the lantern while I do that.'

Dario was a village with little of substance for the gossips, so news of Abel's absence was soon known to every last soul. Such an unusual event brought almost all in a fever to be involved. As many lanterns that could be found were lit and several carts, including Coleman's and Daniel's, were used to take parties of searchers further along the Chineborough road, dropping them off at several places to search. The rain held off, but the moon stayed stubbornly hidden and it was difficult work.

There were so many places he could have fallen, so many stones available to break his skull and so many bushes he could have collapsed into. Eventually everyone was out of candles, out of energy and out of hope. To Christopher's dismay, the searchers straggled back to the inn, and settled in to warm themselves and mull over their lack of success.

'Calm yourself,' Coleman told Christopher. 'You cannot expect more now. We will go out again, when it's daylight.' Several others murmured their agreement.

'What's clear is that he's not lying out on the road,' said Daniel. 'So, he must be in some form of shelter from the night, even if it is under a bush. That is positive, don't you think?' He raised his eyebrows to the distraught father before lighting his pipe with a spill and puffing away as if it was any ordinary night, while in truth it was the first night the inn had been so full for years.

Christopher had no heart for conversation. As soon as beer had been served and he had thanked the villagers and arranged for their return in the morning, he went out into the road and divided his time between walking about and standing still, staring into the night as if he could conjure his son to appear. Once everyone had gone he continued pacing for a while. Eventually, he sent Jane and William to bed. He left the front door propped open and dragged a chair close by, so as to be there the instant there might be any news.

The fire burnt down and he shivered under his cloak. He dozed and woke with a start, but it was just an owl, calling to its mate. He got up and went out into the cold air yet again. It was still several hours before dawn. What if Abel woke from his injuries in the night? What if he wandered, his senses addled by the fall, further from the road? Near where Tinker camped the ground fell steeply away, almost to a cliff. Had Abel stumbled there in a daze and fallen again? All Christopher could do was pray to a God who had never helped him, pace and wait.

The following day was bright and sunny. Everyone's spirits lifted, even Christopher's. But although they searched further and clambered amongst the rocks and furze bushes where Tinker's camp had been, and as far as was safe down the crumbling cliff, they found no sign of him. Christopher took Troubadour and rode until he came upon Tinker, settled into a camp not far from Chineborough.

'I saw no boy,' said Tinker nervously.

Christopher tried not to frighten the man, who had lived in the area all his life and was a simple fellow. 'I'm not blaming you,' he said. 'But Abel is missing, and I would be grateful for any help you could give me. Did you see *anyone* on the road?'

'Only Daniel in his cart,' said Tinker. 'Sometimes he gives me a twist of tobacco.'

'What time of day was this?'

'The sun was still high,' said Tinker. 'But it was beginning to fall, and I was packing up.'

'Then Abel must have just missed you.'

Without another word he left the man and rode slowly home, still looking for any sign of his son.

Daniel was no more help than Tinker. 'Tinker's brain is addled,' he told Christopher. 'I came upon him during the morning. And I certainly didn't see your son. Are you sure Tinker doesn't have him? After all, he is more gypsy than anything. Maybe he has stolen him away.'

Christopher took that back to William and Jane. 'Maybe,' he said to them, 'Tinker should be questioned.'

They looked fearful. 'Tinker has never harmed anyone,' Jane said. 'He's like a child himself. If he's questioned he will be in so much fear and pain that he's likely to say anything to make it stop.'

'And yet, if he knows something . . .'

'He would have told you, I'm sure.'

'It's more Daniel making mischief where none is,' said William. 'In his usual way.'

'The man has no heart,' agreed Jane.

'I would agree,' said Christopher slowly. 'Except he, too, was out, searching with us all.'

'Sitting idle in his cart I heard,' said Jane. 'And hollering up and down when he thought of it.'

'Even so. He could have done nothing.' They were all silent for a moment and then Christopher continued. 'Well, you have known Tinker Black all his life. I will leave him in peace for now. But if we do not find Abel soon he will have to be questioned further.'

The following day, Christopher widened the search. While the villagers looked in every shed, ditch and bush in the village itself, he took the track that led off the road close to the inn. It passed the old abandoned village and ended in the open moor. It was highly unlikely but possible that Abel had mistaken the directions to Tinker's camp. Or, perhaps more likely, wanting to enjoy his freedom, he could have taken a detour onto the moor before planning to ride on to get the pots mended. He did not often disobey his father, but he was a growing lad, and sons did not always obey their fathers in everything.

Christopher felt a shiver of dismay as he approached the tumbled walls of the cottages and the old church. People came this way to cut furze and dig turf for their fires, and to pick berries in season, so the track was not overgrown, but the abandoned village was and was thought to be haunted by the plague dead. Rumour had it that at the end there was no one left to bury the dead, so they lay tumbled just inside the churchyard wall, hidden beneath the tangle of brambles and nettles.

Unlike most of the cottages, the church still had its roof, but it would not be many years before it might fall in. In one place, deer and ponies had broken through the churchyard wall and had left a distinct trail through the undergrowth. In contrast, the original path to the church had become impenetrable.

Christopher dismounted and tied Troubadour to a wind-stunted thorn tree. Before clambering over the church wall, he hesitated. But he feared not finding Abel far more than the skeletons that lay beyond the wall. He hoped, at least, that they were more to be pitied than feared. If the stories were true they did at least lie on holy ground. Besides, surely no demon could cause more anguish than he already felt?

He followed the deer tracks as far as he could before wading fearfully through the long grass to the door of the church. It stood slightly ajar, just wide enough for him to slip through.

Leaves and twigs had blown in over the years, and birds obviously nested here. It smelt of foxes too. It seemed God's creatures worshipped freely here without the interference of men.

It was a tiny church. On the wall opposite, so close he was only a pace or two away, was the unmistakable image of St Christopher, bearing the Christ child on his shoulder. Damp had attacked the painting, but it was still perfectly clear. Christopher thought how bright churches must have been in the old days, before such pictures were painted over. He could imagine how travellers of old, pausing on their journeys, would have been heartened at such an image. He found himself praying for his son to be returned to him. He didn't feel his prayers were heard. He didn't feel God here, or in his heart, but he prayed anyway, using hope as his prop.

The church was empty. His son had not found shelter here.

As he turned back to the door he saw another picture, equally old. It was painted onto the plaster either side of the door and continued above it in an arch, a whole scene of figures in an open landscape, not unlike the moor outside. It was a horrible sight. Everywhere devils had people in their clutches. They were dragging poor souls down into hell, tormenting them with the most hideous tortures. In another part of the painting, devils were being vomited from people's mouths, or erupting from men's and women's stomachs or between their legs in a horrible parody of childbirth.

Christopher recoiled from the painting. For a moment, he feared to pass under the diabolical scene, then he plunged through, emerging with relief into the sunlight. Was it this that would be brought back if the country had another Catholic monarch?

Christopher rode onto the moor. His voice was hoarse with calling, but he kept on crying out his son's name the best he could and then listening for any faint sign that he was near. Even after a few days, if he had a broken leg, perhaps, he could have survived and be even now waiting for help? But by the time darkness fell again, Abel was still not found. When Christopher returned to the inn, Jane had news for him, though not of a cheerful kind.

'Some in the village have beaten poor Tinker,' she said with anger in her voice. 'It was some of the young lads, but I daresay one of the Johnson boys set them on to it. All to do a favour for you by discovering where the gypsies went who took Abel.'

Christopher could not help hoping. 'Did they discover anything?'

'No, sir. They broke his arm, they say, and bloodied him about the face, but Tinker has no secrets, other than who his parents were, and that even Tinker does not know.'

'Where is he now?'

'Some of them had the sense to drive him in his cart to Coleman's yard. They have set his arm, I think, and Coleman has given him leave to stay in the yard until he's better.'

'Coleman has a good heart.'

'He does indeed.'

Christopher looked at his servant. 'Do we have anything we could take for Tinker? I am sorry for his trouble.'

Jane shook her head. 'They have much more in their kitchen than we do in ours, sir, but I'll ask William. He is not long back from searching on the other side of the village. Perhaps he would be able to think of some small thing Tinker would like.'

'I'll speak to him.'

The days passed. Village life resumed its steady pattern and Christopher alone continued to search. Any hope of finding Abel alive had gone. Even so, Christopher could not give up. In the vain hope that his son might have ridden as far as Chineborough and had suffered some misfortune there, Christopher rode to the port several times and asked in the inns and coffee houses, but no one had seen a boy of his description. At least, there were so many wandering boys that it was hard to know if he had been seen or not.

Even Christopher now had to admit the most likely explanation was that Abel had fallen from his horse, hit his head and, in staggering, had slipped off the cliff or lay dead under some bush as yet undiscovered. He had left the road, that much was clear, but how far he had wandered and in which direction was unfathomable. There were so many places: numerous brown pools where turf had been dug, many deep enough to drown a boy, as well as the considerable undergrowth. That was the hardest thing for Christopher to accept, that Abel's bones would lie unclaimed, that there was no body to bury. It was, he thought, punishment for earlier unforgivable deeds. He had fled his wife's unburied body and so God had seen fit to forbid him the consolation of laying his son to rest.

And yet, every time he tried to force his mind to picture his son as a corpse he could not do it. Troubadour was a quiet old horse. Abel had been a good little rider and a sensible boy. Christopher's head knew he was seeking hope where there was none, but his heart wouldn't listen.

ABEL MORGAN

9

I was dreaming of my mother. Having never known her, I seldom dreamt of her, but whenever I did she would be holding me in her arms and rocking me to sleep. My eyes were always closed in these dreams, but invariably she was singing a sweet lullaby and I was filled with an enfolding sensation of being safe and totally loved. As I woke, the feeling was still with me. I had the delicious sensation that the dream had followed me into waking as it never had before, and I wanted to prolong it. I lay on my back gazing up into the sky above. It must have rained, because my face and clothes were damp, but the sun was out now, shining into my eyes. I closed them against the pain, a pain I could not blame on the sun because it came from a deep throbbing at the back of my head. I had never felt such pain. Jane would surely tell me to lie still and would in a moment come to pull the curtains across my window so I could rest, but there was no window, nor was I in my bed.

I was just a boy. Twelve years old. A little young for my years since my father's indulgence had seen to it that I did no labour in the fields, nor follow any master. Between child and man, I was full of a boy's dreaming. The rabbit that would oblige me by entering my snare, the fish that would leap into my cunning hands, the boots I had found in the house and the little knife found hidden within that I kept secret, in case my father took it from me. The vague riches I would present triumphantly to my wondering father. I had been the hero of all my fancies, but now I was in a puzzle not of my making and what I wanted was Jane's mothering. Like a young prince, I expected to be taken up and ministered to. But around that expectation hovered fear. The swaying surface I lay upon, the sounds, like and unlike the rhythm of the mill by the meadow, the pain at the back of my head – I understood none of it. Where was I? What had happened? I remembered nothing, but my father was knowledge itself. He would explain as soon as he arrived to take me home.

'Look lively there!'

It was not my father. I did not know who he was, but he must know my father, for everyone did. As soon as this man knew who I was he would send for him. My father would make everything right. I remember that thought so clearly. The moment such certainties are revealed to be false is a profound shifting of the ground under a child's feet.

The man whose voice I didn't recognise loomed over me. He had a large knife in his hand and an unkempt beard on his face. His free hand, as he grasped me, was calloused and horny, like one who follows the plough. I drew my knees under me and scrambled to get up and away from him, but the ground rocked beneath me. I lost my footing and would have gone down again if his hand had not been upon me. The pain in the back of my head was so fierce that I retched, but there was nothing in my stomach. I stood there, helpless in his grip, swaying with the motion of the floor.

'When you send for my father . . .' I must have said something of the sort, but I don't recall him giving me any answer then, or ever any indication that he either heard or was interested in what I said. I did try many times over the next few days to get him to listen, but eventually, after increasingly severe cuffs, I saw the futility of it and ceased.

Over the following few days I recalled much of what had happened. I had been on an errand for my father and had been riding Troubadour, to where I could not remember. There had been a cart and me dismounting. For a few days more that was all, and then I remembered the face of the man who owned the cart. It was Mr Johnson, Daniel Johnson, who I had always feared. He had ever been at pains to praise me in front of my father, while secretly giving me sly pinches, and once had stepped heavily onto my bare foot with his shod one. I had never mentioned this behaviour to my father through fear of worse from the bully. He was an adult version of some of the boys in the village who liked to inflict pain on innocent cats, dogs and other children. I despised them, and him, but nothing had ever made it stop.

Daniel Johnson was not the person I had been supposed to visit, but he had hailed me on the road and asked for help. I remembered drawing rein, feeling like a king on Troubadour's back, high above my former tormentor. I should have known better. Daniel had hold of Troubadour's bridle in an instant and would not let go until I had agreed to help with his wayward horse. His request for help flattered me, in spite of my being wary. For the rest, all I could recall was sliding reluctantly off Troubadour's back into pain and darkness.

The place I awoke in was revealed by degrees. I could see that the stranger and I were in a large space enclosed by wooden walls, but no roof. The ground still rocked beneath me. It was not my head that made it so. It was something to do with the contraption in which the man and I stood. I could make no sense of it.

The man laughed as I staggered, but not particularly unkindly. 'You'll soon find your legs,' he said. 'Follow me. There's meat and drink for you on deck. Once you've eaten, I'll show you your duties.'

Without further words, he tucked the knife back into his belt and started to leave. Like an abandoned puppy, seeing no other choice, I followed.

At one end of the enclosed space there was a narrow doorway. The man disappeared into it without giving me a second glance. Inside to my left was a tiny cubbyhole, with a narrow bench and table, and a curtained shelf with a grubby blanket and pillow. The only light came from a very steep stairway, almost a ladder. Eagerly hoping for enlightenment, I clambered up after him and emerged as the sun returned from behind a cloud.

It took a few seconds to adjust my eyes to what they were seeing. At first, I couldn't understand. I looked from side to side, searching in vain. Where was the moor, the people, trees, animals? About me was sun and sky . . . and water, such a huge expanse of water. I staggered forwards and gripped the wooden side. I had never seen one, except in my *Orbis Sensualium Pictus*, which my father used to teach me both Latin and Dutch. I knew what it was, even though it was not a galley – *navis actuaria* – nor yet, with its single mast, a merchant ship – *navis oneraria* – but something smaller. The water could be nothing other than the sea, and I was therefore upon a boat.

The waves slapped rhythmically against the hull, sending up the occasional splash of water that moistened my face. Above me, a worn rust-coloured sail bellied out with a steady wind. I licked my lips and tasted salt. I had been in the hold and was now on the after deck. These terms were alien to me then, but it was not long before I knew them all and more. Even then, with proof all around me that I was beyond help, I could not quite believe it. The discovery that a parent is not omnipotent is hard, even for one such as me, who well knew his father's dark, sad moods. But that he would not find me? I wasn't ready to believe that.

Even so, I was in pain, confused and frightened. I couldn't help myself, and perhaps a part of me felt that if I cried hard enough my father would hear, even here, and take away the responsibility for myself that had suddenly been thrust upon me. I sank to my knees with my hands on the deck and gave myself up to howling my grief like an animal.

'Get up, boy.'

His foot nudging my ribs made me curl into a ball of misery, but then he kicked my spine, and I yelped.

'Get up,' he said again, and I did so, wiping the snot and tears from my face. I followed him meekly and sat where he told me to sit, on the deck in the sunshine. With his foot he pushed towards me a wooden plate, with a hunk of bread and some cheese on it. It was a grimy bare foot, which had felt like steel when he had kicked me. I picked up the bread and tried to chew but was so thirsty I couldn't.

'Here.' A leather tankard was slopped down in front of me and I eagerly took it up. I drained the small beer in one draught and looked for more.

'No more until you have eaten,' said the man, with a care for my welfare that an owner might give an animal for which he has no affection but prefers not to lose. 'You need something more than liquid in your stomach.'

By the time I had eaten most of the cheese and all the bread, I was feeling a little better. I sipped the refilled tankard and began to look about me. We were not so very far from the coast. It was much too distant to swim but close enough to see a smudge that might even be Chineborough. Our single sail was still full of wind. Behind me, another man with a big belly and thinning hair sat steering the boat. When I glanced at him he looked away. At the front of the boat I could see another small area of deck. In between, all was open to the elements. I wondered how many people were on board and soon discovered it was just the two men and me. They were the owners of the vessel. It took a while before I realised that they also owned me.

They told me nothing apart from the work they required me to do, but I soon understood that they were brothers. Their vessel carried a variety of goods up and down the coast for whomsoever wished to engage them. They were each capable of sailing the boat alone, but I soon found that they preferred to work together, spending as much time as possible jawing with one another. So, I was made to fetch food and drink, set traps for the rats, wash and keep the decks clear of any impediments to their safe progress, and every day pump the bilge. This last was not difficult, but it was onerous. My soft hands soon became blistered, and then raw. If I had been able to let them heal I would have been pathetically grateful, but other than tipping salt water over them, causing me agony, and giving me rags to pad the pump handle, the brothers showed little concern.

The first night I cried myself to sleep, but after that I was mostly too exhausted to do more than drop onto a woolsack, which was our present cargo, and fall unconscious. Father, Jane and William, the Rumfustian Inn and Charlie too – all were increasingly far from me. I began to look for nothing in the future except for my hands to harden and my chores to become lighter. Sometimes, glancing up from my pumping, I would look out at the coastline with ever-decreasing hope. It was always at the same distance, always visible and always out of reach.

I soon stowed my boots in the hold and went barefoot. It was safer on deck to go unshod. My knife remained safe in my boot because the brothers didn't show any interest in my paltry belongings. After some days my hands began to harden. I got used to the routine and began to feel a little more alive.

By the time we reached the estuary I could almost believe that this life was all I had known and that the Rumfustian was but a dream. It was not what I wanted. I missed my father and Jane, but missing just made me sad and so I tried not to think of them. Boys of twelve are, I think, designed to look outward, away from the confines of family. I had not been ready to leave that embrace, but I found I did not succumb to total despair. I reminded myself that many an apprentice or schoolboy was sent away from home at my age or younger. Indeed, the lack of any explanation made me wonder if all had been arranged by my father, he being too fond and too cowardly to say an honest farewell. Daniel had seemed surprised to see me before his usual spiteful expression settled back on his face, so surely no arrangement had been made with him? But perhaps it had, for why else had I been sent alone on the errand, when before I had only been allowed to trot meekly around the village?

My milk brother, Charlie, already apprenticed to his father, had often scoffed that I would never be a proper man until I had worked. Maybe his father had said the same to mine, who had decided I should be toughened for a while by honest labour. My father was a man of sudden fancies and enthusiasms, but I was sure he always had my best interests uppermost in his mind. That being so, I should be a dutiful son and take every advantage of the opportunity he had given me. That is what I told myself to believe, but resentment that he had not informed me of his decision was no proof against the ever-present fear that he did not know where I was.

In spite of my confusion, I set myself to understand as much as I could about working the vessel, taking as my example the exhortation at the beginning of the picture book I often wished I had with me: *Come, boy, learn to be wise.* Gradually I began to make the most of what I had: life and new experiences. I had always enjoyed understanding new things and there was much to learn about sailing. I was not treated badly, so long as I did my work, which was, once my hands hardened, often enjoyable. Seeing my quick mind, the brothers gave me an increasing role in sailing the vessel, and I was proud of that. I grew new knowledge in my head and muscle where before there had been none. The hope of seeing my family again still smouldered, but I kept it dampened down, as if under a turf.

I had very quickly learnt that a watch must always be kept, so when I noticed a large streak of brown water infecting the usual green I called to Zandar, who was steering. He glanced over to where I pointed and nodded.

'Aye. It's the past rains have done it, bringing mud down the estuary into the sea.'

I had heard of estuaries but had never seen one and was interested to observe it. However, I was also anxious. Our destination appeared to lie up this narrowing channel and I began to fear what might happen to me. I did not want to be with Zandar and his brother, Samal. They were foreign to me in every way, but at the same time I now knew them. They were not unkind to me, especially Zandar. I was fed well enough. In fact, although the diet might be tedious, there was more of it than at home. And I was out in the open air, which I loved. The thought of being carried off to some new place was not something I wanted to contemplate. Although I had told myself that my father was in charge of my destiny, I did not trust the brothers. It was not that they had said they purposed to sell me on, but I could tell well enough that my life was in their hands and I worried about losing what had only recently become familiar. If I displeased them might they abandon me, and how then would my father know where I was? With that in mind, I worked especially hard to please the brothers, in that sad way children sometimes do, to try to avoid a worse fate.

10

Soon, Zandar turned the boat into the estuary, tacking to make the most of the light wind. Now we were sailing into the brown water and I could see more of it pouring into the sea like beer down a thirsty man's gullet. The river looked all brown. It had been raining heavily on and off over the past few days, but I was astonished that rain had so much power over the earth. Surely, if so much soil were lost every time it rained, one day we would be left with bare rock and no means of growing our crops. But I had more to worry about than geography.

As we slowly turned a bend in the river and found the breeze more to our advantage, I saw in the distance what could only be a city. It lay on both sides of the huge river, and as far as I could see there were spires, towers, houses and smoke rising from countless chimneys. Numerous small boats skimmed from one side to the other and nearest to us it seemed hundreds of larger boats with a thousand masts were tied up. I knew that Chineborough was much larger than my village, but this was like its own country. It obliterated the land and imposed its own solidity. What would it do to me?

'Belay that idleness and bring us some food!' Samal was glaring at me, having emerged from the cabin and joined his brother at the stern.

The bread was as hard as biscuits but was edible enough when soaked in the small beer, of which we still had plenty. I cut the remaining cheese into two and took a generous shaving off each piece for myself. By the time I had seen to the brothers' wants and had brought my own meal on deck, we were much closer to the city. Behind the port some magnificent buildings rose up the hill beyond. There were many churches and in the distance a large white tower, surrounded by battlements. But the smoke of kitchen fires smudged the scene in places and we were still too far away for me to tell what sort of people might live there.

At length we were mingling with other boats, all seemingly with the one intention of making for a strip of quayside left vacant by a vessel that was being eased out of the way. We were beaten to it by a boat similar to ours but a little larger. It crossed in front of us and dropped its sail, drifting expertly into the exact spot. Zandar let out a curse and followed it in. Samal fended us off and tied our vessel to the one that had beaten us. This seemed to be the way. There were far too many boats for the quay and so most were in our situation. Some, indeed, were tied four or five boats out from the quay. I couldn't help but hope of some way to escape. Surely, if I could find my way back to Dario, my father would accept that I had spent enough time away from him? If I had proof of my father's hand in my apprenticeship I would bear it willingly, but now, near dry land for the first time, doubt was shouting at me and escape was uppermost in my mind.

'Come here, lad.' Zandar was smiling at me. 'You've done well for us, so I won't put you below while we're gone. You can stay on deck.'

Before my heart could miss more than a beat, he was passing a rope around me and tying it securely. If only I had been wearing my boots! But my little knife was with them in the hold and I felt sure that his knots would be more than adequate to hold me.

Zandar put the flagon next to me along with my tankard. 'There's still beer left,' he said cheerfully. 'No need to be thirsty. Enjoy the sights.'

With that, the two men pulled on their boots and left, clambering over the side of our boat onto the next and so to shore. I watched them go. Zandar had left me enough of a tether so that I could move around a little, but not enough to escape. I gazed over the boats and stared at the tantalising bustle on the quayside. Thoughts of my father and the home from which I had been ripped came flooding back, and I blinked my eyes to chase away the tears. I spent a long while struggling with the rope that held me, ever fearful that they would return before I could free myself. But it was hopeless. Zandar had fashioned a kind of harness that passed between my thighs, making it impossible to bring the knot around so that I could see it. Giving up, I sat disconsolate, staring at the bustle on the quay.

Then, a small figure amongst the throng caught my eye. It was a boy of about my own age, but he was different from any boy I had ever seen. His clothes were splendid like a king's. He wore scarlet breeches and spotless white stockings. His elaborate jacket fitted him perfectly. It must have been made especially for him, which to me seemed a marvellous thing. His parents had to be very wealthy to afford such luxury for a growing boy.

He was carrying a small box, holding it as if it were of great value or as if he were in an important procession. As I watched, something made him turn to look in my direction. I had thought that he was wearing black gloves but now saw that his face was as dark as his hands. The pale blue jacket and snowy linen about his neck framed his ebony face and form exquisitely. He was the most singular and most beautiful person I had ever seen. I thought how proud he must be to belong in such a place, and to so splendidly overshadow everything in it.

And then suddenly, as these things sometimes happen, his eyes found mine. It was as if we were looking into each other's souls: I with my dirty bare feet and roped waist, he with his fine clothes and skin like burnished coal. But the way he looked at me made my blood run chill in my veins. For he was not a haughty foreigner, striding through the bustle as if he owned the quay. Terror was in his eyes. And as if I might have doubted it, a man close by to him turned and spoke to the princely boy. He cuffed him then and the boy stumbled. I could not hear what the man had said, but the boy might have been whispering in my ear. *We are the same*, he was saying. *This is an evil place and I am no less a captive than you.*

The day passed with aching slowness. The knife in my boot, which could have released me, remained out of my reach in the hold. But the look in the splendid boy's eyes had chased thoughts of escape into this place. In truth, I wished Zandar, who had always treated me with a rough kindness, would return. I felt vulnerable tethered as I was in full view of everybody. I was afraid that in spite of my dirty face and straggling hair someone might decide to steal me. But nobody gave me a second glance, not even the crew of the two other boats who used our vessel to reach the shore.

At length, sick of the city, I turned away to contemplate the muddy river and found myself yearning to return to the clean expanse of the sea. I became very hungry, but the food had all gone, and I had had enough of the beer. Eventually, I slept and in the early morning awoke to find that a mist had settled on everything. My clothes and hair were spangled with drops of moisture, as was the rigging. I was cold to the bone, but very soon Zandar and Samal appeared, and at the same time the sun came out.

'Take this and stow it,' said Samal, thrusting a box of provisions at me. 'Then come back up. I have a job for you.' He untied me and watched as I made my way to the ladder. As soon as I returned, he sat me at a pile of short lengths of worn ropes, refastened my tether and gave me a small hook.

'We should have given you this yesterday,' he said. 'Make haste to unpick it. The price of oakum has trebled recently and there's no reason we shouldn't sell some of our own. You've had enough of leisure.'

He had left me a sample of what he wanted. It looked simple enough to untwist and tease out the fibres, but they were sharp and it was sore work, even for my hardened fingers.

'Here, boy.' I looked up. Zandar was standing over me. 'Hold your hands out.' I did so and he dropped a few dark, sticky fruits into my hand. 'Dried apricots,' he said. 'Everything is for sale in this place.' I thanked him profusely and tasted one. It was chewy, gritty, tangy and deliciously sweet.

Soon there was much moving of shipping until at the last we were next to the quay. Two planks were set over the side and several men swarmed on board. Samal went down into the hold. With the shoremen to help, each bale was unloaded. After it was done, Zandar took a turn at the bilge pump. He worked it much faster than I could and soon all was dry.

While the brothers inspected the empty hold, I worked away at picking the oakum, rewarding myself every now and then with another of the fruits. Soon the shoremen began loading us up with timber and barrels. I mourned the loss of my comfortable bed, but Zandar did not propose that I should sleep on tree trunks.

'Too dangerous for you now,' he said when the loading was done. 'You could be crushed.' He dropped my boots at my feet. 'We will find you a different place.'

Once we were under way and drifting downriver towards the sea, he left Samal at the tiller and untied me. He led the way to the front of the boat where I knew his brother slept. Right in the bows were two small bunks. He took my boots and slung them on one. 'You'll do well enough there if my brother doesn't keep you awake with his snoring.'

'Thank you,' I said. 'And thank you again for the apricots. I had never tasted them before. They were delicious.'

Zandar looked delighted. He clapped me on my shoulder and smiled. 'You're a good boy,' he said. 'You remind me of my son that died.'

For the next few weeks we plied our trade up and down the coast, never totally losing sight of land, but sailing north to fetch coal and south to deliver it, while occasionally picking up more exotic imported goods. Occasionally, we would enter some small hidden inlet and goods would be unloaded onto the beach by men who looked as if they lived by night, rather than in the honest daylight. Those men reminded me of the Johnsons and I was at pains to keep out of their sight.

My thirteenth birthday must have passed, but I had no knowledge of the date. The seasons turned from spring into summer. I grew brown, longer legged and more shaggy-haired. And so, when at last we came to Chineborough once more, I was a very different person from the frightened child who had left it six months before.

It was late summer, and my hands and mouth were stained purple with the blackberries I had recently picked. Zandar and I had landed at a deserted beach on an island that lay some way off the mainland. He did business of an underhand kind with a man who hurried away as soon as they had swapped some goods, while I went a-berrying to supplement our diet. Zandar had recently discovered, to his delight, the knowledge of edible plants I had gained as a village boy and he used it at every opportunity. When his business was concluded, we returned to the boat along with the berries and a few barrels that smelt to my nose as if they contained a fine French brandy.

From here, we sailed directly for Chineborough. I had never been there while conscious but realised that between being on the road and waking on the boat I could have been carried anywhere. But I had heard the place described, and when I heard the accents of the men on the shore I felt sure I must be near my home. From that instant, all the memories of the inn and my family returned, as if I had been taken but a day before. I was utterly determined to escape.

It would not be easy. Zandar was somewhat fond of me, but if he was inclined to trust me, his brother certainly wasn't. I told myself that I must not be too hasty. I must bide my time until I had the greatest chance of success. And so, I did not try to run as soon as we tied up. I waited, accepting my tether meekly, as if I had no idea where I was. And then came some news I could hardly believe.

'I must go inland on business and Samal will stay with the boat,' said Zandar. 'I am minded to take you with me. Do you give your word that you will not run away?'

I looked as filial as I was able and nodded. 'Yes. Of course. You have my word.'

'This is plain foolishness!' said Samal. 'Leave the boy here to pick oakum. Or let me go as usual. You do not even know the place.'

Zandar shook his head. 'We have several times thought that we should both know it. The boy is quick-witted and can help me. Besides, he has given his word.'

Samal turned away, after giving me a look of such hatred that it made me even more determined to succeed in my escape. I smiled at Zandar, allowing enthusiasm to show. 'I will be the best help I can be to you,' I said. 'As always.'

Zandar was not a good rider, but he was good enough to guide the hired horse he obtained. I rode pillion and looked about me with mounting excitement as we climbed a steep road inland. Were we going in the right direction? I wanted to throw myself from the horse and run. But there was not enough cover to hide, and even a doubtful horseman would likely be able to run down a boy in this place. I had to wait until I could make certain of my escape. The further we rode from the sea the more uncertain Zandar appeared, and the greater chance I had to make him flounder.

He had to consult a map every now and then. He was loose-tongued, and while we rode he told me to keep my eyes peeled for the abandoned church and churchyard that lay just outside the village of Dario. There was a tomb there which we needed to find.

I stared at the back of his salt-caked shirt as he told me this. Dario! Did he not know that this was my home? I began to tremble so much that I was sure he would feel it and ask what ailed me. But he did not. I wanted so much to run, but I knew that this still wasn't the right time. Above all, I must be patient. In the churchyard there would surely be lots of places to run and hide.

It frightened as well as excited me, knowing where we were going, for countless plague victims had been buried in that churchyard and no one in the village went there by choice. Ghosts walked there and I feared their clutches. Even so, I was sure that my best chance of escape from Zandar would be there. I would be so close to home that, hiding in the heather, I could make my furtive way to the wall that separated the moor from our garden. Once over the wall, I would be safe. If needs be, I would wait for darkness. I knew the country here and Zandar did not. Soon. Very soon I would see my father again! All thoughts of my father being responsible for my absence vanished in my hunger to see him again.

To my dismay, it was going to be less easy than I had thought. When we reached the burial ground, Zandar grasped my wrist in an iron grip. He had been muttering about the undead for the past mile or so and seemed to be as frightened of the place as I was. This fear was a side of him I had not seen before and it added to my disquiet. But I could see the roof of the inn! I was so close to being free. If someone would come by I could alert them to my plight, for all knew me here. But there were none but us in this place. I would have to help myself.

Zandar dismounted, hooked the horse's reins over the branch of an elder and took me with him into the churchyard. It was overgrown and apart from some animal tracks it looked as if no one had been there for a hundred years. I believe we were both trembling. Samal had told him the place he needed was on the other side of the church and so we pushed our way around, taking one of the narrow tracks. He insisted I go first, but still he held onto my wrist so powerfully it felt as if his hand were pincers.

To my astonishment, around the far side of the church a much broader track passed through a gap in the churchyard wall and led out over the moor. Near to us, the track ended beside an ancient yew.

'This is the place,' whispered Zandar.

It was broad daylight, but I felt the presence of evil all around me. Indeed, the track with its ghostly wheel marks shrieked of the dead abroad. I tried to run, but still he had me by the wrist.

Together we pulled away a dead branch. Half hidden by the yew and a dark-leafed holly, a stone tomb stood. Its lid was part off, as if its ghost had left it ready for its return. I believe terror owned us both, but Zandar had trapped me between the trees and the tomb. There was no way for me to escape.

'Now, boy,' said Zandar, glancing into the darkness of the opened tomb. 'Look lively. I'll give you a hand in.'

'No! I . . .'

Zandar looked sorrowful. 'You are a good boy,' he said. 'Evil will not come to such as you. All you have to do is leave this packet on a shelf inside, collect another that will be waiting there and then call to me. I will immediately help you back up and we'll be away.'

Zandar now gripped both my wrists and tried to haul me up to the gaping black hole. I resisted with all my strength and he cursed me. With his knee in my stomach, he released one of my wrists and punched my head so hard my senses floated free. I had no strength to resist as he hauled me to the lip and lowered me into the tomb.

'No!' I begged, dangling helplessly. 'Don't make me go into this place! I will die in there. Please, Father.' At these words I thought I had him. He hesitated for a moment with my legs flailing. And then he seemed to find renewed courage, or maybe he didn't believe I meant the name I had called him.

'Don't make a fuss. It will be over in an instant. I will be here. Make haste.'

With that, he thrust me from him into the darkness. I don't know if I screamed or if it was the dead I heard.

I felt the shelf under my boots and found my footing. Zandar had let me go and was now peering in, blocking all the light.

'I can't see!' I said. He immediately withdrew, and I scrambled down from the shelf into a deeper gloom.

'Where are you, boy?' Zandar's voice quavered from above.

'I'm looking for the packet,' I said, wavering between pleasure to be free of him and terror at where I was. 'Don't you have any light?'

'No. The packet will be on the shelf I lowered you to. So I am told. Do make haste.'

'It's difficult to see.'

I laid the packet I held onto the shelf and picked up the other, which I had noticed in the meagre light. I looked up, but he was obliging me by keeping his head out of the way. I was in a tomb, but I was also freer than I had been for over half a year. If I refused to come out, would he be fearful enough to give up on me and go away? But if he left me, how would I get out? I didn't know if I was tall enough to manage it.

'There is nothing on the shelf,' I called up to give myself more time to decide what to do. 'I am going to look on the floor. Maybe I kicked it off when you lowered me.'

There came a groan from my master. 'Then make haste, boy. We need to be gone.'

I didn't reply. I put my arms out in front of me and felt the chill wall of the tomb. Please God there would be only bones in this place, not a still-rotting cadaver, ready to poison me with the plague. Was there a place to squeeze my body out of sight? If I seemed to have vanished when Zandar peered in, as he was sure to do if I stayed silent, would he think me gone for ever? Should I wail like a ghost to frighten him more? But I was too afraid of the dead to do more than cower as I felt the walls, and almost ready to reach back up for Zandar's hands. There was nowhere to hide in the first side of the tomb, nor the second. As I started feeling along the third most of the light vanished and Zandar's voice boomed down at me.

'Come, boy, don't make me angry now. Hand me up the packet and we'll be gone.'

As I felt for a hiding place in the third side of the tomb, I stumbled into an alcove. It was deep and very dark. The further Zandar leant in to look for me the more light he would block. He would never see me there. All I had to do was to be silent. I felt for the wall to lean against, but there was nothing. I reached out and followed my outstretched hands. Still nothing. Was it a passage to another tomb? A path to the underworld? Was there a pit ahead, ready to swallow me up? I stopped, but then behind me I heard the unmistakable sound of someone climbing down into the tomb. It must be Zandar, but so much horror had me in its grip I feared it could be the returning corpse of this empty tomb. To go on would be folly, to go back was unthinkable, but if I stayed where I was the corpse or its ghost would find me, if Zandar did not.

Terror sped me, caution slowed me down. The dark was soft as soot as I staggered through it, arms outstretched. There came a point when my hands hit a wall and I thought my journey had come to an end, buried deep within the ground, the earth pressing hard upon my head. The wall was rough and jagged against my fingers, but when I felt carefully along it, I found myself turning a corner. On I went, shaking in terror at what I could only imagine lurked there, watching me. All sounds in the tomb were muffled now, apart from my rasping breath and the thundering of my heart. I bit my lip to stop myself moaning. And then, ahead of me, I was almost sure I saw a light. It was no more than the eye of a bird, but something glistened. It must be daylight, shining to me down this terrible path. I hastened towards it, trying to be mindful of dangers, but with hope of escape exceeding my caution. I could be free. I *would* be free. Out in the air of the moor with the bright gorse to welcome me home.

CHRISTOPHER MORGAN

11

Losing Abel was a tragedy that could have been expected to send Christopher entirely into madness, but it did not. It was a close thing, but somehow, he clung to sanity. At first, he dared not take to his bed because each day he hoped to see Abel again. As time passed, the tragedy of his loss seemed to overshadow his instability. Or, he sometimes thought, his melancholy was now so deep it had become his natural state. And yet, still he did not take to his bed. From somewhere he found the strength to carry on. Everything he did, he did for Abel. He considered his son's reaction, whatever he worked at. Instead of abandoning his garden, as he might have done, he worked harder in it, planting all the seeds Abel had sorted and labelled for him. Each plant that thrived seemed to point to his son being alive. Every one that failed told him Abel was dead. He lavished such care upon them all that with William's help they had good eating from the garden that year and plenty of seed to save for the next. Abel was not there to label the packets, but Christopher did it for him, imagining him at his side, his arm about his father's neck while he leant against his father's thigh and made fun of his untidy scribbling.

Christopher had lost the ready laugh that had been his when with his son. As the summer days shortened into autumn it became obvious, even to him, that after six months' absence his son would not return, and that his bones might never be recovered. He wished he could have laid his son to rest. His grief was incomplete without a body to weep over and bury. He had failed both his wife and son in that respect. He prayed for them both every day, although, if anything, his faith was further away from him than it had ever been. He created jobs for himself, to keep despair at bay and his hope in check. Once there was less to do in the garden and the days began to drive him indoors, he decided to block up the locked gate in the cellar. Daniel hadn't tried to use it for a long time. Christopher had won that battle, though it seemed to matter little now. It would be good, however, not to be reminded of it whenever he had cause to go down there. Besides, he had noticed small toadstools in one spot in the cellar, near the gate. Would it be possible to grow mushrooms down there? He wished to experiment. He would need soil, so he would fill sacks and take them down there from the garden. He would pile them up in front of the gate and try various mushroom-growing experiments. It was the right time of year to find specimens to plant. And physical activity quietened his mind.

He worked hard, filling such patched and frayed sacks as he could find, and carrying them through the kitchen and down into the cellar. He knew he tried poor Jane's patience, but since the loss of Abel, she and William had become less like master and servant, and more like friends. They all grieved for the boy and took pains to be kind to one other. Poverty and loss had them all level. So, Christopher tried not to trail too much mud through the kitchen and Jane tried not to scold.

He ran out of sacks when the stack was chest high. It was a pity, but most of the gate was now hidden and he had more soil than he would ever need to grow fungi. He had recently collected edible specimens from the woodland and fields on the other side of the village. He had split a large bracket fungus in an effort to make cuttings. He had planted them with care into some of the holes in the sacks, trying to replicate the trees on which they naturally liked to grow. Unfortunately, they showed little sign of liking their new home, but he persevered.

Near the small cellar window, he had scattered more soil and was busy setting a handful of young field mushrooms there when he heard Abel call him. It happened now and then, always without warning, and as clear as if the boy were by his side. It was, he knew, a trick of grief and longing, but it always pierced his heart.

'Here I am,' he said quietly, which had become a habit with him, as if it were possible to reassure his dead son. But this time, it seemed the disembodied voice was not comforted.

'Father!'

It came again, more urgently, and Christopher found himself looking around the empty cellar.

'Father! Here!'

He stood up, straightening his aching back. He was afraid. He had struggled so long to keep from the madness that was like a baleful twin, constantly dripping poison in his ear. He wanted so much to resist, but his son's voice was so real, and so wanted. He was afraid of hearing it again but yearned for it.

'Father! Help me!'

It was coming from the soil stack, from the good earth within which his son's poor bones should lie but did not. He couldn't help himself. He went over to the stack and put his hand upon the mound as if he could comfort his son that way.

A face was there! His son's face, above the sacks, staring wildly at him through the bars of the gate. For a moment, Christopher thought he had risen from the earth, but he was no pale Lazarus. His skin was as brown as a beech leaf, his hair matted and unkempt. His eyes were wild but bursting with unmistakable life. If this were madness, Christopher could resist no longer. He started to pull away the sacks, heaving them with frantic energy. Soon, he could see more of his son. It was him! He was whole and looked healthier than ever. He was wiry and strong, and the hands he thrust through the bars were rough and calloused.

'Take this. I will help push the sacks from this side.'

Christopher took the small packet his son was proffering and thrust it into his pocket. Abel was in a fever of urgency and his panic infected his father.

'Hurry!'

The sacks had to be pulled far enough away so the gate would open. So much soil was being spilt that he would have to scoop it away. And he must fetch the key when the gate was clear. Was it still in the box in his room? These thoughts raced through his head, even as he longed to hold his son safely in his arms. Questions could come later. Now it was all fevered action and mingled joy and uncertainty. But his son was real. He was. And alive!

Having dragged yet another sack clear, Christopher returned to the gate to see a different face staring at him. This was not his son. This was a man. For a second their eyes met. Fear fizzed between them, and then Christopher felt a blow in his chest as if he had been punched. An unbearable heat, and a noise so loud it deafened him. Everything slowed. He started to fall. He knew he had been shot. He struggled not to let the darkness in. In his mind, he reached out for his son, but Abel slipped like liquid from his grasp. The dark came up behind his eyes and he fell.

ABEL MORGAN

12

The light was nearer than I had thought. And it was not daylight. It looked as if the path ended ahead of me, but a candle or some such must have been set in a niche at the height of my head to cast this feeble glow. I approached warily. For there to be light, there must be someone nearby, and I did not want to escape one to be taken by another. Did the path continue to the right or left? Was someone, even now, listening, waiting for me to approach?

As I drew near, I could see no way to continue. Ahead, the way was blocked by iron bars and a blank wall. But the light was not a candle set into a niche – it was coming from beyond the bars, shining through a gap near the top of the wall. Holding onto the bars, I raised myself, so I could look through the gap. What I saw made me fall back in disbelief. I could make no sense of it, but my heart began racing as never before and I raised myself again. Whatever maturity I had gained from the past half year fell away in an instant and I was a young child again. For it was the cellar of the Rumfustian Inn! I saw a lantern set close by on the floor, and my parent standing by the window!

'Father!'

He did not hear.

'Father! Here I am!'

He moved like an old man, with no urgency in his step until he saw me. Then he moved. He started to pull at the wall and I pushed. It was made of heavy sacks, but he started to drag them away as if they were bags of thistledown. Even so, he was not fast enough for me. I felt buried alive, with freedom so close. Every frantic moment felt like an age. When he stopped to take my hands and to caress my face, tears running down his cheeks, I wanted to be held in his arms, but the bars held us apart. I pulled away and thrust the package I still held at him.

'Father. Take this so I can help.' He put it inside his coat and we both redoubled our efforts. I didn't hear Zandar or see him. But my father did. His eyes widened and he took a step back.

Then it happened. It was done in an instant, but the moment is engraved upon my soul. As my father moved towards me again, a mighty explosion sounded in my ear. A smudge of smoke clouded my sight and, when I could see again, my father was lying motionless on the ground. A red stain was growing over his heart.

Zandar gripped my hair and dragged me back from the gate. The pain was terrible, but not as terrible as seeing my father lying dead because of me.

13

I was soon back on board, shut up in the place where Samal and I slept. The door was barred and my hands were tied so tight I was in agony. I sat on the tiny bunk with only one thought in my head. I had killed my father just as surely as if I had fired the shot. If I hadn't tried to escape he would still be alive.

I was now an orphan twice over and had been the instrument of both my parents' deaths. I had only one hope: that Zandar would forgive me. I had no choice. I would do my best to be a dutiful worker if he would keep me by him. Zandar had begun to think of me as a son. Surely, he would again?

But that was idle fancy. If he could feel sentimental, Zandar could also be unforgiving. What was more, I could hear his brother chiding him for his stupidity with me, and that must have made his mood worse. I stayed locked up for two days, never seeing Zandar, and only getting beer and a little bread from Samal on the second day.

When we eventually left Chineborough we didn't go far. As it began to grow dark, we lost way, and then I could hear the anchor go down. We must have been in one of the many inlets that speckled this coastline. Some gave good shelter in stormy weather, though it was not stormy this night. In fact, it felt very still. I couldn't bring myself to care where I was, but I was not allowed to wallow in my misery. The door to my prison was unbarred and Samal was there bearing a lamp against the night sky. Without comment, he took hold of my arm and manhandled me out into the hold. We made our way without words to the stairs that led up on deck. There was no sign of Zandar. Samal drew me to the side and motioned for me to climb over. At this, a terrible fear filled me. Was he going to drown me? But below was the little rowing boat, used when we lay at anchor close to shore.

'Where is Zandar?' I asked but received no answer. If he was aboard, and I felt sure he must be, he didn't want to see me.

With difficulty I climbed down into the little boat. Samal joined me and immediately pushed off.

'Where are we going?' I was much more frightened of Samal than his brother. It somewhat disgusted me that I could value my own life while having so recently ended my father's, but the desire to live burnt within me. Again, Samal declined to answer.

It was not far to the shore. There was a little beach of sand and shingle, onto which Samal drove the boat. Then he shipped his oars. He pushed me roughly to get out and I did so, splashing through the cool ankle-deep water. Ahead of me, at some way down the beach, a light shone. Samal caught hold of my arm again and pushed me towards it. As we drew near, I looked to see what manner of man was there to meet us. He looked somewhat crooked, and when he stepped forward into the light and spoke his voice was harsh, as if a saw had rasped it half away. My heart filled with dread. He glanced at me as if I were a horse for sale, and a poor one at that.

'What is this?'

'It's the boy Daniel Johnson sold us. We have no further use for him.'

'Why?'

'He's trouble. I would have drowned him, but Zandar is a soft-hearted idiot. He said you would know what to do with him.' Samal sounded surly.

'Give me the packet and be gone.'

Samal's voice had an ingratiating whine to it. 'There was no packet. You were let down by your information.'

The man became very still. He spoke quietly, but every word was clear. 'I was not let down, but it appears I have been betrayed.'

Samal's whine turned to bluster. 'Not by me. I tell you there was no packet. My brother saw so when he went in after the boy. He brought the other packet back with him in case it was not safe to leave it after he shot the man. I have it here for you.'

The man turned his head slightly in my direction. 'You sent the boy to fetch it? And you shot a man there?'

'Not I. My brother. He . . .'

'Search him.'

Samal looked sullen.

The man spoke to us both. 'The boy could have picked up the packet. Did you, boy?'

My mouth was as dry as the dust on a book. I shook my head.

'Search him.'

Samal's callused hands ran roughly over my body. He knocked my feet from me and pulled off my boots. When my knife fell out he grabbed it, but the man was not interested in my knife. 'Put it back,' he said.

Samal obeyed with a frown. 'I don't trust him,' he said. 'He might use it.'

The man glanced at my bound hands with contempt and gestured at my boots. 'Put them on,' he said to me. I struggled into my boots with difficulty and stood up.

'What about the price we paid for the boy?' whined Samal. 'I will take the goods you have for us, but I must also have the price for the boy.'

The man said nothing, but he moved closer, as if to speak privately. Suddenly Samal was falling and the man was stepping back. A blade had slashed Samal's neck and his blood was pouring onto the sand. He jerked horribly several times, and then was still. It was done in an instant. The man stooped and wiped the knife on Samal's shirt.

He took me to a pair of horses tethered to a scrubby tree. I was not required to ride pillion. He boosted me up onto the pack animal, where I sat, trying without success to stop my trembling. Would I be the next to receive his knife? The man laid his hand on my knee and looked at me.

'If you try to escape I will kill you,' he said.

I knew it was true, but I could not answer, for I had discovered something about him that chilled my very soul. The hand on my knee was far heavier than any man's real hand, and it was deadly cold. Its fingers stayed straight, not gripping my knee as I would have expected. I glanced down and saw two metal levers poking out of the leather that covered the hand and wrist. I had never seen or heard of anything like it.

The man swung himself into his saddle. I watched in horrified fascination as he did something with the knobs. The fingers and thumb of the metal hand closed over the reins like a spider gripping its prey. Without a word to me he set off at a steady trot with my horse on a leading rein tied to his saddle.

Once on the road he set a punishing pace. The horses ate up the miles, but I was unused to such long journeys and suffered for it. I found myself slipping between sleeping and waking in the saddle. I wanted to beg him to stop but knew he wouldn't take any notice. Instead, I hunched over my horse's neck and hung on as best I could with my bound hands. I feared falling and longed to wrap my arms around the horse's neck for safety but couldn't. I feared everything: losing my seat, angering the man, our destination and what might happen next. In short, I was as adrift as if I had been alone at sea.

At last I was aware of the darkness becoming thinner. It was almost dawn. The horses must have been tired, but our master hardly slackened the pace. Then, as the sun was about to rise, we left the road and took to a smaller one, a track, which wound its way between two hills. The pace slowed to a walk as the ground became more uneven and I hoped that we might soon stop. When we did, I was surprised, for around a corner we were suddenly once again at the coast.

I had lost any sense of direction during the night and had no idea where this particular bay might be, but it was beautiful in the early morning light. The silvery water lapped at the shingle beach, which sloped gently from the wiry grass where our horses stood, cropping it hungrily. A light salty breeze refreshed my weary face. The bay was almost completely encircled by the hills and would be hardly noticeable from the sea.

In the middle of the bay a ship lay at anchor. She had three masts and looked magical, shadow-dark as she was in the light sea mist. But the mist was dissolving, and the sun was rising behind me, painting the silver sea and the shadowy ship pale gold in the strengthening light. My heart knocked in my chest, for I was certain that this ship was going to take me far, far away. And yet something about her raised my spirits.

As I watched, a boat set out from the ship. Its oars dripped golden sunlit water as it made its way towards us. Two men were aboard. The oarsman shipped his oars and allowed the boat to drift gently onto the shore, where the keel grated on the shingle. The other stepped ashore. He looked at me curiously before nodding to my new master in greeting. My master dismounted, took several packets from his saddlebag and gave them to the man.

'You would oblige me by taking this boy,' he said.

The man looked at me again. 'Should I know anything about him?'

My master shook his head. 'Don't bring him back.'

The other smiled and spoke to me kindly enough. 'Come on then. The breeze is coming, and the tide will soon turn.'

My master pulled me without ceremony from his packhorse. I tried to land on my feet, but my legs buckled beneath me and I fell. I stood up unsteadily, and the man, who had got back in the boat, laughed.

'I'd rather ride the sea than a horse any day,' he said. 'Untie the boy's hands,' he added to my master. 'There is nowhere here for him to run.'

As soon as the rope was cut I cried out in agony. The man in the boat frowned. He stood up, stepped over the gunwale and onto the beach again. He took my wrists in his hands and examined them carefully.

'Once the blood has filled your veins it will be better, but you will be in pain for a while.'

'Put the letters only into the captain's hands and tell him he owes me for a cabin boy,' said my master.

The man from the boat laughed again. 'I will indeed.' He put his hand under my arm to help me into the boat.

'If you are a good boy, you will likely thrive with us,' he told me. 'But you must forget your old life and begin anew. We are going to the Americas, and no, you will not return. Given time, you will not want to. There are fortunes to be made where we are going, so take heart and be resolute.'

No one had spoken so kindly to me since I had first been captured and I felt tears prick at the back of my eyes. I knew he was right. I had no home any more. Jane and William would work for

Daniel, or whoever else might take over the inn. With the death of my father, there was no place for me. Whatever lay ahead, I wanted to face it bravely, but I was not a man. I was still only a boy and, in spite of all my efforts, as they rowed me away, I wept.

CHRISTOPHER MORGAN

14

The sound of his blood was the sound of the sea. It returned him to that day in the Low Countries when he stood on the beach and, feeling so lost, feared he would never see his homeland again. The stone of the flagstones in the cellar seeped cold and damp into his core, as the icy wind had done that day. He would never see what he loved so much, ever again. He was as helpless now, with his blood leaking from his body, as he had been – a lost soul, on that shifting sand. He died and died again. His heart faltered and stopped, gathered itself, tried again and faltered once more. If he could get up, if he could take this weight off his breast, but it lay there like a hot stone, branding his flesh, feeling like heartbreak and worse. And all the while he struggled to live, the name beat with his blood through his brain. *Abel, my son. Abel, Abel, Abel.*

He felt them lift him up. He could hear nothing except the ocean of his blood. He could not see, nor could he speak. He died again, and this time he lay on a battlefield with his Abraham there to raise him up, with love. When Abraham faded, there was pain, so much pain that he wanted his life to stop so he could join him again and lose the pain.

Above the cellar, in the kitchen, Jane heard the shot. She called to William, who was working in the garden, but he had heard it too and was already on his way to find out what had happened.

'Why has he his pistol with him?'

William shook his head. 'I didn't know he had. He said he was going to attend to his mushrooms in the cellar.'

'I hope he has not hurt himself.'

They listened, but all was quiet. William regarded his wife. 'Should we make sure all is well?'

'Yes. But we must not fuss over him. Here. Take him some beer, husband.'

It was not many seconds later that she heard William's voice. 'Jane! Help me!'

Christopher was sprawled on his back amongst a mess of soil and tumbled sacks. His carefully planted fungi were trampled and abandoned. At first, it was not obvious to them that he was shot because there was no gun, and in the dim light his blood-soaked jacket was not obvious.

'We must have mistaken the noise, Jane.'

'Is the gun not here?'

'I cannot see it.'

'Where is he hurt? Has he hit his head?'

'I cannot tell,' said Jane. 'We should get him up the stairs, into the light.'

It was not until Jane tried to feel the beat of his heart that they discovered his wound.

Christopher was heavy, and William and Jane were not young. It was not an easy task to carry their master up the cellar steps and, when they had him in the passage, they knew they would never manage to take him on up the next stairs to his bed. Instead, Jane ran for bedding to soften the floor, and they took him into the kitchen, which at least was always warm.

There was no doctor in Dario, but William took Troubadour and managed somehow to mount and ride him to Chineborough in search of one. All that day, while Jane waited for the doctor to arrive, Christopher hovered between life and death. He groaned on occasion and muttered words she could not decipher, but mostly he lay in a swoon.

The doctor, when he came, didn't give much for the life of his patient. 'His heart is very weak,' he said. 'He will likely die. All that can be said for the good is that the ball went right through his body, so it doesn't need to be extracted.' He uncorked his oil and drizzled some into the wounds. 'And the ball seems to have entered at a fortunate angle,' he added, 'missing his heart and lung. Or he would be already dead.'

'Will you come back again?' asked Jane, gazing fearfully at her white-faced master on the floor.

The doctor shook his head. 'If he lives this night he may get a fever. If he survives that and his wounds don't turn bad, he might survive. In any event, there is little more I can do for him. Give him brandy.'

The doctor had gone, along with Jane's cockerel in payment, by the time William arrived. Troubadour had insisted on ambling his way home instead of galloping, which was just as well, or doubtless William would have lost his seat. William and Jane sat on the bench, gazing at their master. He had groaned many times during the pulling, turning, prodding and poking the doctor had given him, but now he lay deathly silent, hardly breathing. His face was as white as the linen binding his wounds. Jane had tried dribbling brandy into his mouth, but little if any had found its way past his lips.

'We should take turns to sit up with him,' said William. 'He shouldn't die alone.'

'What will become of us?' said Jane. 'Where shall we go?'

William put his arm around her. 'Maybe he won't die,' he said, looking doubtfully at the still figure.

He did not die, in spite of fever and his weak heart. But it was a long time before Christopher Morgan was properly healed. For some days he lay between life and death on the floor of the kitchen. Then, after he had seemed to improve a little and they decided to put him to bed for his comfort's sake, he relapsed with the movement. The fragile clotting of his wounds opened and he bled again, as if freshly injured. For a few days it seemed as if they had killed him by their kindness, but if his heart was weak, his will was very strong.

Stepping between life and death, it was as if his body could not make up its mind. Often, he was not lucid. When he was, he lay for hours, unable to communicate, but alive to the care he was given by his servants. He was aware of their fear for themselves if he should die but could say nothing to comfort them. During the long night hours, when William and Jane took it in turns to watch him, with a single candle illuminating their ageing faces, he was moved by love for them. His parents would have been appalled. He knew very well that had they been alive they would have admonished him many times over the past few years. Why had he not advanced himself with the King while in exile? Why had he not followed him to London and taken a place at court? He could have had a good position by now, instead of mouldering in the countryside on his own.

But his parents had been dead for a long time and Christopher had punished himself enough over the years. He had not enjoyed court intrigue when the court was in exile. How would it be better at Whitehall? He could not regret denying his son false friendships and dangerous politics. And although he had temporarily lost Abel, he knew now that he lived. Seeing him there at the gate in the cellar had suggested to him something he had not known all the months of his vanishment. That Daniel Johnson, who had been assiduous in helping search for Abel, must surely be implicated in his disappearance. Why else would Abel be in the Johnsons' tunnel? So far as he knew, none but the Johnsons knew its entrance. However, it troubled Christopher that he didn't recognise the man who had shot him. It was unfortunate that he couldn't accuse a Johnson of causing his injury. And he couldn't prove the Johnsons were to blame for Abel's disappearance. What if the militia believed that Abel had chosen to run away and join the smugglers? During his slow and painful recovery, he worried away at these thoughts. At one moment he felt optimistic and at the next he despaired at ever finding his son.

As soon as he could make himself understood, Abel's name was constantly on Christopher's lips. While Jane and William wanted to discover how he had a pistol wound with no pistol in evidence, all he would say, in a weak whisper, was 'Abel' and point towards his jacket, which lay on his chair. Jane, having done her best to remove most of the bloodstains and patch the holes, brought it to him and laid it on the bed.

'You want your jacket, sir?'

'Pocket.'

He was too weak to do it himself, so William did as his master wanted and felt in the pockets. He put the contents – a small knife, some twine and a packet – into his master's hand and instantly Christopher stopped fretting.

When, at last, many days later, he was able to tell them what had happened, they found it impossible to believe.

'You have had a fever, sir,' Jane told him. 'You dreamt you saw your son.'

'I tell you he was there, the wrong side of that accursed gate into the tunnel!'

'Sir, you must not become agitated, for your health's sake.'

'And what must I do for my son's sake?'

There was silence, apart from his laboured breathing. Then he pointed at his wooden chest. 'The key to the gate is in there, Jane. Please take it and keep it with you always. Abel may return secretly again.' His mouth worked with emotion. 'We must be ready.'

'Yes, sir.'

'And Jane?'

She paused in her search for the key.

'The tunnel was used by the Johnsons. Seeing Abel there made it clear to me that Daniel must surely know where he is. He must be examined and the tunnel searched. I never wanted to know where it led, but now I must.'

Jane got up and came to the chair by his bed. She had sat in it for so many days and nights, watching over him, that it felt natural to do so now, even though she was a servant. 'Oh, sir,' she said sadly. 'So much has happened in the village since you have been lying here. It was over a month ago when the militia came for the Johnsons. I don't know who betrayed them, but Daniel, along with his sons, were all hanged with terrible speed. Even the youngest, who was a small boy. They say they hardly gave them leave to speak in their own defence. The family is quite broken up and scattered. The soldiers even pulled the thatch from their houses and the very stones from their walls. The ruins of their houses are like lost teeth in a mouth. I don't know why it happened, and God knows the village is better without them, but it was a terrible time, for they didn't all deserve such treatment. The women and babes were left homeless and must be living in ditches, as far as I know. At any rate, none of that family are in the village now.'

Christopher stared at Jane and felt his heart falter. 'All gone?'

'All, sir.'

'Daniel hanged?'

She nodded.

'How can it be?'

The little blood that had returned to his cheeks drained away and his face became grey. He closed his eyes. He had taken too long to recover. He had been determined to have Daniel questioned, but he was too late. It was all too late. It felt as if he were falling from a great height, a falling without end.

For a while, he knew nothing. When he woke, it was to despair, followed swiftly by memory.

'Where is the packet?' He felt on the bedcover but could not find it. He was alone, so he called for Jane. 'Where is it? Abel gave it to me.'

Jane endeavoured always to keep her master tidy, but his bedclothes were constantly disturbed as he became stronger and more restless.

'Calm yourself, sir. It will be here somewhere.' Eventually she found it, lying forgotten under the bed. 'Here, sir.'

'Fetch me a knife, Jane. I cannot undo it without one.'

Christopher did not know what he hoped for. A letter, an explanation, even the slightest clue would be of help now Daniel was extraordinarily, so unbelievably gone. He fretted until William arrived with Jane, bringing with him the scent of cold weather into the sickroom. He slit the cords for Christopher and unfolded the document inside. He and Jane propped Christopher up to see what the packet held. It was an unexpected puzzle, a map that none of them could decipher.

'It is a fortified headland with sea around it, but I do not recognise the place,' said Christopher, struggling and failing to disguise the disappointment he felt. It was unreasonable of him to have expected the packet to contain a direct message from Abel to his father, but that was exactly what he had yearned for.

'Might a sea captain in Chineborough know?' suggested William.

Christopher frowned. 'Maybe. But the map is more a plan of the great castle or palace within the fortifications than the surrounding geography.' He felt suddenly exhausted and totally disheartened. 'Leave me to sleep. I need to recover my strength.'

Sleeping only to wake and fret was the pattern for some time longer.

Several times, Jane and William found their master struggling to dress himself, the wound in his shoulder freshly staining his linen red.

'Why must you give us more work and risk your life into the bargain?' Jane took to scolding him, to little effect.

'You know I must get up and find Abel,' he told them as they eased him back upon his pillows. 'I cannot waste any more time lying in bed.'

'What do you mean to do, sir?'

'Well, Jane,' said Christopher. 'I need you to launder my best linen and air my outer garments, ready for when I am well. And William, if I were to ask you to sell Troubadour, would I have your word that you would drive a hard bargain?'

'I would do my best, sir.' It was obvious both Jane and William wanted to ask about his plans but felt unable to do so.

'The best place I know to ask about such a map is in London,' Christopher explained. 'And if I am to try it, I must have money and try not to look like a pauper.'

'I think, sir,' said William slowly, 'if it is money you are anxious about, you should know that things have been easier since the Johnsons were driven away.'

'The inn is busier, sir,' said Jane. 'It is not a fortune, but there is more in the cash box than for a long time.'

'I had not thought of that possibility.' Christopher sighed. 'But it is so often true that one man's misfortune is to another's advantage. Well . . . maybe we can keep old Troubadour after all. We can have a reckoning one day soon. But I have two urgent jobs to do. I must write a letter and I must get quite well.'

Christopher spent a lot of time composing his letter. In the end, he decided that simple honesty was the best that he could manage. He did not think a reply was very likely, so when, some weeks later, a clatter of hooves outside his window woke him during his afternoon nap, it did not occur to him that it might be a post boy.

Jane took the letter up to him, but he refused to open it in bed. He had been dressed and downstairs several times. This, surely, was a sign that he should fully take up the reins of life again, so he resisted the temptation to read it until he was settled in front of the fire in the kitchen with some brandy at his elbow. With trembling fingers, he broke the royal seal and read the letter. When he had finished, he laid it on his lap and took up the glass. He wiped his eyes with the back of his hand and sipped the fiery liquid.

'The King remembers me. He says his cartographers will study the map if I send it and he hopes to meet me again if I happen to be in London.' He smiled at his servants, who were gazing at him as if he were a magician. 'I am nearly as astonished as you. But I will not trust the map to the King's post. I will take it myself. It is the only link we have to Abel. So, let us count our money and see what we can venture with it.'

Christopher had aged, that was undeniable, but he worked hard on his recovery. At first, it was enough simply to come downstairs every day. Then he began to walk about. Eventually he asked William to saddle Troubadour and, on a crisp winter's day, he took a gentle ride about the village. From then on, he gained strength rapidly, going a little further each day when it did not rain. After riding gently down to Chineborough, spending an hour gazing out to sea, doing some business and returning before dark, he found William bringing some new brewed beer from the brewhouse.

'I wish all my linen washed,' he said, 'and my bag packed. Will you walk with me next Monday, while I ride to the high road? I will take the coach to London and you can take Troubadour back home for me. On Tuesday, a man will come from Chineborough to collect the old beast. I am sorry to see him go, but in spite of our improved circumstances I may need his value in London.'

'Are you sure you are well enough to go, sir?' said Jane.

'I think I am as well as I will be in this life, thanks to your good care. All I ask of you while I am away is that you watch always for Abel and send word to me should he manage to come home. I will send word of where I lie when I know it. And if something should happen to me and I do not return, then I ask that you should care for him as you always have. Apprentice him to a trade of his desire if there is enough money. If not, he may run the inn with you and care for you, his foster parents.'

'Sir' – William worked his hands in agitation – 'I am sure we will see you shortly after you conclude your business with the map.'

Jane glared at him. 'Unless he chooses to stay at court.'

Christopher laughed. It was something he had not done in a long while. 'Don't fret, Jane. I am not made for court life. If God spares me, I will be back soon. I pray it will be with news of where Abel has been taken and how soon we are to fetch him home.'

15

Christopher found the most modest and yet respectable lodging in London he could. After giving himself half a day to recover, he presented himself at Whitehall, feeling so out of place he had to steel himself to remain. His best linen was so patched he felt like a kitchen servant, and he discovered his best suit of clothes to be so out of date he knew he must strike a comical figure.

The letter he had received didn't give any clue as to when would be best to present himself. He hardly expected to be ushered straight away into the King's presence, but he found his heart racing as he presented himself at the gate. It had been many years since he had last seen the King, then still uncrowned. Would he help? Would he even see him, in spite of the letter saying he would be happy to do so? Christopher wasn't concerned about meeting his sovereign. The last time they had met they had not parted exactly as friends. But the King must have knowledgeable geographers who could identify the place on the map. That was all Christopher wanted: just someone who could tell him where he must go to look for his son.

'Your letter of introduction?' The official looked at Christopher's threadbare clothes with an undisguised sneer. 'Name?'

'Sir Christopher Morgan. I was with the King in . . .'

The official moved on to the next petitioner and a guard made it clear that he was not to pass.

After waiting for a while, he and others were told to come back the next day. However, the following day the King was abroad, the next he was indisposed and after that he was attending to the affairs of state. Christopher paced, he sat, and he paced again. He wandered the streets and ate frugally before returning to be told the same things again.

'But I know him!' said Christopher at last, trying to keep his voice from sounding petulant or anxious, though his store of money was speedily dwindling. 'And I have something His Majesty will want to see.'

No one was interested. They offered to take the map to the King but, fearing to lose it, Christopher would not, could not give up this last link with his son unless he were to accompany it, wherever it went.

The next morning, he was sitting as usual in an outer room when a dumpy little man came hurrying past with an armful of documents. As he passed by, some of the rolls of paper slid from his grasp and spilt onto the floor. Christopher went to help.

'Much obliged to you,' said the man politely.

Christopher endeavoured to roll them back up for their owner. As he did so he could see that they were plans of a ship. Where there were plans, surely there might be knowledge of maps?

'I am interested in a ship,' said Christopher, anxious to take advantage of the situation.

The man looked at him doubtfully. 'To commission one? I think not . . . Maybe you wish to find a position on board?'

'No. That is . . . I . . .' The man was losing interest. Christopher tried again. 'The King wrote to me, asking me to visit him. I have a map . . .'

The man's eyebrows rose. He seemed amused, and Christopher felt himself teased. 'A man interested in a ship who has a map! Are you an adventurer, sir?'

'I propose finding my only son, who was captured,' Christopher replied, rather standing on his dignity. 'I have a map but need help in deciphering it.'

The man's demeanour instantly changed. 'My dear sir! I am so sorry. The loss of any child is a tragedy, an only son more so. And under such dreadful circumstances. Was it the Barbary pirates? We sting them when we can, I assure you, and we will do more with the help of new ships such as this one.' He took the plan from Christopher. 'I am sorry to say there are many good Christians in the hands of the Moors.' He adjusted the bundle of documents and gave Christopher a nod. He took a step and then hesitated. 'You say you have a map?'

Christopher couldn't imagine that Daniel would have had dealings with those terrible pirates who raided coastal villages in search of Christian slaves. They were not known for buying slaves, preferring to take by force, slaughtering any that resisted. Besides, Christopher had heard of no such raids on the south coast for some time. All the same, he withdrew the map from his coat in the hope that this man might recognise the place. 'It was taken from his captors and put into my hand by my son,' he said. 'Shortly before he was recaptured.'

The man looked intrigued. 'May I see?'

Christopher unfolded the map but held it fast in his own hand.

'But my dear sir! The legend is Moorish, is it not?'

Christopher shrugged. 'But surely that is just a fancy? I thought it an embellishment. A decoration. Do you not think it a castle somewhere on our coast, or possibly as far as Wales?' He looked at the man in some distress.

The little man gave him a sympathetic glance. 'You may be right, sir, but I am not convinced. I do not wish to alarm you, but I do not know why anyone would give a Welsh map a Moorish inscription. I cannot read it for you, but I am sure Sir John Narborough will know someone who can. I am meeting with him now. If you like I will take the map to show him.'

'That is very kind,' said Christopher, his hopes rising by the moment. 'However, it is all I have to find my son. I cannot let it out of my sight.'

'In that case,' said the man after a moment's hesitation, 'you had better come with it.' He made Christopher a small bow. 'Mr Pepys at your service. I work at the admiralty, hence these plans. His Majesty is in the process of enlarging his navy.'

'Sir Christopher Morgan at yours.'

'Follow me, sir. Oh!' He gasped as the roll of documents threatened to slip again. 'Perhaps you could oblige me by taking some of these?'

'Certainly.'

Christopher followed Mr Pepys into an inner room, one that had so far been denied him. They deposited the documents onto a large table and he helped the admiralty man unroll the plan.

'This, you see, is to be His Majesty's new answer to the Barbary pirates. At least, this is Sir John's fervent hope.'

'It looks a most impressive vessel.'

'Indeed. And it will cost a pretty penny to equip as I, who will be responsible for that task, can tell you.'

Christopher was just congratulating himself on what a fortunate meeting this might be when a commotion was heralded by double doors being opened at the far end of the room. A number of gentlemen entered, all talking and laughing together. For a few moments Christopher thought he knew none of them, but then he recognised the King. Christopher and Mr Pepys bowed. The King, noticing the plans on the table, stepped forward eagerly.

'Mr Pepys! I see you have brought the plans. What news of our ship?'

'She comes on, sire. And I heard from the foundry yesterday. The ordnance will be ready in good time.'

'Excellent! Look, Sir John. I think your quarters will be splendid. And we hope that diplomacy may be one use of them.'

Sir John voiced his appreciation. It was then that the King noticed Christopher. His clothes singled him out, even against Mr Pepys, who was soberly enough dressed.

'I see you have brought an assistant with you today, Mr Pepys.'

Mr Pepys bowed. 'Not an assistant, sir, but one Sir Christopher Morgan, who has a map that you and Sir John might be interested in.'

Christopher bowed, feeling the King's sharp eyes upon him. 'Well, maps are invariably interesting. Let's see it.'

Christopher ventured to look up and King Charles's mouth widened into a large smile. 'Sir Christopher. You appear like a ghost from the past! Gentlemen, this good man was with me in

France and Holland many years ago. We had a falling-out over a girl, as I recall.' His smile became a laugh. 'It piqued me that she preferred this spindleshanks to me.' The gentlemen around him laughed politely. 'Did you marry her, as you swore you would?'

'Yes, sir.'

'And how does she, the pretty Dutch maid you stole from me?'

'Dead these twelve years, sir, in giving birth to the son I now seek.'

Instantly the King abandoned his happy expression. 'I am so sorry. I recall now, the letter you wrote to me about your son's trouble. I asked my secretary to let you know you would find a welcome here. Tell me. Have you heard from your son since he was taken?'

'Once, when he made a brief escape from his captors. In those few moments he gave me a map, which I take to be the place where he is now.'

'He sounds a resourceful boy. Do you have the map with you?'

'I do, sir.'

'Then give it to Sir John here and he can have it examined.'

Christopher looked at his sovereign with a mixture of duty and determination. 'It is all I have to help me find my Abel. I cannot allow it out of my sight, sir.'

The King hesitated. For a moment Christopher was afraid Charles was angry, but he was not. 'Sir John?'

'Yes, sir?'

'Have a cartographer come. Have him bring his materials and set him to copy this precious map.'

'Yes, sir.'

'So, Christopher. I think it won't rain. While we wait for the map-maker we could walk in the privy garden and remember our youth.'

The King led the way and Christopher followed, still clutching his map. It was a very fine day. The peace of the gardens was a welcome contrast to the noise of the court, but it was hard for Christopher to match the King's pace, even though their legs were much of a length.

'You used to keep up the best of all my retinue,' the King complained.

Christopher smiled ruefully. 'I remember. But I am not so fast since I was wounded. I think I am not quite fit.'

'I am so sorry! Let us sit. We will not be disturbed here, if I am not mistaken. Now, tell me of your life since I left you in Holland. It has not been kind to you, I think, and yet you did not write to me for a pension when I came into my own. God knows, parliament keeps my purse almost empty, but I would have been pleased to see you at court.'

Christopher sighed. 'I am sorry, sir. At first, I kept away because of Margarita. You were angry with me in Holland, with just cause.'

'I *was* angry. Remember that last night in The Hague before I set sail for England? All the ladies were mad to dance with me, all but Margarita, and yet I insisted on leading her out three times. It was the anger of a lovesick fool and deeply discourteous of me. I remember how you stood to one side – patient, dignified, waiting for her to return to you. You were more a prince than I then.' He paused. 'I would not behave that way again. But afterwards . . . after she died . . . you could have written then. I would have liked to see you.'

'Afterwards I was seized by a sort of madness,' said Christopher. 'At first, I didn't want the boy to live, then I did. I do . . .'

Charles laid his hand on Christopher's sleeve. 'Sometimes,' he said sadly, 'I think there's no hell like loving too well.'

There was silence between them for a few moments and then the King spoke again. 'No matter. And now things are right between us perhaps you will let me have a glimpse of this precious map. Do you have any idea about it?'

'Yes, sir. Abel was most likely taken by a local rogue, who was hanged before I was able to question him. I don't recognise the place as being on any coast I know, so I thought it is most likely to be a place on a part of the coast I don't know. Perhaps in Wales?'

Christopher drew it out of his coat and unfolded it as he had done for Mr Pepys. He handed it to Charles, who took it as carefully as if it had been a jewel or the egg of a fabulous bird.

'I am sorry to tell you that the script is Moorish,' he said after a moment's study. 'I cannot recognise the place, but doubtless there will be someone here who can and, at any rate, read the legend. I wondered at first if it were our territory of Tangier, but I am sure it is not. Did the man who shot you look like a Barbary pirate?'

Christopher shook his head. 'He appeared as English as me, though I had not seen him before and I did not hear him speak.'

Charles gave the map back, rested his elbows on his knees and set his chin in his hands. 'I will enquire, but I cannot recall hearing of any raids on my coast over the past months. My navy has been better recently at keeping the pirates away from our shores, although Ireland has suffered badly.' He looked at Christopher. 'I hope we can discount your son being dispatched into our navy. We can investigate that.'

'Thank you, sir. I am most grateful.'

For a few minutes Charles gazed, without speaking, at the small neat hedges and gravel paths of his privy garden. Christopher waited. Rather than being forced to linger while his map was copied for the King's possible use, he wanted an answer now. He wanted to be told exactly where to go to find his son and what to do to release him, but much in life had taught him that things were seldom so easy. He schooled himself not to sigh, which might insult the King. When the King spoke again, it was briskly.

'Do you remember lending me your shoes?'

Christopher found himself surprised into a smile. 'I do, yes.'

'It was such a kindness. You had to go barefoot until my mother could get me a pair made.'

'It was not for so very long. It was fortunate that our feet were the same size.'

'Let me return the favour, Christopher, and find you a pair. You cannot go shod like that, in court or anywhere else.' Christopher looked at his feet, which were, certainly, poorly shod by any standards. The leather was split, and betrayed not just an old fashion, but also overuse and lack of proper repair. Next to his feet were those of his king. They were encased in exquisite shoes, with elegant heels and profuse embroidery. They were not the shoes of a man who needed to walk outdoors. And yet he had. The flowers and leaves stitched upon them were dusty with the gravel path. The fabric they were made of would not last long, used this way. Such shoes would be no use to Christopher, but he could not say so.

'I insist,' said Charles, misreading Christopher's lack of reply. 'You must not be so proud. There are men at court living on pensions given to them twenty years ago for small things done for me. You have asked for nothing, and now when you do it is only to find help in reading a map! You cannot deny me the pleasure of paying you in kind for your favour in the past.'

Christopher did his best to look grateful. 'Thank you, sir.'

'Good. I will enjoy ordering them for you.'

He stood up. A gentleman who had been hovering some way off started towards them. 'If I am not mistaken, here comes word of our cartographer. Let us go in. Maybe your son is not so far away and will soon be recovered.'

16

If Mr Pepys was annoyed at having to wait while the King renewed his acquaintance with Christopher, he didn't show it. He stood politely to one side while Christopher and the map-maker were settled together at a table, and while several gentlemen offered opinions on the map.

'Tangier!' said one. 'This has been made by our enemies who seek to take our territory!'

The King turned to Sir John. 'What do you think?'

The man peered thoughtfully at the map. 'The shape of the promontory is similar,' he said. 'But these aren't English fortifications, nor are these English buildings. And look at the bottom of the map. I know of no islands like these off the coast of Tangier. I am pretty sure this is the capital of the Ottomans, Constantinople, and this place here is the Sultan's palace.' He gave Christopher a hard look, almost as if he suspected him of some sort of subterfuge. 'I have never seen a map with so much detail of the forbidden interior of the palace.' He cleared his throat and addressed the King. 'It is, in my opinion, sir, a map of the very heart of the Ottoman Empire and I think the legend will confirm it.'

There was an air of excitement amongst the gentlemen, but Christopher was not interested in their pleasure, only in the feeling of dread that filled his heart. 'I must go there at once!' he said in a louder voice than he had meant.

Charles glanced at him as if he had almost forgotten he was there. 'Passage cannot be got overnight,' he said. 'However, you are welcome to remain at court until you have a resolution by letter from your son or find passage on a ship.' He turned to the others. 'I am sorry, gentlemen. I am out of time. I suspect I am already late for a meeting and will be taken to task by my ministers. Our business will have to wait.'

Christopher stayed by the cartographer until the map was copied and returned to him. But after that, he decided he must stay on in London until a ship was found. Back at his lodgings, he wrote to William and Jane, asking for word to be sent should a letter arrive from Abel, hoping they would be able to make out the words well enough to understand his message. He also asked for more funds. His determination to find his son wasn't dimmed, but he was deeply shaken at the destination. Although his plans to rescue Abel had been vague, he had assumed it would entail a ride, a ransom or escape, and the risk of violence. Now, he had to contemplate a long sea journey to a place entirely foreign to him, with a language he did not speak and a culture he did not understand. In truth, his wanderings on the continent after the war as a penniless outcast had cured him of wanting any more foreign travel. Thanks to that time, he had, as well as his native tongue and passable Latin, enough Dutch and French to get by. Arabic, however, was another matter. He had never even heard the language spoken. If it was as much of a mystery as its writing it would be impossible to understand. And yet, apparently there was at least one at court who could decipher it. He would have to seek this person out and beg instruction.

This was as far as he had got with his thoughts that evening. As he sat disconsolately by his window after supper, a small commotion in the street made him look out. He could not see who was knocking so loudly beneath him, but after a few seconds his landlord came up to him.

'Your presence is needed,' he said.

'We are directed to take you to Whitehall,' said one of the two men at the door.

Christopher looked in vain for any badge that would proclaim them the King's men. The two were dressed too well to be common thieves, but only a fool would follow strangers in this seething city.

'I have just come from there!'

'Even so, you are to come with us now.'

Their appearance was bewildering and alarming. Christopher had seen enough soldiers in his life to recognise these two, even though they were dressed almost as gentlemen. 'Am I arrested? If so, can I enquire why? And by who?'

If he was not arrested, it seemed neither was he quite free. His sword and pistol remained upstairs, and they were both armed. He had no choice but to go with them. They had brought a horse for him, and for a few moments he was afraid they would bind him. They did not, although he had the impression that they would not hesitate to do so if he became difficult.

For a little while, their route made him fear he was being taken to the Tower, but the men had spoken the truth. They took him not exactly to the palace but to a building close by. In a plain room he was asked politely enough to wait. There was a bottle and glasses on the table, but Christopher did not trust the wine enough to drink it.

At last, two different men arrived. They immediately poured wine for themselves and him. He began to feel slightly reassured, but without introducing themselves or any other courtesy they began questioning him. Over and over again they asked him about the circumstances of his receiving the map. Christopher could tell them little, but he did his best to satisfy them.

'Does your son often carry sealed packets about the country,' asked one, 'when any honest man would use the King's mail?'

Christopher tried to curb his anger and frustration. 'My son is a young boy and has been taken from me. I do not know how he came by the map, except I am sure he wanted to tell me where he was being taken. He could not have known I would be in the cellar, so he must surely have secretly taken it from one of his captors, intending to leave it for me to find. In the event, I was there and he gave it straight into my hand.'

'Did he say anything?'

Christopher tried to think. 'He said, "Here, take this" or similar words. In truth we said little. I was in a fever to uncover the gate, so I could unlock it and rescue him. It was a matter of minutes only . . .'

One of the men pushed his glass of wine to him, and Christopher took a deep draught to steady himself. 'I'm sorry. I find the memory distressing.'

'Could it be,' said the other, 'that your son was secretly acting as a message boy for someone? I mean, without your knowledge?'

Christopher stared at him. 'He was hardly out of my sight until he was taken. And we live in a small village, not a great city with all its opportunities for subterfuge. Who would he take a message to . . . or from?'

The men looked at each other but did not reply.

'My son is not a spy!'

'Do you think your son knew what was in the package?'

Christopher scratched his head. 'Why would he give it to me if he did not?'

'Well, sir.' The two men drained their glasses and got to their feet. They seemed very pleased at what had transpired, although Christopher was no more informed than he had been at the start. 'Thank you for your time.'

They went to the door, but the one who reached it first paused and looked back at Christopher. 'I hope your son returns, sir. But if I might give you a little advice?'

'Yes?'

'It would be to return home and continue to live quietly. That appears to have done you well in the past.'

Christopher could not help his bitter response. 'It has done well enough to lose me my son.'

For a moment the two men were silent. Then the other said, 'If you go to that place you would be advised to leave the map behind.'

They both bowed and left, closing the door behind them. Christopher was left with the remains of the bottle of wine and myriad unanswered questions. At length, being alone for some while, he tried the door and found, somewhat to his surprise, that it was unlocked. There was no sign of the men, nor of the two who had brought him there. He considered going to the palace as it was so near, but he did not have the stomach for it. He could hardly ask the King about what had happened, even if he had been on familiar enough terms with him. In spite of the King's kindness in speaking with him and offering him a gift of shoes, Christopher was certainly not of his sovereign's inner circle. He also knew he was too innocent of court matters to know if those men had been for the King or for some other interest. It would probably be better not to ask anyone about it. In the end, after some indecision,

Christopher made his way slowly to his lodgings. He arrived back much muddied about the legs, regretting his lack of horse.

He went to court the following morning somewhat nervous, but it was as if his questioning had never happened. He discovered that Sir John Narborough would soon take his fleet to the English port of Tangier, with the intention of confronting the Barbary pirates. Sir John did not have time for the likes of Christopher, but he was not impolite to him and did not definitively deny him a passage on one of his ships. It was the best Christopher could hope for.

While he waited, he pondered. His questioners' warning to go home and stay there was no help to him. He feared becoming entangled in any form of spying, and he recognised that innocence in such circumstances could be dangerous, but what else could he do? He could not abandon his son if there was any chance of saving him, no matter what was involved. So, yes. He would leave London as soon as possible. But he would not go home. Not unless word came from them that Abel had returned.

The very next day he had another visitor. His jangled nerves were somewhat gentled by it being the King's shoemaker and his assistant, come to take his measurements. A little while afterwards, a pair of stout, practical shoes arrived, made of excellent leather. He felt pathetically grateful at the King's thoughtfulness. He soon also received a suit of clothes, not of the latest fashion but only lightly worn. Along with them came another pair of shoes, worn but very fancy, matching the clothes and obviously meant for court wear. He had owned similar clothes as a young man, but never so fine. Christopher was touched that the King should send him his discarded clothes but couldn't help wondering that if his questioning by the two men had gone badly he might have received nothing at all, or worse.

He tried on his new wardrobe that evening. The clothes would not need altering if he regained his usual weight, and both pairs of shoes fitted very well. Glancing at himself in the glass, Christopher felt new-made. His past few years seemed to fall away, like the discarded husk of an insect, almost as if his son had never existed. It was a vertiginous feeling and left him uneasy.

He went to court almost every day and would have liked to personally thank the King, but his sovereign was always surrounded by garrulous company and although he nodded at Christopher a couple of times in a not unfriendly manner, it was always a very slight acknowledgement and at a distance. Not being a person to ingratiate himself, Christopher expressed his thanks in a letter, which he gave to the King's secretary.

After a few more days, he received a laboriously written note from Jane at home: *No news, sir*.

While he waited, Christopher studied the language of the Arabs and learnt as much as he could about the great empire of the Ottomans. It seemed Barbary pirates were being increasingly dissuaded from raiding English soil by decisive action from the navy.

'And there is a plan to expand trade with Constantinople,' one of the gentlemen at court told him. 'I hear His Majesty is writing to our ambassador to the Ottoman court, instructing him to seek an audience with the Sultan. Our King hopes a desire to improve trade will encourage the Sultan also to resolve the matter of the many Christian slaves he has toiling in his empire. Some of the letters received from prisoners are truly distressing.'

Christopher's heart tumbled in his chest with conflicting emotions. 'Will the instructions go by sea?'

The gentleman smiled. 'Of course. One of the newer ships is being equipped this very moment and I feel sure the fleet will be ready to sail soon. Several business interests will be represented on board, so if you desire also to sail you should apply.'

Christopher leapt to his feet.

'Rest easy! They won't be ready for another two or three weeks.'

That did not seem soon to Christopher, but he could not rest easy. He was in agony to depart. He found himself pacing at night and unwrapping and poring over the map twenty times a day. There were some things he could do. He must write again to inform his servants what was happening. He must buy provisions for his journey and gather as much money as he could in the hopes of finding and ransoming his son. With little sadness he sold the flamboyant hat that had arrived with the suit of clothes from the King and bought a more practical one. The sale added a few more welcome coins to his store.

All was finally ready, but then the winds were not favourable. For three extra days Christopher waited, each day going out into the countryside where he walked at a furious pace, very much as the King liked to walk in his garden. Then, on the fourth morning, it was so still that hardly a leaf trembled. This would not do and Christopher was racked with impatience. But as he was about to set out pacing again, a message came for him to go to the ship.

When he arrived, there was much bustle at the dock. To Christopher's great surprise, the King was there with some of his gentlemen and he approached Christopher with a smile.

'You find me at one of my favourite pastimes,' he said in greeting. 'Inspecting my ships gives me much pleasure and I am pleased to say the building of my newest vessel is coming on at a great pace.'

'I wanted to thank you again for the fine shoes and clothing you sent me, sir,' said Christopher.

The King waved away his thanks. 'I was glad to do it. Now, I was told your ship was ready to depart and am glad to find you here. I think the wind is set to change and the estuary will be busy.' He reached out his hand behind him and a gentleman put something into it. It was a document, which he offered to Christopher. 'I promised you a letter of introduction to my ambassador John Finch, commanding him to give you every assistance in finding and delivering to you your son.'

Christopher bowed. 'I am very grateful.'

'There may be little he can do, but we will hope and pray for good news. Keep it and yourself safe on the voyage, Christopher.'

'Thank you, sir,' said Christopher. 'I will keep it close, along with the map.'

'Yes, that map.' The King looked away from Christopher and observed the dark water of the river. 'My cartographers were startled at how much detail there was of the palace. Much of it is forbidden. Even the ambassador is only welcome in some of the outer courts.' The King looked sober. 'Christopher, show the map to no one except John Finch. I doubt the Sultan, should he hear of it, would want any man to have such information. Show it only to Sir John.' His expression cleared. 'Now I must greet your captain. Come with me and I will introduce you.'

Christopher followed the King as he made his way onto the deck. 'This is our good ship *Henry*'s second voyage, Christopher. I commend her to you. She is an excellent vessel. And, between you and me, I always consider that a second voyage is the very best. All problems have been found and put right, while the ship is new enough for her timbers to be sound. Is that not so, Captain?'

The captain bowed.

When a sudden breeze caught a pennant and set it flapping, the King looked pleased.

'There, Christopher! Here comes the wind. And the tide will be right within the hour. I almost wish I was sailing with you. But I will pray for your son to be restored to you safe and well. Bring him with you to see me on your return. I would like to hear your traveller's tales, and to meet your son.'

Christopher found his eyes filling with tears. It was quite beyond him to make a courtly reply. The King, however, was adept.

'I have many faults, as my ministers are often pleased to tell me,' he said, gracefully ignoring Christopher's embarrassment. 'But forgetting my friends is, I hope, not one of them, even though I must ration my time with them. I wish I could do more.' He handed Christopher a small purse. 'If you wish, you may call this a payment, for sight of the map. We are extremely pleased to have been given the opportunity to copy it.'

The *Henry* was beginning to tug at the lines that held her and the breeze was strengthening. The King rejoined his gentlemen on the dock, where he waved a brief farewell before mounting his horse and turning its head away. Christopher watched him go. How simple it seemed to make things happen when in a position of influence. Seemingly on a whim, the King had conjured up clothes, a ship and money, all without the slightest effort. Or perhaps that was just how it looked to someone who had, over the past decade, found it difficult enough to keep from utter ruin. Feeling a little furtive, he opened the purse and regarded the coins within. Not a king's ransom, certainly, but enough perhaps to buy the freedom of an unimportant boy.

Christopher heard the sudden slap of sailors' feet drumming on the deck as they hurried to make ready. With every moment the wind was strengthening and, with the tide's pull, the *Henry* was eager to be gone.

Christopher was in the way. He was in a quandary as where best to stand, but a gentleman dressed in a warm cloak took his arm. 'This way, sir. We will be quite out of the way here and you will still be able to watch as we leave England.'

'Thank you,' said Christopher, taking in the well-fed appearance of his fellow passenger. 'Sir Christopher Morgan at your service.'

'Ethan Ford at yours. I go to the Orient with goods to sell, and perhaps to buy.'

'Goods? What sort of goods?'

Mr Ford laughed. 'What to buy is yet to be decided. But my father dealt in spices and I mean to expand the business if I can. As for selling, I have samples of fine woollen cloth from our Cotswold sheep. What is your reason for travelling, if I may ask?'

'To find my son, who I believe is held prisoner in Constantinople.'

'I am most sorry to hear it.' The strengthening wind caught Ethan's plumed hat. He snatched at it and gave Christopher a rueful smile. 'I would not wish to lose my best beaver hat!'

Both men watched as the *Henry* slipped quietly from her mooring and slid out into the channel. The ship drifted faster and the helmsman had to beware the many other craft taking advantage of wind and tide.

It wasn't long before the river met the sea. At the mouth of the estuary, Christopher gazed at the expanse of marshland bordering the water. It was full of water birds. As he watched, a flock of geese came in to land at the water's edge, disturbing a group of ducks, which grumbled noisily. Overhead, countless gulls floated on the wind, crying like frightened children. The breeze was strong now, blowing them away from England, and Christopher was glad of his old cloak. The ship shuddered as it hit the waves, the captain called for more sail and the *Henry* found a new rhythm. Like the ship, Christopher turned his face away from England and towards the open sea.

17

Christopher had brought his journal with him and wrote in it every day. He also attempted to make his own copy of the map, but the paper was not large enough and he had none of the cartographer's skill. He noted down the ship's position and the day's weather, but he wrote mostly about Abel and the love he felt for him. It was as if by writing his son's life he was ensuring he stayed alive. He had nothing else to remind him of his son's existence. He had not thought to bring any memento with him. If only he had Abel's first shoe or his early attempts at writing. Those things lay as treasures in his room at home and he wished he had them now. They would reassure him. Being on this ship, wearing unaccustomed clothes, approaching unknown places and unmet people had disorientated him. The wooden walls of his tiny cabin creaked and groaned as if sharing his agony, while the floor was a trickster. One moment it would tilt alarmingly, causing him to stagger and hit his head. The next it would settle into a smooth rhythm, as if all was well in the world. Nothing was certain, and he craved certainty. The old inn, with its solid walls and stone floors – he had not known how much he had come to love it. He missed it, with a similar ache to the remains of grief for his long-dead wife.

The *Henry* was well furnished with ordnance and carried few passengers as its main purpose was to help subdue the pirates, while also carrying the King's mail. Many letters were destined for the garrison at Tangier as well as those for the ambassador in Constantinople. Ethan, in a surfeit of enthusiasm about his knowledge, told Christopher that Christians were enslaved in many places: in Morocco, Tunisia and Algiers as well as elsewhere. Some letters being carried were to the son of a friend of his, who had been in the English navy until his ship had been sunk and he had fallen into the hands of the slavers.

'The conditions are truly dreadful,' Ethan told him. 'They have very little food, and in his recent letter he said that a dreadful pestilence occurs every summer, which last year carried off above 1,800 Christians. My friend is offering to ransom his son, but so far there has been no response. Now he tries a more generous offer.' Ethan noticed Christopher's appalled expression and tried to ameliorate his insensitivity. 'But your son would not be given men's work,' he added hastily. 'Besides, you say he is in Constantinople. In that great city things will be very different. Much better, I am sure.'

Ethan had a rosy look about him. Christopher could imagine that he had never wanted for anything, nor suffered any ill treatment. However little he understood Christopher's anguish, he was a good-hearted soul and obviously wished to be friends. Christopher had always been something of a loner and without friends for a long time. Indeed, he had more or less ceased to see the need for them, not being ready to admit even to himself that was how he regarded his servants. Ethan ignored his ambivalence, and Christopher found himself won over by the time the sea turned from green to blue and they entered the Mediterranean.

'Did you know that the City of London still distrusts the King in the matter of business,' Ethan told Christopher one morning as they took the air.

'I did not. Perhaps that is why you have passage on one of

his ships,' said Christopher. 'To help alter the city's mind?'

'I think it is more to do with the number of times I visited the Admiralty and left certain small gifts,' Ethan replied with a smile. 'Almost anything is to be had for the right price.'

Christopher thought of the purse in his cabin and wondered not for the first time if he had the price for his son's freedom. As if Ethan could hear his friend's thoughts, he spoke again in a kindly voice. 'When you have your son restored to you will you look for business opportunities in Constantinople?'

'I am unlikely to have the means to do it,' said Christopher, 'but if I did I think I would be cautious. I remember my father-in-law telling me about the fever to speculate in tulips that made and broke so many men in Holland before I was born.'

'Caution is good,' said Ethan, 'but a good businessman knows when to be brave and take a gamble.'

Ethan had been to Constantinople once before, when he was a boy. That trip with his father had made a huge impression on him, as Christopher could tell.

'It is,' said Ethan one fine afternoon, 'a place of mournful cries and needle-like towers. You will see faces there the like of which you will never have seen before. It is a place of wealth and splendour, squalor and filth.'

'It is a place,' growled the captain, who happened to be nearby and was not inclined to poetry, 'of shifting currents and cursed morning mists. We will need to engage a good pilot, who will no doubt attempt to cheat us by demanding double his usual rate because we are Christians. But first we must get there.'

These were beautiful but dangerous waters. Sudden squalls could founder a ship if her captain was not vigilant and the north coast was prey to the pirates.

'Villages on the Spanish coast have all but vanished,' said the captain. 'So many have lost their inhabitants to slavery. The majority of the population has gone inland where it is safer. But the *Henry* is a swift vessel and well protected by her cannon. The pirates prefer easier prey. They have come to fear the English navy, as well they might.'

The night before they reached their destination, Christopher went to his bed and could not sleep. Terrible images came into his mind. He had managed so far to thrust most thoughts of the privations and horrors of slavery into the back of his brain, but now they came crawling out, and every vision had his young son's face upon it. Abel pulling a cart, his bare feet cut on the sharp stones of the road, his back lacerated by the slaver's whip. Abel in the palace, not waiting gracefully at table, well fed and clothed, but Abel sent to the harem, castrated and left to live or not, to be a slave to the women, or else his mutilated body cast outside the palace walls to rot where it lay.

At length Christopher could bear it no longer. He got up and felt his way on deck. As he paced, he cast his mind back to the day when his dear son had disappeared. What had happened to him between that evening and the day, months later, when he had suddenly appeared, as if by magic, at the gate in the cellar? Where had he been? What had he been doing? He had grown, that much was clear, and he had been brown and weathered. He had been out in the air, not confined in some cell. He had been thin, but not emaciated. He had been so very, so suddenly alive! And then, almost instantly, he had been wrenched away again.

To his shame, after Abel's first disappearance, Christopher had privately tried to make himself believe that his son had gone for ever. He knew that was what his servants and everyone else in the village felt and for his own health's sake he felt he should concur. But then, like a miracle Abel had turned up again. That fleeting appearance and dreadful recapture had made Christopher determined never, ever to give up on his son again while breath might remain in his body.

In this spirit, Christopher had his first view of the great Ottoman city. The night was beginning to fade, but it was still too dark to see. As he stood on deck, his face to the breeze, there was nothing to focus on and he was thinking more about Abel than at what lay hidden. Then, slowly, he could see that the fading darkness was revealing a thick mist. It hung on the rigging and settled in his hair and the shoulders of his cloak. As the sun began to rise, the mist became suffused with a pale golden light, the beauty of which made his heart leap painfully in his breast. There was still nothing to be seen. They seemed to be sailing through a celestial cloud rather than the sea.

Soon they were hardly moving at all. The command was given to extinguish the lamps and a hail from aloft caused the captain to curse and call for the steersman to mind his job. After a few moments, a cry came from somewhere off their bow and the captain strode to the side to reply.

Christopher watched as a shadowy boat appeared in the mist and the pilot came aboard. He wore baggy trousers and a cloth around his head. Christopher had expected his skin to perhaps be brown, but his face was flat and his skin yellow.

'I said there would be many different faces,' said Ethan, who had just come on deck.

Christopher nodded, but he had no heart for conversation just now. Instead, he listened to the strange sound of the words spoken by the pilot. The captain, who had a little of the Moorish tongue, replied as best he could. A deal was being struck when, all of a sudden, a wailing cry came from somewhere beyond the ship. Christopher started and stared with alarm into the golden mist, but the few grey shapes discernible were impossible to define. The cry became a haunting chant, which was taken up by others until they were surrounded by a sea of ethereal voices.

The pilot took from his waist a small cloth and laid it carefully on the deck. Christopher had heard of this way of worship and turned his gaze politely away from the man, not wanting to appear rude. The pilot, however, seemed oblivious, concentrating totally on his preparations for prayer.

Slowly, as the haunting voices ceased, the mist thinned, turned to wisps and disappeared. The city was revealed in all its watery splendour with tall, slim towers and many curious buildings. The pilot finished his prayers and calmly folded his cloth, ready now to begin his work of bringing the ship to a safe harbour.

'There is the Sultan's palace. They say he has a thousand concubines there. Maybe it's ten thousand. Who can tell?' Ethan was pointing at a great wall, close to the water's edge, with many bastions. The wall stretched in both directions and enclosed a huge fortress on the headland. Behind the wall were several domes and many tall, thin, delicate towers reaching up into the sky. Trees behind the wall hinted at pleasure gardens, but the wall itself spoke of security. This was a palace in a supremely defensive position. With a jerk of recognition, Christopher felt sure it must be the palace depicted on his map. He stared at the little he could see, as if he could will Abel to appear. His son felt suddenly close and at the same time mournfully distant.

Guided by the pilot, their ship crept forward and rounded the point. Christopher could see that the wall still ran along the edge of the sea until at last it headed inland. According to the map, the palace walls enclosed the entire headland, holding back the city, which clamoured right up against them. Within those walls must surely be where his son lived, even now maybe rising, little knowing that soon his father would come to take him home.

Christopher found he was trembling. If only he had wings to fly straight to where Abel lay! At this instant his heart rose, loving this city, this place where they would be reunited. The golden mist, the haunting song, the minarets – all were known to Abel and were now known to him. How lucky he was that the King had been kind enough to facilitate this journey. Maybe Abel would know of some speciality of the city they could take back to delight the King.

Christopher knew he must be patient. It would take a while for the ship to dock, for him to find the ambassador's residence and to present his letter of introduction. No doubt more time would pass before he was able to meet the Sultan and ask for his son's return. He should take this time to acquaint himself with his surroundings. Determinedly, he tore his gaze away from the palace and crossed the deck to look out in the opposite direction. As he did so, he got a surprise. His map had not shown this part, but it seemed that more of the city lay here. Constantinople sprawled on both sides of the water, with yet more minarets as well as a wider tower thrusting up into the sky, and many houses and other buildings too. The channel was much wider than the Thames, far too wide for any bridge. In the infant daylight, numerous small boats were beginning to cross over, carrying people, goods and even horses, as he noticed on one of the nearer vessels. Constantinople was a city divided by the sea, a sea in this calm, early morning sunlight that looked like pale liquid gold.

In spite of Christopher's determination to remain patient, he couldn't help being distressed to realise that the *Henry* was going to moor on the opposite side of the city to the palace.

'Calm yourself, friend,' said Ethan. 'The ambassador lives up the hill on this side. I must report to his office, as must you, once we have found lodgings. Would you care for us to find a place to stay together?'

There was a gentle bump as the ship nudged into the jetty.

'That is very kind of you, but my letter of introduction to the ambassador requires him to find me a place to stay.'

Ethan looked impressed. 'You are fortunate, sir. I wish I had the ear of the King!'

Leaving their boxes on board, the two men made their way onshore as soon as they were able. The narrow streets were busy and, although it was still early, the sun was warm. It was very different from London. Much of humanity was here, with a few pale, lumpish European faces mingling with tawny Arabs and flatter faces with almond eyes from the East. The food for sale looked and smelt different from the pies and vegetables Christopher was used to. Ethan wanted to linger and pay attention to the numerous vendors who bayed for business, but Christopher refused to dally.

'You must eat!' complained Ethan, pushing some food into Christopher's hands.

Christopher looked down. Ethan had given him a large, warm piece of puffed-up bread. It must be bread, although he'd never seen the like before. It was very different from the heavy loaves Jane made. This was fragrant and soft. When he bit into it, it collapsed and steam rose from the hollow within. He folded it in half and took another bite. It was very good.

'Thank you.'

Ethan gave him a cheerful grin. 'I think we are coming to Pera, where the ambassador's residence is. It's hard to remember clearly.'

They did appear to have reached a richer part of the city. The houses were large and the streets less cluttered. Christopher looked about him for someone to ask where the English ambassador lived. Several people were coming towards them and Christopher approached one. The man was dressed in a long robe but looked European.

'Excuse me . . .'

The man inclined his head politely.

'Can you tell me where the English ambassador has his house?'

'Yes. It is just a little way along this street.' He had a strong accent that Christopher recognised straight away.

'Forgive me. Are you Dutch?'

The man smiled. 'I am. Jacob Borch at your service, sir. I live nearby, as do most of us who serve our ambassadors. I take it you have just arrived in this city?'

Ethan broke in. 'Indeed, we have! And are eager to learn. I have to find somewhere to live, although this lucky fellow is to be housed by order of our king.'

Jacob looked anew at Christopher. 'Then you will soon be comfortable. And you, sir,' he added to Ethan, 'will not have difficulty in finding lodgings nearby. When you are settled,' he went on, between their thanks, 'I would very much like to hear the news from Europe. Our nations are now at peace and there is no reason why we should not be friends.'

They parted at the English ambassador's house. Christopher's letter from the King got him swift entry and almost immediate access to John Finch, the ambassador, who seemed at a bit of a loss how to help him.

'I am, of course, happy to accommodate you at the King's pleasure,' he said uneasily. 'But I fail to see how I can otherwise be of any help. There are thousands of Christian slaves throughout this empire, many of them English, with families wishing to bring them home. Unfortunately, because you have not heard where he is, to find your son is well-nigh impossible.'

'But I am persuaded he lives in the palace,' insisted Christopher.

John Finch looked even more uncomfortable. 'Indeed?' Christopher waited a few moments while the ambassador picked up a small brass vase from his desk and studied it as if he'd never seen it before. At length, he replaced it and looked at his visitor. 'I can and do have general conversations with officials about the problem of Christian slaves. However, I do not think that making enquiries about one who may or may not be in the palace would be a sensible idea. It is not for me to ask about the Sultan's own slaves. At the very least, it would be thought impertinent.' He looked at Christopher and sighed. 'At Whitehall, I dare say if you loiter outside for long enough and make enquiries you will learn every servant's name and where they dwell. Here it is very different.'

'But I have this map. Surely, sir . . .' Christopher struggled to find the most diplomatic words. 'Surely with this it might be possible to make my way to him . . . once I found out what part he lives in . . .' He handed the map to the ambassador, who glanced at it impatiently, then took a closer look and blanched.

'Where did you get this?'

Christopher started to explain, but the ambassador interrupted him. 'No. I think I would rather not know.' His eyes flitted to it again and he spoke very quietly. 'Does the King know of this?'

'Yes.' Christopher matched his whisper. 'Indeed, he had a copy made.'

'Then, if you take my advice, you will burn it and bury the ashes.' He thrust it back at Christopher. 'If that map is accurate . . . or even not, it is a smouldering fuse. If you were found carrying such a thing, you would be arrested. I could not save you. Nor would anyone else. Even in this residence I cannot be certain there are no spies.'

'But the King . . .'

'Our king is a long way from Constantinople. You are in a foreign country and the Sultan's word is law. That' – he hesitated – 'thing . . . looks to include details of the most private apartments. Believe me, if the Sultan knew such a map was in your hands, your death would not be a happy one, nor swift. It is not just slaves that are kept captive in that place. I suggest you know nothing of the politics of this place, nor the dynasty that rules it. Better to keep away if you value your life.'

Christopher took a deep breath. 'Sir, it matters little to me whether I live or die, except that I must live to save my son. This is all I have to show me where he is. Is there *nothing* you can tell me to give me hope?'

John Finch's eyes flashed with anger. 'You know *nothing* of this place or my difficulties. I do what I can diplomatically every day. I can perhaps mention your son to an official if you leave his name and description with my secretary, along with your offer of ransom, but I have to tell you that you would have more chance if he were in a private home or working on a farm. Forgive me, but you are unlikely to have enough money to interest the Sultan.'

Christopher refused to give in. 'If you could at least discover if he is there.'

John Finch looked exasperated. '*You* tell me he is.'

'I believe so, but as you say I have no letter. If he could be given paper, of course, at my expense. If I had a message from him . . .'

'And then what?'

'I have little money, it's true, but might the Sultan be interested in trading the map for my son?' He stopped at the horrified expression on the ambassador's face. For the first time, Christopher became truly aware of just how alien Constantinople was. This man was the representative of their king and yet he obviously felt powerless to help his subjects. And he seemed, quite frankly, frightened of the map. Christopher suddenly felt a very long way from home. The ambassador was not the first person to have told him to keep the map's existence to himself. He did not know enough about this place or the people within it to make any sensible decisions. His blundering was like a child trying to stroke a viper.

'I'm sorry,' he said, trying not to sound as bleak as he felt. 'I realise you take me for a fool.'

'I realise your pain,' said John Finch stiffly. 'And I am sorry for it. If I could give you hope I would.'

'You are saying there is no hope?'

'I am saying there is very little. I will ask, but it may not be soon. Diplomacy takes its own time and you must remember: you are not the only person to have lost a child, a parent, even a wife this dolorous way.' He got up and escorted Christopher to the door. 'Do as I say with that thing. I do not want it in this house. As for the rest, live your life, Sir Christopher. Live your life.'

18

Christopher thrust the map inside his shirt, bowed to the ambassador and allowed a servant to lead him to his quarters. It was a modest room, with a window shuttered against the sun, giving onto a small courtyard. His food would be found for him, so he would have little need to spend.

As soon as the servant had gone, he pulled the map back out of his shirt. What to do? How could he destroy the last thing his son had given him? But the ambassador had made it clear that it was not to be in this house. The map was, at the moment, the dearest thing he had, and yet seemed at the same time a dangerous document that only served to point out his ignorance. Should he throw up his hands in defeat and go home? Was it now that he should do the unimaginable and abandon all hope? Should it be here, in this foreign city? He had determined never to contemplate such a betrayal. But Christopher felt old and worn down with care. Every time he thought he was making progress he was thwarted. There were too many obstacles, not enough clues, and he was the only person in the world who cared.

He sat on a stool in the gloom and bent his head. Sir John Narborough, however many cannon he had, would not sail all the way to Constantinople, sack the palace and release the slaves. He might dissuade the pirates at the mouth of the Mediterranean from raiding the English coast, but he would not rescue those already captured. It was for the King's ambassador to use his diplomacy to help their cause. And as far as Christopher could see, the ambassador was a timid, ineffectual fool. He didn't care about the King's subjects. No. If anything was to be achieved, Christopher was going to have to do it himself. He should stop feeling sorry for himself and remember that Abel was in a far worse situation. He, Christopher, was free to come and go at will, while his son was a captive. He would be relying on his father to not give up. There were too many things about Abel's disappearance he didn't understand, so he must, surely, keep the map until he had explored all its possibilities.

Christopher took a deep breath and raised his head. Burning the map was not the answer. It made him uncomfortable to disobey the ambassador, but he was angry with him now, and yet the idea of looking for a different place to stay was not attractive to him. Surely, this little part of England was safer than anywhere else in the city? And he needed to keep himself safe for Abel's sake, as well as to save his money.

He folded the map carefully and put it in the inner pocket of his coat. While he waited for the ambassador to raise his case, if he even intended to do so, Christopher would make it his business to learn as much as he could about the city: its streets, shops and businesses; its parks, buildings and the people living in them. He would watch and listen, roam the crowded alleys and hope that one day he might even see, in the slim figure of a trusted slave out on some errand, the unmistakable face of his beloved son.

Crossing the stretch of sea that divided the city, Christopher felt as if he were approaching the maw of a beautiful monster. He had lived too long in the country. London's cacophony had been shock enough, but crossing the Thames was nothing to this. The crowded sea chopped and spat at the small vessel until he wondered if he would ever reach the further shore. When he did, it was not easy to disembark. A crowd of people surrounded him as he stepped ashore, all demanding or offering something. He waded through them, rejecting them all, but they hardly retreated. Eventually, he out-strode most at the jetty, but more appeared wherever he went. There was no way he could observe anything with such a riotous entourage. He was beginning to despair when a man in a long dark robe approached. With hardly a word from him the crowd melted away, leaving them in a small oasis of peace in the busy street.

'How did you do that?'

The man smiled. 'Speaking in your language will not help,' the man said. 'You must do this.' He moved his head in an abrupt manner. 'That will show them you are not as foreign as you look. And you can say this too.'

'What does it mean?' asked Christopher, trying to get his mouth to make the same sounds as the man. The Arabic he thought he had learnt in London had not been pronounced like the language spoken here.

'With the head and the tongue, you are saying that you want nothing and that you are local. They will see with their eyes it is not true, but they will also see and hear that you know enough to mean what you say.'

'Thank you. It is similar in London, but there I know how to refuse.'

'A stranger offers an opportunity and they are poor people.' He touched his hand briefly to his breast. Before Christopher could think to do the same in politeness the man had turned away and was already being swallowed up in the crowd.

Christopher plunged at random into a side street, in the hope it might lead to the palace. The walls were lost to him with so many buildings blocking his view, but he was fairly sure he was going in the right direction. Eventually he came to a more open space. There, in front of him, was a beautiful domed building with slim minarets on either side. He approached it curiously but was alarmed by a number of well-armed men in his way, wearing colourful robes and tall hats. The map in his coat felt uncomfortably obvious, although he knew it was nervousness rather than the map that was showing. He turned and was about to retrace his steps when he saw a gateway set into what looked very much like the palace wall.

There were gatekeepers at the entrance and, although many people seemed to be passing in and out freely enough, some were turned away. Christopher sighed. He needed to know the etiquette of this place and what documents would be required. He should give himself the very best chance of being admitted. Perhaps this was not even the correct entrance for making enquiries. He wondered if any of the guards would speak his language as fluently as the helpful man in the dark robe and wished he was with him still. At the edge of his mind were the seeds of a mad plan involving disguise, the climbing of walls and secret use of the map. Being so close to the palace made him itch to do something, almost *anything*, to gain entrance. He was full of excitable energy and could feel his brain beginning to overheat in a familiar manner. He wanted to roar his son's name in the hope that Abel might hear him, but he did not. He must not blunder unwittingly into difficulties. He sat for a while, taking pains to calm himself, but the sun was climbing higher and Christopher was getting uncomfortably warm. Perhaps if he returned to Pera he could find Jacob the Dutchman and a shady place to sit so he could ask him what he knew of the great city. Pleased with this idea, and hopeful that some useful information would result, he headed once more for the shore and found a boat without difficulty. The sea was even more choppy than before. By the time he landed, he was quite wet through.

'Christopher!'

It was Ethan. Lingering by the food stalls at the water's edge appeared to be a favourite pastime of his.

'How goes your day? Here, have one of these. They're delicious.'

Christopher took the small ball of spiced meat Ethan

handed him and put it in his mouth. It was indeed delicious.

'Where are you going?'

'I've just returned.' Christopher waved his hand in the direction of the water. 'From the other side.'

'Oh.' Ethan looked disappointed. He made a small moue of displeasure, but couldn't keep a smile from his mouth for long. 'I was going to cross with Jacob, but he had business to attend to here. I am determined to go tomorrow . . . unless, having met you, you would like to go back with me now as my guide?'

Christopher wiped the grease from his lips and shook his head. 'I doubt I could guide you after one visit. And I was hoping to speak to Jacob. Do you know if he'll be free later?'

'I do. We are going to meet at the hammam.' Ethan laughed at Christopher's ignorance. 'It's a bathhouse. My father took me when I was a boy and I'm looking forward to going again. Jacob knows of a good place. Join us! You can speak to Jacob then, while we wash off our long journey.'

It was early afternoon by the time Christopher returned to his lodgings. The cool, quiet room was welcome after the day's noise and heat. Feeling tired after his exertions, he lay on the bed and closed his eyes.

He was woken with a start by a banging at the outer door. He heard the servant speaking to someone and was already drawing on his coat by the time the servant came to tell him that Ethan and Jacob were there.

The hammam was a circular, domed building with walls and floor of marble. Christopher gave himself up to the ministrations of the young bath attendants after first asking each if he knew a boy called Abel.

'Come,' said Ethan. 'They don't understand you. And surely the chances of them knowing him must be slight in the extreme. Didn't you say he is a slave in the palace?'

'What's this?' said Jacob. 'Your son, you say?'

Christopher told his story while the heat drew the travel weariness out of his body and reduced his overwrought mind to a semblance of peace. By the time they had been washed and sweated and washed some more he felt calmer than he had done for a long time. Unfortunately, Jacob knew nothing of the palace, although he had plenty of advice about the best markets to go to and which bankers to approach. He, like Ethan, was involved in trade and preferred to leave politics and officialdom as far as possible to the ambassador and his staff. Listening to them talk, Christopher felt alone with his troubles.

The following day he tried to see the ambassador but was told he was not available. Back in his room he unfolded the map yet again and studied the maze of rooms in the palace, as well as noting all the possible entrances. He made his way down to the jetty and once again took a boat across the Golden Horn.

This time, instead of hurrying past all the shops, he loitered, picking up the atmosphere while looking to see what was for sale in this great foreign city. After dawdling through the narrow streets for some time, he stopped at a metalworker's to admire the considerable skill of the artisan at work. The man looked up. He began to smile at his assumed customer, but then his smile faded into an expression of alarm. Before Christopher could turn to see what had so alarmed the man, his arm was gripped in a vice-like hold and he felt the point of a knife held close to his ribs. No words were spoken, but by the prodding of the knife he was propelled inexorably along the crowded street with his assailant as close as a lover.

Christopher had no option but to obey the knife's point. He wondered about calling for help, but who would help him in this place? He so feared the blade sliding into his body that he kept his breath as shallow as he could. He had little doubt that his captor was taking him to a quiet place where he would be robbed and murdered. If only he could run, but his arm was too tightly gripped. He was sure that if he attempted to pull away, the knife would do far more than scratch him. His heart was thudding with mingled fear, anger and despair. How cruel to be cheated of life in this most casual way by a street thief. And even if left alive, how terrible to be robbed of the map and his chance of finding his son. Apart from the clothes he wore and a few coins it was the only thing he had with him.

It was too much to hope his murderer would understand English, but when they came to a halt just inside a covered market, next to a stall selling fine silks, he attempted to speak to his captor.

'I will willingly give you what I have,' he said. 'In return for my life. I am a friend of the English amba—'

The knife found its way through his jacket and shirt. It sawed at his skin between two ribs. He couldn't help leaping forward. He stumbled and found himself imprisoned behind the stall. The stall-holder refused to meet his eye and moved away without a word. Death felt very close. Prodding like a callous surgeon into the cut, the knife pushed Christopher agonisingly on, straight towards an embroidered curtain that half hid a doorway. They went through into a twisting, private passageway.

Before his eyes had time to adjust to the gloom, a hood was thrown over his head. Not being able to see was fearsome. His limbs trembled uncontrollably. He began a muttered chant, which he thought was his son's name but then realised it was his long-dead mother he was calling for. It was hard to breathe, but the knife sent a maddening pain into his side every time he hesitated. His journey, it seemed, was not yet done. Stumbling constantly and feebly outraged that he could not see the face of his captor he was pushed on, changing direction so many times he was completely disorientated. Suddenly, the point of the knife, his only guide, was withdrawn. He was turned again, and the hood was pulled roughly off his head.

He gasped, drawing welcome air into his lungs. He was in a rug shop, or at least the back room of such a place. The small room was almost filled with Turkey carpets made in rich colours. Christopher had seen one similar piece at Whitehall, but here there were many, some piled and others hanging like tapestries, making the place more like a stuffy cave than a room. There was no window, but several hanging lamps, whose light made the carpets glow. At his ease, sitting in front of him was a man. He looked as English as Christopher, but over his linen and breeches he wore the same sort of long robe as had the man who had been so helpful in the street the previous day.

'Would you like some tea?' The man's voice was polite, even friendly. He sounded as English as he looked. He was acting as calmly as if they had met by arrangement, while Christopher's heart was still pounding. Suddenly, fear seemed out of place. Had he dreamt the vice-like grip of an assailant? But the scratch in his side, from which blood had trickled, still pained him. He had imagined nothing. One moment he was expecting to die, and the next he was invited to drink tea. It was impossible to know how to respond, but the man was obviously expecting an answer, so Christopher said the first thing that came into his mind.

'I do not know your name.'

The man seemed amused. He smiled but made no answer. 'Please, do sit down.'

Christopher hesitated. He was still stuck between horror and hospitality. There was no stool, only a low heap of rugs in front of him. He wished to turn his head, to look about for a seat, but his flesh shrank at the thought of his assailant still behind him and he did not quite dare to do it.

The man laughed. 'Come, sir! Sit! If you want my help I will need to hear your story.' He glanced at the person behind Christopher with an expression that seemed full of tenderness. Surprised into a lack of fear, Christopher turned his head. Behind him stood a tall African man, who looked at his captive impassively. There were no chairs.

'Make no mistake about Ahmed. He is no slave, nor servant, and doubtless far wealthier than you. He is mute and illiterate but has a prodigious intellect and we understand one another perfectly. He will bring us some tea once you are sitting. Please.' The man extended his arm. Instead of pointing at the rugs, the fingers of his hand remained curled inwards. It was however obvious what he meant and so Christopher sat.

Ahmed brought a small table and placed it between the two men. It made Christopher feel like a child, sitting as he was a little lower than his host. He fought his inclination to get up and walk about. Soon, on the table were two tea glasses and a small metal dish of sweetmeats. Ahmed poured the tea and the green liquid sent up a fragrant minty steam. He acknowledged Christopher's thanks with a nod and melted back into the shadowy rear of the room. The man picked up one of the glasses and raised it to Christopher.

'Now, sir, please forgive the way you were brought to me, but Constantinople can be a dangerous place and it is not always a good idea to broadcast your business. As you see, it is already common knowledge that you were looking to meet me. Here, however, we have privacy, so perhaps you will tell me why you need my help?'

'But I do not know you! How could anyone know I want your help when I do not?'

The man looked surprised, even slightly offended. 'Are you not in need of help?'

'Who in the world would not welcome a helping hand in one way or another? But how can you judge what I need? And the way you had me brought here, not like any civilised . . .'

'Bluster ill becomes you, sir.'

His tone was still perfectly even, but there was a steeliness in his eyes that had not been there before. Christopher took a sip of the fragrant tea to steady himself.

'I am sorry if I appear impolite. Perhaps our ambassador or one of his people have spoken to you of my quest?'

The man left the question hanging in the air between them, not choosing to reply or to say anything on his own account. The longer it hovered there the more ridiculous the question seemed. Christopher felt obliged to say more. 'I don't yet know the ways of this city, but your methods seem more like . . .'

He had been going to say 'more like a bandit than a diplomat', but humour might not be in this man's canon, particularly if he was in fact a bandit. Nervousness was bringing Christopher close to hysteria. If he had a sword or pistol they might be more even, but this strategic silence was too much for him. He took another sip of his tea, rested his hands on his knees and took a breath.

'I have a son, sir. One who is lost. I need to find where he is in the palace, so I can bring him home. Is this what you think you might be able to help me with?'

His host looked unimpressed. 'So not entirely lost if you know where he is?'

'I had hoped the ambassador would intercede for me with the Sultan, but he seems unable to accommodate me. I . . .' Christopher faltered. He had been about to mention the map but stopped himself just in time.

The man put down his glass. 'Show me.'

The hairs on the back of Christopher's neck prickled. 'Show you what, sir?'

Silence. It stretched again beyond the bounds of politeness and became oppressive, but still the man did not reply. Christopher's fear, lulled earlier by his captor's politeness, came tumbling back. The man's face remained open, even bland, but his eyes hardened until their hazelwood hue became obsidian.

Christopher spread his hands in what he hoped was a conciliatory gesture. 'What is it you want of me, sir?'

'What *you* want is your son. What *I* want is my map.' The man's tone was still conversational, mild and even, with not a hint of menace. Only his eyes betrayed a different truth.

Christopher fought his inclination to say, 'What map?' Such a hasty rejoinder might make things a whole lot worse. This man, whoever and whatever he was, could prove himself to be as dangerous as a loose cannon on board a ship. So, what should he say?

The map Abel had thrust at him in Dorset could not be the same map this man wanted. How could it be possible? Yet his map depicted the palace in Constantinople and here they sat, in that very city. He remembered how alarmed the ambassador had been when he had seen it, with his warning about spies. If what he had and what this man wanted were one and the same, it could only be that someone in the ambassador's house had communicated the fact to him. Yet only the ambassador had seen it. What had he said? He had mentioned the rooms in the palace. It could have been enough for someone who had overheard the conversation to know what they had been talking about. And yet no one else had been in the room and the door had been closed. What about the window? That had been mostly shuttered against the sun. Even so, someone outside might have been able to hear what was said.

Perhaps the most important thing to consider was who this person might be working for. Presumably, the most dangerous would be if he was in the pay of the Sultan.

Did he want to bargain with him or, if he admitted to the map, would he simply take it and get Ahmed to dispatch him and dump his body in an alley somewhere? All Christopher had were questions that he could not ask. Did this man know where his son was in the palace? Might he need the map to release other Christian slaves? Somehow, that didn't seem likely.

The silence was stretching out. What to do? If he drew the map out of his pocket and offered it, would he then have his son delivered safe to him? Would the second follow on the first? Somehow, he could not believe it. So, what was the worst that could happen? The loss of the map, his life and his son. Therefore, he must play his only card as well as he could. This man might be honest or not, cunning and insane or open and intelligent. It was impossible to tell.

Christopher strove to keep his voice even. 'I cannot show you now. I do not have it with me, but if it will help you to deliver my son to me I am happy for you to have it.' To keep himself steady he lowered his eyes. They fell on the man's hand. He didn't seem aware that his left hand, still curled into a fist, was leaning on the edge of the dish of sweetmeats, spilling the contents. Christopher wondered why the man didn't move it. Then he realised that the hand was not real. It looked a fair representation, covered as it was in pale leather, but there was obviously no feeling in it. Christopher noticed two metal knobs, or levers, protruding from the wrist. What they could be for he couldn't imagine, but the thing invoked a feeling of horror and fascination in equal measure.

The man removed his mechanical hand from the table and leant back in his chair. On the crushed metal dish was a clear imprint of the fist. Christopher found it impossible to look away. Rising unbidden into his mind was an irresistible image of that hand. He saw it unsheathed, in its raw metal state. Would it be burnished steel, blue and silver, small plates overlaid on the fingers like old-fashioned armour or the carapace of a woodlouse? Or would it be black as iron, like those large nimble spiders that run around the edges of rooms, seeking another to devour? He dragged his gaze away, but not until an image came to him of the man laying that hand on Christopher's naked flesh, gently trailing the cold dead fingers down his spine and on down with Christopher helpless to resist. Something of the shame he felt must have shown in his face, because the man glanced at the hand and back to Christopher with an expression that told him he knew very well the erotic thoughts the hand engendered.

'So, let us say for the moment that you do not carry this map on your person . . . I hope it has a safe resting place.' His gaze settled on Christopher's coat.

'Indeed.' Christopher shifted his position on the rugs. He began to wonder if the man had magical powers that allowed him both to conjure erotica and to see through broadcloth and into pockets.

'I can enquire about the boy while you fetch the map. Bring it to the market tomorrow afternoon. Ahmed will find you. Please don't think to cheat me. You will find I can be a reasonable friend but a very bad enemy.' He got up and came round to Christopher's side of the table. Before Christopher could rise, the man rested his mechanical fist on his shoulder. The weight and pressure made him feel like a man trapped in battle under a dead horse. He was so close that Christopher could smell mint on the man's breath, along with a slight scent that reminded him of overripe plums lying in the sunlit grass, being eaten by wasps. There was something about his closeness that made Christopher more frightened than he had ever been in his life, while at the same time his flesh was caught between desire and distaste. He closed his eyes. If the hand drew him closer, he wouldn't be able to resist.

After a few more seconds' pressure, the man took away his hand. When Christopher dared to open his eyes, he was quite alone. For a few minutes he stayed where he was, trying to get air into his lungs and to still his racing heart. When he eventually made his way out of the back room, the shopkeeper was busy serving a customer and paid no attention to him.

James Bramble, for that was his name, watched Christopher Morgan secretly from behind a gap in the rugs as he left in obvious confusion, and not a little fear. It had been a most satisfactory meeting. Since the day his father had run him over with his cart and caused his terrible injuries, James had felt entitled to make others suffer for his pain. Even before his accident, he had preferred cruelty to gentleness. It was inconvenient to remember that he was partly to blame by not obeying his father's instruction to stay out of the way, and so he chose not to remember. In fact, he was quite able to believe that his injuries were taken with courage during the war, and to tell others so. Whatever was convenient for him became his truth.

From being the intelligent and injured son of a carter, sitting ignored in the corners of rooms, he had discovered how valuable eavesdropping could be. From that small beginning, he had created a network of spies, people he had charmed, paid, or threatened to provide him with what he wanted. Mostly he wanted information, for that brought power, sold well, and with his convoluted string of puppets, was difficult to trace back to him. At first, his only desire was to stop the boys' mockery of his twisted body and lack of hand. When fear made those who knew him smile instead of tease, he grew more ambitious. Next, he wanted a new hand, a mind-numbing expense for such as he, but last year he had it, his cunning hand, made by the finest German armourers, a thing of enormous satisfaction.

Now what he wanted was absolute power within his sphere, and he almost had that too. Servant to none, he sold his secrets piecemeal. He prided himself on knowing everything about his world, and so, today had given him much amusement. He remembered that boy, and where he had put him, but there was no money or influence to be had by telling that to Christopher Morgan. He was obviously a poor man, with nothing to offer. The map would not be payment, for did it not already belong to him? Its loss had been most inconvenient. One of the places he lived quietly when in England was on the moor, not so very far from Dario. Although he kept himself apart from the village he had benefitted from using the Johnsons for some years. The need to destroy them for his own security was another irritant, because

Daniel Johnson had then to be replaced by another man, in another place. In short, the whole situation had been trying, but thanks to his network here, the map was nearly his again. He did not doubt that Christopher Morgan would bring it to him. Thinking he would see his son again would make most men reckless. Ahmed could kill him once the map was theirs.

But James Bramble had seen something else in Christopher. It was not simply fear for and confusion about his son. No, there was more. He had seen that unmistakable frisson in the man's face, the twin revulsion and desire that had not been acknowledged but would now haunt him. For in spite of his perilous situation, a part of Christopher had wanted James Bramble's hands upon him. The most secret, forbidden part of his nature had been revealed to them both, putting him even more in his tormentor's power. Perhaps it would be a waste to kill Christopher Morgan. Perhaps he might be useful in the future, in some way. That being so, it would be amusing to give him a gift he would not want. It would ensure he was remembered, and James Bramble liked to be remembered almost as much as he liked to be feared.

Unaware he had been studied, Christopher tried to retrace his steps, keeping in mind where the rug shop was, but it was impossible. The covered market was vast and there were many shops that sold rugs. He found himself wandering like a lost child, at a loss how to exit the place. Eventually, he emerged into a poor alley where naked children played beside the corpse of a cat. He picked his way through the filth and, after passing along several similarly malodorous alleys, he found himself in a series of rather better streets. At last he entered a large space, with an open gate in front of him.

There was a bustle here. It seemed to be some other kind of market. He entered freely and saw to his horror that it was a slave auction. Had Abel been here? Christopher wondered if they might keep any sort of record.

A collection of young women was being auctioned and there were no children on offer that he could see. There seemed to be a lot more spectators than buyers, some of them European. Christopher found himself standing by a Frenchman, who in spite of Christopher's nationality was prepared to be friendly.

'We Christians must support each other in this country. We cannot afford to let politics get in the way so far from home.'

Christopher nodded his agreement. 'Where have these women come from?'

The Frenchman shrugged. 'From many places. These are second-hand slaves. They have already been trained, so command high prices.' He nudged Christopher. 'That one is wasted as a domestic servant. A pity we are not allowed to buy.'

'Are we not?'

The Frenchman laughed. 'Had you set your heart on her?'

'Certainly not!'

'It matters not. It is usually possible to find a local willing to bid for you. Would you like me to ask?'

'No! That is' – Christopher bowed slightly – 'thank you, but no. I only called in out of curiosity. I was looking for the sale of children . . . boys . . .'

The Frenchman raised his eyebrows. 'You have the wrong day. Of course, the best are taken for the palace, but there are a few traders who specialise in such tastes.' He observed Christopher's horrified expression and murmured an apology. 'I seem to have misunderstood, sir. Will you excuse me?' He pushed his way through the crowd and out of sight before Christopher had thought to ask him about record-keeping.

After leaving the slave market, it took Christopher an hour of dead ends and false turns before he found himself back at the sea. He made his way to a jetty and waited for a boat, feeling sick at heart. It was vital not to make a false move so far as that man was concerned, but Christopher had small idea what a false move might be. Even so, as he got into the boat and was rowed out into the choppy channel, he knew he would go to the market tomorrow. He had to. He would give the map to the man with the false hand because that man had said he would make enquiries and had sounded more able than the ambassador. The poor copy he had attempted to draw while at sea was almost useless, but he comforted himself that there was, after all, as a matter of last resort, a fair copy safe at Whitehall.

19

The following day, Christopher went straight to the market for the map's owner to find him. He did not have long to wait. He was almost pleased to see Ahmed and followed him willingly to the carpet shop. The nameless man was not there, but Ahmed held out the hood and this time Christopher was allowed to put it on himself. After another disorientating walk guided by Ahmed's hand on his arm instead of the knife, Christopher found himself in the storeroom of a spice shop. Plump sacks were stacked up from floor to ceiling around the small room. The spicy aroma completely masked the usual street odour of excrement and rotting vegetables. Ahmed leant against one of the stacks, teased a dried chilli from a small hole in the sacking and chewed on it appreciatively.

There were no chairs, no table and no offer of refreshment. Only the man was there, and he wasted no time in getting to the point. He held out his good hand.

'The map.'

Christopher's own hand went unwillingly to his coat and pulled the map out of his pocket. 'What did you discover about my son?'

'Have you a wife?'

'No.'

'A pity. Still, wives are to be got.'

'What has this to do with my son?'

The man looked irritated. 'Why, get a wife to get a son.'

Christopher swallowed with difficulty. 'What are you saying? You are speaking in riddles! Are you telling me Abel is dead?'

The man snatched the map without warning from Christopher's grasp and unfolded it. Ahmed gave a hiss. The man made no sound, but it was clear by the muscles tightening in his face and the way he gripped the map that both men were strongly affected by what they saw.

'Where did you get this?' Perhaps his voice was a little higher in pitch than usual.

'From my son.'

The man stared at Christopher. He spoke slowly, as if to an idiot. 'And where did he get it?'

Christopher swallowed. 'I don't know.'

Ahmed moved towards him and Christopher backed away, feeling behind him for the doorway. His hand met an open bag, into which his fingers plunged, meeting a soft powder. He withdrew them and tried, with as much dignity as he could muster, to explain.

'He had been captured by . . .' He spread his hands. 'I don't know who, but I suspect a local smuggler. He had momentarily escaped and gave me the map seconds before he was recaptured, and I was shot almost to death.'

Ahmed leant back against the sacks and pulled another chilli from its fellows.

'Where did this happen?' said the man. 'In England, I daresay. In the West Country, perhaps?'

Christopher took his turn to stare. 'Yes, you are right. How did you know?'

'Well, well.' The man's expression was unreadable. He folded the map and handed it to Ahmed. 'As you have returned what belongs to me, even though I did not wish it back in this country, I will let it pass.'

'But, sir,' said Christopher with a desperation he couldn't help but show. 'My son! If that is your map you must surely know where my son is!'

'Must?' The man looked at Christopher as if he were no more than an annoying flea. 'Doubtless God must know where your son is, but I do not see him here. Do you?'

Christopher felt as if he was being played with, as a cat torments a mouse. 'I have given you what is yours. Will you not give me what is mine?'

The man with the metal arm hesitated. He spoke rapidly in the Arabic tongue to Ahmed. When he had finished he looked again at Christopher. 'Listen to me. You have become entangled in something you know nothing about. I can see you are obsessed by the thought that this map will show you where your son lies. But I tell you it does not. What's more, it is a severe inconvenience for me to have to send it again.'

181

Christopher's eyes were drawn to the man's hands. With his real fingers he was playing with the levers in the wrist of the other hand. Like some kind of machine, the artificial fingers opened and then closed, with the thumb completing the fist. He smoothed the soft leather covering the mechanical hand as one might stroke a dog. Without looking at Christopher he spoke again.

'If I hear gossip in this country or any other, about a map linked with this city, I will know it comes from you.'

Ahmed made a sound and the man paid him close attention as Ahmed signed to him with rapid movements of his fingers. He shook his head and turned to Christopher.

'I cannot give you your son now, even if I wanted to, which I do not. So, choose another. Then you will embark for home. If you continue to be a nuisance I shall kill you, or Ahmed will, or perhaps we might share the pleasure.'

He raised his metal fist and tapped Christopher on the temple. 'Now go, and be grateful you have your life.'

Christopher stumbled from the storeroom into the shop. His temple pained him badly where it had been knocked, but not as much as his heart. He made his way out into the dim jumble of passages that made up the great market with its domed roofs. Feeling tears threaten, he rubbed them away with his hand and instantly his eyes felt as if they were on fire.

He could see nothing, and the pain was terrible. He stopped and leant against a heap of rugs, but their owner shouted at him and he lurched away. He stumbled against someone and the man started to berate him, but then muttered something and took his arm. He spoke no English, but it was evident that he wished to help. Christopher allowed himself to be led a little way. Tugging at his arm, the man made him understand that he should sit.

Christopher sank gratefully onto a rug. More than anything he wanted to rub his streaming eyes, but the man spoke urgently to him while pushing at Christopher's wrists to keep his hands away.

Another man came over and translated for Christopher's benefactor. 'He asks if you have been to a spice shop.'

Christopher nodded. 'Yes.'

'Then you doubtless have chilli powder on your hands.'

There was a rapid conversation and then the translator spoke again.

'They will bring water. They will wash your eyes for you. You must thoroughly wash your hands. Do not touch your face or you will make it worse.'

It took a while, but eventually Christopher could see again, and the burning sensation lessened. He gratefully accepted a glass of tea and looked for his benefactor to say thank you, but the man had gone. Christopher left a coin for the tea and went back into the crush of people in the market. He wandered aimlessly for a while, not knowing or caring where he went. He ceased to hear the vendors as they shouted their wares and drifted as helplessly as a twig whirling in a swollen river. Eventually, he emerged out of the dim market into the fierce sunlight. It was late afternoon and the heat was seeping out of the buildings. He had no idea where he was and couldn't bring himself to care.

It was almost dark when, more by chance than design, he finally reached one of the jetties. He climbed into a boat and sat like a stone. He didn't seem to understand that he should get out at the other side and had to be chivvied by the boatman. When prompted, he found some coins and put them into the impatient man's hand. They were enough to pay for the journey ten times over, but Christopher wandered away before any could be returned.

For the next two days, Christopher stayed in his room, pleading illness when Ethan and Jacob called. He went over and over every moment of his time with the man who had refused to introduce himself. He had said he could not give his son back now. Why now? Was he saying that he could at some time in the future? Or did he mean that he could have done so in the past, but that Abel was now dead? There was no resolution in this. He was no better off now, having travelled all these miles, than when Abel was first lost. What should he do now? Where should he go? There was no reason to stay here. If he had been given his son's body to weep over, it would be something, but he had nothing, not even the map. If only he knew. If he knew for certain that his son was dead, he could grieve, but he did not know. That man had taken what he wanted and given nothing in return.

At length, early one morning, having slept very little, he could bear the room no longer. He went out into the street to wander once more. At the jetty, he was approached by a man he hadn't seen before.

'You are looking for a boat?'

Christopher felt in his purse for coin. 'Yes.'

The man led the way to one of the small boats that plied the channel and Christopher stepped in. He was the only passenger and it soon became obvious they were not making for the usual landing.

'Where are we going?' asked Christopher.

The man looked at him gravely. 'To fetch your son.'

It was as if thunder had rolled out of the sky and into the slopping water at his feet. 'What did you say?' But the boatman turned away from him to pull on his oars and refused to say any more, no matter how hard Christopher pressed him.

When they arrived at a jetty he had not landed at before, Christopher spoke to the man again. 'Please tell me again what you said. I'm not sure I heard you right. I thought you said we were going to fetch my son?'

The man looked at him, but he might as well have been mute for all the sound he made. He made no attempt to force Christopher as Ahmed had done, but simply began to walk away. Christopher followed him closely, anxious not to lose him. His heart was thudding in his chest as if it might break free and his legs trembled as he walked.

They headed quickly towards a part of the city Christopher had not visited, eventually stopping in a quiet alley. The man pushed open a small door in the wall and led the way into a courtyard. There was a stone building with a large arched opening, which was barred like a cage. Christopher could see several young boys behind the bars, but the man took his sleeve and led him through a door in the building before he could tell for sure if Abel was there or not. They went down a passage, at the end of which was yet another door, leading out into an untidy garden. It was very quiet.

In the garden, the man paused. He pointed to a low shed. Suddenly it seemed he could talk again. 'Do you want to see one being cut?' He made a chopping motion with his hand at his groin and Christopher stared at him.

'What do you mean?' As it dawned on him where he was, he felt revolted. This must be where boys were turned into eunuchs. 'For pity's sake. No!'

The man laughed at his horrified face. 'After they are cut' – he was leading the way as if giving a guided tour to an interested tourist – 'they are buried up to their necks in sand.'

'In God's name, why?'

The man shrugged and then smiled broadly. 'It keeps the flies away. There is one in the sand now, but I think he is dying. You want to see?'

'No! I do not want to see.' But what if that boy were Abel? 'Yes,' he said, the word crawling from his throat in a groan. 'Where is he?'

The man led him to a spot in a shady part of the garden. Christopher could tell at once that the ruined boy was not Abel. His skin was dark and his hair was in tight curls. Christopher backed away with his hand over his mouth. He felt horrified pity but also overwhelming relief that the suffering boy was not Abel.

'It is indeed regrettable,' the man agreed conversationally. 'So many die, it is hard to make a good profit.' He hesitated. 'Some Christians pay handsomely to be shown what you refused to see.' He waited, as if he might have expected Christopher to change his mind or pay him anyway, but Christopher said nothing, and the man shrugged. 'The boys who live,' he went on, 'they can become very influential and rich. Then they bless what we did to them.'

Christopher could not bring himself to make a reply. All he could do was to pray that Abel had not been brought here. After a moment, the man shrugged again. 'Well, come back this way.'

He led the way back, closing the doors carefully behind them.

Christopher followed him in dread. Why was he being shown all this? Was it some kind of fiendish joke or punishment perpetrated by the owner of the map? It certainly felt so. If Abel were dead he wanted to be allowed to grieve, not to be shown some of the horrors he might have suffered.

'I want to see every boy you have here,' he said to his guide's retreating back.

As soon as they returned to the courtyard, he went up to the arched opening and stood looking through the bars. There were about a dozen young boys, most sitting on the straw that littered their cell. When he approached, some stood up, but others stayed where they were, huddled towards the back of their prison. The guide took a stick that was propped up against the wall and rattled the bars, speaking some words in his own tongue. Instantly, they stood up and arranged themselves so that Christopher could see them all.

It was a pitiful sight. Some could have been no more than five or six years old – all were still children. Abel was not among them. In spite of himself, for a few seconds Christopher had hoped, and his disappointment was hard to bear. This was the moment when he felt, despite all his efforts to remain optimistic, that Abel was further away from him than ever. His despair was total. The only thing left for him was to go home. He turned away from the caged children, but his guide tugged at his sleeve.

'You must choose . . .'

'What do you mean?' For a few appalling moments he thought he was being asked to choose the next victim to be castrated.

The man pointed with his stick at the boys and Christopher tried to pull away. 'No! Not to save my life!'

The man protested. 'But it is paid for you to take a son. You must choose.' He looked alarmed that Christopher might not let him do as he had obviously been bid.

'Choose? But none of them are my son. I don't want just any boy. No!'

'But you must! Look. Any of them. This one here perhaps.' He pointed with his stick and Christopher glanced back.

'Sir?'

It was a small voice, coming from the smallest child: a naked little boy with very pale skin and tumbling, wavy black hair. He looked like a Spaniard but spoke English with an accent that was not Spanish.

'Sir? Are you English, sir?'

Christopher found his voice. 'I am.'

At that, the other boys in their various languages began calling to him like birds, stretching their thin arms through the bars and entreating him piteously. But the little boy who had spoken first stood quietly, asking nothing.

'Ireland, sir,' he said when Christopher asked him his country.

The lump in Christopher's throat made it hard for him to reply. 'What is your name?'

'Turlough, sir.'

'Well, Turlough. Would you like to come with me?'

Turlough thought for a moment and then looked up at Christopher. 'Where are we going?'

Christopher looked at the little boy through blurring eyes. 'I will take you back to your father, Turlough.'

For the first time the child's resolve threatened to desert him. His mouth twisted as he fought not to cry. 'My da was killed by the pirates.'

Christopher mastered himself for the boy's sake. 'Then I will restore you to the rest of your family, Turlough,' he said in as sprightly as voice as he could muster.

'This one,' he said to the guide. He tried hard to avoid seeing all the other children's faces as they realised they had not been chosen, but it was impossible. He felt sure they would haunt him for the rest of his life.

'I will not take this child naked through the streets,' he said when Turlough was standing by his side. 'Find him something to wear.'

The boy was given a filthy garment that at least covered him to his knees. Once he had put it on, the guide led them to the outer gate, hardly allowing them through before he slammed it shut behind them, remaining himself inside. Christopher found a small hand taking his as they set off through the crowded streets. It took a while before he got back to a part of the city he recognised. By that time, Turlough was stumbling. Christopher picked him up and carried him. At a stall, he bought him some more suitable clothing, some slippers, a piece of fruit and some puffy bread. In the ferry he sat quietly eating, sitting as close to his saviour as he could.

Christopher was in turmoil. What was he to do with this orphan? He supposed he would have to take him back to England with him. Once the child told him his village, no doubt there would be someone he could return him to, but it would be an expense, and time and trouble that he didn't have the stomach for. All he wanted was to get home so that if Abel did ever manage to escape again, he would be there to welcome him.

Back at the ambassador's residence, he asked for some water and gave Turlough a thorough wash, looking carefully at him for any sign of fleas, lice or ticks.

'Now. Let's put your shirt and slippers back on.' Turlough did as he was bid. He was touchingly delighted with his slippers and slid about on the cool marble floor in them. Christopher was pierced by a memory of Abel being equally delighted with his silk dressing gown. It was unbearable, being so reminded.

It wasn't long before a message came from the ambassador, summoning Christopher.

'Stay there and be a good boy,' Christopher told Turlough. 'I will not be long.'

It was an uncomfortable interview. John Finch was halfway to working himself up into an apoplectic rage.

'You come here with your dangerous . . . cargo and the next thing I know you are bringing some wretched catamite into my home. This is a good Christian household and I am the King's representative. I will not have my good name or his dirtied by your un-Christian practices.'

Christopher looked at him wearily. He didn't have the energy for an argument.

'He was a slave, is a Christian child from Ireland and I am returning him to his homeland. All I need to know is when the next ship might be leaving for England. God willing, I shall be on it.'

Without another word, he went back to his room, where Turlough was waiting patiently. Christopher packed his belongings into his box and closed it.

'Come, Turlough,' he said. 'We are going to go and see a friend.'

Leaving word that his box would be collected later, he and the child went back out into the sunshine. It was a quiet time when many people were resting indoors, out of the heat of the afternoon. Ethan was at his lodgings. He looked very surprised and then overjoyed to see the little boy holding Christopher's hand. Christopher shook his head and Ethan stopped his congratulations in mid sentence, looking thoroughly mystified.

'This is Turlough,' said Christopher. 'It has fallen to me to return him to his family, but our ambassador accuses me of unnatural practices. I cannot stay under the roof of such a man. Can you tell me if there is a room available here?'

Ethan held the door wide. 'Come in. I will enquire. If there isn't, you can both lie with me tonight, though sharing a bed in this heat is likely to make us melt! But what of your son?'

Christopher looked sorrowfully at his friend. 'No news. I am persuaded to go home in the hope he may yet return to me.'

There was no ship leaving for England, but after a week one was bound to Holland. Christopher negotiated passage for himself and the boy. He was quite defeated by John Finch, who continued to show no sign of asking about Abel at the court. Jacob kindly mentioned Christopher and Abel to his own ambassador, but nothing came of it. Even if the threat from the man with the metal hand, whose name Christopher had not learnt, had not been hanging over him, it would still have felt to Christopher as if it were time for him to go home.

When the day came for them to leave, Ethan walked with them down to the quay, while a porter wheeled Christopher's box. Ethan carried a parcel and, when they arrived at the quay, he gave it to Christopher.

'What's this?'

'Call it a trader's speculation if you like.'

'But what is it?'

Ethan laughed. 'Nothing to be alarmed about. Just a few bulbs to plant in your garden. And perhaps you might like to give a few to His Majesty.'

'I hadn't thought to go back to court, though I suppose I owe the King an account of my travels. Thank you,' he added belatedly to Ethan.

'I don't need thanks,' said Ethan. 'But if I could write to you with news of any interesting goods I might find? I remember how the King addressed you as a friend. If you could also be a friend to me and lay before him things I might send you from time to time . . . ?'

Christopher couldn't help returning his smile. 'I see your gift is more in the way of a transaction.'

Ethan started to bluster and then blushed. 'I don't mean to use you, Christopher. There may be advantage to some things and not others. I don't ask you to lay out money in speculation, but just to go to court occasionally if something arrives from me that you think might be liked.'

'I can't promise,' said Christopher. 'I'm not sure I have the stomach for it, but I will try once at least. I will promise you that.'

Ethan took Christopher's hand. 'Thank you. I have money to speculate that you do not; you have the ear of the King, which I do not. It is the basis of a good partnership, but if you want to have no more of it after a while, just write and let me know. I will understand.'

'And if I could ask you to let me know if you hear anything . . . ?'

'Of course, I will.'

Once they were aboard and had cast off, Turlough tugged gently on Christopher's sleeve. Christopher looked down at the small child, who had been like a shadow since he'd been freed.

'Are we leaving this horrible place?'

Christopher looked at the beautiful light on the water and the delicate minarets reaching up into the sky. The further they slipped away the more beautiful it all appeared. Was everything in the world like this? Was it only possible to see true ugliness at close quarters? He had read of instruments with lenses that showed insects so closely that they could be seen in all their terrible ferocity. What would a page look like if you could inhabit the ink? Would it, too, have its own horror? He glanced down at the child. It was also that beauty and ugliness depended on a person's experience. He remembered the strange charisma of that man with the metal hand. He had pulled him inexorably towards him with undeniable eroticism. It wasn't just the mechanical hand, with its peculiar combination of fear and sensuality, it was also the man himself. It wasn't because Christopher hadn't lain with a woman for a long time. It was more that the man had about him something of a boy at school who could lead the rest of the class to the height of folly, simply by the strength of his personality. Such boys knew their power and so had he. Thinking about the man even now brought Christopher a rush of guilty desire, although as well as his missing hand he had not been comely, and his voice had an ugly timbre.

Turlough tugged his sleeve again and Christopher remembered that he had asked a question. Poor child. He must have suffered so much and, even now, feared more to come.

'Yes, Turlough,' he said kindly. 'Don't worry. We are leaving and returning you to your home.'

The little boy smiled up at him with such trust that Christopher felt a terrible jolt go through him. How could he possibly boast that he would take this child to a place of safety when he had not even been able to keep his own flesh and blood secure? Did such a place even exist?

As the Dutch ship carrying Christopher and Turlough made way, it had passed one from England, heading into port. Christopher had gazed at it with longing. How much easier it would have been to sail straight home than to be obliged to go first to the Low Countries! But if he had known what that ship carried he would have been grateful to be escaping now. For the English ship carried letters, one of which would have ended his life had he still been in the city.

As the English ship arrived in Constantinople, carrying its incendiary cargo, James Bramble was lying on a marble bed while his body received with somnambulant pleasure the ministrations of the man who kneaded his flesh. James was pleased with himself. He had regained the map that purported to show every detail of the secrets within the Sultan's palace. Of course, it did no such thing, but he had spent a considerable amount of money and effort to make it plausible enough to send to his contact at the English court. He had just that morning written, telling his contact that, although the map had been delayed, it would, by secret means, arrive soon. Little did he suspect that later that day he would read in a newly delivered letter that his contact would tell him not to bother with the map. *For the King now has one, no doubt a better and more accurate one, delivered to him by a fellow known personally to the King.*

James Bramble's certainty of making a good profit from the English king, only to find that he would not, would infuriate him, and if Christopher had still been there, the city of Constantinople would have been his agony and his tomb. But chance, which had first entangled the Morgans in James Bramble's web, on this occasion threw Christopher free. For a while, James still imagined a satisfactory death ready for Christopher when he returned to the Rumfustian Inn. But Daniel Johnson was no longer there to carry out such a deed, and Christopher Morgan might yet be of some use. Besides, in England, some wealthy fool whose son, brother or father was missing would buy the map, in the fond hope that it would aid a slave's return. There were many Christian slaves and many gullible families. The matter was of small moment.

And James was brooding on other things. When he returned to the city he loved, he also returned to the man he loved. Sometimes, he could convince himself that Ahmed loved him in return, but in his heart, he knew he did not. They would never be more than business partners. It plagued him not to be possessed by the man. He longed for that more than anything, but Ahmed would not stoop to such depravity, as religion had it. Perhaps, James considered, for a contented life to be possible, no man could have everything he wanted, because if he did, he would want not to have everything, or else to die. Life was not a life if there was nothing left to achieve. But not being able to master Ahmed made it very difficult to master himself, however hard he tried.

ABEL MORGAN

20

The *Angel* shuddered and heeled over. The surgeon's instruments I had neatly laid out tumbled off the bench and skittered across the scrubbed oak timbers.

'Abel! Look sharp!'

I slithered after the instruments. The light wasn't good below deck. The lantern hanging from a beam swung wildly, casting shadows all around. I managed to gather the saw, along with both dismembering knives, but I couldn't see the bullet extractor. I was cursing myself for taking it out of the chest, for it was not a large instrument and might not be needed, when the ship righted herself without warning. I lost my footing on a puddle of blood, lurched to avoid the injured sailor who was waiting for treatment and was flung onto my back with all the breath knocked from my body.

The surgeon, Ptolemy Moore, was on me in a moment. 'No bones broken? Get up, boy. And take more care.'

'Yes, sir.'

I struggled to my feet. I could hear the slopping of waves against the side as the *Angel* wallowed while her sails searched for the wind. We were desperately vulnerable in this state, but if we had kept our course we would have been caught in the bay. Our captain had no choice. We *must* run for the open sea. Already, one ball from our attacker had found its mark, smashing into the upper deck and injuring two men.

The *Angel* was slower than she should be due to the weed adhering to her hull. We had been going to careen her, but as we had made for what we thought a safe place on one of the small islands that dotted the Caribbean, we had been ambushed.

'Bring him over. Steady now!'

Two sailors brought the casualty over to the table. It was Jim Carew. His leg was smashed and I could see no help for it. It would have to come off.

The ship felt steadier as her sails filled and she leant into the wind. The waves began to slap with a rhythm as she picked up speed. I started to hope that we might yet escape without further mishap, but at that very moment something made me look up and I saw death approach.

Bursting through the side of the ship crashed a great cannonball. It flew straight at me. It splintered the vessel's great timbers as easily as tearing a wall of paper. It brought shards of timber with it, each one as deadly as a spear, but I had eyes only for the ball. Its force almost spent, it dropped onto the deck and growled towards me along the oak planks. I was transfixed, awaiting my death like a man drugged. I could not move, even to save my life. And yet somehow the iron ball missed me by the width of a finger and hit a sailor standing next to me, smashing his lower leg and taking off his foot.

My senses returned, and with them the screams of the wounded and the smell of hot blood meeting the shocking green aroma of the sea, draining in as it was through the shattered timber. All was chaos. I looked in panic to my master for instruction. Mr Moore was bent over Jim Carew, seeming his usual calm self. Then I noticed the shaft of wood that had punctured his back. It had gone right through his body and skewered him to his patient. I went to help, but they were both quite dead.

The only remaining able-bodied man was already shouting for help. He was contriving to fix the piece of tarpaulin that had conveyed Jim Carew to us over the hole the cannonball had made. It was just above the waterline, but the hole gulped water like a parched mouth. The carpenter arrived and, with the sailor's help, he was soon at work making a temporary patch.

I went to the man with the smashed leg while keeping a wary eye for the iron ball, lest the motion of the ship should set it rolling once more. I thought the man had fainted, but then I could see that he, too, was dead. I was angry at that. His injury should not have killed him, but my master had told me that God's ways were not ours and we could not presume to know His mind.

Up above I heard a great crash and much shouting as another ball found us. We began to lose way again. The carpenter finished his work and took the sailor with him, leaving me with the dead.

If they had been alive, my master would have been taking off Jim Carew's leg. Maybe he would have invited me to do it. I had helped him perform such an operation twice before, as well as dealing with many other procedures, and he had recently commented that I was strong enough at last to wield the saw. Now he would speak to me no more.

My master had been like a father to me and I wanted to afford him some dignity in death, but try as I might I could not loosen the spar that horribly pinned the bodies. I struggled for some moments before hearing Mr Moore's calm voice, as if he were yet alive. *Pay no attention to the dead, Abel, but attend to the living.*

The *Angel* had almost completely lost her way and was listing badly. I went on deck to find a mass of tangled sailcloth, rigging and spars draggling over the side. Almost all the men were desperately hacking at the rigging. I went to help, but one of the crew waved me away. It was well he did or I might have been killed by a spar that, just then, being freed, fell onto the deck.

Eventually, the immediate danger of capsizing was passed, but much sail and rigging still dangled, obscuring our gun ports. The men stood where they were and gazed sullenly at our captor. She was standing a little way off with all her gun ports open, favouring us with the promise of a broadside should we make any further resistance.

I approached Richard Darte, who had been a particular friend of our surgeon. He, like the rest, was regarding the vessel that had attacked us. I had been long enough in the Caribbean to recognise the black flag that had been unfurled and flapped in the breeze. I strove to stay calm while a longboat full of pirates approached us, but my guts churned and squeezed as it drew alongside.

As a privateer, some would call us little more than pirates ourselves, and indeed we had several times traded with them, but this ship had made it clear that it did not wish to trade.

Mr Darte felt me at his shoulder and half turned. 'Is the surgeon coming up?'

'I regret to say Mr Moore is dead.'

There was real pain in his eyes at the news. 'Did he . . . ?'

I shook my head. 'He was gone in an instant.'

Mr Darte put his hand on my shoulder. 'Ptolemy was very fond of you.' He was quiet for a moment, but then looked at me again. 'Stay close by me until we see which way the wind blows. And hang on to those tools of your trade.'

I looked at my hands and realised to my surprise that I was holding the saw and one of the knives. I had no recollection of picking them up, but I must have done so without thinking, after trying to free my poor master.

As the pirates came on board, our captain stood forward to receive them. They were well armed and wore flamboyant combinations of clothing, gaudy silks and satins being favoured, though much stained and frayed by wear. Once on board, the leader of the band entered into a low-voiced discussion with our captain, and I found my attention straying to their vessel. I wondered what life was like on board. Some said that a pirate's life was for the most part easy and democratic, with riches being distributed so none would feel badly done.

Raised voices drew my attention back. The pirate leader appeared calm while our captain was very agitated.

'Yet I *will* have your ship,' said the former in a mild voice. Without warning, he calmly raised his pistol to our captain's breast and shot him. The captain fell and lay groaning on the deck. The pirate leader, a slight, wiry man, lifted his voice to us, cutting through the tension on board. 'This ship is our prize,' he told us. 'You may choose to be put ashore and make your way to the town on the other side of this island, or ask to join us or resist.' He paused. 'I do not advise the latter, and in truth we are many and not in need of extra hands.'

A buzz of discussion rose up, but I took no part in it, knowing my duty. I pushed my way to the captain and knelt beside him. There was a hole burnt in his jacket and his life's blood was spreading over it, changing the blue to black. He tried to say something. His voice was gone, but he fixed his eyes on mine and held them for a long, gurgling breath. Then he gave up the ghost and I closed his eyes.

A booted foot prodded my master's instruments, setting them to rattle together. I looked up. It was the leader of the pirates. 'Are you the surgeon's mate?'

'I was,' I said angrily. 'Until your attack killed him.'

He sucked his teeth. 'And we in need of a sawbones ourselves.'

It came to me all at once how it was. I had been a captive on the *Angel* and would be on the pirate vessel, unless I took my future into my own hands. 'If you will have me,' I said, 'I will join with you and be your surgeon. Although I am young, I have much practical knowledge, my late master's books and his instruments.'

I gathered the saw and knife and stood up. I was a little above the pirate leader's height, but that didn't seem to bother him. He looked me over with a critical eye and then glanced at his men.

'What say you?' he asked them. 'Shall we try him on Will and Black Tom?'

I held myself straight and purposeful.

'Aye.'

'Let's try him.'

'It seems we have an agreement,' said the leader to me. 'So, young Master Sawbones, take my hand on the deal and then, if you will, go gather your belongings and put them into the longboat. You are needed on the *Revenge*.'

I looked him in the eye. 'I will want my fair share of any prizes,' I said.

He laughed. 'If your doctoring is as good as your resolve, you'll do well enough. What is your name, lad?'

'My name is Abel Morgan.'

He held out his hand. 'I am Rowan Mantle, present leader of the ship *Revenge*. Be welcome.'

We clasped hands over the body of my dead captain. A warning voice called out from behind me. 'You'll hang if you're caught, Abel.' It was Mr Darte. A few minutes before I might have listened to him, but I was done with other men's advice. Several years ago, I had seen my much-loved father shot and killed, much like the captain just now. Today, the surgeon I had come to love and respect and from whom I had learnt so much had been horribly slaughtered. I resolved never to love as a son again, nor to respect as an apprentice. It hurt too much when people I cared for died. I was as tall and broad as a man now. I would be my own person and determine my own fate. I would not be dragged onto a pirate ship. I would go there of my own free will.

I went below decks to collect my few belongings. I wanted to take the surgeon's unguents, oils and books, as well as his instruments. He had no further use for them and, if I was to make my way as a surgeon, I would need them all.

It was melancholy going into his small cabin where we had spent so many hours discussing medicine. He had been a well-educated man, a physician who had, I think, become adrift during and after the civil war, although he didn't speak much of it. At one time a fugitive, he had lost the will to settle back in England. He told me he had no family left alive, as indeed was my situation. We had taken comfort in each other's company, Ptolemy Moore and I. We were, I think, each other's family in all but name. At least that is how it felt to me, but now he was dead, a few short steps away, and I must once more make my own way in life.

There was too much to put into my bundle, so I opened his sea chest and packed everything inside. Even a year ago I would have been unable to lift it, but now I could manage with the help of one man. A hostile muttering broke out as the crew realised I was deserting them, but I hardened my heart and left nothing behind. They had only to trek across the island to where they had been told there was a settlement. I would need to prove myself if I was not to be thrown overboard, and Ptolemy's medicines would, God willing, help me to survive.

A mahogany-skinned pirate with merry eyes widened his mouth in a grin. 'We'll row you across,' he said. 'You have two patients waiting.'

He and another man, heavy limbed, with large hands and feet, took the oars and in a few moments we were at their ship. I climbed up and looked about me. In the shade of a rigged piece of sail lay a man. I didn't wait for my box, but hurried to him, anxious to make a first assessment of his condition, praying it was one I would know how to mend.

I could see straight away he had a fever. He was conscious, but his eyes were glassy. Then I noticed the discoloured bandage on his leg and my blood ran chill. My future might depend on saving this man, but I knew the odds were not in my favour.

'I must look at your wound,' I told him. 'Is it painful?'

He nodded slightly. He clenched his teeth as I bent to unwrap the cloth. A jagged tear in his calf had been badly stitched. His leg had swollen and the skin around the wound was an angry red. To my relief there was yet no sign of rot. I prayed I was soon enough, for both our sakes.

The merry-eyed pirate and his companion had brought my chest on board and were watching me closely. 'His wound is angry,' I told them. 'It needs cleaning. I will need you to hold him while I do it.'

Merry-eyes nodded. He seemed satisfied at my decision, though his lugubrious companion was less comfortable. 'Why not take off his leg?'

'I hope I am in time to save it,' I said, trying to sound confident. 'But if that is not possible I shall certainly remove it.'

I freed the wound from the stitches and washed it with oil. The procedure was bravely borne, although the man must have been in severe pain. Afterwards he looked a little easier and even found me a nod of thanks before the sleeping draught I gave him took effect. I took my time to prepare a good plaster for the wound with the materials in my plaster box. I had a supply of silken thread, some already waxed, and I knew the needles, like all the instruments, were clean and free of rust for I had lavished much time on their care. I hoped the swelling would reduce and I would be able to stitch it again. I knew I could make a good job of it. I could hear the surgeon's calm words in my ear. *Have great respect to the true beauty and former comeliness of the wounded part.* This was what he had always said about stitching.

The second patient, lying in his own filth in his hammock with vomit on the planks, was much simpler to deal with. I was fairly sure a goodwife could have given him the herbs he needed to settle his guts. He was over-purged and needed rest from all food for a while. At least I hoped it was so and that he did not have some kind of disease with which I was not familiar. When

I was done with him I went thankfully back on deck and drew a bucket of seawater to wash my hands, something my master had always insisted upon. I had thought him overly fastidious, but it had soon become a habit with me too and I saw no reason to change it.

I was satisfied with my work as I emptied the bucket over the side. As Ptolemy always said: *We do what we can, but God makes the final decision.*

'Their fate is in God's hands,' I told the two pirates who still loitered nearby. 'And while they wait for his judgement, sleep will ease their suffering.'

'With a young lad as their nursemaid,' grunted the lugubrious one, still glaring at me with undisguised suspicion.

They said no more, leaving me on deck as they went below. They returned a few minutes later, along with several others. To my surprise, all began climbing into the longboat.

'Where are you going?' I called out.

Merry-eyes laughed. 'Why, can't you feel our old vessel wallow?' said he. 'The worm has her and like as not she'll sink any time. But don't you worry. Being so lightened with us all gone she'll probably last another hour or two, maybe even for the rest of the day.'

My mouth must have dropped open in shock. I wanted to call after them as they pulled away from the *Revenge*, but my words died in my throat. I would not plead. I would not snivel and whine at my situation for I knew it would be of no use, but all the same, I was fearfully afraid. The worm was much to be feared. Ships' timbers lasted only a few years in these waters. I had heard stories of ships disintegrating as they sailed, too late to get to port before the worm holes destroyed the timbers and all drowned. I had heard, too, of pirates taking another ship with the only purpose of abandoning their own vessel before it sank. Indeed, privateers did the same on occasion. But the captain had said they needed a surgeon. He had shaken my hand on it. Why now renege on the agreement and leave me to drown?

I could clearly see my former shipmates, looking a small company compared to their captors, being herded into the boat and rowed safely to shore. I bitterly regretted offering to join the pirates. If only I had kept silent about my knowledge and had stayed with the men I knew! They had simply to trek across the island until they came upon the town, which the pirate captain had assured us existed, whereas I was to drown. The pirates must have no need of a surgeon but had brought me here to ease their comrades' last hours, knowing they were going to abandon the sick men along with the ship. I had heard the pirate captain say that he needed no more crew. Is this what they did with sick men, then? Perhaps it was, though I had not heard of it before. Why had I thought that I, a mere boy, not yet fifteen, would be thought capable of being a surgeon? I had made a terrible mistake and would pay with my life.

I gazed after the longboat, wishing with all my heart that I were aboard. I fancied, now it had been brought to mind, that this ship was indeed wallowing somewhat. She already seemed to be lying lower in the water than when I had arrived. I listened fearfully to the quiet ache of the rigging in the sunshine and the calm lap of the sea. All seemed well enough. But the teredo worm worked its evil out of sight and every seaman feared its work. I wondered, should I dive into the sea and swim to the *Angel*? It was not far and I could swim quite well, having learnt in the river at home. But I doubted the pirates would allow me on board. They would more likely shoot at me for sport and fend me off if I tried to climb aboard.

The sun beat upon my head while I wandered the deck and watched my old shipmates being landed on the island and the longboat returning to the *Angel*. I looked disconsolately for signs of the *Angel* being readied to sail, but it had swung around on its anchor and I could not see if they were cutting away the rest of the damaged rigging. For a wild instant, I thought of raising the anchor of this ship and sailing it myself. Surely, I could at least set her drifting towards the island? All she needed was the muscle and the will to put her in motion. If I could do that I could hope to be reunited with my shipmates! I set to haul the anchor up, but before I had hardly felt its weight I let the cable drop. What if she drifted *away* from the shore instead of nearer in? If she sank where she was I could surely reach the island by clasping a barrel or a spar. If she drifted further out to sea I would certainly be lost.

I looked around me and spied the water barrel. Once emptied, it would make a very fair aid to keep me afloat if I could find some nails to attach the lid.

Black Tom was still sleeping, and his colour looked better. I went below and glanced at the other man, who was sleeping deeply in his stinking hammock. Their ends would be easy enough if they drowned while still drugged, but I didn't intend to finish my life here.

By dint of searching, I came across the carpenter's hoard and took some nails and the means to drive them home. Well pleased with myself, I went back on deck. I decided to drink heavily of the sweet water as well as to fill as many pots and tankards as I could. I did not intend to wait until the ship began to sink, but I was at the same time reluctant to trust my life to the sea until I had to. While the ship was afloat, it afforded me safety from sharks and from the pirates using me for target practice if they saw that I was escaping.

I did not know how quickly the ship might founder, so I set to and filled every vessel I could find with water. The rest I let run into the scuppers. When it was all drained out, I nailed the lid tightly on. It pleased me how secure it was. I was proud of myself for finding such a simple solution. To give me a secure hold on the barrel whilst I was in the water, I took a length of rope and tied the barrel up like a parcel, leaving a good loop for me to hang on to. I would be able to thrust my arms through the loop and so not risk losing my lifesaver.

I decided to rest before leaving. I did not know if there were any currents between the ship and shore which might tax my energy. As a consequence, I joined Black Tom in the shade of the tarpaulin. I stretched out but took care to have an arm through the barrel's loop. It would be sheer stupidity to risk being too far from it in the event of a sudden sinking. I also kept the hammer with me in case either of the pirates recovered sufficiently to try and wrestle my lifesaver from me.

I was dozing peacefully when I heard the unmistakable sound of the ship being boarded. Hardly before I had time to sit up and take hold of the hammer, they were on board. I stood up as Merry-eyes, along with several others, climbed aboard. They looked in some surprise at my stance, but I was determined to hold them off until I could jump into the sea with the barrel. I might lose my life, but I would die while trying to escape, not like a cringing cur. I hefted the hammer and waited.

'What's this?' said Merry-eyes, seeing the hammer in my hand. I expected him to be wary, but he laughed into my face. 'What? Are you carpenter now as well as surgeon?' He gestured to the hammer. 'And look, Simon, how our little barber thinks to lay about him with his weapon!' He laughed again.

'Did you hope we had forgotten you and think to take our ship for your own?' said the man Merry-eyes had called Simon.

I shook my head.

'Not him,' said Merry-eyes, hardly able to speak for laughing. 'He was more like to abandon her since I told him she would sink within the hour. Or maybe he thought to mend her planks with a few nails.'

Simon laughed then as did the rest of the men and I could feel my face reddening. I *hated* that I had been made a fool of. I laid the hammer down with as much dignity as I could, though I would far rather have smashed the foul Merry-eyes' mocking mouth with it. I stalked away from them, not trusting myself to speak. While I strove to control my temper, I stared out to sea, waiting for the blood to leave my face and for my breathing to ease. And I vowed that if ever Merry-eyes was in need of my ministrations he would not find me a gentle surgeon. I would *not* forgive and I would *not* forget. I knew how highly good surgeons were regarded by all seamen and meant to have the respect my calling demanded, young though I was. Respect was not, however, to come my way this day. Instead, when they saw how I had appropriated the barrel, Merry-eyes set me to undo all my work. I don't know if they would have flogged me, but he threatened it and I did not dare cross him. It was easy enough to undo the rope. The knots were not so very tight. The nailed-up lid was another matter. I had driven them in so well that removing them was all but impossible. Simon, who was the man in charge of all carpentering, threw down a couple of tools to help me. He had laughed, but showed an appreciation for my difficulty, for which I was grateful. I didn't make a very good fist of it though, and by the time I had the lid off it was badly split.

Merry-eyes kicked it with his toe. 'You will have the cost of providing another removed from your first booty,' he told me with contempt.

'I can mend it well enough,' said Simon mildly. I learnt much later that he couldn't bear to waste anything if it could be mended, and in time we both came to see certain similarities in our professions. His love of wood and care of it reminded me a little of Ptolemy's care of the human body. But all that was in the future. Maybe if I had been younger I would have taken the tease for what it was. I had weathered many such jibes in the past from my milk brother without resentment. But we are all made by our lives, and mine had not been easy. It seemed to me, then, that a dignified man would never forgive a slight but would avenge it in his own way and in his own time. Ptolemy would not have agreed, that I knew, and I could hear him dispute it with me in my head, but he had his respect, while mine was still to be earned. I took my own counsel, for it was all I had.

When I was released from my labour, I found my patient below decks wakeful and in need to take his ease. As there was no bucket to hand, I assisted him on deck and afterwards sluiced him down. While engaged in this malodorous work, I decided that I would demand a surgeon's mate to take such mean duties as soon as was practical. Merry-eyes and his companions made ribald remarks to me and the recovering pirate, but I could see they were impressed that he was on his feet, though weak. One of his friends found him a clean hammock and tied the soiled one over the side so the sea could wash it clean. And when Black Tom awoke, free of fever, I basked in the knowledge that I had done what none of them could do. If I had not been there he would have surely died, and the pirates knew it.

I eventually discovered that the absence of the company of pirates had been no more than their commonwealth customs dictated. All should be present when booty was found, in case any thought the distribution unfair. And far from abandoning one ship for another, they had looked over the *Angel* and decided it would do them very well as a second vessel. None of them included me in these conversations, but they were not secretive about their business, nor did they treat me like a captive. They seemed to accept that I had volunteered to join them and would be with them for the foreseeable future.

They planned, as had our dead captain, to careen the *Angel*, but would not risk it on this shore. Instead, both ships set sail for another island they had used in the past. And so, several days later, we dropped anchor in a hidden bay on an island I had never seen before. The *Angel* had fallen a little behind us and we had the best part of a day before she arrived. We had anchored a little way out so that when she arrived she was able to lie close in to the beach, ready for careening. All of us, including Black Tom under my care, had come ashore and spent several hours at our ease.

As soon as they landed, Rowan Mantle hurried over to greet Merry-eyes and the others. He smiled at Black Tom, leaning on the crutch I had asked Simon to fashion for him. I had not wanted Tom to risk the wound by clambering into the longboat, but his friends had lifted him and no damage had been done. God willing, thanks to my care, his neatly stitched wound would continue to heal well.

'He needs to be careful,' I said to Rowan. 'But he is healing well and his fever has gone. I have saved his leg.'

Rowan Mantle seemed both amused and impressed. 'So, young Sawbones,' he said, 'it appears you are as you said. Well, you can enjoy your leisure now unless administering to any hurts. It will take a while to careen your old vessel and fit her out for our purpose.'

So began the fairest time I had known since I was taken from my father's care. A pirate's life can be hard and dangerous, with the shadow of the gallows always near at hand, but it can also be merry, and they *were* merry in this beautiful place. The men who had chosen a pirate's life had chosen freedom over servitude. In some ways, they reminded me of my milk brother's father, Coleman, the village blacksmith. He worked hard when needed but, being his own man, could take time off from his labours with no one to say him nay. But, unlike our village, these pirates worked in a community where *everyone* was a free man and no one man served another. The only master was work, and when that was done all could take their ease.

The *Angel* was emptied and beached. Over a period of days, she was turned this way and that with willing hands to repair and clean her of the weed that adhered to her hull. I helped, too, and a richly stinking job it was when the sun hit the weed. When work was done for the day, I rambled freely over the small island, gathering such fruits and greens as I recognised were good to eat. Several of us fished from some rocks at one end of the beach, further adding variety to our eating. I made myself a bower and there I kept my journal every day, using a blank book I had discovered in Ptolemy's sea chest. I made drawings of the less familiar fruits and flowers, hoping I might one day identify them. I kept away from Merry-eyes and he spent no more time trying to bait me. I think he knew I didn't like him.

I had a few small services to perform. Several men had stood on sea urchins and needed the spines taken out. Another gashed his arm and needed it stitching. Through these small offices, my standing grew until I felt respected by the band and secure in my place.

As soon as the *Angel* was upright in the water once more, the *Revenge* was beached and careened in her turn. She was fit enough to be kept afloat and the decision to run both vessels was a very popular one, especially as we had men enough to sail them. Much discussion, accompanied by a great deal of rum, took place that evening on the beach. How to split the company fairly, who was to lead the second vessel, even which of the two should give me a place – all was argued over before decisions were made. When it became clear Merry-eyes would be voted leader of the *Angel*, I asked to join Rowan's company.

'For you invited me originally to join you,' I told him. 'And my first loyalty is to you, although I will of course attend to any in either ship that need my help.'

To my relief, this was thought a very honourable plea, and my place on the *Revenge* was confirmed.

Before we sailed, I asked if I might look in my dead captain's cabin for books, as apart from Ptolemy's small collection of medical treatises I was without reading matter. Rowan was happy to agree and Merry-eyes saw no profit in objecting.

'But watch your step, young Sawbones,' said Rowan. 'We are still making changes to your old ship. I wouldn't want our surgeon to be injured, for who would doctor you?' He laughed and slapped me on my back, as was his habit.

In spite of the warning, I was taken by surprise when I went aboard. Fore and aft, all impediments had been demolished, and the open deck lay flat and uncluttered like the *Revenge*. It made the *Angel* look bigger than I had remembered, and it would allow easier boarding of other vessels. The changes weren't all restricted to above decks either. Below, all the bulkheads and partitions had been removed, apart from the captain's cabin. The other small cabins were all gone, including the surgeon's. All was open space. More, the carpenter had opened two new ports below deck. Even now, they were bringing a couple of their cannon on board to augment the *Angel*'s complement. Both ships together would be, I could see, a formidable force.

I made my way into the captain's cabin and saw that his possessions had already been ransacked. On a small shelf, however, behind a rail, sat several volumes. I went to them eagerly. One was the bible, but I had Ptolemy's. Another was a journal, which would be useful for its remaining empty pages. There was also a slim volume of poetry, inscribed to him from a lady. I had not thought the captain a romantic man. I wondered if she waited for him yet and if she would ever hear what had happened to him. Of his log there was no sign, but the last volume was a book of essays. I took it, the journal and the poetry.

Both ships were nearly ready. The *Angel* was rerigged where the cannon had done damage, both had been careened, and the final day was spent cleaning and refilling the water barrels. The men were in high good humour for I think none liked to feel the earth for too long under his feet. I came back from my usual ramble to be greeted by Black Tom, who was by now able to get about very well with the aid of a stick.

'How do you like our new figurehead?'

I squinted to look. The *Angel* was floating nearby, but it was hard to see clearly into the setting sun.

'What have you done to her?'

Black Tom laughed. 'An angel is too good for the likes of us, so I have shared my name with her. With the help of some pitch she now has the same colour skin as I. We have named her the Black Angel, and she and I will be shipmates. I hope you will wish us good fortune.'

'Of course,' I said, more heartily than I felt, for I had come to like Black Tom very much and hoped he would have chosen to sail with the *Revenge*. 'How is your leg?' I asked him.

'It does well enough,' he said. 'But it itches badly, and the stitches are troubling me.'

I was pleased when I took a look at it. 'I will remove them,' I said. 'But you must promise me not to overuse it for the next couple of weeks. I don't want to get a signal from the *Black Angel*, asking me to stitch it back up again.'

'I will. You do know how grateful I am to have both legs?'

I laughed. 'You are most welcome. Your wound gave me an opportunity to show Rowan that I am indeed a competent surgeon. I might not be here now, had I not the means to prove myself.'

We embarked that evening and set sail at dawn the following day. I had not expected to be given a cabin, for almost all the men, the captain excepted, bunked together. However, there was a tiny place for me and my medicines.

'Why, sir, thank you,' I said, much pleased.

Rowan looked almost as pleased as I.

'We have been without a surgeon for a long time,' he said. 'And now we find we have a likeable young man, no more than a boy, who is less a sawbones and more a physician. I have seen men

215

suffer in terrible pain and want to save them from such a fate if I can. I wish to make your time with us a pleasant one and hope that as you have joined us freely you will want to stay.'

I thought of the many pirates that had been hanged without consideration and reflected that no man has only one story to him. Rowan Mantle was indeed a cold-hearted killer, but also a man of feeling. Over the past days I had heard several of the pirates talk of their lives: Black Tom had suffered as a slave on the plantations of the Americas; Simon, like me and several more, had turned pirate when his ship had been captured; others had turned to thieving rather than starve when orphaned and had escaped the rope to find themselves sent to sea. It seemed clear that few had been *born* villains. As for me, when I was a boy, I had played at pirates with my friend Charlie but had anyone suggested I might become one both, he and I would have laughed heartily. So, life takes us and rattles us around like dice in a box, never telling which way the spots will fall.

We now sailed with all speed towards the place where our leader hoped to find riches to plunder, and it was not long before a small merchantman hove into sight. Once both the *Revenge* and the *Black Angel* raised the black flags, not even a warning shot was needed to bring her to heel. She dropped her sail and waited while we approached. She had no gun ports and but one small cannon I could see on deck. Even so, I felt the same pull in my guts that I had felt whenever the *Angel*, as a privateer, had taken a prize. There was always the risk of hidden weapons or some hothead who would defy us against all reason.

We drew alongside while the *Black Angel* stood a little way off with several of her gun ports open. Our boarding party swarmed over the side and we took her without a shot being fired. As surgeon, I was not expected to take an active role, so I had been standing well back, but once she was safely secured I moved closer. The captain of the vessel and his crew had been herded near to where I stood and were being guarded while their ship was looted. I looked at them curiously. No doubt they were happy to have their lives spared, if not their livelihood. I wondered if we might keep their ship and add more to our fleet.

'She is too slow for us,' Rowan told me when I asked. 'And even if she were right for us, the crew might give trouble and we would most likely have to toss at least some of them overboard. You may think us bloodthirsty dogs, young Sawbones, but it always unsettles us to do that.'

'I am glad to hear it,' I said.

'I remembered your quest for books,' Rowan added, handing me a salt-stained volume. 'Another for your library. Are you not now a very well-set-up young fellow?'

I agreed and congratulated myself for the decisions I had lately made. I had become my own man. My decision to abandon my shipmates and go willingly with the pirates had been excellently made. I had impressed the pirates by saving Black Tom's leg and now I found myself surgeon not just to one ship but two. My only enemy sailed in the *Black Angel* while I kept company with my friend the captain in the *Revenge*. Being surgeon, I would be obliged neither to climb rigging nor risk my life in a boarding party. In short, I had fallen like a cat, on its feet.

What was more, my share of any prize was generous, whereas I had hardly a penny to my name as Ptolemy's mate. And, when we had called at Port Royal and the other places where a privateer was welcome, Ptolemy had not allowed me ashore. He had kept me innocent of women and that had rankled. Now I looked forward to joining my new shipmates in the stews and inns that I had heard so much about. And when I was rich, I told myself, I would give up this life, sail home and lord it over the village from whence I had come. I would avenge the death of my father, drive out the Johnsons and make Charlie, my childhood friend and milk brother, my general factotum. How everyone would admire my fine clothes and carriage!

In spite of dreaming of being lord over an English village, the pirates' democracy is something I still greatly admire. I wish society could aspire to it, though how such a device could work well for more than a few dozen men I am at a loss to explain. For pirates consider that each man is equal to the other and all debate the articles until agreement is reached. The leader is voted for and is followed only for as long as he has the support of his fellows. My one-and-a-quarter share of the booty was awarded to me in recognition of my value as surgeon and physician. Sums are awarded to the injured for their hurts and all share equally the food and drink available. Work is done when needed and the rest of the time all take their ease. I would the world was thus for every man. It is, however, impossible.

We were not far from that island they call Jamaica and all on board were minded to sail at once for Port Royal to change goods into gold and gold into entertainment.

'It will make a man of you,' said Rowan, who seemed to take it for granted that I had not been there before. 'I will take you myself to my favourite inn and get you a willing girl. Only the best will do for our young Sawbones!'

I remember so clearly land being sighted and the long hours that dragged until we finally arrived at the busy harbour. I remember the beauty of the island with its wooded hills and the stone buildings, like those in an English town. I was, however, given little time to admire the place. Rowan's offer to make a man of me was a popular suggestion and it seemed most of the crew wished to be involved. As a result, I was almost entirely swept from my feet and carried ashore by a laughing wave of pirates. The cry went up to take me into the first inn on the quayside, but Rowan refused.

'D'you want a surgeon riddled with the pox?' he demanded to ribald laughter. 'I say we take him to the Serpent.'

He got his way, and so they carried me on, half laughing and half protesting until we arrived at the door of an inn several streets back from the harbour. I recall the first few drinks, the back-slapping and the jokes, half of which I understood. I became as merry as the best of them, loquacious and with a feeling of such belonging as I had never before felt with any other group of men. I was finding it hard to focus and harder to sit upright, but I do remember Rowan asking me what sort of girl I would like.

I looked up and saw, collecting the used tankards, a girl with long, tangled black hair, eyes as bright as ripe currants on the bush and skin the colour of rich mahogany. My hand felt weighted, as if it held a heavy stone, but I did my best to raise it and point at the girl.

My friends shouted in what I supposed was approval and I remember smiling at them as if I had said something clever. One of them must have gone over to her, for in a few minutes she was standing in front of me, holding a brimming mug. I don't remember if she spoke English to me – I think not – but she offered me the drink.

'What is it?' I asked. I hadn't asked what I was drinking before, but perhaps I thought this drink, offered by the girl of my

219

choice, might be some sort of love potion. She replied, but I didn't understand. My friends were roaring at me to raise my mug, but I roared my question back.

'WHAT IS IT?'

Black Tom took my arm in his hand and shook it in high good humour. 'Just rumfustian,' he told me. 'Drink it down. Rumfustian is good.'

Immediately, and with no warning, the tears began to spurt from my eyes. I don't think I made a sound, but I stared at the mug with the tears blurring my sight. A slow silence fell over the group as they all noticed that I wept.

'What ails him?' asked one.

'Is he a maudlin drinker?' said another.

After a moment, Rowan put his arm about my shoulder and helped me to rise. 'He weeps because she is too beautiful for him,' he said, and laughter was restored. But he and the girl took me upstairs between them, and Rowan made some financial arrangement with her while I continued to weep into the bed.

'Are you ill, lad?' he asked at last. 'Do you wish to return to the ship?'

I shook my head. I couldn't speak for grieving for my dead father and the rest of what I had lost.

'Drink and women combined make some men weep,' he went on. 'Think nothing of it. Talbo will look after you, and if you want me I shall be downstairs. All right?'

I must have nodded because I felt his hand briefly on my shoulder and then he left. I remember nothing of the rest of the night and have no idea if I lost my virgin state or not. In the morning, there was terrible pain in my head and I was alone in the bed. I was grateful to get back to the ship and collapse into my bunk. I was in no state to rebuff the jibes and teasing that came my way, but I bore it all in good part, knowing that from my friends it was fondly done. I was glad of a few days' peace at sea to mend my head and stomach before we fell upon our next prize, for, unlike the small merchantman, this vessel gave me work to do.

21

In search of a prize, we sailed close to a route many traders took. There was the risk of meeting navy vessels or privateers, but we had two fast ships and Rowan was confident we could repel or escape should the need occur. Even so, remembering Ptolemy's instructions, I set out my table for the treatment of any wounded whenever Rowan decided to engage.

I was on deck when the call came from above. 'Sail ho!' There was tension while we waited to see what sort of vessel she was. At last it was decided she was a merchant ship and a large one at that. With the *Black Angel* we changed tack and with full sails sped to catch her. At first, she did not seem to have seen us or thought us harmless traders, but then she hoisted more sail and increased her speed.

Rowan chuckled. 'She thinks to outrun us. But we will have her.'

It took us a while, but by afternoon we were much closer. Rowan ordered our gun ports opened and the cannon made ready. I went below to light the lantern and check the instruments but couldn't resist going back on deck when all was done.

Once we were within reach, Rowan ordered our black flag raised and the *Black Angel* did the same. We were soon in a position to steal the merchant vessel's wind and our prize had to accept the inevitable. It seemed the captain was minded to be pragmatic and give in without loss of life. Their ship's several gun ports stayed closed and the crew waited, hands at their sides. The *Black Angel* was closest to the prize, so she drew alongside while we kept watch.

Merry-eyes led his boarding party. He leapt aboard first and made for the captain, with his men beside him. At that moment some several members of the merchant vessel let fly with the pistols they had hidden about their persons. And more, a small cannon, which we had not seen, was fired directly at the boarders.

Our company was not so naive that we would send a boarding party without the means to protect themselves. However, damage enough was done by the time they could retaliate. Three of the *Black Angel*'s men lay wounded upon the deck with several dead. Rowan immediately sent our own boarding party to secure the prize. They swiftly dispatched the merchant's crew – everyone – without mercy and tossed the bodies overboard.

I went below and packed up my instruments. As soon as the prize was secured, I called for my box to accompany me while I boarded to assess the wounded. One man had taken a shot to his arm, but the ball had exited cleanly. After pouring soothing oil into his broken flesh, I told him to go back to his ship, to await my further attention. Another had been unfortunate enough to receive at close quarters the ball which the small brass cannon had fired. It had mangled both his legs above the knee and I knew they would have to come off, if indeed I could save his life, which I doubted. There was no point in trying to move him. The other wounded man was Merry-eyes. I went to him with a heavy heart. Ptolemy had always told me that I should never let enmity stand between me and a wounded man, but I knew I could not do it. I would be professional, but no more.

He was conscious and told me he had slipped on another man's blood. While down on one knee, he had been fired upon by the captain. Indeed, I could see that a pistol ball had entered at his neck and gone down into his chest. If it hadn't gone too far, I thought I had a reasonable chance of saving him.

'These two must be treated here,' I told Black Tom, who seemed the most in command of himself and the others.

The man with the shattered legs was looking grey and his breathing was slight. 'Give him some brandy,' I said, hoping it might stimulate his heart. 'But I cannot promise it will help.'

When I cut away his trousers, I found the damage to his lower body was far worse than I had first thought. Maybe a man with more experience might have been able to save him, but I knew I could not. I called for something to cover him and someone brought a fine woman's shawl of embroidered silk. I took off my coat and made of it a pillow for his head.

'I will stay with Sam.'

It was Black Tom. I could see that he knew, as I did, that the man would not live long. Tom eased himself down onto the deck beside Sam's head. I made a strong draught and gave it to him.

'If he is in pain, give him this. If he prefers to stay awake, hold off.'

I went then to Merry-eyes. I found my hands shaking as I examined my adversary.

'I won't bite.' He spoke through gritted teeth. His collarbone was shattered and he must have been in terrible pain, but I could not feel pity. His comment irritated me. Could he not see that he needed to be respectful, not sniping?

Our faces were as close as lovers as I examined his wound. I tried to concentrate on my skill as a surgeon. 'I need a probe,' I muttered. I took one from my box and a cloth to mop the blood so I could see more clearly. I laid the bullet extractor ready, too, though I could not yet see the bullet.

I confess it: the wound was a tricky one. I could remember Ptolemy cursing over a similar case. Splinters of bone must be taken away or they would cause constant pain. Every scrap of cloth driven into the wound by the bullet must be removed or it would fester. The bullet must at all costs be found so I could be sure all the cloth had been taken out. Ptolemy had told me to look at the angle of the wound to estimate where the bullet most likely would be. I was trying, but it was difficult. He'd had me to mop the blood and hand him his instruments, but I must be my own apprentice when I needed most to keep my eyes only on the wound.

Then, as I mopped away another seeping of blood, I was sure I spied it. Ignoring the groans of my patient, I took up the probe again. If I could touch it and feel metal on metal I would know I had it right. It was then it happened.

A sudden spouting of blood occurred, like the foetid spray from a whale. It was the bright gushing of his life's blood and it refused to be halted. For a few moments I could see nothing for his blood in my eyes. I pulled back and wiped them clear. He looked up at me and such an accusation filled his dying eyes that it chilled my heart. He blamed me for his dying. He was saying I had not taken enough care. It was my fault. He could not speak but said it all with his eyes in those last few moments. Then it was over. His life's blood had drained almost all from him and his eyes no longer held any spark of life. I closed his eyes, but there was no relief for me in that act, for his unspoken accusation lived on in my mind.

Sam, too, was dead of his wounds. As I collected my instruments I didn't look at Merry-eyes' body. Both men's friends would grieve for them, but I could not feel sorrow for Merry-eyes. They would sew him into his hammock and send him to the deep, but I was afraid that his eyes would haunt my sleep. I had sluiced as much of his blood from me as I could, but it would take more than a bucket of water to make me clean.

I heard one man mutter to another, 'We are doctored by a mere boy. When will Rowan find us a proper surgeon?'

Back on the *Revenge* I couldn't think of anything but the dead man's eyes. His wound had been severe, it's true. That great artery which lies in a man's neck could have been damaged by the bullet. But I had treated him with less gentleness than I might have done because I disliked him and that might have hastened his demise.

I needed to wipe the instruments, dry and oil them well before putting them away, but as I did so I felt a great weariness of spirit. All my optimism had left me. I had lost two of the three injured men, one the captain of the *Black Angel*, a man who had been popular, though not with me. Would the men decide they did not want me any more? Was I to be tossed overboard with as little ceremony as any other untrusted man? My heart began to hammer in my breast. I could not bear the confines of my tiny cabin. I must walk, so I hastened on deck and paced from one end to the other. There was much clutter because the prize was being emptied of her goods and everyone was in my way. I was in theirs too.

The *Revenge* was too small. I had a sudden longing for the open moorland where I had roamed as a boy. And, like a little child, I wanted my dead parents to hold me in their arms, to convince me that I was not to blame. I wanted to be an innocent infant again and to be comforted. I was too young to have such a heavy load of responsibility. It was not fair to expect so much of me. I had acted like a schoolboy, but that is what I should be. I should have taken more care, though if I were a schoolboy a whipping would suffice for carelessness. I should be paying for a boy's folly with a boy's punishment. As it was, I was doing an expert man's work and now might suffer the fate of a man. There was a bitterness in my heart I had not felt before.

If only my mother hadn't died. She would have taught me better. If only my father had married again or, if not, he had been more a father and less a feckless playmate and irresponsible parent. I was not at fault for who I was! I had ended up here through no fault of my own and now might be thrown overboard through not being able to do an impossible task. It was not fair. Not fair!

'Gold aplenty! Gold enough and more!' It was Rowan. He, at least, was happy. 'Don't mope, boy,' he said. 'There are riches to spend when we reach port.'

'They question my competence and in truth I did let dislike . . .'

He gripped my arm and looked angrily at me. He spoke in a low voice, so only we could hear it. 'Say no more. Don't sulk at hearing resentment instead of praise. I do not want to hear what lies on your conscience. You think you are the only person who has allowed petulance to be a killer?'

I think he could see the shock on my face. He gripped my arm even tighter for a moment and then let it go. He made his voice loud. 'You have a heavy responsibility and you have lost two men, in spite of your care. I dare say it was a blow, though to me it looked as if both would die, no matter what. Forget not,' he said more quietly, 'I am the one who threw us at this prize. Their deaths are on my head. You try to save life. I, as captain, must risk it. You

226

are young,' he added, as if he was being kind, 'but you have skill. Don't allow this misfortune to spoil you.'

For a while, in my quiet times, I found myself returning often to my captain's words. Even now, after so many years, I can remember the scene so clearly. The thump of cargo being moved and the sound of bare feet on the deck. The heat of the sun raising the stink of the blood still under my nails and clotted in my hair. The sharp smell of sweat and Rowan's face, burnt dark, his black eyes flinty and hard, his Welsh voice strangely mellifluous in that unforgiving place. He liked me. I know that. But I was also only a commodity he wanted to keep efficient. I learnt much from him, more than I realised at the time. Above all, I learnt that there is little profit for a man in being soft.

There was no reason not to head for Port Royal now we had a hold full of goods and purses full of gold. Some of the men wanted to keep the ship to add to our burgeoning fleet, but Rowan's distaste for a vessel that had cost lives won the day. Without more ado, we let her go and soon she had drifted a good way astern of us.

I stood aft, gazing in the direction of the drifting prize with unfocused eyes. A surgeon got a good proportion of any prize, but if the pirates were unsatisfied with me they would vote my share down, no matter what their captain said. He commanded only because they had chosen him. If they decided I was of no use, they could still throw me overboard. It was up to me to prolong my usefulness.

I turned my face away from the abandoned ship and leant my back against the side to feel the breeze on my face. As I did, there came a noise like the firing of a great cannon and my heart set up a great hammering in my chest. I leapt away from the side. Had an enemy vessel crept up to us unobserved? Were the timbers splitting? Should I be lost into the sea? But the *Revenge* was as solid as ever. And on the sea was no enemy ship.

'What has happened?'

Rowan, accompanied by several others, had hastened to join me. The captain pointed out to sea. 'The prize ship is afire!'

Smoke was drifting up into the clean air and a fire blazed amidships. As I watched, the sails began to catch. Soon the whole ship would be burning.

'How could this happen?'

Rowan looked troubled. 'None of us set a fuse. I wonder, did the captain think to set us a trap?'

I grinned at him. The unexpected fire had quite restored my mood.

'Never mind,' I said to Rowan. 'You did not want the ship. It matters little if it burns.'

'What worries me is . . . GOD SAVE US!'

A much larger explosion rent the air and set my ears ringing. The burning ship seemed to leap out of the water, as if pursued by a whale. Flames shot out of her broken belly, taking with them all manner of things. I stared, but my captain was not inclined to do the same.

'Look lively! Fetch water there. Cover the hatches!'

Some of the pirates scrambled to obey Rowan while others hastened to furl our sails. I wondered why until hot ashes began to fall upon us like rain from hell. Then I knew well why all made such haste. If our sails burnt we would be helpless, and if hot ashes got into the hold they could ignite our powder and we, too, could explode.

Soon, all that could be done was done. With the sails dampened as much as possible and a watch on them being kept, Rowan rejoined me. 'I wish we had taken her powder and shot,' he said.

'We would then have discovered the mischief in her depths. But in truth we did not need them.'

'Rowan!'

He and I turned together at the urgent voice.

'The *Black Angel* burns!'

A trickle of smoke was rising close by from my old ship. Fear grabbed my heart and squeezed. Were we yet to be in trouble?

It was not easy to see the source of the fire with the smoke blurring the deck. For the first time I saw Rowan look indecisive. 'We could send our longboat over to help . . .'

His mate shook his head. 'Better we save ourselves. If we set sail now we can outrun any further fire. If we stay and the *Black Angel* explodes we will all be lost.'

There was some muttering of approval at this, but Rowan looked angry. 'Are we in the habit of abandoning our fellows? Those sailing the *Black Angel* were our shipmates a little while ago. And remember that they have recently lost their captain. They will vote another in but may now be drifting rudderless in a time of difficulty. Would you have us abandon them?'

More muttering broke out. The crew was divided and with every minute that passed the *Black Angel* might pose more of a risk to herself as well as us.

'I will go and aid them.'

It felt as if the whole crew was staring at me and, in truth, I had surprised myself. 'I will go,' I repeated more firmly, thinking of Black Tom. 'Some may be injured. We should not abandon them.'

For a moment the silence held, then Rowan broke it. 'I will not risk my surgeon, but I do ask for volunteers to come with me. The sooner we go the sooner the fire will be out, and we can head for Port Royal.'

Without waiting for an answer, he made for the longboat which lay alongside us. 'Richard Trewson, you are captain until I return!'

His tone was so heroic, and his attitude so determined, he took the crew entirely with him.

'I will go!'

'And I!'

'Let us take what buckets we have. Make haste!'

In no time, half a dozen men were in the boat with Rowan.

They pulled away with a will and were soon at the *Black Angel's* side. Richard Trewson and I watched as they clambered aboard.

'I see no flames,' I ventured nervously. He didn't answer, being a taciturn man, but only kept his eyes fast upon the smoke. Very soon it was reduced to a trickle and I began to breathe easy, but then a new column rose up, blacker than the first, and all of us remaining on the *Revenge* held our breaths.

'It has the better of them,' muttered one man.

Another said, 'The fire is in their hold. We should set sail with all speed.'

The prize that had exploded was now astern of us and far enough away to cause us no more harm, but I swear every one of us had her earlier destruction uppermost in our minds as our grisly future to come.

'Our hatches are battened,' I reminded them. 'And our sails and deck wet. We are well placed to resist a few ashes and have time to take our comrades on board before we flee.'

'Aye. That's maybe true.' Richard gave me a cursory nod. 'The young surgeon speaks well enough. Besides, the smoke pales again. And look, observe how they cast the fire into the sea.'

We watched as a quantity of goods was thrown overboard,

trailing smoke as it went. Our captain didn't seem in any hurry to return to us but appeared to be ordering matters to his satisfaction before he left. At length, the longboat put out with our crew members aboard. In a short while, it was alongside. The *Black Angel* was already raising her sails as our captain climbed aboard.

'Set sail,' he said into the clamour of men. 'We will go straight to Port Royal while we may. No more pirating until we have enjoyed the plunder we have.'

This roused a cheer, to which I added my own voice.

'I would have returned earlier,' added Rowan. 'But I wanted to satisfy myself that the hold was clear of smoulders. They had been more tardy than us at covering the hatches, and one box of plunder, various charts and clothing from the captain's cabin, started to singe.'

'Could you save none of it?' asked Richard.

'It pained me to lose the charts,' said Rowan. 'They were well-nigh destroyed except for this, but I don't recognise the country or the legend. Here,' he said, thrusting the charred article into my hands, 'make of it what you will. I don't think it is of these waters.'

Before we sailed, I asked if the crew of the *Black Angel* had elected a new captain. Rowan sucked his teeth. 'They are still debating, which is not good for any vessel, so I suggested Black Tom as he seems to me the best person to take control.'

'Will they choose him?'

Rowan nodded. 'I think it more than likely. Black Tom would be a good captain to sail under. If I am voted down I would be proud to sail under a man such as he. Oh, I almost forgot, I have something else for your library.'

He held out something that looked like a charred piece of bread.

'What is it?'

'It is from the ship that exploded. Black Tom said it landed at his feet along with a mass of ashes and debris. Here, take it.'

It was part of the cover of a book. The pages had all burnt away, but this piece of leather with a few letters of the title had been propelled high in to the air to land upon the deck of the *Black Angel*.

'Thank you.'

Rowan had thought it a fine joke to give me such a useless piece of a book, but I found it a great curiosity. The only legible words were *The Won* . . . I pondered often about what the title could have been and kept it as a memento of that day of life and death. I wrapped it in a piece of linen and stowed it in Ptolemy's box. Sometimes, when I was feeling a little melancholy, I would take it out and wonder about the dead hands that had perhaps turned the pages of this book with gentleness, reading aloud to a wife or child. It was likely it had held a special place in someone's heart. In the confines of a ship, only items that mattered found their way on board. The murdered owner's flesh was doubtless all picked from his bones by now. How long would it be before his family heard that the ship was lost? How long would they wait before realising he would never return? At least I had known straight away when I was orphaned.

My father's bones would be lying at peace in the churchyard, and I had no doubt that Jane and William would tend to his grave. It was sad of course that he was dead, but the physician I now was wondered if he had suffered from a disorder of his mind. He had been a very loving father but, considering my memories from a distance, it seemed to me that he was too brittle and unadventurous to make a success of life. Well, he was long gone and it was a mercy that I did not need to concern myself with his welfare, for that would be a drag on my own life. I had been saved the dolorous responsibility of caring for an aged, sick parent, something I know I would have resented, especially as I felt sure he would have been horrified at the company I kept. I honoured his memory but was proud that I had already done so much better than him in my life.

CHRISTOPHER MORGAN

22

It was a difficult journey home from Constantinople for Christopher. The weather was generally good, but the lack of a ship heading to England, having made it necessary to take one bound for Holland, troubled him greatly. It would be easy enough to find passage from there to London, but The Hague was the last place he wished to be because that was where Margarita's parents lived. He had not visited her family after writing, eventually, to inform them of their daughter's death. He had neglected to take Abel to meet his Dutch relations because he couldn't bear to be reminded of his dead wife, and now Abel was lost to them all. Christopher knew he should visit the family since he would be in their town, but his head invented myriad reasons why he should not. How could he inflict this small, unwanted Irish child upon them when he had never taken their own grandson to see them? Besides, they would surely not want to see him after all his years of neglect. With luck, a ship to London might be got almost immediately, making no time for a visit. And yet, the embarrassment of perhaps meeting them by accident would be extreme and unforgivable. He would have to force himself to offer a visit, against everything his mind created as one impediment after another.

In the end, he sent them a note, finding that no suitable ship would be leaving for a couple of days. He received a surprised but generous invitation, including Turlough. To make that visit was the hardest thing Christopher had ever done. He took Turlough to the market to buy him a set of more respectable clothes, including a pair of shoes that were made wearable by putting him into two pairs of stockings. He had nothing to take as a suitable gift, so he made do with some sweetmeats, which might have come from Constantinople, but had not. He expected, even hoped, to be berated, but was not, which made their sympathy even harder to bear.

'I am sorry . . .'

'We all are.'

It turned out to have been a good idea to take the child. He had quite recovered himself during the voyage and seemed to be a natural comedian. His antics charmed and amused them all, distracting them a little from their sadness.

'Do you purpose to raise him as your son?' asked the merchant.

Christopher shook his head. 'He will, I am sure, have some members of his family somewhere. And, just as no one could replace your daughter, my wife, so no child could replace our lost son. I will make enquiries and take him back to his own people as soon as I can.'

'God has entrusted his safety to you,' said Margarita's mother, watching the child play with their kitten. 'His family will be most grateful.'

As they were leaving, she pressed a toy into the child's hands. 'It belonged to Margarita,' she told Christopher. 'Our other grandchildren have grown out of it now and Abel would be too old for it, so this child may as well have it.'

'We do regret not having met our daughter's child,' said the merchant, his tone at last betraying his anger and pain. 'All I would ask now is that you inform us at once if he comes back to you and that you do then bring him to see us.' He looked at Christopher helplessly. 'Did you not consider all these years that we might have been able to help? We wrote . . .'

Christopher took his hat from a servant and bowed his head in shame. He had not been able to school himself to write a reply to that long-ago letter. 'I have no excuse except for my grief, which made me foolish and unreasonable. I do promise to let you know as soon as I might have any news of Abel.'

As they made their way back to their lodgings, Turlough more than countered Christopher's silence.

'I have *shoes*!' he prattled, going through a litany of his new possessions. 'Shoes, and stockings, linen, breeches and a cat with wheels!'

'Don't put it down in the street!' Christopher told him crossly. 'It will be filthy in no time.' The street was, in truth, much cleaner than any in London, but Christopher did not want to slow his pace. 'You can play with it in our lodgings,' he added in a kinder voice.

It was not the child's fault that Christopher was so out of sorts. In truth, having managed the meeting a little better than he had feared, he was now burdened with a new problem, for Margarita's father had given him a sum for prayers to be said at her grave. That night he had a terrible nightmare, which took him right back to the day he had discovered her body. He had opened the window to let her soul free, but in the nightmare her physical body also rose from the bed, trailing bloody sheets, the smells of birth and death entwined. As her body brushed past him, its dead eyes fixed him with a dreadful, accusing stare and the hand she raised to touch his cheek was made of cold, hard metal. He awoke at dawn, sweating. That his love for her should be tangled with the desire he had felt for that fearful man in Constantinople was unbearable. He lay in the grey light and tried to still his unbiddable heart.

He had sworn never to return to the place where she had died, but now, in all conscience, he would have to. He would have to go to the church, try to find her resting place and follow her parents' wishes. He couldn't bear it, but he must. He owed that at least, to them and to her. His mind rebelled. He could not help wondering when *his* wishes might be recognised. Duty was thrust upon him. He did not want any of it. He had not wanted to lose his wife after less than a year of marriage; he had not wanted to bring up their son, although that had turned out to be a blessing. He had not wanted to lose him, nor travel to Constantinople in vain. He did not want to look for his wife's grave, nor take responsibility for the child sleeping at the end of his bed. None of this had he wanted or in any way asked for.

He glanced at the little boy and felt nothing but resentment. If he could have risen from his bed then, walked away and left him, he would have done so. It was only self-preservation that stopped him. He knew all too well that another abandonment would only add to his guilt. He must not allow himself to hate an innocent child and yet he did hate this extra burden, along with every other aspect of his life. He hated it all through the tedious journey to Norfolk, with the rain and thunderstorms suiting his mood and making him even more tetchy with the child. He tried to sympathise with Turlough's fear of the storm but would far rather have been alone with his thoughts. In the end, the child crept onto his lap and fretted himself asleep, giving Christopher at last some quiet in which to fear and worry about what lay ahead.

It could have been so much worse. For one, he was able to leave Turlough at his lodgings, playing with the innkeeper's daughters. Also, to his relief, no one at the church remembered him or Margarita. He remained silent about his connection to her, muttering that he was a messenger for her parents, which was true enough. The priest looked in the church records with him. They found a note of her burial, although no name. Had Christopher in his all-consuming pain neglected to leave her name along with the money for her burial? He could not remember. But the date was right and Margarita was noted to have been Dutch, dying in childbed. The priest was sorry, but he had no knowledge of which of the three rough wooden markers in the churchyard might be hers.

Christopher gave the priest the generous amount of money for prayers, adding what he could from his own purse, and asked that they should be said every year on the anniversary of her death. He stayed while prayers of thanks were made for this pious gift. Afterwards, in the quiet of the empty church, he began to feel a little peace. Although he doubted God's forgiveness, perhaps he could begin to forgive himself for abandoning her body in his grief. And truly, standing in the churchyard, he felt himself to be quieter about her death than he had for many years. She did at least lie in this green hallowed place, even though he didn't know exactly where. He wept, then, for the girl he still missed with a constant ache. He wept for their life together that could have been, but also in gratitude that she had not, as he had so long feared, been thrown into a ditch. Before leaving, he spent some time in prayer at each rustic marker, praying for whoever lay in each spot. At the gate he hesitated, looking his last at the church with its round tower and listening to the rooks cawing in the tall elm as the mist gathered in streaks over the flat marshland. If tragedy had come to them in this place, he realised, then also they had known a few weeks of great joy. He should remember that and try to be glad for it.

From Constantinople to Amsterdam, The Hague to Norfolk, and briefly to Whitehall to deliver the bulbs Ethan had given him. There, he was invited to the theatre to watch the latest play by Astrea and felt he couldn't refuse. He found the play disturbing. While he thought it tragic, many in the audience found much to laugh about. He wished he had more time. There was much learned conversation to be had at court and he would have been interested to discuss the play, but he had his young, unwanted charge to consider. His self-imposed duty must come before his own interests. Besides, he knew himself to be very tired and he was not unhappy in the morning to turn his face at long last to home. If only he could walk in to find his son sitting in the kitchen, astonishing the servants with his escape. He could not avoid hoping. But there was no Abel waiting for him in the kitchen.

'Where is Abel?' asked Jane, as if Christopher might have him hidden in a pocket.

Christopher shook his head. He did not wish to explain his lack of success, nor the appearance of this lively, tousled cuckoo child. 'This is Turlough. Please make him a bed in the attic, Jane. I have to make enquiries about his family, so I can return him to them, but I am so weary I must sleep before I can do any more.'

Sleep is what he did for many hours. He stepped into his familiar bed, noticing with pleasure how his furniture had been kept faithfully polished and the bed aired against his return. After so much salt water, mud and bone-aching jolting, it took him a little while to still himself. His body was soothed by the much-washed, butter-soft sheets, but his mind was still hearing the creak of the coach and the horses' hooves splashing through the rain-soaked ruts. At last, the simple sounds of home entered his soul and he slipped, effortlessly, peacefully into sleep.

23

He woke late in the morning, luxuriating in being in his own bed. He stretched his long limbs out, smiling to himself as his toes met one of the familiar oak bedposts. There was something wonderful about being home. He felt safe, rested, and somehow his soul felt, if not exactly healed, at least soothed. Later he would think about the future. At the moment he was content to know that he had journeyed far, experienced much and had returned safe and well. Latterly, he had also faced some of his demons and won. Fate or God's plan had sent him home via Holland to make his peace with Margarita's parents. He had survived seeing his beloved's face replicated in that of her mother. He had managed that difficult encounter and gone on to visit the very place in Norfolk where she had been laid to rest. Why had he spent so many years believing he would die if he had to go back? True, he had avoided going near the house. That still troubled him. The room where she died would always haunt him. But he had discovered his worst fear had no foundation. She had been buried in hallowed ground and, although his money had not stretched far enough to pay for a stone, the records could not lie. She was at peace and surely in heaven. With this knowledge, much of the weight he had carried for so many years dissolved into gratitude and relief.

He gazed up at the faded canopy of the old bed. For too many years guilt had infected the open wound that was his grief. Now, after more than a dozen years, perhaps he could begin to pardon his mistakes. He was tired, though rested – a dozen years tired. He felt tears leak from his eyes and turned over, letting them soak into his pillow. He wished her by him, but his grief was quieter now, less raw. *There is no point in wanting anything from love. It is not a bargain. It is itself, and that is all. Anything else is a chimera.*

She would not have agreed with that. She would have teased him, would have told him not to take life so seriously, she who was almost always merry. But she had been surrounded by love: her parents, friends, sisters and brother, and him. Everyone had loved her, even a king awaiting his crown. So, for her, love was something bounteous and it had been easy for her to shower a basketful over him, the shy, awkward young man by her side who wasn't quite sure what he felt. She'd used it to make him happy, to see him laugh, which gave her pleasure. She had not experienced the loneliness of love.

He wiped his eyes. Into his head had flown the image of the young man he had shared a stable with during the war, when both had become separated from their regiments while foraging. What was his name? It had gone from him for a moment, though he would never forget the man. He remembered reading about his sad demise in a broadsheet Abel had brought him once. Abraham! Of course. That was it. Dear Abraham. There had been love in that one night. They had talked for hours and then lain down in the straw, trying to find enough space away from their horses' hooves. They had taken off their coats and weapons, but kept them close, fearing discovery by the enemy. Christopher had fallen quickly asleep, but awoke in the night to find his companion's arm thrown over him, breath close upon his neck. For the rest of that night they lay together, kissing, caressing, murmuring to each other in a sweet embrace. The next day they had both been shy. Christopher had wanted to give his companion a farewell kiss, but somehow, they had found themselves leading out their mounts, booted, with swords at their sides and neither had quite dared. Christopher had wished so many times that they had met again, wondering if Abraham had felt the same. He had told himself for years, when he happened to recall it, that their coupling had been no more than mutual comfort, sought in a time of war, but that had not been the whole truth. There had been something good about it, something that answered a question in his heart. Given a chance, he was sure there could have been a deep love between them, and today he found he could now at last admit that to himself. If he was unnatural to have found love with both a woman and a man then let the world condemn him, but he could not hate himself. Both had places in his secret heart and it was a kind of solace to him to admit it. These past few days had brought him to a reckoning, he supposed, and closer to a kind of peace about much that had happened in his life. He was letting much of the painful past go, making more bearable the unresolved loss of his son.

He sat up. A few of his books lay next to the bed. They were other companions he had missed, but before his outstretched arm could pick up the Donne, a sound floated up to him that had him instantly alert, his heart pounding with sudden joy and excitement. He was half out of bed before his brain caught up. He had in that moment forgotten Turlough, but it was that child whose voice he could hear in the garden, playing with the dog the inn had acquired in his absence. He sat back upon his bed to catch his breath. It was time he took hold of the day. There was much to do.

But there was not *so* much that Christopher needed to do. Since the dramatic downfall of Daniel Johnson and his family, there were no more sleepless nights, fearing attack. They were still poor, but life had been harder. Dario had changed from an anxiety-driven smuggler village to one that dozed in the righteous afternoon sun. Jane and William were more than capable of running the inn, although since Christopher had been shot and then been away, much of his garden had run to weeds. Only the vegetable plot thrived under William's care. It was too late in the year to sow seeds, but Christopher hacked back the rampant undergrowth and cleared a plot for the few bulbs he had kept back from Ethan's gift.

He spent no time with the little boy, leaving him entirely to Jane. It wasn't that he didn't care. He had bought him clothes, food and a passage to safety. He had even tried to comfort the child when he was fearful. But Turlough did not belong with him and Christopher did not want him. He had rescued a boy because he had been forced into it. Of course, he was glad that one less child should suffer, but given that Abel had not been there, who was to say that his choice was right? Had another boy been more deserving? Or with more potential? Could one he had left there have been capable of being the next Harvey, or Homer, or Raphael? These questions were unanswerable, and he told himself he was foolish to entertain them, but he couldn't avoid them passing through his mind. Even if he had become fond of this particular child, the questions would remain, but he had not. Turlough was an unwanted obligation to deal with, and deal with it he would, even though he found the mere sight of him at the inn unbearably painful. Every favour shown to the child by Jane wrenched at his heart because Abel was not there to receive it.

He had almost convinced himself that, because of his age, Abel would have been spared mutilation, but that led to more fevered speculation. He had now been to the East. He had seen a slave market and heard terrible stories of the treatment slaves could suffer. He knew it likely that his son would be worked to death on a farm or a building site, if he had not already died. It broke his fragile heart to know that he had perforce rescued the wrong boy, but in spite of that he still had a job to complete and could not allow himself to falter until it was done. In lieu of saving his own son, he must finish the task of returning another's to his family.

Before tackling his garden, Christopher had written in haste to the village priest of the place where Turlough told him he belonged, but even after he had laid waste to the weeds, planted the bulbs and made plans for the next year he received no reply. He had written in English, having no knowledge of the Irish language. Perhaps he should have written to the priest in Latin. He knew nothing of Ireland, other than it having always been a troublesome land, which Cromwell had failed to tame.

Jane and William had saved some small store of money from their judicious running of the inn so there was enough to pay for Turlough's passage home and for Christopher to accompany him. For, as he told them, 'Having brought him all this way I cannot now but finish his deliverance in a proper manner. I cannot allow such a young child to travel alone nor will I be comfortable until I see him properly restored to his family.'

He suspected that the money had been saved to pay for a suitable homecoming feast for Abel, but he could not help that.

Leaving the child at the inn, Christopher went to Chineborough in search of a ship and information. He was pleased to discover a lively trade in sheepskins and leather goods between Cork and Chineborough and, if he was not too particular, passage could easily be found. Turlough had mentioned Cork as his home and so this seemed ideal. Christopher paid for their passage and went home to make ready for the journey. Turlough was overjoyed.

'I will see my dog again!' he said, stroking the ears of the dog that lived at the inn. 'And my ma.'

He hugged Jane, who over the course of a few days he had already become fond of, and William shook him seriously by his little hand. Christopher almost objected when Jane packed an overly generous number of honeyed cakes for the journey. He couldn't help recalling that throughout Abel's young life such things had been beyond their getting, though since Turlough's arrival it seemed they could afford a comb for the kitchen. He knew he was being unfair. The Rumfustian was doing better and it was natural, he supposed, for a woman like Jane to want to fuss a child, but it was hard to know that his son had been denied such things. He managed to hold his tongue because in his heart he knew that Jane would have lavished much more than honeyed cakes on Abel, should he have returned. Indeed, that honey had probably been bought in the expectation of his son's rescue.

The wind was favourable and the journey not too irksome. In truth, Turlough's excitement infected Christopher at least a little. Having seldom crossed the sea before his voyage to Constantinople he found he had become something of a sailor and that it agreed with him. His exile as a young man in Europe had made him wish never to travel again, but now, to his surprise, he found he was enjoying another journey. With his new-found confidence, Christopher hired a horse and obtained directions to the small fishing village near Cork from which Turlough had come.

'But you'll not find a soul there,' the owner of the stables told him. 'Since it was raided by pirates some while back, no one lives there any more.'

'There must be some who avoided capture,' said Christopher. 'I am come to return this child who was taken to Constantinople and who I was able to release. Surely he will have family there still?' He felt his heart sinking, as Turlough's mouth turned down and tears rolled from his eyes.

The man looked at Turlough and then back at Christopher with both astonishment and scepticism. 'What's his name?'

The child answered for himself. 'Turlough O'Reilly.'

The man began to speak to him in his own language, and Christopher waited, trying to remain patient. 'There are O'Reillys farming inland from the village,' the man told Christopher at last, gazing at him with more respect. 'They may know what happened to his parents or be prepared to take him in. Take the coast road west out of the city. Once you reach his village, turn inland. Do you have a pistol?'

'Yes.'

'Then keep it ready. English voices are not well received in the country. Get the boy to speak for you. That would be best. And look after the horse. I'd like him back.'

After the bustle of the city, the coast road was eerily deserted. Every small house they came to was empty. Christopher remembered what Ethan had said about the south coast of Spain, deserted because of the raiders. The people here had, perhaps, abandoned their homes because of the pirates, though he had heard tell that Cromwell had also terrorised this beautiful land not so many years ago.

When they reached his village, Turlough cried to be put down and so Christopher did. 'Be careful,' he warned, but the child ran heedlessly down the deserted street, past several smoke-blackened cottages, calling for his ma. Christopher followed slowly on the horse. At last the child came to his own home. It had not been burnt, but there was no sign of life. Several hooded crows flapped lazily away from a collection of old bones that lay near the threshold. The flesh and most of the skin had long gone, but the bones were about the size of a dog.

'There's no one here,' said Christopher, anxious for the little boy not to recognise the bones as the remains of his pet. 'We must go on to find your family.'

In later years, whenever Christopher had occasion to recall this search he remembered the bravery of the little child, who called out at every farm to protect Christopher and to ask about his lost family. All Christopher could do was to smile encouragingly at the suspicious people and hope for the best. No one spoke English or would admit to knowing the language. At the third little farm Turlough looked resigned.

'This is my aunt,' he said, not looking at the careworn woman at the door. Unshed tears filled his eyes, but he blinked them away. 'She says she will be my ma.'

Christopher tried to ask Turlough gently about what he had discovered and whether he was happy to be left here, but it was beyond the child to reply. Instead, he wriggled to be put down and that action spoke for him. Christopher handed Turlough the remaining honey cakes, telling him to be sure to share them with the toddler who gazed up at them, his dark eyes huge in his grubby, pale face. He handed the woman the bundle of Turlough's clothes, and, wondering whether to embrace the little boy or not, ended by giving him an awkward hug, which Turlough returned with embarrassing passion. Christopher found himself handing more coins than he could afford to the woman, hoping the gesture was not misunderstood, not being sure himself what he meant by it, except that the woman and her homestead looked even poorer than he had been at his most destitute.

He had not dismounted throughout the exchange and when he looked back after walking the horse a few yards from the house, Turlough and the woman had already disappeared inside. Christopher had done his duty as far as he possibly could. There had been a few scrawny chickens pecking at the door and a little red and white cow peering over a stone wall. He reminded himself that the family might have looked ragged to him, but there would be precious milk and eggs, and no doubt a dog or two around for Turlough to love. It would be a healthy life in this beautiful green countryside, back where he belonged.

Mindful that he now had no native to speak for him, Christopher urged his horse into a canter. When he regained the empty coast road, he allowed the beast to trot and arrived back in the city of Cork with no mishaps. There were plenty of English voices there and it was a simple matter to find lodgings for the night and passage home the next day. He was woken very early by the unaccustomed noises of the port. Immediately, he recalled that night's dream; indeed, it felt as if his waking had disturbed it, before it was quite ready to end.

He was in the theatre, but not in London, as recently. It was more like some country performance where everything was rough and unfinished, but he had never experienced such a thing in his waking life. The play was, he knew straight away, about him, but not seen from his point of view.

Centre stage, under a sign that read LONDON, the swarthy king was being restored to his rightful place after years of exile. Most of the audience cheered. He took the painted orb and sceptre and sat, careful to keep the ill-made throne from tilting. Far to the right, Norfolk lay, where Christopher, with theatrical gestures of affection, kissed the actor portraying his grotesquely pregnant wife. Lewd comments were offered by the audience, who were thoroughly enjoying the show. Mounting a hobby horse, Christopher galloped across the stage, pausing only to doff his hat as he passed the King. He arrived stage left at Dorset, where, before a painted coastline, seagulls jerked on strings, their joints creaking like mewing babies. Abandoning the horse, Christopher jabbed enthusiastically at the planks with a child's spade, to mime finding at least some of the coins he had hidden with his father during the war. More cheers and laughter as, capering with glee, he stuffed the discovered money into a purse, into his pockets and even under his hat.

While the actor playing the King sat in state, bestowing gracious smiles on the audience, Christopher spilt money into the apron of a Dorset innkeeper. Soon, the man was staggering with exaggerated pleasure at his new-found wealth. He handed a model of his inn to Christopher, who tucked it under his arm before leaping once more astride his horse. He began to trundle back across the stage, urging his steed to ever greater effort by thrashing its wooden flanks with his hat. Their progress was slow. In spite of Christopher's eagerness to rejoin his wife, he stopped in London to buy her ribbons, a hat and an embroidered pair of satin shoes – all of which he showed off to the audience as an infant might delight in showing his parent a pebble.

By the time he had once more passed the King, his wife's pains had come upon her and the audience, seeing her distress, fell silent.

She writhed and howled in her agony but none of her shrieks were heard by her husband. In happy ignorance, he made his way towards her, pausing often to admire his purchases, in spite of the audience's exhortations to him to make haste. By the time he arrived, black crows made of paper had been perched about her bed and the sprawled corpse of the actor lay still, partially covered by a sheet coloured with splashes of blood-red dye. The black 'O' of Christopher's horrified mouth stretched upon his chalked face made the audience shiver. Hat, shoes, ribbons, remaining coins – all tumbled to the stage as he fell in anguish from his horse. He howled his theatrical misery, writhing in a pathetic aping of his poor wife's final moments.

He had never remembered a dream so clearly. As he lay in that unaccustomed bed with the early light beckoning him to rise he wondered how instead of his usual grief and guilt at remembering that part of his life he felt neither. It was all so far away in his past it might as well be a play. His wife was long dead and her pains long over. To his surprise, he knew as certainly as he knew anything that his were too. He had put his wife to rest, he had returned the child to his homeland and he had survived Daniel Johnson. As for his son, his sadness was mingled with hope. Life had taken its toll, but Christopher was not an old man. Plenty of life was there in front of him to live.

Once at sea, the wind turned against them and the voyage back to Chineborough was arduous, but with every mile gained Christopher felt his spirits lifting even higher. He was free! Free of guilt over his dead wife and free of the child he had never wished to be burdened with. As for Abel, he would keep in touch with Ethan, in case he ever had any news.

With Ethan in his mind Christopher recalled the offer made in Constantinople, for them to try a trading relationship together. Why should he not try it? He would never make his fortune at the inn and this would be an opportunity to improve his financial situation with little risk to himself. He had liked Ethan. It would be the action of a friend to help him with his court connection. It might be tenuous, but he did know the King and was welcome at court. It would be a while before the bulbs flowered, but what if Ethan could discover other plants to send? The King might be interested in unusual items for his privy garden. It would cost little enough to return to London and try his luck. It was a good plan and he would set it in motion as soon as he reached home. It would be a fine thing to practise diligence in a new trade.

ABEL MORGAN

24

I studied my dead master Ptolemy's books diligently and learnt much from them. I so wished for a mate to help me, but, apart from Will Mather, who was almost deaf and so most helpful when a man had to be held still for treatment in spite of his screams, there was no one on board with the inclination or ability to become a surgeon's mate. As the months became years I doubted I would ever find a mate such as I had been to Ptolemy Moore. Then fate sent me help from a most unexpected quarter.

We were in need of supplies and had taken a small merchant vessel without mishap. The captain looked a brutal man, a corpulent fellow with a big belly that spoke of idleness and greed. I'd warrant he took his ease while his five crew slaved for him. Our boarding party had herded the captain and his crew together, and from where I stood I could see them well, for their vessel was tight alongside ours. The captain had his meaty hand on the fragile neck of his small cabin boy, a delicate-featured child with coffee-coloured skin. The very sight of his hand on that boy repulsed me.

As I gazed upon them, the child looked up at me. The next instant, he had broken away from his master, had clambered over the side and was on our deck at my feet, clinging most piteously to my legs. He was lucky no one had shot him, as usually happened when a crew member tried to escape.

'Save me, sir!' he begged in good English while his master roared in impotent anger. 'Take me with you. I'll die if you don't.'

I looked down at his ragged figure to remonstrate with him.

'I cannot do that,' I said. He only clung the harder, looking up into my face, his eyes seeking mine. I felt my heart turn over. He was so young and so very frightened. And he was undoubtedly a slave, obliged to suffer his master's every debauched whim. It struck me that I *could* rescue him if I wished. We were kings here and he was as much a prize as the rest of the cargo. I did not want him, but he might be useful on board and I could ensure he was not brutalised while with us. I supposed we could free him at some landfall if he proved a nuisance.

'Very well,' I said and was rewarded by a tremulous smile and glistening eyes as the boy struggled not to cry. 'I will look after you.'

Will Mather tossed a sack onto our deck and a few peas leaked from it. He grinned at me. 'Yonder captain wants his toy back,' he said, 'but I see it has taken a fancy to you.'

I found myself blushing. 'I know it,' I said. 'But I could not leave the child with that brute. Perhaps I can find him a better master in Port Royal.'

Will gave me a quizzical look before shaking his head. 'Too pretty for a good master,' he said.

I looked up to see Rowan with his weapon pointing directly at the child.

'Don't shoot,' I said quietly. 'The child means us no mischief.'

'Do you mean to turn slaver?' Rowan enquired with a slight smile. 'Or whoremaster?'

I felt myself blush again. I knew I did not want a boy in that way.

'At any rate, you have made an enemy of yonder captain,' added Rowan.

I looked over at the drifting merchantman. We had just cast her off and her captain appeared to be shaking his fist in our direction. Rowan levelled his pistol and took a shot. It was too far to do damage, but the captain ducked, and we laughed.

'Maybe the child can make himself useful,' I suggested.

'If not, we can sell him at Port Royal.'

The child clutched my legs even harder. 'He won't eat much,' I said. I looked down at him again and saw that his eyes were magnified with unshed tears. 'We won't sell you if you are useful.'

I turned to Rowan. 'May I have him as my share of the booty?'

He regarded me seriously. 'No man owns another on this ship, but I have no objection to him joining the crew so long as he can pull his shrimp-like weight. Take my advice, however, and don't let him have a knife until you are sure you can trust him. I would not want to find my surgeon murdered in his bunk.' He gave the child a hard look. 'Nor any of my men. If you cause trouble we will toss you overboard.'

My new charge was a very attractive child with his smooth, unblemished skin and his tousled black curly hair. He told me his name was Jack and said he thought he was ten years old. His story was a sad one, but not uncommon, I think.

'I was born in the Americas,' he said once he was calmer, realising he truly had escaped from his master. 'I am the child of a

254

maid and her master. My mother was unable to spend much time with me when I was a baby because she was required to work, but now and then the master took it into his head to dote on me. My mother said like a pet . . .'

He paused, and I could see he was remembering.

'I thought he behaved as a father would, having no other child. When I was older he liked to speak to me. He said he would teach me my letters and sometimes allowed me to run beside him when he rode around his estate.' Jack's eyes filled. 'On two occasions he lifted me up onto his horse. He could see I was tired and let me ride behind him.'

'Indeed, that does sound a little like the behaviour of a true father,' I said, remembering my own lamented parent.

Jack shook his head. 'But it was not! Two years ago, he married and his wife made plain that she didn't want me near him. I was instantly removed from the house servants' shack and sent to live with the rest of the slaves, away from my mother and all I knew. He would not allow me to be taken into the fields or to be beaten. I was grateful for that, but such treatment didn't endear me to the field slaves. They had seen me ride pillion behind the master. Once I was brought down, I found I had no friends, nor the love of my father or any more the life I had been accustomed to in the house where I had sometimes eaten off china and even drunk a little wine.'

'I am sorry for it.'

Jack looked earnestly at me. 'Last year my father died after a fall from his horse. He had made no provision for me and, as a result, his widow made swift arrangements to sell me. I was sold to a . . . a . . . fearful house.'

I waited until he was able to go on.

'I ran away, sir,' he said in his high, sweet voice. 'I know I shouldn't have, but I couldn't stay.' He rubbed at his eyes fiercely. 'For a while I lived a roaming life. I got far away from the town in which I had been dwelling and came eventually to the coast. I was in constant fear of discovery as a runaway, but one day it was so long since I had eaten that I went to an inn, offering to do the meanest job for a crust. It was there the captain saw me and took me with him. I thought it would be better than starving, but . . . there is nowhere to run on a ship.'

Jack bent his head and buried his face in his hands. His narrow shoulders shook as the tears fell.

I was moved more than I can say. That this blameless person should be treated so ill pained me deeply. I put my hand on his shoulder to comfort him, but he flinched so I hastened to remove it. What horrors he had been subjected to since he had been sold I hated to imagine. I decided then that I would not let him leave my side until I had found him a position that I could be certain would give him safety and dignity as well as honest toil.

We had hammocks to spare, but he insisted on sleeping just outside my door, so I found some sailcloth and other fabric, and he made himself a nest there. It would hardly do if we came into rough weather, but while the sea was calm it did him well enough.

I admit I was flattered by his attachment to me. He followed me like a puppy and did my bidding with a readiness that was most pleasing. After a few days I wondered if I might teach him something of my calling. He was too young and not strong enough for many of the duties of a surgeon's mate, but there were things he could do if he were only clever enough.

'Come on deck, Jack. And bring this box with you.'

We settled ourselves and I took the box from him. 'Here are some of my instruments. See how they are oiled and free of rust?'

He nodded. I took a small roll of cloth and undid it. Within were the few pieces Ptolemy had originally given me for my own. 'These have not been looked at for a while, but should my others become damaged I might have need of them. Do you think you could clean and oil them, so they are as fair as the others?'

I gave him the materials and he set to with a will.

'What is this for?' he asked, holding up a probe after cleaning it.

'It is sometimes necessary to look into a wound and this instrument helps me to do that.'

He looked at me with awe. 'Are you a barber, sir?'

I shook my head sternly. 'I can indeed shave a man and pull teeth, but I was trained by a great physician and surgeon and am myself the surgeon for both our ships.' Jack was silent a moment and then he held up the bullet remover.

'Can you tell me what this is for?'

I felt a jolt of pleasure. He was young, but he was deft of hand and was showing interest. Maybe he could be my apprentice, as I had been Ptolemy's. I explained, showing him how to turn the screw to make the remover the right size to grasp a bullet within a man's flesh. When I handed it back to him his face was a study in concentration as he worked it.

'Were you able to learn your letters, Jack, after your father died?'

'No, sir.'

'Would you like to learn?'

He looked up with such a smile on his face I had to return it. 'Oh yes, sir!'

'Then I shall teach you. And if you are willing I will teach you a little of my skills too.'

'Yes, please, sir!'

I was the happiest I had been for a long time. I wished I had an English version of my old picture book, which had been in Dutch and Latin. It would have been very useful, but Jack was a quick learner and very keen, even without a book of words and pictures to help him. He practised his letters at every opportunity, writing mostly with charcoal begged from the cook and using the deck as his paper. As one of his duties on board was to swab the deck he was constantly erasing his own work, which meant he had a never-ending surface. I wondered if Rowan might object to the school I had set up, but he was amused and happy I was teaching the boy.

'Teach him to shave a man,' he advised one afternoon. 'For once we have another prize we will head for Port Royal and many of the men will want smooth faces then.' He winked. I knew what he meant. There were plenty of women there of all types who would not object to a dalliance with a pirate, especially if he had plenty of gold to spend.

'And for goodness' sake,' Rowan added before moving on, 'find the poor child some means of keeping his work. He looks so regretful every time he must wash his carefully made letters away.'

Rowan had noticed what I had not. I hadn't realised my pupil cared that he had nothing permanent to show for all his efforts and I was sorry. I did not think he was a fair enough hand to warrant having paper from one of my precious journals, but I rummaged through my chest and found the scorched chart Rowan had given me from the vessel that had exploded.

The chart was of the entrance to the Mediterranean and so of no use to Rowan, but the reverse would give Jack space to practise writing on a finer medium than the deck. His young face lit up as if a lantern shone from within when I gave it to him.

'This is very different from writing with charcoal,' I said as I trimmed a nib for him. 'It will take practice to master a nib, so don't get disheartened.'

'I won't.' He looked up at me with serious eyes and then he couldn't help breaking into a wide smile. 'I am in heaven!'

I doubted that but said nothing to spoil his pleasure.

A pirate ship is not often a heavenly place to be and it wasn't long before Jack had his first taste of bloodletting. He acquitted himself well, not shrinking like a girl from the gore, but nimbly handing me instruments and mopping blood when required. He was so keen to learn that his few early mistakes were easily corrected. After a few months, the way he anticipated which probe, knife or clamp I would need made it hard for me to imagine how I had ever managed without him. His ready smile soon won over the men and his deftness made them seek him out to pull splinters rather than me.

'The child has a gentle touch,' said Will when I came upon them one afternoon on deck. Jack had just drawn a large splinter from Will's palm.

I looked at the hand carefully. 'Such wounds can fester,' I told my protégé. 'Be sure to pour some oil and honey into it.'

The child nodded obediently, but I had already noticed the unguents ready at his side. I wondered if I might feel some jealousy at the child's popularity, but I did not. In truth, he had brought a welcome cheer to all our lives. He had become something of a mascot for the men and at the same time his loyalty to me was unquestioned.

I began to give some serious thought to his future. Although we had embraced the pirating life, it had not exactly been a free choice for me or my protégé. We risked hanging if we were caught and the thought of that end for Jack disturbed me greatly.

I remembered that Ptolemy had told me of a lawyer in Port Royal who was to be trusted. Perhaps the next time we were in port I could take Jack to see him. Would it be too much to hope that he might find the child some worthy and safe occupation? I had money aplenty now. I had learnt not to drink and whore it all away and kept a reasonable amount in Ptolemy's chest. I could settle that on the boy for his lodging and apprenticeship if one could be found for him. I would sorely miss my little surgeon's mate, but it would be years before he would be strong enough for much of the work and, if I were to hold his best interests at heart, I could see no other way.

I decided to tell no one of my plans, not even the boy himself. I did not want to be dissuaded from doing my best for him. I rummaged in the chest and found the note in Ptolemy's hand of the lawyer's name and lodging. It was melancholy to see it. I remembered so well him writing it down and telling me to be sure to search out this lawyer should anything happen to him. I had not needed this Mr Chepstow, but now I was grateful for the information. It was hard to know who to trust in Port Royal, but I felt sure I could trust a man of Ptolemy's choosing.

I had done as my old master had with me and not allowed Jack ashore in Jamaica. This time it would be different. I would take him: not to the inns and whorehouses as Rowan had done with me, but to the lawyer to settle his future. So, I watched our approach to the island with mixed feelings. I wanted to do right by the boy, but I would sorely miss him. It would have to be done before I was quite unable to let him go.

25

The lawyer was a well-made, handsomely dressed gentleman. His study was filled with papers, books and many interesting curios. He remembered Ptolemy well and was effusive in his condolences when he heard of the surgeon's demise.

'He was a man of good family,' said Mr Chepstow. 'Set adrift after the war in England. I did my best to convince him to return to his homeland, but he had too many sad memories of that place and enemies, too, I fear.'

'I know it,' I said. 'We sometimes spoke of our lack of family and how ill winds had blown us to the same ship. He was like a father to me.'

Mr Chepstow nodded. 'Very like, I dare say.' He looked over to where Jack sat quietly on a stool, waiting in his innocence for me to finish my business. 'Before we go further may I ask what business this young person has in your affairs?'

'He is actually the reason I am here, though I have not told him of it. He is an intelligent boy who knows his letters and is adept at assisting me in some of my lighter surgeon's duties. I fear a life such as mine is full of danger and I would prefer him to have a safer trade.' I smiled encouragingly at Jack, but Mr Chepstow looked unimpressed.

'I have money,' I continued, signing Jack to return to his stool, from which he had risen, looking most anxious, 'to pay for his lodging and apprenticeship if honest employment can be found for him.'

Mr Chepstow looked scathingly at me. 'I would have thought,' he said 'that Mr Ptolemy Moore would have taught you better. Honest employment is best suited to an honest person who does not dress herself in a boy's clothing to take advantage of a poor fool.'

I stared at him, unable to take in what he meant. At that moment Jack rose again from his stool and without a word to me sped out of the room.

'Jack!'

'I would advise you to let her go.'

I barely heard him. I raced to the open door and caught a glimpse of Jack weaving deftly between two laden donkeys. I gave chase. The narrow street was crowded and slippery underfoot, but if it was hard for me to move fast the throng must also slow his progress. Surely I would catch him. Him? It was impossible to think of him as a girl. It could not be. But trickling into my mind were questions I could do nothing to stop. Thinking, not looking, led me to run right into a woman with a basket of fruit on her head. I fumbled for my purse and threw her a coin, apologising profusely, but by the time I had renewed the chase Jack was nowhere to be seen.

Port Royal was a dangerous place. For someone so young, unarmed and with nowhere to go it could be desperate. I looked everywhere, even down some dark alleys I would not usually dare to venture. Several times I thought I had him, only to find it was some other dark-haired, pale-brown-skinned boy, a real boy, ragged of clothing and dirty of face, as most were in this place. Eventually, as it got dark, with leaden steps, I made my way back to Mr Chepstow's office, hoping he would still be there. I felt sick. I didn't want to go back to my ship. There was no one I desired to confide in. I didn't want to admit to Rowan that I'd lost my mate, nor did I want to know if I was the only one who thought him a boy. Had the whole crew been hiding their laughter behind their hands? I very much feared it must be so. Well, I would not go back to the ship to be met by their derision. If that was the way they purposed to treat me, they could do without their surgeon. Perhaps Mr Chepstow would know of a respectable inn where I might sleep. In the morning I would search for Jack again and take him to task for deceiving me.

Mr Chepstow was on the street, locking up for the night. When he saw me, he scowled, but put his key back in the lock and beckoned me in. He stood his lantern down and relit several candles before sitting once more at his desk.

I halted at the door and glared at him. 'You have it wrong! He is a good, honest boy. He had good reasons for his . . . deception . . . and would have told me when he thought . . .'

'Then why did she run?' The lawyer sighed. 'You must know you would not be the first to be tricked by a girl in boy's clothing.'

'It's impossible!' Even as I blustered to save my dignity I thought of ways in which Jack could have kept the secret of his sex. I had teased him about his modesty in never disrobing in front of me, especially once, when we needed to wash after performing a particularly bloody operation. But I had thought it a result of the way he had been used in a debauched manner in the past. That would be enough to make any boy try to keep himself safe. But that could also have been a story to take advantage of me. I could see the argument, but I could not see the person I knew as Jack being other than honest. And yet, he . . . she . . . had run when discovered.

I felt . . . I knew not how: bewildered, yes, and I admit it, hurt at not being trusted, even bereft. But while I reeled from the knowledge that I had been tricked I still fretted after Jack's safety. I went to the lawyer's desk and sat down. 'What should I do? If I can find her, I should still like to set her to gainful employment. A safe place for her is what I need.'

Mr Chepstow looked impatient. 'Doubtless she is a runaway slave,' he opined. 'And as such not legally yours to dispose of.' He scratched his head. 'Depending on your proclivities I would say the safest place for her would be with yourself, but it appears she doesn't like that option.'

'He' – I corrected myself – 'she . . . didn't like the idea of being sent away, but there must be someone . . .'

He looked at me with something approximating contempt. 'She didn't want to be sent away so she left? And why should there be someone?'

I had no answer for him.

'Mr Morgan?'

I looked at him wearily.

'There are other matters to discuss.'

I tried to pay attention, but I was tired and sick at heart. I berated myself for being such a poor judge of character but could no more feel anything but care for my Jack. 'What other matters, sir?'

'Financial matters pertaining to you and Mr Moore.'

I tried to gather my thoughts and pay more attention. 'Well, Mr Moore did tell me he would invest my few pennies when he came to see you, but I doubt they are worth considering. I earned very little as his mate.'

'Indeed. In fact, I have to tell you that Mr Moore neglected to invest anything in your name.'

His words got my attention. 'Really?' I felt stunned. It seemed that I was no judge of character at all. Not only had Jack deceived me, but the man I had thought of as a second father had done the same. Was this lawyer he had recommended to me also not to be trusted? How could I tell? I sighed. It was too late and too long ago to remonstrate with Ptolemy, even in thought. The best I could do was probably to hear Mr Chepstow out and then politely take my leave. 'Well,' I said. 'No matter. Ptolemy has been dead for a long while and I will not speak ill of the dead. Besides, I am no longer a pauper.'

Mr Chepstow cleared his throat. 'As to the matter of investment . . .'

I set my face to look mildly interested, although I would not be giving him care of my gold and I did not feel very patient.

'It appears that Mr Moore . . . neglected to invest any sum of money in your name whatsoever, but . . .'

'Yes?'

Mr Chepstow raised his hand. 'The surgeon invested no money in *your* name,' he said in a level voice. 'That is correct. However . . .' He shuffled some documents on his desk, and then reached over and pulled another from a shelf. 'He did name you as his only heir.'

I sighed. 'Well, that was kind of him. I must confess, knowing he had no heirs, that I took his chest and his instruments for my own use. His few books too. I am heartily glad my action would have had his blessing.'

Silence filled the room, apart from the street noise that entered from the open window.

Mr Chepstow held the document like a weapon and shook it at me. 'This is his will. All his possessions, property and land he left to you without condition or mortgage.' A slight smile turned his mouth. 'Unlike his shipmates, your surgeon was a cultured man with great presence of mind. He was not, I think, inclined to drink his wealth.'

'That is as he told and advised me,' I said. 'I really have no complaints about him. He treated me very well. His wise instruction gave me a profession and his instruments are both payment and interest for the small amount of money he had of me.'

'You see,' said Mr Chepstow, leaning his elbows amongst the papers on his desk. 'You had such a little quantity of coin that I advised putting it with his to get a better return. We didn't purpose to fleece you.' He looked at me as if he could tell that I doubted him. 'You are, as a consequence, a very wealthy young man.'

I was in no mood to hear a lecture. 'Indeed, I do consider myself such. I did not have to pay for my apprenticeship and my calling has served me well. I do not wish to make a complaint.' My mind kept wandering back to Jack, wondering what she purposed to do now and feeling sad that she had not felt able to fully confide in me.

Mr Chepstow looked exasperated. 'You do not understand me, Mr Morgan. Mr Moore's will leaves you a fine stone house in Port Royal, at present rented out, several other houses and offices also rented out, a large plantation with over a hundred slaves bringing in a healthy income from sugar, with many fine valuable trees which would find a ready market as building timber. In addition, he wrote an account of his life for you to read, as his adopted son.' He cleared his throat. 'There was, of course, the matter of his . . . um . . . surgeon's income, which I have done my best to disguise so as not to admit it coming from privateering.'

He looked at me as if awaiting my comments, but in truth I could think of none, being too astonished for words.

'If you want my advice . . .' He got up and closed the window onto the street before regaining his seat and leaning towards me over the desk. 'You would do well to leave your employment this instant, change your name and live quietly on the plantation. On the high seas, pirates may feel like kings, but things are changing here. As a surgeon you may never have killed a man . . .'

'I—'

He shook his head slightly. It was obvious that he didn't want to know. 'But that will count for little if you have been profiting from plunder. Men once welcomed here are now being hanged and their wealth confiscated. Mr Moore made you a rich man. Don't squander your life before you have had time to enjoy it.'

I struggled to understand this new revelation. 'But Port Royal has always been a haven for pirates!'

Mr Chepstow shook his head. 'You people come with your booty and go with sore heads, not seeing how the wind blows on this island of ours. Your namesake, Sir Henry Morgan, has recently been charged with ridding our seas of pirates and buccaneers. He goes about his business here with the same zeal he last employed in plundering his prizes. No one is immune. Three days ago, he hanged several of his old shipmates for doing what he used to do.'

He looked at me with such intensity I could not doubt the shocking truth of what he said. Seeing he had my attention, he nodded. 'Yes, even a young surgeon's mate who has never killed. Even you should beware the admiral's reach. I fear he becomes rapacious, even to his own kind.'

I swallowed. 'What should I do?'

'Do nothing to connect your person with any sort of questionable activity. On no account go back to your ship. Do not associate with any of your former shipmates. Change your name. Shed your old life as a snake discards her skin.'

'But I should warn them!' My heart was hammering in my breast. 'And my instruments! My sea chest. All I have . . .'

Mr Chepstow held up his hand to quell my protestations. 'It may be that your shipmates will enjoy their carousing tonight and will live to sail once more, but I *cannot* counsel you to search for them.' He lay his hand back on his desk. 'Mr Moore asked me, if he died, to be your guide away from the life he had and into the one he wished for you both. He did not live to enjoy the life of a plantation owner, but you can, if we take care. You are very young. Mr Moore wanted you to live and prosper.' He smiled. 'Do not regret your sea chest. You will have all you need in your new life if you will be guided by me.' He hesitated. 'Even to surgical instruments if you so desire.'

I took a deep breath to try and still my pounding heart and racing mind. Should I put my well-being in this man's hands? I had sworn to be my own man after Ptolemy's death, but Mr Chepstow was offering me his professional advice, based on what Ptolemy had wanted.

I was adrift in my thoughts. Life was crammed full of what was known and what was not. In the space of an hour or two I had discovered that a boy was not a boy, that I could not trust what Ptolemy had said, although he had done more for me than I had ever imagined, and that I was totally unqualified to make any sort of decision about the man in front of me. This was not the first time my life had been completely altered by others. Was it even possible to ever be in control of my own path? I felt like a child in a sea of fancies, without the ability to tell what was imagining and what was real. More than anything I wished Ptolemy were here so I could thank him. It was melancholy to think that he had planned to take me with him when he retired to his property on this island but had never thought fit to tell me of it. Was it that he didn't trust me to keep the knowledge to myself in case the pirates got wind of it and held us against our will? Or perhaps he feared we would not live to enjoy the idyll he had planned, as it had in fact turned out for him.

I tried to push thoughts of self-pity away from me. They had no place in the mind of one who had just been given so much. But I couldn't help thinking of my losses as well as my gains. My poor, sad father, dead on the floor of his cellar. Ptolemy, dead in the act of practising his calling, and Jack, the child I had thought to help in turn, but who I had also lost. How many buildings, how much wealth would it take to make me forget these losses?

I hauled in my bitter thoughts and forced myself to be in the present. I owed it to my benefactor's memory to fall in with his wishes and count my luck. Besides, what Mr Chepstow said made sense.

'I will, in memory of Mr Moore, do as you suggest,' I said.

Now the words were out I felt a sudden panic in case my decision was too late. 'I need a safe place to stay tonight!'

Mr Chepstow looked relieved. 'Yes, you do. There is the plantation house, but I would not suggest you ride there in the dark through country you do not know. There is a quiet, respectable inn a little way along this street. With luck, you should be safe there tonight.'

He snuffed the candles. Once the outer door was locked, he pointed the way. 'A few steps that way is an inn called the Sugar House. Tell them I sent you. If you are agreeable, I will call for you early in the morning and take you to your plantation.' He touched my sleeve. 'Take my advice and spend a sober night. Do not draw attention to yourself. It would pain me after all the care I have taken, to see Mr Moore's wealth forfeit because his inheritor is hanged for a pirate. My house lies in the opposite direction, so I will bid you goodnight. Oh! And consider your new name, what it is to be. I will have documents for you to sign.'

In an instant he was gone with his lantern and I turned my face the other way, my mind in turmoil. So, it seemed I was wealthy, though it was hard to comprehend it. But what use was wealth without a soul to share it with? I was to abandon the pirates, had lost my young mate and could hardly call Mr Chepstow a friend.

I wondered, as I tried to master my feelings, was it common for men to feel like children, although they were grown and should be confident in all they did? Was adulthood a thing of dusty mirrors? If so, I was indeed grown.

As I set my feet in the direction of the inn I felt a tug at my sleeve. I pulled my arm away and put my hand to the sword I wore when on shore. I was not a competent swordsman, but I felt safer wearing it and I was not about to let a beggar or cutpurse take advantage of me. An anger that must have been simmering in me since I had learnt of Jack's deceit burst out of me and I rounded furiously on the person who had dared to touch me. I was confronted by a face that had been recently sliced open by what must have been a very sharp blade. The voice came faintly.

'Mr Morgan, sir.'

'Jack!'

Her eyes fluttered in her head. As she fainted I caught her in my arms and lifted her up. I carried her the few steps to the inn and called for the landlord.

'A room. The best you have. And water in a basin, soap, linen. Ho there!'

The pot-boy stared at us and fled. A woman with tangled hair came from behind the bar and stood with arms akimbo. 'Who makes a disturbance here? This is a good house.'

'Mr Chepstow sent me,' I told her, calming my voice. 'He is my lawyer. Now show me to the best room you have. Make haste!'

The most imperious voice I could muster while appearing calm seemed to convince her. She glanced at the blood weeping on the wounded cheek and made up her mind. 'Follow me,' she said.

As I carried Jack up the wide stairs I was thinking what I must do to tend the wound. I was praying the knife had not gone too deep and that the palate and tongue were safe, but my hands and arms were not listening to my professional thoughts. They were telling me without doubt that under the ragged clothing a young woman lay unconscious in my arms.

'Put her on the table. I will not have so much blood on my sheets.'

'I will pay for the bedding,' I said as I laid her gently down. 'Now bring me warm water and cloths as I have asked.'

The woman left us, grumbling as she went, but soon a boy appeared with what I had asked for.

As the door closed behind the boy, my Jack's eyes fluttered open. She began to rise, but I pressed her gently back upon the bed. 'Rest easy. I must look at your poor face.'

Knowing her trade, she mumbled awkwardly, 'There is no blood in my mouth.'

I satisfied myself that she was right and then bent to the wound, cleaning it gently so I could see the extent of the damage. She had been lucky, if such a cut could be deemed fortunate. It had been made with a very sharp blade and ran in a curve from beside her mouth to the outer corner of her eye. It was more than a scratch, but not a bad wound and should heal well enough.

She struggled to speak again. 'I thought . . . if it needed stitching I would rather you did it than any other . . .'

I felt tears prickle behind my eyes. Ptolemy's gift, the fear of arrest, Jack's true gender, her departure and the manner of her return for my help – so much change had come tumbling, one thing after another. It was as if the earth had carried me away on a fantastical earthquake and returned me into a different geography. I sat myself down on the bed against the trembling in my body and took her hand.

'I have no means with me to stitch the wound, but I think it will knit well enough without help. Even so, I will keep a careful watch on it.'

Her voice was so small I had to bend to hear her words. 'Thank you.'

She made no attempt to withdraw her hand, so I raised it to my lips and found myself kissing it.

'I tried to steal a fish to eat, but the fish-wife saw me and lunged with her gutting knife.'

'She might have killed you.' I looked at her and saw that she wept. 'The salt will pain your cut.'

She winced as her tears watered the red line on her cheek, but she made light of the sting. 'They will help it to heal.' She gripped my hand. 'I did not return simply for your skill as surgeon. That man, Mr Chepstow, saw me straight away for what I am. I was frightened of your anger.'

I tried to speak, but she stopped my mouth with her hand. 'I am sorry I misled you, when you have been so kind. Please don't send me away. I will work hard. Even though I am a girl I am growing stronger every day. I will fill all the responsibilities of a surgeon's mate if you will let me remain. We can be as before. I will do anything . . .'

'No.'

She turned her face away from me then with a kind of hopelessness that tugged at my heart. I hastened to reassure her.

'I thought I had lost you when I had just discovered you! Don't cry. I don't want you to leave me, but I can no longer call you Jack. Tell me what your name is.'

She turned back and looked earnestly into my face. 'So, I may still be your assistant?' What she read there disappointed her. Her eager expression turned to one of distrust and she pulled her shirt about her neck as if to protect herself. 'I will not be your doxy.'

I think the horror in my voice gave her pause. 'No!' I protested. 'I do not want that! I would marry you.'

I shocked myself. I did not know I would say it, but when it was out I saw that I meant it.

'You don't know me.'

I felt reckless with outrageous happiness. 'I have known you for the best part of a year! I know your intelligence, determination, cheerfulness.' I paused to refill my arsenal. 'Good humour, loyalty, resourcefulness . . . all I have *not* known is your sex!'

She looked at me and there was despair in her face. 'I am a fourteen-year-old runaway slave with a scarred face and I am not a maid. Even before that sea captain . . . he . . .'

'I care not!' I took her hand again and spoke seriously. 'Except that if he hurt you I will find and kill him.' She shook her head slightly, but it was not to deny his cruelty.

In spite of Jack's hurts, I felt a rising desire to caper like a mummer. I had never before felt this extraordinary mix of desire, trepidation and exhilaration. New feelings that I could only call love buffeted around in my heart and my loins. 'I will be your Romeo to my Juliet!' I told her. She looked at me in puzzlement and I laughed. I had an overwhelming desire to share in five minutes all the book learning I had gathered at my father's knee. Such dizzy thoughts were a happy kind of madness. Well, I would soon, it seemed, be able to afford as many books as I wished. Meanwhile, I had an object of my new-found affections that but an hour ago had not existed! The stews of Port Royal and other towns were all very well, but they had afforded me only animal couplings. I would not be alone on my plantation. I would take her with me and together we would enjoy everything my good fortune could bring us. What a life we would live!

CHRISTOPHER MORGAN

26

Christopher had always told himself he was not cut out for court, but since he had successfully discharged his duty to Turlough he found his mind entirely altered. It was obvious that Jane and William were more than capable of running the inn without him. Christopher could feel himself emerging, as if from the cocoon of a moth. He was a changed man. Buying the Rumfustian Inn had felt the right thing to do at the time, but neither of the people he had thought it would shelter were with him. It was time he made a new life for himself.

The more he thought about it the more he relished the opportunities London and the court offered. At home he had starved himself of intelligent conversation, while the court was awash with it. Men discussed the latest scientific experiments and theories, including ones pertaining to plants. His abandoned attempts to cultivate fungi in the cellar came back to him. He should ask someone about such things.

It was as if he were waking from a long sleep. His spirit bounded upwards like soap bubbles in the breeze. At court, he had heard a wonderful young composer's anthem. The King had also been enamoured of Mr Purcell's genius, so perhaps there would be more sublime music to listen to, in the company of others who could appreciate it. Never could Dario furnish him with such experiences.

He reminded himself that a gentleman needed money to stay at court. Well, if he was careful the inn's profits could be stretched to keep him there perhaps a week in every six or eight. Perhaps that would be enough to discover how he could improve his financial position. As well as enjoying the best of court life, he would scurry about his business, seeking profitable enterprise. He had already written to Ethan, asking for more interesting plants to be sent to him, and eagerly awaited his reply. Every gentleman of fashion wanted to emulate what the King favoured. If he could interest the King, he would have a slew of willing customers, gentlemen all, with gold to spend. And then he had another thought. He had a connection with Holland, where skilful gardeners had great success. Why should he not ask his father-in-law to introduce him to a Dutchman willing to teach him or to supply him with other plants? There were possibilities everywhere when he began to look.

If Abel returned, he would take him to court and help him to make a good marriage. If he did not, at least Christopher would have something to distract himself from his loss. It was more than time to look forward.

Christopher could not tell why flowers meant so much to him, but they did. Maybe it was simply that their beauty soothed his soul. Whatever the reason, it was a fortunate interest. When next in London, he visited gardens and growers whenever he could, learning much. Ethan needed no urging to facilitate his plans, sending more bulbs and searching for unusual roses, flowers which

Christopher particularly loved. He was far from being the only person involved in the horticultural trade. London was a great centre, but it wasn't long before Christopher decided to send the royal plant and garden fashions to the West Country, and that proved a wise decision. Within two years, his contact with Ethan was providing him with some wonderful new plants and his trade in Bristol and roundabout was beginning to thrive. He still bought much from the London growers as well as from Holland but was starting to build up a stock of unusual plants of his own, which was giving him much more profit.

On his return to the inn one day, he could hardly contain his excitement as he presented Jane with a tiny plant in a pot.

'What is it?' she asked, never having had a great regard for plants unless they were useful.

'It's an auricula,' he said. 'The King's gardener gave it to me. He says it has a colour and stripe he has never seen before and he cannot recall where it came from. He wondered if I had supplied it to him, but I know I have not. I wonder if it will set seed for me? It is a very pretty thing.' He regarded it with pleasure. 'And I wonder more if the seed will be true? But I will grow and sell them as having come from the King's garden. They will be very popular, whatever they look like!'

'And to think,' said William in his lugubrious manner, 'that in days past, producing a cabbage was an achievement.'

Christopher favoured him with a laugh. 'I am still early in learning and I fear I will never learn to love digging and weeding, but propagation and breeding are fascinating sciences. William, can you find me a couple of good boys to help you? I have it in mind to increase my nursery, and to do that we will need more land and more help.'

That evening, when Christopher retired to bed, he sat at his desk for a while, drawing the tiny flower. He had a new journal now and it was filling with drawings, lists and descriptions of plants and flowers, as well as a growing list of wealthy customers who wanted to speak to him personally, rather than to simply buy his plants from the man he supplied in Bristol. Everyone wanted the latest fashion in plants as well as clothes and houses, and that meant knowing what went on at court. Making the acquaintance of Sir Christopher Morgan was fast becoming a fashionable step to take.

He got into bed and, as always, stretched out comfortably. Rather to his surprise he found he was an excellent businessman, while somehow not compromising the fact that he was a gentleman. Money was coming in, more than he had thought possible. He had fortuitously discovered a hobby which had become both a passion and brought a handsome income. He was almost entirely a happy man. He still wrote to Ethan asking about Abel, but there was never any news. If he still lived, he would be a grown man by now, and yet Christopher kept his son's room the way it had always been. If he did ever return, Christopher would not wish him to think his memory had been obliterated from the inn. At least there was a pot of money now with which to ransom him, if they could ever discover where he was, and to buy him clothes fit for a gentleman instead of his slave's rags.

ABEL MORGAN

27

Ptolemy, far more than my father, gave me what I needed to survive in this world. I wish sometimes that I knew more about him. He told me little about his early life and the account he left me is so closely written I find it hard to decipher. Perhaps one day I will get it copied by someone, so I can read it, but really, it does not matter. It is all he did for me that I remember with gratitude.

As much as the wealth Ptolemy left me, my surgeon's skill has continued to open doors. For even the mightiest of men are disinclined to suffer pain when they can avoid it and will welcome any who can give them relief. What's more, doctoring is my passion. The body is an ever-wondrous thing and I suspect no man will ever learn all there is to be known about it. Medicine will, I feel sure, interest me until my eventual death.

At seventeen, I had experienced much and managed not just to survive, but to prosper. Perhaps I can be excused for making mistakes in the one life skill of which I had no knowledge: women. Expressly in the form of Marie. Her perfidy at not sooner revealing her true sex to me hurt. I thought I had been trusted, but I swept the hurt away because, in my new realised passion for her, I did not wish anything to render her imperfect. And so, I fell down immediately on one of my tenets. I know the puppyish affection I had for her was no more than a boy's desire, imagined to be a great love, but at the time it laid me open to her manipulation, which included not taking the advice of my lawyer, Mr Chepstow. I insisted on marrying her because *she* insisted on it before she would allow me access to her delicious body. She could not pretend to be virgin, so why protest so much? But we had struck up a friendship on board and discovering her sex turned me romantic. I wanted to see romance and nobility in our situation, and so, because I thought I loved her, and she I, we wed.

Let me explain a little more. Recall that I am a surgeon, with at that time little knowledge of the female body. If I had thought of it, I could have doubtless purchased a girl to conduct examinations and experiments upon, but I have never, nor ever wished to, practise medicine on any but willing patients. So, it was not just my boyish ardour that trapped me. In addition, the temptation of knowing that I would every night have the body of a young woman in my bed, a woman eager to teach me her form's contours, abilities and secrets, was not to be passed up. It may seem a curious premise for a marriage, but it was, I know, at least a small part of my great enthusiasm. That and the feeling that suddenly the world was laid out before me, with wealth, a home and a woman there for the taking. I turned none of it away. I cast off my name for safety's sake and became a newborn man, one Sir Jack Moore, come into his new-found land. Moore had been Ptolemy's family name and so honoured him. Jack, of course, had been the name Marie called herself as a boy, and my title I took for myself, knowing for a certainty of my father's death.

Everything was awash with newness. Has anyone had such a turnaround in their fortunes? I cannot think it. I almost felt myself a foundling discovered to be a king. In truth, pirating had brought me gold enough. A surgeon's share is a generous one, but the life is always hazardous.

At first, I felt myself at immediate danger of being discovered for who I had been, because that former pirate Henry Morgan had been knighted, made governor of the island and was in the process of hanging his old friends. However, having abandoned my shipmates so precipitously and living quietly on the plantation under new names as a married couple gave us both cause to believe that all would be well. Cut off as we were from society, we had only ourselves for entertainment. I admit I was like a child with a honeycomb. My ardour knew no limits, except for my body's occasional exhaustion, due entirely to overuse. Her body was a constant delight to me and I know mine was not unpleasing to her. We lay abed for most of the time, only rising to eat or drink, our needs being met by an elderly slave woman, who said little to either of us.

Eventually, Marie swore herself in need of other entertainment, and so, although I would have been happy to remain indolent a while longer, she shrugged off my advances and insisted on exploring our immediate surroundings. I did not see then, but understood eventually, how single-minded she was. I had thrilled at her intelligence when I thought her a boy, so eager to learn about my work. I had not understood that it was ambition that drove her, not interest. As soon as she no longer needed to practise medical matters she cast them entirely aside. Always for her it was ambition. She had escaped ill use by throwing herself on board at my feet. I had proved to be a happy choice then and was even more of one now I had come into my fortune. Did she love me? I do not think I will ever truly know, but I cannot blame her for trying to escape the miserable life she had led until meeting me. Now, she had every intention of taking up the role of plantation wife, a change of life that was a miracle to us both. So I trailed behind her like a puppy as she thoroughly explored the house. It was, I thought, a good house, though small. Having been raised in the fusty old Rumfustian Inn, I found the large windows and front porch very pleasing, but Marie, who knew of these things, said that the house was much too small for a resident owner and must be improved. I had been assured by Mr Chepstow that there was money and to spare for any improvements I might wish, and so I told Marie she could have a free hand. I wasn't particular because I was more interested in her body than her plans, but being temporarily thwarted in that respect I decided to match her in maturity by discovering all that was to be known about my plantation. And so, a few short weeks after we became man and wife, our new life truly began.

The plantation had an overseer who dealt with everything and had been answerable to Mr Chepstow. Mr Ballam rode the plantation every day and so if I were to learn what I owned I must ride too. Apart from the nag hired by Mr Chepstow to get us to the plantation from Port Royal I had not been on the back of a horse since leaving England. I knew nothing of horseflesh but ordered Ballam to find me a good riding horse. The one he bought was too spirited for my inexperience, but I had more tenacity than the horse and over the course of a few weeks I had the measure of him. I did not like Ballam and I daresay he did not much like me watching him as he worked. Maybe he thought to dissuade me from accompanying him by providing me with such a horse, but I was not going to allow that to happen. This was my plantation and I meant to know everything about it.

I had another reason to want to know all I could. Marie, having been born on a plantation, seemed to know much and had an opinion on everything, which often varied from mine. Even on the slave policy, where I thought she would agree with me, she did not. Remembering my father's gentleness in never beating me, I found Ballam's treatment of the slaves overharsh, but when one evening I told her how I purposed to change his regime she remonstrated with me.

'Leave it alone,' she told me.

'But it seems to me he would get better work and even loyalty from the slaves if he treated them well,' I argued. 'Surely you cannot advocate severe punishment for small wrongs? It could be your mother being whipped for being tardy, simply because she was caring for her sick child, who could have been you!'

I had never seen Marie so angry. It shocked me that she could be so unfeeling towards those whose blood she carried in her veins. Granted, the only outward sign of her ancestry was the colour of her skin, which with her European hair and features could almost, in some lights, have been Spanish, but for her to so deny her blood surprised and appalled me.

'Do you think kindness makes any difference?' she shouted. 'Their only reason to live is to escape. You know *nothing*!'

It was our first serious disagreement, beyond the bickering we had begun indulging in. I felt like striking her, but instead I turned and left the room. I snarled at a slave to saddle my horse and galloped angrily towards the place high on my land that overlooked the sea. At that moment, if I could have been back on board ship, I would have far preferred it to being a young husband with a wife I did not know how to tame. Looking down at the waves far below, crashing unceasingly on the rocks, I felt trapped in a life that had at first felt perfect but had too quickly turned sour.

My horse moved under me and I yanked cruelly at his mouth. I hated myself in part for this behaviour, but another part of me felt that Marie was to blame. I slid my feet from the stirrups and dismounted, leaving the horse free to wander as he wished. It would be the slave's fault, I told myself, if the damned horse went home without me and the slave would answer for it. I have no excuse for my childish behaviour, other than youth and disappointment at my honeycomb days so swiftly turning to gall. I did not know how to recover those first days when Marie had seemed as pliant as her alter ego, Jack, with the added pleasure of her true sex revealed. I felt more at sea than when I had been on board ship and there was no one here to give me advice.

I was in no mood just then to ponder her words about the treatment of slaves. I was more concerned with feeling outraged at her, a woman, daring to defy me, but over the following months and years I came to think much about the question of slavery and how best it was to be managed. Some had it that slaves were no more than animals, others admitted them to be more like children, but I never saw less than full humanity in all its many guises. They had been taken in Afric wars and sold by their captors to the merchants that ploughed this harvest of humanity. It was otherwise the tribal kings' habit to slaughter them. By bringing them here, to labour in the fields, their lives had been saved and they were taught to be Christians, so also saving their souls. I knew I was doing God's work by giving them their lives, but at times I wished they could have been less resentful and more grateful. I did rein back some of the harshest treatment of my slaves and did also physic them when needed, though at first, I had a hard job to convince them of my genuine concern for their well-being. Sadly, Marie was proved right in that none of this stopped slaves trying to escape. It took me a long while to understand this. Why should they not work for food, shelter and physic? But that is not it at all, is it? For my slaves, like that beautiful boy I had seen when I had been a captive myself, had not chosen the life they had. They had not asked to sail to Jamaica, to toil in the terrible heat of the sugar fields. And unlike any free man, the only way they had to improve their situation was to run away. What the answer is I do not know, for the demand for sugar is so high and plantations need more men to labour in the fields than could be provided in any other way. The Irish sent here as slaves are not able to withstand the climate, so the problem is more than I can fathom.

My horse did not wander far, and so, having calmed myself, a little I remounted and returned home to my wife. Neither of us referred to our falling-out. For a few days things were awkward between us, but then she gave me news that made me forget my sulk. For Marie was with child, which gave me much joy. We were, I know, in spite of our differences, fond of one another and both had found each other's bodies attractive. Many marriages have, I think, succeeded on less than this, but I did not know that then and Marie had been forced to subjugate her natural wilfulness through necessity for so long that she could no longer suppress it, nor wished to. In addition, pregnancy must have made her feel even more secure in her role as my wife, so it was not long before we took to bickering again.

I thanked God I was a surgeon, having the knowledge to make draughts, because that was my recourse when argument failed. I did not wish to beat her to make her compliant. In truth, I feared it would take more than a slap to bring her to heel. She was not easily cowed and might even retaliate in kind. I did not wish to risk serious violence, especially while she was carrying my child. Instead, when her tongue goaded me beyond all managing, I took either to my horse or to administering a soothing concoction that made her drowsy, disguising my true purpose by telling her that it was a simple tonic for the child's sake. That, and her pregnancy, reminded me of my calling. I could tell that administering a plantation was never going to be of any great interest to me. Let Marie pick fights with Ballam instead of me. He could not answer her back, which would keep her temper more even and be better for the child.

I sent word to Mr Chepstow, ordering new instruments and medicines as well as the latest books. I would use some of my new-found wealth and leisure to learn of the ills of women and children, as well as the diseases of this island. Until the materials arrived, I spent more and more time away from home, riding in the woodland away from the fields. Sometimes I could almost imagine I was back in Dorset, riding old Troubadour quietly around, under the proud and watchful eye of my father. But the pretence never held for long. The climate was too hot, the trees too different and the sea was the blue of the Caribbean, not the much-missed, ever-changing sea off the coast of Dorset.

On this particular day, the trees were hissing in the wind as I arrived at my favourite dawdling place. I rode idly along the track, the reins slack in my hands, thinking with pleasure of the books that would soon arrive. I should have kept closer control of my horse, but I was sure I had his spirit beaten and he was adept at avoiding tree roots and other obstacles. I had thought I was safe on his back, but I was not. I saw nothing to alarm me, deep as I was in thought, but he took a sudden skitter sideways, which made me raise my head. To my horror, a ruffian clad in rags, brandishing a pistol, erupted from the undergrowth. My life seemed to slow to a crawl. I had no time to wonder what a highwayman was doing on my plantation, why he was not on a horse like any self-respecting gentleman thief in England, and that I should spur my horse to escape being shot. Why my first thought was not to gather my reins I do not know, but I paid for that error. My horse reared onto his hind legs at the sight of the raggy man. I fell backwards and landed heavily on the track. The horse bolted, and I was at the mercy of a desperate man.

28

The breath had been blown out of my body by the fall, making me temporarily helpless. I cursed my foolishness for neglecting to carry my new pistols as protection. I tried to ready myself for what was to come as his face drew nearer, his eyes staring into mine. He was a filthy specimen of humanity, but with both relief and an equal sinking of my spirits I recognised him.

'Abel. Are you hurt? I am sorry to have alarmed your horse. Let me help you up.'

I had hoped to leave my past securely behind me, but there he was: Rowan Mantle, a shadow of his former swaggering self, but flesh and blood, here, on my plantation.

'What are you doing here?' I asked in astonishment as he helped me to sit up. 'I thought you to be long gone from this island.'

Rowan gave me a hard look. 'Black Tom and I have been evading the militia for the past several months. It seems you have been doing so in rather better style. You look as unlike us as is possible to imagine.'

I shook off his hand and got to my feet, shedding leaves and twigs from my clothes. Rowan had a haunted look about him and when he explained what had happened I could see why. It seemed the very morning Mr Chepstow had guided me and Marie to our new home, the militia had entered the inn where most of the crew lay, half insensible after a night's carousing.

'Black Tom and I had not partaken as they had,' said Rowan. 'And we had risen before the rest of the crew to discuss re-provisioning our ships. We had heard that pirates were less welcome here than before but thought there was enough time for the men to enjoy their time ashore. Ale and a woman. It's unheard of to land here and not spend some gold that way. But the crew paid with more than gold for their pleasure. They are all, I fear, dead or captive. Black Tom and I only just escaped after hearing the commotion.'

I was shocked at the news and felt even more pleased I had heeded my lawyer's advice. 'So where is Tom?' I said, him being the person I most cared about.

'He took a cut to his arm and lies not far from here in some bushes. We saw you by chance a few days ago, but you were with another man and we dared not approach.' He looked at me curiously. 'Where did you go when we got onshore? And how are you riding about this place as if you own it?'

I told him briefly of how I had come into my good fortune. Rowan smiled bitterly.

'You joined us freely and left us freely too. All luck to you and none to us, but I cannot blame you for it. I daresay any one of us might have taken the opportunity if it had been offered to us, although speaking for myself I far prefer the sea to the land.' He looked around him at the peace of my woodland and frowned. 'The sea is clean and wide open. Here, there is danger I cannot see. I don't trust these trees and hate skulking in bushes as Tom and I have been obliged to do. And all because Henry Morgan, God rot him, pretends outrage at our business, which in all but name was also his.' I kept silent and after a moment he continued. 'Well, will you come with me for old time's sake and doctor to Black Tom's arm?'

I had saved his life once, why should I doctor him again? I would get no payment for it, nor did I owe him anything. I wanted to say no, but something lay between us. Past friendship, yes, but mostly fear. What if I refused to help these two and they were eventually captured? How loyal would they be to me then? Might they even decide to trade my life in the hope of saving theirs?

'Is he nearby?'

'No more than two hundred yards from here.' Rowan hesitated. 'It would be an added kindness if you could find your way to bring us meat and drink.'

'Of course I will!' I said in as hearty a voice as I could manage. 'I would suggest you come to my house, but it would not be safe for you. Take me now to Black Tom and I will look at his arm. Then I will fetch you something to eat and drink. It will take a while. My horse took even more fright than me and it will take me a while to walk back.'

Rather than apologise for the loss of my horse, Rowan pulled up his shirt to reveal his swollen belly.

'And if you could bring something to ease the pain in my belly.'

'Food will soon cure that,' I said, anxious to bring our meeting to an end.

'I fear not,' said Rowan wryly. 'For it began to pain me while we were at sea this past year, only it has recently got worse.'

'May I feel it?' There was no mistaking the lump when I laid may hands upon him.

'I regret to say,' I said sadly, 'even if I had my medicines or instruments with me I could do little to help you.'

Rowan looked bitterly disappointed but made light of it. 'No matter, Abel. No matter. It seems I am a dead man whatever I do.'

He had hidden Tom deep in a thicket, close to a rocky outcrop. It would have been a good lair for an animal, but it pained me to see two men who had each commanded successful ships to be brought so low. Once I had crawled in, I looked at Black Tom's wound. He had taken a sword cut to the left shoulder. The wound should have healed a long time ago, even without being stitched, but their exertions and lack of food had not given it enough opportunity to do so. If I'd had a bucket of seawater I would have sluiced it down. And if I'd had my medicine box I would have washed it with oil and made a plaster, as I had done so successfully with the cut on his leg. However, I had nothing but my eyes and nose, which told me that in spite of all Rowan's care the cut had gone bad and would certainly be Tom's end. I think both men knew it.

'The best treatment is rest and good eating,' I said, seeing no point in spelling out his death. 'The first you have in this place and the second I will bring you.'

I began to crawl back out of their den. Rowan would have followed me, but I refused his company.

'You need rest too,' I said. I hurried away from the place and regained the track. I was astonished to find my horse standing a little way on, looking very sorry for himself. Ballam's horse was there too, tethered to a branch, and the man himself was dismounted and feeling the legs of my mount. He straightened up as he heard me and, although my heart had begun to bang in my chest, I put a smile on my face and hailed him as if I were mightily glad to see him.

'The devil threw me,' I said, 'and bolted. I had thought him to be home by now!'

Ballam's expression was one of distaste, quickly replaced by his more usual subservient demeanour.

'I was alarmed when I saw him riderless,' he said. 'And he is lame.' He left it a moment before continuing. 'I wondered if you were lying injured somewhere.'

'As you see, I am not,' I replied.

Ballam waited, not quite daring to question me. Going to my horse's head and giving him a stroke, I looked the manager full in the face. 'As you are here,' I said, 'you can give me your mount and walk my horse back for me. I trust he has not irreparably damaged himself?'

'I expect it is just a sprain,' said Ballam. 'He should do well enough, given time.'

I took his horse and resisted the urge to look back at where Tom and Rowan lay before I rode away.

I had thought I would not speak of it to Marie but, finding her in a mild temper, I changed my mind. In truth, I was in need of an ear and another mind to help me decide what to do for the best.

'If I had the right materials for Black Tom there is a slight chance I could save him, and with food and rest they might both appear well enough to find a new ship . . . so long as they left the plantation as soon as they were able . . . No ship would take them as crew as they are but . . .'

'I curse the ill luck that brought them to this place,' she said. 'Or did they know you were here?'

'How could they? They were astonished at my good fortune.'

Marie laid her hand on my arm. 'There is only one safe solution,' she said.

'What is it?'

'You must shoot them.'

I stared at her.

'Rowan was my captain, Black Tom my friend.'

She shook her head. 'If you truly cared for them you would have offered them better rest than the den they have made in the bushes. If you really wanted to help them you would not be debating now how to absolve yourself from them.'

I could understand her argument, but to shoot them? In cold blood? I could not bring myself to go that far.

'Listen to me,' said Marie with steel in her voice. 'You say yourself Black Tom is wounded and suffering.'

'As is Rowan,' I admitted. I told her of the cancer in his belly and to my utter disgust she laughed.

'You see! They are neither of them long for this world, no matter what they or we do. What is the matter of a few weeks or months when it will be full of suffering? You would be helping them to a peaceful end.'

I tasted bitter anger. 'Being shot to death by a friend is not a peaceful end.'

She hardly paused, and a smile still hung about her face. 'More peaceful and quick than dancing at the end of a noose or dying of starvation and disease. If they betray us,' she continued in a hard voice, 'you are hanged, and I most likely returned to slavery in the Americas. Do you wish your child to be born a slave?'

She had me silenced. And so, filled with poison, I left her.

I rode away from the house, not knowing in which direction I went. It was as if I struggled to shake off a snake that had me by the neck. I did not want any of this. I did not want to be a murderer of friends, nor did I want a shrew of a wife to drive me on to it. Equally, neither did I want to dance at the end of a rope or see my child a slave.

What she had said was true, but I did not want her to have been the one to say it. Was there no other way? Could I not shelter them somewhere until they died of wound and disease? But where? Nowhere was safe from the eyes of slaves and if I was discovered to have harboured two outlaws it would go even worse with me. I was in a fury of indecision. I turned my horse and cantered back to the house. Flinging the reins to a slave, I crashed back in, scattering anxious house slaves as I went. I paused only to collect my new pistols, powder and shot before escaping once again. I did not see Marie and was glad of it. My resentment at her was like a stone in my chest. I hated her for saying what I had not thought through for myself. I cursed myself for speaking to her of it. I should not have been so weak, but I would be weak no longer. In a fever to rid myself of my dilemma I rode back to where Rowan and Tom lay. I drew rein at a little distance from them and tied my horse to a tree. I had no plan, other than to put an end to my trouble, but as I primed my pistols I remembered that I had never tested them. They had cost much, but how accurate were they? How close would I need to go to be sure of my shot?

I told myself that all would be well and with that thought I felt tears prick my eyes. It was what my father had so often told me when some childish trouble had worried me. Why, after so long, could such occasional memories so unman me? Why, especially at a time like this when I needed to be bold and strong? What did those words even mean? All would be well for whom? Even as a child I had known that what is good for one person is not always good for another. I rubbed my eyes and thrust these unhelpful thoughts away. I had spent some time after my father's death trying to live in a way I thought he would have approved of. But my father was no longer living and I had led a violent life. I could not gain his approval, even if I wished to. I had to do what was right for me now, in the life I found myself in. I had to make all well for me. I could do it. I *would* do it *now*. All I had to do was call the men out of their lair and shoot each one as he emerged. They were cornered. They could not possibly escape, and with two shots I would be free.

I approached the place cautiously. I must think of them as no more than the murderous dogs I knew them to be. I couldn't allow myself to falter because of past comradeship. Above all I must not remember the liking and respect I had for Tom or the admiration I once had for Rowan's leadership. I had to remember how they were so often the first to board a vessel, cutting down any who resisted. That was not bravery. It was murder. They were killers I had been obliged to spend some time with, not friends. I was the son of a gentleman and so much better than them.

The bushes and undergrowth were tangled, and the path to where they had hidden themselves was not at all clear. I pushed my way on and called Rowan's name. I stumbled over a root and stopped to steady myself. It wouldn't do if I fell, discharging the pistols by mistake. I wouldn't be the first man to shoot himself that way.

It was then that I heard a sound to my right. I was so tense I reacted without thinking. I turned and fired both pistols at once. As I did so I saw Rowan in front of me. He held a dead rat and a knife in his hands and I knew with pitiful certainty that he had been about to skin and cook it to feed himself and Tom. I saw his fleeting expressions of pleasure and relief at seeing me turning to puzzlement and then to disbelief and last to anger. His feelings swept over his face in the blinking of an eye, but I have never managed to banish them from my mind. I saw no fear in him, but with total certainty could tell that should he survive to escape me his intent would be murderous revenge. The flash and smoke obscured my view, and I confess I feared the knife he held, for I was now unarmed. The breeze soon swept away the smoke and revealed him sprawled amongst the greenery. I feared he lived still. I couldn't believe I had killed him. Was he not teasing me as he sometimes liked to do? Was he playing dead, only to rise and shake the rat in my face, my shots having gone wide? Or was he gripping that knife, waiting until I bent over him, ready to plunge it into my heart?

But it was not so. The force of the shots had knocked him onto his back. Both had landed in his chest. There was not a mark on his face, but it was horrible to behold when I ventured to push back the leaves that obscured it. His mouth was open, making a dark hole in his face as if another shot had taken him there. His eyes were open, too, staring up into the cloudless sky.

I don't know how long I stood there, but I don't think it was very long. I had been deafened somewhat and was shaken into something of a stupor by what I'd done. I roused myself angrily. I was wasting time. I would need to go back to the horse, where the spare powder and bullets were in a saddlebag. Tom would have heard the commotion and be wondering what had happened. He was not too wounded to throw his knife, so I would need to be careful. But it was too late. Already Tom was emerging from his lair and I had no means of finishing him, while he held a pistol and a knife. He saw me, but before he could speak I rushed to give my story.

'Oh, Tom! A terrible thing has happened.'

He looked at the pistols in my hands and then at my face. 'Was it you who fired?' he said. 'What is amiss?'

I said the first thing that raced into my head. 'It was my fault!' I said. 'I saw Rowan and went to meet him, but I stumbled, and both my pistols fired.'

'You shot Rowan?' Consternation filled his face for he had relied on his care.

'It was terrible,' I said. 'And he is quite dead.'

'Where is he?'

'Just here,' I said, indicating the place.

Tom came towards me with his pistol lowered and his knife loose in his hand. I wondered if I should try to snatch the pistol, but Tom was no fool. He would be alert for any treachery, as are most desperate men. He looked at Rowan and then at me.

'So now I am a certain dead man,' he said. 'For my wound will not heal and I cannot survive without him.'

'I am heartily sorry,' I said, and it was no less than the truth.

'It is a bitter thing that the land he hated living on has contributed to his death,' said Tom sourly.

'You are right,' I said, having a sudden idea. 'But here we are close to the cliff edge. I feel sure he would rather choose a watery resting place than a shallow grave. Will you help me return him to the sea?'

Tom stuck the knife in his belt but kept the pistol in his hand. 'Very well,' was all he said.

I put down my spent pistols and together we dragged Rowan towards the cliff, though I had the greater part of it. It wasn't simply that Tom had little strength to help me. I could tell he doubted my explanation of Rowan's death and so kept himself out of my reach. At length, when we were almost at the cliff edge, he let go of Rowan's arm and moved further off. He sat on a rock, watching me struggle, his pistol still in his hand. It was horrible work, dragging Rowan's lifeless body. His head jounced through the undergrowth, as if he was engaged in some silent but lively conversation. It had been hard enough with Tom's slight help, but now it was almost too much for me. Then, at the edge of the cliff, his shoulder got stuck on some hidden obstacle. After trying without success to shift his corpse or the rock that proved to be in the way I stopped to take my breath. I hoped Tom would take pity on me and help again, but he sat on, watching me carefully. Although I had indeed killed Rowan by accident, that hadn't cancelled my intention to see both men dead and I knew Tom had grave suspicions. He and Rowan must have discussed my good fortune and the risk they posed for me.

I raised my arms from my sides and looked hard at him. 'I know your shoulder pains you, Tom, but will you not help me to move Rowan away from this rock? I cannot bear to leave him lying here, and you have your pistol, do you not, while you can see mine have been discharged and lie on the ground?'

He got up and approached carefully. 'I know I am a danger to you while I live,' he replied. 'But you must know that I would not willingly betray you.'

'Rowan's death was an accident,' I said in reply. I think he could hear the truth of it in my voice. He got up and with his good hand helped me pull the body away from the rock. Now we were right at the edge. All we needed to do was to roll the body over and Rowan would be gone.

It was then I took my chance and made a grab for Tom's pistol. We grappled together, he and I, feet sliding on the loose stones that made the top of the cliff. For an instant I thought he had me over. My left foot went from me and could find nothing but air below it. In desperation I clung to him. We hovered there, in balance between life and death until, being the stronger, I pushed him back and regained my footing. At the same time, I had my hand on his pistol. I wrenched it from him, but it slipped from me and fell. It went over the cliff, far away from us both, and landed with a silent splash in the sea. We stood at the high cliff's edge, with Rowan's body beside us. Tom had his knife in his hand and I was still unarmed. More than that, I had squandered my small advantage of surprise. He now knew for certain that I intended him harm and so would need to kill me in self-defence. Neither of us spoke. Only our panting breaths betrayed our recent tussle.

Without warning he turned, took several paces away from the cliff and threw his knife. It buried itself in my upper arm. I screamed in pain and dropped to my knees. Tom glared at me.

'Now we are equal,' he said. 'Though I am more of a man than you will ever be.'

His words cut me as sharply as his knife. I had no words for him, thinking only if I could run before he could wrestle with me again. I felt faint and his slender knife was still in my arm. I had never shrunk from removing such things from others but found it a different matter now. While I steeled myself to remove the blade he was already on me. Before I could react, he had grabbed its handle and yanked it from me. To my shame I screamed again, feeling a stream of hot blood issuing from the wound. I struggled not to faint, while he stood back, watching me.

I was now completely at his mercy. My stupidity had altered me from one with all the advantages to none. There was no point in begging for my life, but I couldn't help looking up to him in supplication. All I saw was contempt.

I cowered with my eyes screwed up, waiting for the blow that would end my life, but it did not come. He did not engage, nor did he say anything to me. I forced myself to open my eyes and saw his bare feet in front of me, the flesh horny, each toenail scuffed and broken, the result of barefoot years at sea. Still he remained silent and I could not resist raising my gaze again to his face. His body was alert, ready to repel me, but his eyes looked far away. At last he reached down and took hold of Rowan's arm once more. He stepped lightly over him and off the cliff.

He fell all the way in silence, but Rowan's body rolled and grated on the stones as Tom's weight pulled it after him. I heard a faint double splash, as both bodies hit the water.

I had difficulty mounting my horse. The pain in my arm was very bad, but it was the first time I had taken such an injury, so I had nothing to compare it with. When I got home I called for oil and honey, and tended to my arm. I would not speak to Marie or allow her to minister to me. I knew well that she wished to know what had happened, but I would not oblige her. I would speak of it to no one. I could not. I prepared the sleeping draught I had kept for her, took it myself and went to bed.

29

More than the cold steel of Black Tom's blade had entered my body. In time, only a small scar was visible, but the wound to my pride and self-esteem was very great. I had spoken to my wife when I should have deliberated alone. I had bungled the murders, with no honour, and had heard Tom's last terrible words, which had seared themselves into my soul. I could not allow that I was half the man of Tom, a common pirate, yet I feared I was. A speechless, impotent fury entered me that left even Marie atremble. I almost wished to emulate Tom's final action to prove to myself that I could die just as well as he. Several times I stood on the spot but knew I could not do it. I tried to believe him cowardly, but knew he was the opposite.

With no word to anyone, I visited Mr Chepstow, desiring to rid myself of all the wealth I had got when on the *Revenge*. Gold is gold, wherever it comes from. It has no morality, but I suffered a violent distaste for the coin I had won while on board and told Mr Chepstow so.

'I wondered . . . if it might pay for a school . . .'

He raised his eyebrows. 'I see you are determined to risk your liberty by entering Port Royal.'

'Or do some other philanthropic deed . . .'

He cleared his throat and ran his fingers along his desk, as if he was feeling for a tumour. 'As it happens, I think you will be reasonably safe here now. There have been so many hangings that I cannot imagine any are left to denounce you. My advice

300

though would be not to make free with your money before you are integrated into society. You would draw attention to yourself, which would not be wise. I suggest you start quietly, humbly. There is a suitable house for sale nearby. Install yourself there and offer your services as a medical man. Perhaps allow your wife to take care of things on the plantation? Ballam tells me she is capable.'

I stared at Chepstow, but then recollected that Ballam was his man. Well, if Ballam could stand Marie's tantrums he was welcome to them. If Ballam had told my lawyer of Marie's knowledge of plantation life he would also have told him about our arguments. I would be surprised if the house slaves did not report to him, too, through Ballam. He had, after all, supplied the slaves for our use. I would, I decided, do as my lawyer advised, but would be careful to buy my own slaves. I wanted no more spying, if spying there had been.

'I will take time to look about for a house,' I said to Chepstow.

It was a good decision. Hurling myself with all my energy into a new enterprise stopped me from dwelling so much on myself. Port Royal was much in need of another physician and the welcome society gave me was a soothing balm. With much effort and determination, I succeeded in banishing almost all thoughts of the plantation, my wife and that terrible day at the cliff.

Five months later, I held in my arms my infant son. To my shame, that my wife had been safely delivered was of little interest, although I tried to be glad for her. Although it had not been her fault that I had confided in her about Rowan and Tom, and in spite of her giving me a son, I found I could not reconcile myself to her. Perhaps we could be friends or at least polite acquaintances, but it seemed neither of us wished for more.

I had many invitations to toast the health of my infant son. What was more, my recent success in operating on a merchant's stones made my reputation. Mr Gerard's full recovery was remarkable, and he became one of my greatest advocates. Receipts from the plantation had dropped a little, but I cared little for the fluctuations of business. My true profession was bringing me all I needed in the way of gold, friends and social regard. I was much relieved to live a steadier life.

One afternoon, I was called to good Mr Gerard for his wife, who suffered from debilitating headaches. After her consultation she took to teasing me about my son.

'I don't believe you have either a wife or son!' she said. 'Neither having been seen. I would love to dandle him on my knee, my own daughter being well past the age when she would tolerate such behaviour.'

We all laughed, for Alice was a beautiful but wilful girl, fifteen years old.

When they had gone, I recalled that it had been almost a month since I had seen my boy. I decided to ride up to the plantation and spend a few hours there. It was a beautiful afternoon. As I rode out of the town, the breeze enlivened me. It was good to be away from the noise, bustle and stink of the town for a while. The wind brought memories of my first days on board ship and the kindness shown to me by Ptolemy. I thought how pleased he would have been to see me so well-set-up in my profession. As I arrived at the house I was wishing that both he and my father had lived to see my son.

I saw Christophe straight away. He was outside with his nurse, sitting on a rug in the shade. I was very pleased to see that he had learnt to sit up unaided and went to him immediately, scooping him up into my arms. For a few moments he seemed as if he might cry, but then he reached out and caught hold of the moustache I had recently grown. I gently took his hand away, for his grip was causing me some discomfort, and smiled at him. He regarded me seriously but did not protest. I entered the house with him in search of Marie, wanting to politely praise her for my son's excellent condition. I did not call out to her because she often liked to rest during the hot afternoons. Quietly, I opened her door. She was indeed abed. I do not know how I could have missed the truth before my eyes, but I did. I took several steps into the room before what I saw entered my mind. Even then, concerned not to frighten the infant in my arms I spoke no words, but stood stupefied for several seconds. It was Christophe's crowing that alerted his mother, rather than my rage.

She must have thought his nurse had brought him to her. Shameless, she sat up, naked in her bed, stretching out her arms to take him. Seeing me, she hastened to cover herself – from me, her husband! But it was not her false modesty that angered me. It was the body lying next to hers. If I had been carrying my pistols I would have shot him as he lay. Instead, I pulled the covers from him. It gave me no pleasure to see him cowering. I simply wished undone what I knew I would never be able to forget: Ballam.

'Get out of my house and off my land. If you return I shall kill you.'

I kept my voice low, but even so, my son began to cry. I waited, hushing Christophe, while Ballam gathered his clothes, and then I kicked the overseer out of the room. He stumbled and fell so I kicked him again. There was no pleasure in it. Not then. Later, I was pleased I had shown him just a little of the violence of which I was capable.

Marie huddled in bed, her face as pale as I had ever seen it. I said nothing to her but took the child back to his nurse. When I returned, Marie was dressing.

'Do you lie naked for your paramour and dress when I am here?' I threw her back upon the bed and took my husband's rights. She must have expected a whipping, but my anger had become a passion which was a furious mimic of our honeycomb days and nights. When eventually I was spent, I forced myself to rise from her stinking bed. I washed myself and went out upon the porch. Night had fallen and the air become cooler. I called for wine and tobacco. Slowly, the wine stilled my blood. I lay back in my chair and watched the smoke curl up from my pipe. The stars rocked to and fro in the sky and my senses swam with the wine. All was peaceful, except for my heart. I must think what to do. I should rise and inform the slaves who guarded the house and garden that Ballam was to be repelled if he tried to re-enter. Ballam no doubt had thought he was safe, being Chepstow's man and his mistress's lover. As for Marie, I had no words. I would be a laughing stock. I should think what to do. Instead, I let my pipe fall upon the ground and allowed my eyes to close.

When I woke the night was almost over. I rose stiffly and stretched. Going first to my son's room I woke his nurse and instructed her to pack their things. I then went to my wife's room. She had put a chair to the door, but it was no defence against me. She was fully dressed and I doubted she had slept. A lamp was lighted by her bed and she was sitting up. She shrank from me as I entered, but I was not there to do her violence.

'You will stay here and take Ballam's place. I expect to see this plantation increase its profits since I suspect he has been taking more than you from my estate.'

She stared at me, her eyes glistening.

'If you show yourself assiduous and repentant, in good time I will allow you to come to my house where you may see your son again. But if you at any time stray from behaving properly as my wife in society, I will put you aside and you will never see your child again.'

'No . . .' Her tears began to fall, but I would not acknowledge them.

'Do you understand?'

She nodded meekly. 'How long must I . . . ?'

'That is for me to decide.' I do not say that my heart softened, but she had been nursing our son and something of her distress made me a little less cold. 'I will appoint a new overseer when I can and bring you to Christophe when I am persuaded that you will not shame me again. I wish to have the accounts. I will take them for Chepstow to examine. *Has* Ballam been cheating me of my profits?'

Her reply came as a whisper. 'I truly do not know.'

'Very well. Now go and fetch the accounts, and then make your farewells to the child.' At that, her tears fell faster, and a sob came from her beautiful, treacherous throat.

Soon after daybreak I took him and rode away. As soon as I was home, I called to Mollie, my personal slave. She showed great delight in meeting Christophe and they were soon good friends. I asked her how she did, and she told me the sickness she had felt for the past week was much improved. She was forward enough to kiss the baby and also me, which did a lot to restore my good mood.

When I called at Chepstow's the following day, I tossed the accounts onto his desk.

'I want Ballam banished from the island or hanged.'

Chepstow looked up in alarm. 'What has he done?'

'What has he not done? He is lucky I did not kill him,' I said. 'I want you to go through the accounts. What concerns you are his financial dealings. He has betrayed your trust, which reflects badly on you, as you endorsed him. I want him not just off my plantation, but also off this island. If he can hang or be branded a thief, all the better.'

I do not think Chepstow had been aware of Ballam's thieving, which was soon proved. However, I suspect he had wind of his behaviour with my wife. Perhaps he had decided I was unlikely to find out or indeed would not care, having already left her. He was wrong, but in the end, I could not hold it against him. Since I had first met him, Chepstow had been assiduous in his care of my business, from saving my life the first day we met to helping me into society. He had made his opinion of Marie clear to me in the politest of terms, while remaining more gentlemanly towards her than she deserved. I had no doubt that he was as good a lawyer as there was on this island and I duly retained him.

Christophe was soon crawling everywhere and pulling himself upright to stand, though he had not taken his first step when I sent for Marie. I had visited her several times over the months and had determined that she was truly sorry for what she had done.

The first test for Marie was Mollie's swollen belly, but she said nothing and remained meek. I had not had congress with my wife since that day when I had discovered her with Ballam and I told her I didn't purpose to resume relations with her but would rather form an alliance with her. If she would support me in society as my wife I would allow her to stay here and take a full part in our son's upbringing. She would have all the dresses, furniture and so on that she desired. I would arrange for her to have riding lessons and buy her a gentle mare to ride, if she wished. She could go about and make friends.

'All I ask,' I said, 'is that you should be loyal to me in comradeship and, if you desire a liaison you will inform me, and keep it discreetly within the household, as I do.'

She looked at me in great surprise.

'I realise it is a controversial theory,' I said. 'But I have come to believe that both sexes can feel desire. I doubt Ballam forced you, did he?'

She shook her head defiantly. 'No.'

I allowed myself a slight smile. 'Then let us be practical. You would not be the first wife, I think, who kept a personal slave, as I have Mollie. But we will need to make sure that any man you might allow in your bed does not believe it gives him any power over either of us.'

'No other man will have power over me!' She glared at me, then relaxed and wryly returned my smile.

'Even so. I would make it plain to any man that such an arrangement is my wish and within my gift. That should help to protect us both.'

She could not refuse, but she agreed with good grace and I was well pleased with our compact, as I believe she was too.

There was also the matter of the second child she now carried in her belly.

'I cannot not tell who the father of your unborn child is,' I said. 'But it might be me. I will accept the child as mine, no matter when it is born, so long as you keep to the bargain between us.'

I was her husband. She had no power in any of this, but she considered, as if she had several choices. After a few seconds she looked keenly at me and then offered her hand, as if she were still in her male disguise. 'I agree.'

I took her hand and we shook on the deal. Her handshake was firm and purposeful. I admired her bravado.

After she had been restored to our son for no more than a week he took his first step. It happened that we were both there when he did it and I must say that moment brought us together more successfully than any bargain or punishment could have done. It was not that we were abruptly reunited in love, but we forged an even stronger understanding, united in love of him. From that moment our alliance was steady. I do not say we never argued, or that Marie never tried my patience or I hers, but we became akin to business partners. We were much better at that than marriage. What's more, I soon forged an amiable friendship with a gentleman from London who had come to visit our island. His company gave me much respite from Marie while he was there. Hans Sloane had a desire to learn about the flora of the place, so I took him on many rambles, first having found a knowledgeable slave to carry our requirements. I learnt almost as much as Hans and, when he returned home, we continued our friendship by occasional letter. I was proud to receive a copy of the book he wrote about the plants, which he inscribed to me.

30

Time has a habit of passing quickly when children are growing, but after almost a dozen good and successful years, a day came that altered all our lives most terribly and ended my life on the fair island of Jamaica.

It was even hotter than usual, airless, and the small rumblings that shook the ground here were blamed for the insufferable heat. I called for my horse to be saddled. I didn't see Marie before I left, but Mollie had her three children as well as Elizabeth and Christophe in her care, as usual. I remember that Christophe asked if he could ride with me, but I had business unsuitable for him to share. This was my visit to Caroline, a young widow who would no doubt be awaiting me in a delicious state of undress in a darkened room. I decided first to ride up out of the town to try and find a little breath of unsullied air. It would not do for me to arrive early. God knows, tongues wagged even when there was no impropriety between doctor and patient. Caroline cared little for chatter, but I didn't want to be barred by jealous husbands and fathers from treating some of the more interesting female diseases. I will not say that Caroline was the only young woman who had offered herself to me, but she was the most brazen. I was walking a fine line with her. I had no wish to marry her, even if I had been free, nor did I want a scandal. Perhaps in future, taking Christophe would be a good way of avoiding her ardour.

Once we reached the country, I gave my horse his head and he settled to a comfortable canter. It was a relief to feel my hair lifted in the breeze and the movement of air about my face, but I knew I couldn't prolong the pleasure for too long. Caroline would take me to task if I were late.

The town lay below me, almost surrounded by the still blue waters of the Caribbean. None of the noise and filth of the port could be seen from this position and it was a very beautiful scene. I could see my fine stone house, set in one of the best streets of the town, and the several ships that lay at anchor, waiting for the wind.

Suddenly my horse shied, almost unseating me. At the same time a nearby tree toppled without warning to the ground, wrecking the peace in a most unexpected way. It took me a few minutes to soothe and control my mount as well as to still my thumping heart. When I had him calm, I looked with interest at the tree. It was not so very old. How intriguing! Was it riddled with rot? I dismounted, walked a few paces and then stopped. My mount was pulling at his reins and rolling his eyes in fright, but it was what I saw on the ground that alarmed me.

The ground was cracking like a walnut and opening a gap across the track along which we had just ridden. It was this underground disturbance that must have loosened the tree and felled it. I allowed my beast to lead me back to the security of the rocky outcrop where he stood with his legs trembling and his coat dark with sweat. I found I was trembling too. I had seen such fissures many times, but never one in the making before my eyes.

I was looking once more at the town, wondering if my wife and children had felt the tremor, when a deep rumbling came from all around me. With a scream of fear, the horse leapt sideways and ripped the reins from my hand. In a moment, he was gone, crashing through the trees and away in the direction of his sometime home at the plantation.

I was a distance from the sea and yet it felt as if I were aboard ship in choppy water. I looked at the ground and saw small stones shaking as if in a sieve. Then the shaking stopped, and all was quiet. Relief turned to anger at my horse. I would be very late and would arrive at Caroline's hot and dusty, and without my bag of tinctures. I would have to go home and bathe, making me even later. I was in a quandary. She liked to tease and might refuse me entry if I were very late. Which was the greatest risk, to go dirty or late? She was capable of complaining about me to her friends whatever I did.

I looked at the town again to reckon how long it might take me to reach her. There was something wrong with the view. At first, I thought it was my eyes at fault. I seemed to be looking at the town through a mirage or a wavering glass window. The whole port was trembling. Buildings swayed, and the great leaves of the palms waved as if there was a strong wind. And then, to my horror some of the buildings began to collapse. From my position I could not be sure, but it seemed as if the very ground was melting, sucking the town ever lower. And then, with the quay seemingly sunk, the sea began to race inland, swallowing up streets with their stalls and hubbub of customers. I stood transfixed while the street where Mr Chepstow had his business became like a river.

I tried to see Caroline's house, but such dust had arisen from the fallen buildings it was impossible. I don't know how long I stood there. It felt like hours but must have been little more than a few minutes. To my shame it was only then, when I roused myself from my horrified stupor, that I considered my dear children. I prayed Mollie had kept the children at home this day. The house was strongly constructed, with good foundations. Surely it and Caroline's house would stand? It was the poor in their hovels who suffered most in any disaster. Even so, I determined to make all haste to discover how my family did. They were my priority now.

I leapt across the narrow chasm to gain the undamaged part of the track, eager to make my way downhill. I don't know why I took another look at the town, but as I did I stood transfixed, for an even more terrible sight hit my eyes.

A great wave was rearing up from the tranquil sea. It snapped the lines from the vessels in the harbour and drove them from their moorings. They tossed about and then rushed inland, pushed by an implacable fist of water. Most soon lay dashed and broken, hurled against buildings and stove in. One, a large merchant vessel, was carried on before my unbelieving eyes and came to rest perched on top of one of the more solid buildings.

At last the great wave spent itself, and receded, but either the sea had risen, or the port had sunk for much of it still lay underwater. I stood for a few more minutes, wondering what other disaster would happen, but all that occurred was that a gentle breeze began to blow, the breeze we had all wished for.

I made all haste towards the town. It was not so very difficult. Little damage had been done to the hill I stood on, apart from a couple more cracks like the one that had toppled the tree. I managed to cross them without mishap and soon reached the town. It was a terrible sight. Some buildings stood intact, while others were almost completely ruined. I looked over to where Caroline's house had stood, but it had entirely gone. A melancholy thought struck me. But for our rendezvous, she might have been out this day, riding her mare, and so might have avoided what I felt sure must have been a sudden and certain death. And then I realised that had my horse not bolted we would both have been within, and if I had taken my son, he would have died too.

Many buildings had partly sunk into the ground and were stuck at extraordinary angles, and yet, so soon after the disaster, I could walk on the once more solid ground. I could only surmise it must have in some way melted before instantly setting again. How could such a thing possibly happen? I confess I walked with much trepidation.

Everywhere people were dead or injured. Some unfortunates had been caught like the buildings in the melted ground and were now held fast. Some were crying pitifully to be released while others were clearly dead, their vital organs having been crushed. Some had been injured by falling debris, many more were drowned, floating horribly in the flooded streets around the harbour. Several inhabitants recognised me and begged for my help.

'I am going to fetch my medicine box,' I called to them. 'I can do little without it.'

Some people, unharmed by the earthquake and its aftermath, were busily looting what they could. Port Royal had ever been a lawless place and I suppose I should not have been shocked at such callous behaviour, but I confess I was much saddened.

I made all haste to my house. It leant drunkenly, on one side buried to a height of several feet. Some of the masonry had fallen and cracks had appeared in the walls. It was clearly uninhabitable. But where was my family?

There was no sign of the slaves but, cowering in the damaged drawing room, I found my wife and our daughter.

'Where is Christophe?' I asked.

Marie didn't reply, only holding her daughter to her ever more firmly.

'Are you hurt?' I asked her.

She stared at me, still speechless.

'How does Elizabeth?'

In spite of her reluctance, I took the child gently from her and stifled the cry of grief that threatened to escape my throat. The beautiful little child I had accepted into my home was quite dead, her dress turned white with dust and her face the same hue. I could see no obvious sign of injury until I examined her head and found the back of her skull shattered. I did not want to put her down, but I knew I must, so I laid her gently on the floor and went back to my wife. 'Do you know where our son is?'

She looked through me. Indeed, I do not think she saw me at all. If she did, she did not know me. I left her with her daughter, then, and began to search the house. It was dangerous work. The floors were aslant, the furniture for the most part broken and the plaster dropping from the ceilings. It didn't take me long to discover that my son was nowhere in the building. Nor were Mollie or her children. They had, I suppose, fled, but to where I had no idea. I returned to my wife. She was in the same position in which I had left her. Now Elizabeth was no longer on her lap, I could see blood staining my wife's dress. A quick examination revealed a cut on her leg. It was deep but should not threaten her life if it was attended to.

I recovered my box from the study. Thankfully, it had survived intact. I cleaned Marie's wound. Then, after taking up Elizabeth again, I helped my wife from the house. All the while she said nothing to me, nor made any sound.

Outside, I sat her on a block of fallen stonework while I went to see what remained of the stable. Two horses were within. One was in a lather and had a broken foreleg but the other, Christophe's pony, stood quietly enough, in an obvious sweat and with his head hanging down, but physically unhurt. He was pathetically pleased to see me and stood willingly, like a pet, when I saddled him. I blessed the day I had disregarded my son's desire for a spirited animal and had bought him a stolid pony. I put Marie on the beast, laid her poor daughter in her arms and tied my box behind the saddle. It was a heavy load for the pony, but he made no protest as I led him away.

I had it in mind to set my wife and child down at the cemetery, where they would be clear of most falling buildings, while I returned to search for our son. However, as we approached, it became clear that the ground had melted here too. We were met by several stinking corpses, still in their wrappings, lying as if tossed aside by some ghoulish funeral party. One had tipped up out of his grave and sat as if alive or as if he had heard the trumpet calling him on Judgement Day. I took a different route and eventually reached higher ground where there were no tall buildings, nor ungodly raised dead.

Many others had made for the same place and there was a multitude of patients clamouring for attention. I wanted to think of nothing but my son, berating myself, of course, for neglecting to take him with me when he had asked. I hoped he had run from the house and, like us, had headed for higher ground. Perhaps he was here already and would soon find us. In any case I knew my duty. I had to do my best first for the injured.

I put Marie in the care of a lady I knew, untied my box from the pony, and set to. More and more survivors continued to arrive. Some were unharmed, but many carried wounds. I did my best, but it was little enough, with my medicine box soon depleted.

The town had been full of slaves that had been trained to work in our houses, but I saw few here. I warrant many had escaped, feeling no loyalty to the people who owned them. I could not blame them. I, who had some experience of captivity, would have doubtless done the same.

At length, a few unharmed souls came to help me, for which I was most grateful. I had attended to the worst cases but knew that many more would be lying helpless in the ruins of the town. It frightened me that I had not yet seen Christophe. What if he were one who hadn't been able to flee the town through some injury? I had to go back and search for him, and to help the rest of the injured there.

A few well-organised people were discussing searching for water. Everyone here was in need of a drink, but all the water was contaminated with salt. When I went to look at Marie, she was sitting where I had left her, still holding her dead daughter.

'She will not give her up,' said the woman looking after her. 'I have tried, but she will not be parted from her. Nor does she speak.'

'She has retreated from the situation and gone somewhere we cannot follow,' I said. 'I am going back into the town now to do what I can for the poor souls still there. I will bring something to use as a shroud for her daughter and will deal with my wife then, if you are able to continue to care for her in the meanwhile.'

'She is no trouble,' said that good soul. 'And if water can be found, I will make sure she has some.'

I loaded my box on the pony, regretting the medicines I now lacked. Maybe I could find more in the town, and if my house had collapsed no further I could certainly collect more from there.

I tried to think where Christophe might have gone. He was not, as a rule, allowed to wander alone around this lawless town, but there were no rules now and I had no idea where to look for him.

It wasn't until several days later, when I had searched the town as well as I was able and eventually taken my wife to the plantation for her safety's sake, that the truth about my son was known. Imagine my joy to find him there and unharmed! It seems he had had an argument with his mother and had, without leave, purposed to secretly go to that place where he was always happiest. But, rascal that he was, he had decided to confuse her by hiring a horse, rather than take his own pony. By doing this he hoped to make her fret more, feeling sure she would think he had not gone far without his pony. His ruse had worked, but on me, not his mother, whose wits had not returned.

'You deserve a beating for your behaviour,' I said.

'I'm very sorry, Father.'

I sighed. 'There has been enough violence and sorrow in this place,' I said. I held out my arms to him. 'And I feel far more joy seeing you alive than anger at your behaviour.'

'Will we live on the plantation now?'

I had no stomach for it. 'Christophe, life has utterly changed. So many friends gone, Port Royal destroyed. And that is without what has happened to our family.'

He fell to weeping in my arms. 'I'm afraid for Mother. And I miss my sisters and brother so!'

I had not entirely lost hope of finding Mollie and the children, but the possibility was slight. If they had survived, they had almost certainly gone to the lawless mountains where I would not dare to follow. They had been pretty about the place, but my son had always been of more importance to me. No medicine on earth could help his mother return from the place she had gone to in her head, but the plantation did very well without me and I had money aplenty.

'Listen,' I said to Christophe. 'Sometimes a disaster can also become an opportunity and I think I know what to do.'

He gazed up at me through his tears, a frightened boy looking to his father to lead.

'A ship is expected very soon to take timber from our plantation to England. It is time you learnt something of the world.'

'Don't send me away!' he begged, clinging to me. I took

hold of his shoulders and held him away, so I could see his face.

'Do not be afraid, Christophe. We will go together.'

Until this moment I had not considered returning to England. I had believed both Ptolemy and the man with the metal hand when they told the boy I had been that I would never return. It had been a matter of distress to me on my original voyage to the Caribbean, but I had come to terms with it and came eventually never to look back. Now, however, I had the financial means to return and a son whose education would benefit if he visited the old country. Perhaps I might send him to Oxford, as my father had wanted to do with me. I could write to Hans for advice. I had never been to London or Bristol, nor almost anywhere else in England. Christophe and I could experience these places together. It would be wonderful!

'But what of Mother?'

I sighed. 'I think a long sea voyage might cause her even more distress,' I said. 'She is calm here on the plantation and I think that is because it is familiar to her. To wrench her from here would do her a disservice and maybe endanger her life.'

He looked bewildered. 'We cannot abandon her.'

'She will not be abandoned. She will be on our estate, looked after by people she knows, even if she does not speak to them. I will ask our manager for regular reports to be sent to me, but I do not expect her to return to her senses soon, if ever.'

'Maybe when we return, that will make her wake up?'

'It is in God's hands, Christophe. All we can do is make sure she is gently cared for and kept safe. He will decide.'

I wrote to Hans that evening but expected that we would arrive in London on the same vessel as the letter. No matter. Now I had decided on this plan I was in a fever to execute it.

Before I retired to bed, I went to Marie's room. I had instructed a slave to be with her at all times, in case she suddenly recovered herself, or indeed tried to harm herself. Anything was possible. She had been put to bed for the night, and looked cool and comfortable, but just as remote from me as ever. I sat beside the bed and told her of my plans. She showed no reaction at all. My mind was made up. I might as well be as dead as her daughter. Even Christophe could not reach her. Staying here would simply cause Christophe constant distress, but travel would almost certainly prove diverting for him. For the sake of my son, as well as my own inclinations, we would leave her here and travel to England.

CHRISTOPHER MORGAN

31

Christopher Morgan's coach made its way to Bishopsgate in London and stopped outside Grisham College. His was not the only coach. Others were arriving, too, for what promised to be an interesting lecture. Christopher had originally been invited to join the Royal Society by Charles II, who had enjoyed the new plants he had presented to him on several occasions and especially his success in the science of breeding new roses.

The country had gone through much turmoil since the unexpected and untimely death of Charles. To Christopher's great relief, with the self-imposed exile of Charles's brother James and eventual crowning of William and Mary, the country felt a little more at ease with itself, although for a while he, like many, had feared another civil war. Christopher hadn't particularly liked James and didn't know King William at all, although he had seen him once, long ago, in his own country.

Christopher was happy to be away from court. For more than fifteen years he had revelled in it, loving the way his king had encouraged experimentation and ideas by the formation of his Society, as well as patronising the arts. He had been fortunate to have met and had good conversation with some great men. His years at court had helped make his business a most fashionable and profitable enterprise, but Christopher was of no significance to William or his queen, and now, in his sixty-first year, he preferred to let his agent conduct his business for him.

He had remained interested in the Royal Society and liked to attend occasional meetings, although these days he tired easily and could not always recall what questions he wished to ask at the conclusion of a meeting. Today's lecture was to be given by an eyewitness to last year's earthquake in the Caribbean that had ruined Port Royal in Jamaica. It was extraordinary how the ground could open up in some countries and he was looking forward to hearing this account. As he found his seat, he could hear some discussion going on behind him.

'They say the quake in Jamaica was most unlike the ones suffered from time to time in Europe.'

'I hear this fellow will speculate that it was caused by excessive heat trying to escape from the earth.'

'Not at all! I heard that the island is nothing but sand and from time to time the grains settle further into cracks in the rocks, causing buildings to fall.'

Christopher was tempted to turn around and tell the two gentlemen that they would find out soon enough and so why speculate. However, he did not. His increasing tetchiness with age displeased him and he did his best to curb his tongue. Instead, he leant on his stick and waited, hoping he would not doze off. It was a warm day and he did have a habit of falling asleep unless he was exceptionally interested in what was going on.

He did not have long to wait. Soon, the visitor from Jamaica was introduced as one Sir Jack Moore. Christopher sat straighter in his chair in order to listen.

The man was tall and slender, and dressed in the latest fashion. Christopher's eyesight wasn't as good as it had been in his younger days and he was in his preferred position at the back of the room, so the man's features were unclear, but his pleasing tenor voice was strong and Christopher had no difficulty in hearing him.

The first part of his lecture was very interesting, especially the way he described the land melting, which was something Christopher had never heard of before. However, Christopher hadn't realised the man was a doctor. Soon, the lecture became an account of the injuries suffered by the inhabitants and the measures taken to help them, which didn't interest him so much. The room was warm and he began to nod. Only his stick falling with a clatter to the floor roused him just before he was about to slide from his chair and join it. He jerked upright, saving himself just in time. However, he was embarrassed to find that the speaker had interrupted his talk because of him.

A gentleman sitting nearby leant over to address Christopher. 'Our speaker has just asked if you are unwell,' he said.

Christopher waved his arm towards the speaker in what he hoped was both a reassuring and an apologetic manner. 'Quite well, thank you. I do apologise. Please continue.' He recovered his stick and wedged it between his knees, determined not to embarrass himself again. At the end of the meeting, he hastened to leave while the gentleman was surrounded by members wanting to engage in further conversation. He thought he had escaped, but a voice followed him to the door.

'I hope you are recovered, sir? Is there anything I can do for you?'

It was the gentleman from Jamaica. His voice boomed over the heads of the crowd. Christopher affected not to hear. He had already put on his hat and now he kept his head turned away, not wanting to engage in a discussion about his health with some foreign sawbones.

In the coach, Christopher leant back and closed his eyes. As so often when he attended Royal Society meetings he wished Abel could have been there with him. He had been such a bright child and so interested in everything. His son, that lost boy, was never far from Christopher's mind. If a day passed without some thought of him, he met him in his dreams, or discussed the day with him when resting in bed. Increasingly, over the past few months he had felt his weakness increase and knew he was not long for the world. He had never been on particularly good terms with God, but he prayed often to be reunited with his son in death.

Death did not frighten him. His life had been full of loss. Mother, father, wife, son. And yet his life had not been all unhappy and he was thankful for much of it. It was his son's unknown sufferings that still caused Christopher pain, even now. And so, if he could have changed anything in his life, it would have been not to have sent Abel out on his old horse that fateful day. He would still hold that regret in his heart when death took him at last.

It was well after dark by the time he reached home, and Christopher was exhausted. Sally's husband brought in his luggage. Christopher sat quietly in the parlour with his eyes closed while he waited for Jane to bring him her special concoction to help his heart and restore to him a little energy. When he was well and in London, he liked to speak of it to his friends at the Society.

'This drink, like so much of life, is not what I expected. When Jane first brought it to me, I expected rum and there is none in it!'

He would wait for the chuckles to cease before continuing. 'I tried several times, as a young man, to discover how to make it, but always failed. My mistake was to insist on rum. The inestimable Jane made it on a day when I was quite unwell. It revived me and I take it now whenever my heart dictates. I would recommend it to you, gentlemen, but I fear her recipe is a secret she guards like a lioness.'

It was well he was home at last. Christopher's heart was behaving like a trapped butterfly in a window. He could tell by Jane's face when she brought him the drink that he must look most unwell.

His hand trembled so that he could not hold the cup. She took it before it could fall and held it to his mouth. As soon as he smelt the fragrance of the drink and tasted the hot, sweet mixture of egg and cinnamon he felt a little better. The brandy within it gave the drink a fire that stimulated his heart and he began to think that he might survive another night.

'Get up,' he whispered between sips as she continued to crouch before him with the drink. 'You do your joints no good.'

She got up and sat in the chair next to him. When she offered him another sip he took a long draught this time and smiled at her.

'That's better.' He took the warm cup from her with almost steady hands. 'Now, tell me,' he said, pretending to them both that he was quite well, 'what of my garden?'

'Such roses!' she said. 'I swear it has been the best year yet for your roses. Tomorrow you must sit in the arbour and take in their scent before the last petals fall. I have had the boy collecting them and am drying them for the bowl in your bedchamber.'

'Thank you, Jane. And how is William?'

'He does well enough,' said Jane. 'He is in bed. He would have been up to greet you, but we didn't expect you until tomorrow. The aches and pains in his bones trouble him, but that is nothing new.'

Christopher smiled. 'Ah! We old men. We are a trial to you, Jane. And yet we so depend upon you to scold us and keep us in order!'

ABEL MORGAN

32

How fortunate to have known Mr Hans Sloane in Jamaica! That serendipitous friendship brought me great good fortune once in England. I had known he was well thought of, but his modesty in his letters to me had not prepared me for the society in which he moved. Thanks to his friendship, I had the great honour of being presented to Their Majesties! Very soon afterwards I was invited to give a lecture about the great tragedy at Port Royal at the Royal Society. Hans is secretary, which has been a great help for my advancement in society. After my lecture, in which I described many of the injuries and my role in ministering to the injured, I was swiftly being consulted as a physician. Hans even assured me that I would one day make bone-setting a respectable profession! It is a source of great joy to me to have access to learned society in London. Returning to the country of my birth was the best decision of my life. I add to my library every day and frequently take chocolate with Hans and his friends. He has made his concoction quite the thing to drink within his circle and it is certainly delicious. Both Christophe and I had a little difficulty adjusting to the change in temperature, but I find I now relish the seasons, and Christophe eventually came to terms with the lack of sun.

After some months in London, we were beginning to feel quite settled. As well as familiarising ourselves with this great city's streets, Christophe and I had visited the theatre several times, but not wishing him to grow into a rake, I took Hans' advice and engaged a tutor for him who would take him to Oxford and see him get the education fit for a gentleman. Christophe did pine for news of his mother at first, but eventually a letter arrived. When it came, it described no change in Marie's mood except that day by day she needed more help with her personal requirements. I called Christophe from his tutor and gave him the letter.

'Much of this is about plantation business, but you should read this part about your mother.'

He stood by me to read it. Barnstable's writing was not easy to decipher, but I helped when Christophe got stuck.

'What does it mean?'

'I think it means your mother is declining in health. You should prepare yourself. We cannot tell how this may turn out.'

He turned pale. 'I want to return to Jamaica to see her.'

I remonstrated with him in a kindly manner, but it was important he was not deceived. 'You must accept that if you were there she would still be unlikely to know you,' I said. 'Besides, she may already have died. The best thing we can do is to pray for her.'

My boy was inclined to be angry with me.

'You don't want me to see her again! You never loved her. You should have brought her to England with us. You are a physician. You should be caring for her!'

'I did what I thought was best for her, Christophe. You know that.'

'Then we should have stayed with her!'

'She is not simply far from us in miles. Her mind has taken her to a place where we cannot reach her. No one can.'

At this he sobbed, and I put my arms around him. 'Why don't you write to her, Christophe? Tell her all the things you have been doing and tell her too how much you love her.'

'But she might already be dead!'

'But your love is alive. Who knows but that the dead may hear our words even when we do not speak them aloud? And if she lives, she may take comfort from the letter, even if she shows no sign of understanding it.'

He wept a little more, but became calmer when I told him we would, next Sunday, ask that prayers should be said for her in church. I dispatched him to his tutor then, with a message to say that lessons were to be abandoned until he had written as long a letter as he wished to his mother. I also wrote to Barnstable, demanding an immediate reply and instructing him that Marie was to have every care in her decline. I added that I had other sources of information and that it would go very hard with him if I heard her nursing had been anything but the gentlest and most caring. I did not, but it would do no harm for him to think it. I could do no more.

Since returning to England I had meant to visit the place where I had been raised, but autumn had turned into summer and still I had not done it. Now would be a good time. It would be a distraction for Christophe and in the nature of laying ghosts for me. My violent removal from home and my father's murder in front of my eyes had affected me for a long time during my youth, but that was far in the past and it would be amusing to show Christophe my childhood home. So, it was on a warm June morning that we took a hired coach and spent a leisurely night in Bristol. The following morning, we headed further into the West Country. The dried ruts were very jarring and with so much dust we were obliged to keep our windows up, even in the heat. I several times wondered if I had made a mistake in my calculations, but Christophe was too excited at the trip to bother about any discomfort and I found I was impatient to see the old place.

I had wondered briefly if I should still be afraid of the Johnsons, as no doubt the family still reigned in Dario. But I reminded myself that I was a grown man of considerable wealth, not a frightened boy. Having ensured that both coachman and our servant were armed, and having with me my pistols and sword, I felt that I and my family were safe enough. The Johnsons were rural ruffians, preferring to terrorise those weaker than themselves, so I would not allow them to frighten me from my pleasure. In fact, a part of me hoped I would see Daniel Johnson. He would be an old man by now, if he lived. How good it would be to parade my wealth and success before him. He would think I had come to avenge the wrong he had done me all those years ago. Maybe he would be sitting in the inn, smoking his pipe as his father had done before him. I smiled to think how he would hurriedly scuttle home, his neck in his imagination feeling the harsh embrace of the noose. No, I had no reason to be afraid of the Johnsons.

We had a picnic with us, but I hoped the inn might have come into better times and would be able to offer us a decent meal. I doubted there would be comfortable rooms on offer so had decided to spend the night at Chineborough, where we would be sure to find decent lodging.

'We will stop at the Rumfustian Inn,' I told Christophe as we left Bristol. 'And I will enter in the hope that it may not be as run-down as when I lived there. If I decide it is safe enough you may alight too. I would dearly like to take you in and have a drink with you in my old home.'

Christophe looked pleased. 'And will you take me to the river you told me about?' he said. 'The one where your friend used to swim and fish?'

I laughed. 'I will.'

I thought of the people from my past I would like to see. Surely some would still live in Dario? I felt sure Charlie, if he lived, must have taken over his father's forge. I wondered if he was married and had children. He would be astonished at my changed circumstances. Here I was, a wealthy man with a well-grown son, travelling in a coach. How different from the scrawny boy I had been. Would he even recognise me, or me him?

Most of all I hoped my dear foster mother, Jane, might still live, though she would be very old by now. I had never known her age, but she and her husband, William, had ever seemed ancient to me. If either of them lived, I longed to see them. More, if they lived in poverty, as was likely after my father's death, I would offer them relief from their woes. If they would let me, I would set them up in a small cottage somewhere, with a pension to see them comfortably to the end of their days. I wished I had thought of it before and made enquiries when I first came into my fortune, but England seemed a vanished land to me then, with no reason to consider the past. I would be a happy man if

I could make amends. I would, of course, visit my father's grave and spend some time alone, before allowing my son to pay his respects to his grandfather.

As we drew closer to Dario, I began to recognise the landscape. Just outside the village had been a huge old oak tree struck by lightning many years before. To my joy it was still there, lacking all its branches now, taken no doubt for fuel, but the trunk remained, standing like a sentinel guarding the entrance to my home.

'See that!' I said. 'We are almost there!'

And then I was bewildered. For after driving down the old main street that I remembered so well we reached the end of the village without passing the Rumfustian Inn. I called to the coachman to stop.

'Where is it?' asked Christophe, peering out of the window.

'I think we have missed it,' I said. 'There has been some new building done and that has confused me. When I lived here it was the last building at this end of Dario. When I was learning to ride, my father took me up and down this part of the road. Further on is the track to the deserted church and round another bend is eventually the first glimpse of the sea.'

I opened the carriage door and got out. If I walked instead of rode, the past would surely come back to me.

'I will come with you, Father.'

'No. Stay . . .' One look at the boy's face, and I reconsidered. 'Very well.'

There could be no harm in it. I closed the door of the coach and told the coachman to wait.

'Come, Christophe. Let us see if your poor old father can remember where he lived as a child.'

My son laughed and took my hand. Together we began to walk. We had travelled beyond the village and had a little way to saunter before we reached the first building. I didn't recognise it. It was faced with fine ashlar in the modern style with a good wall to either side. Through a small gate in the wall I could see an attractive formal garden planted with low hedges and gravel paths. I was surprised that anyone of quality would want to build such a fine house next to an inn, but then I realised that the Rumfustian no longer existed. It must have been knocked down after my father's murder and the land sold to the man who had built this house.

I followed the wall until it joined the house. Beyond the dwelling ran another wall, a brother to the first, but with a much larger gate, big enough for a carriage to pass through. Was this where the Rumfustian Inn had been? I could not tell, for all trace of it had vanished.

'It is not here,' I said to my son, looking down at him and feeling suddenly bereft. 'I fear it does not exist any more.'

'Why not?' said Christophe.

'Because . . . because it was old . . . and . . .' I was making my way to the second wall as I spoke but stopped suddenly at a door in the centre of the building. 'I think I remember this . . .' I put my hand on the old door. It was studded with ancient nails, banded with iron, and looked a little out of place, framed as it was by a pair of fine stone pillars while above the lintel was a steep, triangular pediment. 'Not the stonework, Christophe, but this door . . . I am almost certain . . .' I stood back and gazed at the front of the house. As I looked I could see the Rumfustian Inn, lying disguised within the fabric of this new building. The uneven thatched roof had gone, as had the small windows either side of the door. The inn had been fronted with dressed stone and was balanced with large windows and a new roof. It was nearly swallowed up, but still it existed, like the ghost of an almost forgotten memory.

'Well,' I said to my son, feeling somewhat winded. 'It seems we cannot avail ourselves of the Rumfustian's hospitality, but . . . here it is.'

'This is it?'

'The central part is it, yes, though it has been much altered and added to.'

My son squeezed my hand. 'Never mind, Father. It is a very fine house.'

'It is indeed. A very fine house.' I shook away all fond thoughts of eating a meal in the inn and thought of my son. It mattered little to him if the inn existed or not. At least I had come and seen it. I should return to the coach and guide our coachman to the river, where we could spread a cloth and have our picnic. It was a fine day for dining out of doors. But even as I turned my back and we retraced our steps I could still on the skin of my palm feel the door I had touched. The nails, the warmth of the wood – they struck such a memory in me that I could almost believe I was a child again.

We reached the river with some difficulty. I had forgotten how narrow the track to it was, with many overhanging trees. I am sure it had never been made with fine London coaches in mind. However, we got there without mishap, set out our picnic by the river and had an enjoyable hour or so in the good country air. Christophe tried to catch a trout the way my friend Charlie had been accustomed to, by lying on the bank with his arm in the water and lulling the fish into a dream by tickling its belly. When young, I could never bear the cold water for long enough. Charlie had the trick of it, but I never did, and I fear my son needed a better teacher than I.

After we had eaten, our servant packed away the basket. We were ready to visit the church, but I wanted first to make enquiries about Jane and William. 'We will visit the forge before we carry on,' I said. 'It is nearby. Whether or not my childhood friend owns it, someone might know what became of my father's servants.'

Soon I could hear a hammering start up and shortly afterwards I saw the familiar building. This at least was as I remembered it. I found a smile hanging about my mouth. What a shock Charlie would have, if he were here!

I knew him almost right away. He had not changed, except to mature and grow taller. I would have recognised his way of standing anywhere. It was a stance that his father had before him, a way of holding himself before taking the next blow at the anvil.

'Charlie!'

I had the advantage of him. He was dressed as I remembered while I was very much changed. 'Charlie! It is your old friend Abel.'

He took a hurried step towards me and then stopped. He laid the hammer down with exaggerated care and watched me approach. It wasn't until we had almost reached him that he truly recognised me. 'Abel? Is it really you?' A grin I so well remembered stole across his face. 'How is it possible? And' – he waved his dirty arm at my fine clothes – 'and you looking so well-set-up.'

'I am a little surprised myself,' I said. 'And yet here I am with my son, despite many years ago having been sold, a captive, and sent out of my own country. It is well for the Johnsons that I am not bitter.' I saw his face. 'What is it?'

'So, the Johnsons were indeed responsible?'

'Of course.'

'Well then, you got your revenge.'

'What do you mean?'

'They were rooted out after you were lost. Every last one of them. Men, women and children. Mostly hanged, some of the young ones were sent to the Americas.'

It was the last thing I had expected. 'Because of my capture?'

Charlie shook his head. 'No one knew what had happened to you. My father told me you had most likely fallen over the cliff.'

I stared at him and shivered. It felt as if a shadow had passed over my tomb.

'The whole village searched, to no effect.' Charlie looked at me as if he still had trouble believing I truly lived. 'It is astonishing to see you . . . and so well! But tell me. What of your father? He must be so happy to know you are alive.'

The world slid from me and then froze. 'My father?'

'Yes.'

'My father is dead, Charlie.'

Charlie looked puzzled. 'Of course he's not. At least, he was alive yesterday. Though he is frail, and I hear his heart is weak, but . . .'

My own heart trembled and then beat wildly in my breast as if it would escape and fly up into the air. I felt weak and strong at the same time. I feared I might faint and yet desired to run.

'Where does he live?'

Charlie looked even more puzzled. 'Where he has ever been, of course.' Then his face lightened. 'At the old Rumfustian, but the inn is no more. It is named Rumfustian House. Your father is a wealthy man and has extended the place. You probably . . .'

I left him without a word. I had no words in me. I abandoned my son to the care of my old friend and ran. It was not far, but far enough for me to fear I might be too late. Good living had slowed

335

me, and I was no longer the boy who had run this path several times a week. By the time I reached the place I was quite out of breath. However, I knocked at once on the old door, and impatient to be answered I went then to the double gates, meaning to get in that way. As I struggled with the latch an old man came out of the door towards me, shaking his head.

'Do not be so impatient, sir. You must give me a little time to answer your knock.'

He was bent with age and frail. I was about to announce myself and embrace him when I realised that this was not my father.

'William?'

The old man nodded. 'I am he. Can I help you?'

'William, it is me, Abel. I am alive, and I hear my father also lives. Please tell me it is true!' My voice was trembling, so I wasn't sure if I made sense, but William understood.

'Abel? Alive? But is it really you?'

He came up close and stared me in the face. William had always been a cautious fellow and steady. He would not want to take an imposter to his master. I stood his scrutiny willingly, seeing within his watery eyes and lined face the honest servant I had known so well.

At length he nodded. 'I would not have believed it possible,' he mumbled, his voice shaking with emotion. The colour had quite left his cheeks. I wondered if he might faint and made ready to catch him, but he did not. 'It is true! Oh, sir! You remind me much of your father when first I knew him. Come in, sir, and welcome. I believe your father is in the garden.'

In through the door I saw the great fireplace I remembered so well. Instead of the wooden surround, it now had carved stone pillars and an under-mantel decorated with leaves and flowers. The room served as a kind of hall with doors off it to the newer parts of the house. I wanted to explore but felt constrained. I was a visitor here, which was a strange, unsettling feeling.

William led me to the passage that went to the kitchen. He took me into the small parlour and put his hand on my arm. 'Wait if you would while I call Jane. Your father is not well, and she will know best how to tell him with the least shock.'

I did as I was bid. To know the three people I had most loved were still in this world was such a joy to me! There was a chair, but I could not sit, nor stay still. I could scarcely breathe.

After a few minutes, Jane entered, much lined in the face and with a walk that favoured one of her hips. She, too, was breathless, and anxious as well as happy. I could not restrain myself and gave her a heartfelt embrace. There were tears in both our eyes when we had done.

'Your father is weak, sir,' she said when we had recovered ourselves. 'I fear for his heart when he knows you are here. It will be a shock to him after all these years, but he will be happy, so very happy to see you well and prosperous.'

'I will go quietly to him,' I said. 'I should tell you I am a surgeon and understand something of weak hearts. If I tell him softly and am there to prove it, he may, I hope, take it calmly.'

Jane nodded. 'I think that a good plan. For if I tell him and then you approach there will be a few seconds when he is not sure. The anxiety would not be good for him.' Her eyes filled with tears again and she laid her old hand on my sleeve. 'A surgeon! Pray God your father is well enough to hear your story. Of course, he will wish to, as do I.'

I took her hand. Without another word she led me back into the hall and on into a new room. It led to another, which in turn opened into a room that looked out onto the garden. A door was standing ajar in the balmy afternoon air. William was standing outside, gazing at me as if I was a thing of wonder. At some way distant was a rose arbour.

'He has been sitting there a while,' said Jane pointing at the still figure in the arbour. 'Among his roses. It is his favourite place, where I feel sure he often thinks of you.'

IN ARTICULO MORTIS

33

Abel stood at the door, his heart overflowing. He could hear a horse on the road, trotting smartly on, before it stopped amid curses and then galloped away, but he heeded it not. The world turned, men and beasts lived their destiny, boys too, but for him, at this moment, life stood still. Out on the road, Fortuna had brought James Bramble to ride past Rumfustian House, upon his most recent purchase, a fine, pale stallion he had bought from a dealer he knew in Constantinople. He didn't usually ride in this direction. There was an easier road from Chineborough to his isolated house on the moor, but he wanted to test his horse's stamina on the steep road. He was quietly pleased. Having allowed the animal to walk for a little while he urged it on at a fast trot through the village of Dario. It was only about a mile on the now level road until the crossroads. There he would take the track that wound through the heather to his house. He was thinking of the young idiot to whom he would sell this horse. The wealthy fool would not be able to manage it, and yet he wanted to race him at Bibury. James Bramble foresaw an amusing accident to the empty skull of the wealthy young man.

He continued to think of the future. He schooled himself never to think of the past, because past mistakes were never his fault. He did not choose to remember Ahmed's beautiful, dark body, spilling its carmine life at the thrust of his jealous knife. But there was the potential for death here. He should have been paying more attention.

Seemingly from nowhere, two young boys sprinted out of a gap between two houses. They were already halfway across the road when time seemed to stand still for Abel in the garden. The horse saw them first and had but a moment to react. The boys saw the horse. One stopped dead; the other could not decide whether to sprint harder or go back. He split a second with wavering, making it inevitable that horse and boy would collide.

James Bramble was still an excellent horseman, but he was now nearly sixty years old and his reactions were the slowest of all. The horse half reared, trying to turn from the boy, his hind hooves milling the grit of the road. The boy slammed into the horse's side and was spun away by his speed, combined with the turning of the horse. James Bramble lost his stirrups but leant over his horse's neck and did not fall.

The boy rolled over in the dust and lay still, finding it hard to believe that he was not dead. He got up and wondered ruefully how he would explain the holes in his stockings and the dust on his breeches and shirt. His knee was bleeding where it had made contact with a sharp stone. His head ached where it had collided with the rider's knee. His companion joined him and made an effort to dust him down. Then they shrugged, knowing there was nothing to be done, and scampered on their way.

The horse's haunches powered him on. Thoroughly alarmed, he bolted, in spite of James's efforts to control him. James Bramble's thighs were not as strong as they used to be, nor were his knees. His feet could not find his stirrups, although his good hand was still holding his reins and his metal hand was firmly clamped to them. The horse was running as if he was already in a race, as if he had not climbed the steep hill out of Chineborough, as if he did not have five more miles to travel across the moor. James Bramble was now entirely in the present. He was thinking of how he must not fall, must not fall, must not fall.

ABEL MORGAN

34

Before going to my father, I stood, somehow, now the moment had come, reluctant to disturb his peace. My father! Never had I thought for one instant that this would happen, except after death. I was conscious of Jane and William, standing back to give me privacy for my reunion, but unable to leave for care of their master. I took a breath and went to him.

My shoes crunching on the gravel path announced my coming, but he didn't turn to see who approached. Indeed, he was mostly hidden from my sight, sitting as he was within the arbour and with his profile towards me. I moved quietly to stand before him. I could see him well, but he had the sun in his face. He was resting his head on a scarlet cushion against the back of the arbour and his eyes were closed. A stick was propped against the seat and a few creamy rose petals lay carelessly on his lap. He was so much older than I remembered him, old and pale, and the skin on his hands where they lay amongst the petals was wrinkled and flecked with brown.

My throat was constricted. 'Father?' It came out as a whisper and he still didn't stir. For an awful moment I thought his heart had stopped, cheating us of our meeting. I swallowed and looked for a sign that he lived. He did breathe. I was almost certain of it. I swallowed and spoke again.

'Father.'

Not opening his eyes, he lifted his hand and calmly patted the seat. 'Come and join me. Tell me about your day. I have been expecting you this past hour.'

A trickle of fear ran up my back, making me shiver. Had he turned necromancer? What dark magic was at work here? Then another thought, equally unwelcome, entered my head. He had reacted as if I had been gone but a few hours! It was a totally unnatural response unless . . . Neither Jane nor William had told me he had lost his mind and lived in the past, but it must be so. He was not so very old, but it was hardly impossible that he had become feeble-minded.

It was too much. To have thought him dead all these years and then to discover he lived, only to have him insensible to the present day. How could I bear It? I would not be angry. It was not his fault, but I raged against fate that had cheated me at the last. I railed against myself, too. Had he fallen into his dotage very recently? Would he have known me had I come straight away, last autumn, when I reached England? Could I stomach being his boy to please his feeble mind? Could I play his young son, with none of the long years that stretched between us? I wanted him to see me as I am, full grown, with a son of my own. I wanted him to marvel at my success and yet, as I thought all this, I also wanted to weep in his arms, as if I were his child again.

What should I do? My heart was so full. I wanted to beg him through my tears to acknowledge my long absence, but he was too frail for such a show of emotion. Instead, I steadied myself as well as I was able, did as he bid me and sat beside him, the scent of the roses all around us.

'So, have you had a good day?'

'Father.' I took his frail hand and held it in mine. 'It is I, your son, Abel. Please . . . don't alarm yourself.'

But his eyes and mouth had flown open and he jerked his head from the cushion. His free hand went to his breast. He held it there against his heart and breathed with difficulty. After a few seconds he turned to look at me. His eyes took me in, lingering on my face and then travelling over my body, looking at my good clothes, even down to my buckled shoes. At the last he observed his old hand in my strong one.

He spoke carefully, with effort. 'I see it is indeed you, Abel, grown to be a fine man.'

He saw me! Maybe he would lapse into dotage again at any moment, but in this instance, he saw me as I was.

I smiled at him through my glassy tear-filled eyes and spoke softly. 'You see me as I am?'

He withdrew his hand from mine and peered at me. 'Of course I see you as you are. Do you think me lack-witted?'

I found myself laughing at his tetchiness. 'No! Of course not! Only you seemed at first so unsurprised that I was here . . .'

He waved the comment away. 'Let me look at you again.'

He was trembling and tears spilt from his eyes. He held out both his hands and I embraced him gently. He was thin and worn, but his hands held me tightly for a long time, with surprising strength, while he muttered endearments to me.

'It is really you . . . my dear, dear son . . . I never gave up hope, but after so long . . . who would have thought it . . . So many years, Abel.' He hugged me tight. 'So many years . . .'

At last he let me go and looked at me again.

'I expected all my life to rescue a ragged boy or man,' he said. 'But I see you had no need for my concern these past years.' Another tear leaked from his eye and he rubbed it away. 'I am more glad than I can say that you live, but . . .' He bit his lip. 'I would wish you had thought to send word to your grieving father that you were well and alive.' His face looked full of regret and sadness.

'But I thought you were dead!' I slid from the seat and knelt at his side. 'I saw you shot and blamed myself for your demise. I have been abroad and have only this past hour learnt that you live! It is not my fault I did not seek you out! I thought I was to blame for both my parents' deaths and now I find my mother is the only parent I killed.' I was a little boy again, with the thoughts I had not felt for years suddenly assailing me. I put my head on his knee and wept.

After a moment I felt his hand on my hair, caressing me in the way I remembered from so many years ago. 'I did not know you blamed yourself for your mother's death, Abel. You must not do that. It was not your fault. And you see that I live. There is no blame. But I am so very sorry you thought me dead all these years.' His voice broke. 'I searched for you so long and never quite gave up hope that you lived. I followed you to Constantinople, but never found any word of you . . . and oh!' He held his heart again as if it would break. 'Your grandmother in Holland died some two years ago and she *so* longed to know you!'

He sat back in the arbour and let his emotion take him. All I could do was hold his hands and wait for the storm of weeping to pass. At length he became a little calmer.

'I am so sorry. I should be rejoicing to see you and all I do is weep. But I do rejoice, Abel. I do. It's just that my heart is overfull.'

'I understand. But tell me why you went to Constantinople. I was never there. I have spent all these years in the Caribbean.'

He stared at me. 'But you gave me a map of Constantinople!'

I could not think what he meant.

'On that dreadful day in the cellar. You gave me the map, so when I was recovered from my wound I went in search of you.' He saw my face. 'You did not know about the map?'

'No! It was just a packet I had picked up . . . I can't quite remember why I gave it to you. Instead of simply dropping it, I suppose, so I could help make my escape.'

'Oh. Well.' For a moment he looked displeased, but then he gave a shrug and laughed. 'That map did not lead me to you, but it did bring a comfortable living, by degrees.' He gestured at the sweet-scented roses that flowered around us. 'This is one of the first I bred from the roses my partner sent from the East. It is still my favourite. I called it God's Breath, which is the meaning of your name, as you know. They now grow in several of the royal gardens and their oil is much prized.'

I was too full of emotion to speak.

He looked at me seriously. 'When you were a baby, Abel, you saved my life. You saved me because I knew that I must save you, so don't blame yourself for the demise of either of your parents. I'm sorry you blamed yourself. I would not have wanted that for the world. And now . . . when I felt my life was ending you come to refresh it once more. I hope you can stay here a while,' he added anxiously. 'Your room is . . .'

'I long to spend as many hours in your company as possible, but I have left my son at the river with our servants and coach. I must send word to them . . .'

'You have a family?'

'Your grandson. Christophe. He is eleven.'

My father struggled to stand, and I helped him up. 'Will you bring him here? Are you able to stay? There is room and to spare. I would wish to meet him . . . as for your servants and coach . . . we can make all comfortable, I believe . . .'

He was becoming agitated and I did my best to soothe him. 'All shall be well, Father. All shall be well. We were going on to Chineborough, but that is of no importance now I have found you alive! There is time aplenty. If you have someone who can take a message to my son, I will stay with you. Don't worry, Father. I *will* stay with you.'

I took his arm, gave him his stick and slowly we made our way back to the house. Jane and William had gone from the garden. My father showed me where he wished to sit, in a chair filled with cushions, next to a window looking out at his garden. I wondered if he had taken a physician's advice, if he took any stimulant for his heart, but now was not the moment to ask. He wished me to find Jane, and so I reluctantly left him and went to the kitchen.

To my great surprise, Christophe was there, sitting on the very bench on which I used to perch to beg titbits from Jane. He was with another boy and a stranger, some sort of workman, as well as both Jane and William. They made a very merry group. I did not hear what the stranger had said, but he had them all laughing. As soon as Christophe saw me he ran to me.

'Father!' He indicated the boy. 'This is Richard, whose father has the forge. He found me by the river and told me my grandfather is alive! We ran here together as soon as we had directed the coach to come. It stands outside.' He stood tall in his child's attempt to be an adult. 'Have I done well, Father?'

I put my hands on his shoulders. 'Yes, you have done well.' I called to Jane, 'Jane? My father wishes you to go to him.'

She began to bustle. 'His drink is ready. I will take it now.'

I looked again at my son. 'Christophe! Your clothes are a disgrace.' I glanced at Charlie's son, Richard, who could almost have been his father when a boy. He was regarding me with what looked like trepidation in his eyes, but it was my son who was in trouble. 'Your stockings are in holes and your knee has been bleeding. Your clothes are covered in dust. What have you been doing?' Both boys looked at the floor and said nothing. I sighed, remembering my own escapades with Charlie. I lifted my son's chin, so he was obliged to look at me. 'Fighting with the son of a smith is not fitting for a gentleman,' I said in a soft voice. 'You will change your clothes and wash before you present yourself to your grandfather.' I looked over at Charlie's boy. 'I am obliged to you for bringing Christophe here, Richard. My compliments to your father. Now you may go.'

'Yes, sir.'

The boys exchanged secret glances as Richard sidled past us to the door, but neither spoke to the other. No doubt they would seek each other out again, but I did not want Christophe rolling in the dust with his new-found friend.

While Christophe went to make himself presentable, I returned to my father. He had been agitated, Jane told me. He had risen from his chair to find me but had knocked his stick to the floor and could not bend to reach it. It had been difficult to make him sit again and wait for me.

'I thought you had gone.' His hand was tight on mine.

'I told you I would not go. I am here.'

I took the drink from Jane and held it for him. I had to hold it to his lips because his hands trembled so, but as he drank he became calmer. I would have to ask Jane what she put in it.

'I want to know what happened to you, Abel, but for now I simply wish to see your face and hold your hand.'

We sat this way, mostly in silence, for some time, until his grip grew slack and his eyes closed in sleep. Even so, I dared not leave his side in case he woke and became distressed again, nor did I wish to. I could hear the sounds of the house, and the great door being opened and closed several times. William would speak to the coachman, I was sure, and Jane would deal with my son. I gazed upon my sleeping father and marvelled anew at how he lived. My heart was quite overfull.

I had many questions. We had lost so many years, he and I. From penury he had gone to obvious comfort, with several new young servants I had already seen about the house. And all this it seemed through gardening! I remembered very well our attempts in that patch behind the inn. I had enjoyed grubbing in the soil with him and picking the fruit from the old trees, but to have gone from that to the large elegant garden full of flowers and herbs was a mystery to me.

At length Jane came back so that I could take my ease. I went to find Christophe. He had done as I required and changed his clothes. To pass the time while his grandfather slept, I took him up to my old bedroom, where to my delight I found the few toys I had possessed. Although much of the house had been altered, that room had not. It was like walking back into my childhood. It reminded me, too, that I was heir to this place, and so he and I explored freely together. Looking out of an upstairs window, I saw that the garden was only part of the land under cultivation. Much more had been set out as a nursery, with rows of plants of various sorts, and several men and boys were working there. It struck me that although the nursery was much smaller than my plantation, and very different, we had both made our fortunes from the soil.

The tipsy staircase was as I remembered it, but the kitchen was now more of a parlour than a working kitchen, having a much larger, better one newly built behind it, with new bedrooms above, looking over the garden. When we returned to the old kitchen we found the stranger still sitting at the table with William. William struggled to his feet and the stranger, who was covered with even more dust than Christophe had been, leapt to assist him. He was so forward as to approach me as if my equal and greeted me as if I were the stranger. I did not like his informal manner, the mug of our ale at his hand or the good English platter filled with ham and bread and onions which he had been devouring. He, however, appeared happy to see me.

'I am so very pleased to meet you at last,' said he.

I looked to William for explanation, but he had never been comfortable with words. Before he could introduce the man, to my surprise my son rushed to do so.

'Of course! You were with Grandfather, so were not introduced.' Christophe's eyes flashed with excitement. 'This is your brother! He insists I must call him Turlough, instead of Uncle, and so I introduce him to you as Turlough.'

I looked at the man in astonishment. He was not a gentleman and it seemed clear to me that Christophe was confused. 'You are right, Christophe, as you are but a boy, to call any man "uncle" or "sir", out of courtesy. If he wishes you to use his Christian name you are free to use it, but you should know that I have no brother.'

The man had proffered his hand, but I saw no reason to take it. 'You are a nephew of William's?' I enquired. 'Or perhaps some kind of cousin?'

He took back his hand and shook his head. 'No, sir. I am the one-time boy your father adopted some years ago. I have my own home and workshop in Chineborough but come to see him as often as possible. At present I am making repairs to Dario Church and so he has got into the habit of seeing me every day after work.' A puzzled frown crossed his face. 'Did our father not tell you of me?'

I felt outraged. How dare he act as if we shared a parent or consider himself so important as to be uppermost in the first conversation between a long-parted father and son? I was angry with Jane, too. William was a doddering old man, but she should have told me about this cuckoo before I even saw my poor old father. I would have to speak to her about the man later, when he had been got rid of. However, I would not wish my father distressed in any way and I would not show myself an uncaring man to any.

'We have not had the time to speak of trivialities,' I said to this Turlough. 'But doubtless we will.' My manner must have appeared stiff, but that my father could have adopted this person to replace me was a great shock. Indeed, I could not believe it, but William had not demurred, so there must be some truth in the man's words. Even so, I was not inclined to call him 'brother'. Certainly not until I had discovered more about him.

'William tells me our father is weaker today,' said the stranger, disregarding my coolness. 'I am sorry for it, but will not stay many minutes with him, as I am sure you will want to spend much time together while you are here.'

'My father is sleeping,' I told him. 'And not well enough for casual visitors. I tell you this as his son and physician. I suggest you finish the food you have been given and call another time.' I turned from him to go back to my father, but William called to me.

'Wait, sir! You do not understand. This is no casual visitor! Your father will be likely dismayed if he and Turlough do not spend a few minutes together as usual. As you have seen, sir, he can get distressed if people are not there when he expects them.'

'Under those circumstances he must certainly see my father this day for a few minutes, as soon as my parent wakes,' I said coldly. 'I am going now to see how he does and will send someone back to inform you if he is well enough to see Master . . . Turlough. Christophe, come with me.'

35

So, it was concern for my father's heart that forced my son and I to stand by while the labourer went to him, kissed him and told him he would return again. Seeing them together caused me great pain. I would rather have been absent from their fond conversation, but my father, when he learnt Turlough was in the kitchen, called at once to see him, refusing to let me or my son leave. On the contrary, he seemed to think it would be a source of great joy for us to meet the interloper.

'My two sons and a grandson! How blessed I am today,' he said. 'You must become good friends, because my love unites you.'

I was heartily glad when the man left. He was, at least, sensitive to my need to have private intercourse with my father, but I doubted he realised the size of my disquiet. I feared he was taking advantage of my father's kindness because I could not see that my poor father would have wished to adopt such a person and yet he appeared quite under the man's spell.

I freely admit that a part of my dislike of Turlough was my own circumstances. I had been ripped from my father's love, while he had seemingly lost no time before replacing me. It was a hurt that reached my very soul. And it made me consider my own son, Christophe. What of the inheritance that should come to me? It was not right that I or my son should be disadvantaged by this man, whoever he was. I would dispute it if necessary in law. I had powerful friends in London and many questions for this Turlough. I would protect my son's rights and my own. Where was Turlough's mother? Had she perhaps tricked my father into thinking her child was his?

I said none of this to my father, not wishing to distress him. However, as soon as Jane, William and I were the only ones not abed I tasked them to tell me everything.

'The master came upon him while abroad, searching for you,' said Jane.

I think she was trying to make things sound better for me, but I was not minded to be soothed. 'So, are there a host of other "sons" that he collected while I was parted from him through no fault of my own?'

'No, sir! He can better tell you the circumstances but, in any case, he returned him at once to his people.'

'It was a full two years later when the child turned up again,' said William.

'Three,' said Jane. 'He was about nine years old by the time he ran away from the people in Ireland. He had been used most cruelly, sir, and his parents were dead.' She shuddered. 'Killed most horribly they were, by pirates, who took the little child to be a slave in the East. Having returned him to Ireland and restoring him to who appeared to be his aunt, your father thought that all would be well but, by all accounts, he was almost as much a slave in Ireland as he would have been in Constantinople. Naturally, he made his way back to the one person who had shown him any kindness.'

'He was hardly my father's responsibility!'

Jane looked at me reproachfully. 'Your father has a soft heart, sir.'

'Just so! It is easy to take advantage of a man with a heart that is over-soft.'

'He had not wanted to be a parent to any other than you,' said William. 'But in time we all came to love the child for himself.'

'He was never a replacement for you, sir, nor never could be. Don't ever think that.'

I made no response, though I am sure Jane meant what she said.

'Your father was away on business when Turlough arrived,' she added after a moment. 'We didn't know what to do, but when the master came home he said we must care for him, so we did.'

'I assume he is a papist, with that name of his and his nation,' I said in disgust. 'How sensible do you think it was to give him shelter?'

Jane sighed. 'Perhaps he was born that way, but we took him to church with us and that is how he has worshipped ever since.'

William coughed. 'Your father apprenticed him to a stonemason in Chineborough when he was of an age. He works hard, sir, and has repaid your father's kindness manyfold. He has been dutiful and does not forget his benefactor, although he is successful in his work and has had no need of help for a long while. He asks for nothing.'

'What's more,' said Jane, 'his liveliness and good humour cheered your father and helped him to bear your loss.'

'I can see,' said I, 'that you are determined to excuse him, whatever my doubts. As you say, Jane, my father does have a soft heart. It sounds as if you and William have allowed him to be taken advantage of.'

William looked at the floor, but his wife gave me a searching look and the memory of her role in my childhood made me feel somewhat uncomfortable. 'I am sorry you think that,' was all she said.

'Well,' I said. 'I will say no more. Ours is not the only nest in the land to have admitted a cuckoo, but I take it he resides in Chineborough? I do not expect him to treat this place any more as his home, coming and going as he pleases.'

'I will ensure his coming and going will be at the master's desire and no other person,' she said, rather pertly, it seemed to me.

I went to bed somewhat downhearted. It was a miracle to have found my father alive after he had been dead to me for so many years. I should be brimful of joy, but my joy had not lasted above a few hours. I had come here in part hoping to find our old servants still living and to be their benefactor. Of course, it was wonderful to find that all lived, but no one needed me. Was that what ailed me? A desire to be needed? That and Turlough the interloper, stealing my father's love. And for how long had I been missing before my father had shaken off his poverty and shifted for himself? Then, he replaced me with another, who he supported, when he had not paid a penny for *my* education.

I was, I could see, inclined to feel sorry for myself. Even Jane, who I had loved almost as the mother I had never known, didn't support me over Turlough. What was more, my marriage had not been a success, my wife was mute and most likely dying, if not already dead. I berated myself for counting my misfortunes instead of my blessings, but I could not prevent these miserable feelings from stealing my rest.

I felt tears pricking my eyes and a sob fighting to burst free of my throat. What was the matter with me? It all felt too much. I no longer needed to feel guilty for being the agent of his death, but discovering my father alive had not brought the feelings I might have expected. Some part of me, the remnant of the child I had been, wanted him to pick me up, hold me to him and take away all the hurts and fears of the years we had been apart. It was not reasonable to want that, but it was how I felt. Part of me also wanted him to admire the successful adult I had become, but he, too, had become successful and needed nothing material from me. It seemed that no part of me could find a place here. Perhaps it would be better if I went back to London, where I was respected and had many friends. My father had been dead to me for too long for him to be alive now.

I hated this room. Christophe had begged leave to sleep in my old bed, so I lay here, in part of the new building. The bed was comfortable, but the walls were too straight and pale-plastered, the window glass too clear and the stonework too recently carved. It made me feel a guest instead of a returning son. I did not want to go back to London feeling this way. I wanted to love him and be loved by him as in the distant past, but how do you restore past feelings? Our special love, decades away, was long gone.

I turned over in bed and buried my face in the pillow to stifle my sobs. I was deeply ashamed of the tears that dripped from my eyes, but I was overfull of emotion. I felt like a wild animal that howls its distress, but I must muzzle my misery and be quiet. At length, when my eyes had enough of tears and my sore heart was somewhat calmer, I wondered if I might sleep at last, but I could not. I wished the day was here so I could pick up my life again, but it was the middle of the night. I thought of my father and decided to go to him, to make sure he was comfortable and not in need of anything.

His door stood ajar and a little light spilt through. I pushed the door wider and stood there, looking at his shadowy form in the bed. A small fire illuminated the room, but no one was with him. I went quietly to his bed. He was lying on his side, with his hand by his cheek. I listened and could hear his breathing, a little rasping, but otherwise calm and steady. All was well with him, but I was chilled in my nightshirt, so went to the fire. When I set more coals upon it, he awoke and turned in the bed.

'Abel?'

I went to him. 'Yes. It is I.'

'My son. I thought I had dreamt it, but there you are! So tall and handsome. But you must be cold. Take my gown there and put it on.'

It was a fine wool gown and very warm. I put it on, remembering the silk gown he had owned when I was young. The long fraying threads had fascinated me when a child. I had so loved the bright colours, but it would be long gone and forgotten now.

I sat in the chair beside his bed. For some minutes he was quiet, and I wondered if he had gone back to sleep, but then he spoke again.

'I am often awake in the night,' he said, 'and doze in the day. If you are not too tired, Abel, would you like to stay with me for a while? There were too many people today. Now it is just us two, like in the old days.'

'I would like that.'

'Then can you help me with my pillows? And pour wine for us both? There is some on the table.'

'Would you like me to light the candle?'

He shook his head. 'I like the firelight . . . unless you need it . . . ?'

'No. I can see to pour the wine. Here you are.'

I handed him the glass and he took a sip. I felt shy of him somehow. I did not know what to say, but I wanted to say something.

'I'm sorry.'

I had not known I was going to say that. He looked at me with surprise in his face. 'What are you sorry for?'

I turned the glass in my hands. 'I wish I had come sooner.'

'You thought me dead. I realise that.'

For a few minutes we stayed silent. So much of his room was as I remembered it. The bed, where I had always felt safe after bad dreams, his night table and large wooden chest. But I was grown and he was old. I thought about taking my leave, so he could sleep, but his eyes were wide open and eventually he spoke again.

'I am sorry too, Abel. So sorry that I lost you.'

What could I say? That it didn't matter? That I didn't blame him? I took a long drink, but the wine didn't make me feel any less awkward.

'What happened to your boots?'

I stared at him. 'My boots?'

'Yes. The ones you found under the seat of the old settle.'

'Oh! *Those* boots.' I hadn't thought about them for many years, but I remembered them now. 'I lost them along the way . . .' I took another mouthful of wine. He was watching me, waiting for more.

'I was sorry to lose them because the knife would have been useful. I might even have managed to—' But he interrupted me.

'Knife! You had a knife in your boot?'

'Yes. I found it with the boots. There was a loop inside one boot that I thought had been made for it.'

'I never knew!'

I smiled. 'Perhaps I thought if I told you, you would have taken it from me.'

He laughed. 'At the least I would have been concerned about the safety of your foot!'

He reached out his empty glass with his slightly trembling hand. 'More wine, Abel. To soothe my fear about your boyish foot! I feared so many things for you, but a knife in your boot never occurred to me!'

'Maybe,' I said, thinking of the great disaster in Jamaica, 'it's the things we don't know that we should fear the most.'

'Life has made you a philosopher! But certainly, I sometimes feared things I didn't need to, while some I had not anticipated were so frightening I would have run from them if I had known about them in time.'

I passed him his glass, but he gripped my hand instead and I was forced to return the wine to the table.

'Abel, we have both had to face fears not of our making nor imaginable until they happened. And yet, here we are at last. I thank God you thought to visit your old home before I died. It means the world to me that you are here.'

I felt tears pricking my eyes again, but my heart was in less pain.

'Come,' he said, letting go of my hand for a moment. 'Come and sit up here next to me, like we used to after you had dreamt a bad dream. It was always better after we talked, to chase the dream away.'

So I did, bringing the wine with me. We sat up in bed together, my father and I, drinking our wine and talking of the past.

We spoke of so much that night. I tried to tell only the more cheerful parts of my lost years and I daresay he did the same for me. I told him a lot about Ptolemy, which made him recall his own experiences after the war and how so many who had fought were set adrift, not being able for one reason or another to return to their earlier lives.

'I owe that man so much,' he said, on hearing that my profession and wealth had come from the surgeon. 'I wish I could have met him and thanked him for his care of you.'

'He wrote an account of his life for me, but I could not understand much. His hand was not easy to read.'

My father looked at me sternly. 'You must persevere! If he wrote it for you, then you have a duty to read it.'

'Maybe in London I will find someone to help me,' I said, trying to remember if the papers were with my London lawyer and if they had even survived the disaster in Jamaica. 'You are right. I will see to it. Then I will be able to tell you more about him.'

I had been concerned about admitting my time with the pirates, but I did not need to be. My father simply assumed that after Ptolemy died I had immediately come into my inheritance and had ceased to roam the sea. He was very ready to believe that a life in the Caribbean was not quite as lawless as the broadsheets liked to make out. There was a part of me that regretted not confessing that dreadful day when Rowan and Black Tom died. Perhaps the telling would have purged my guilt at planning to kill them, but it would have been unkind to burden my father with that. If I had, I would have been hard put to avoid talk of my piracy. At the time, I had been pleased at the expediency of my decision, but I knew he would be sorely distressed at me having walked freely into the profession.

The thing he took hardest was my estrangement from Marie and her subsequent illness. He seemed determined to see her only as a sweet English girl and was inclined to blame me for our falling-out, although he did not say it in so many words. I was glad when he finally accepted the end of our relations. I would have been hard put to describe truly some of her behaviours, not to mention her life on board as a boy and her birth into slavery. It was all better unmentioned.

As for my father, he did not have so very much to tell. Apart from his brief journey to the East and subsequent adoption of Turlough, his life had been uneventful. It had been fortunate for him that he had met his business partner, otherwise his life would undoubtably have been much harder. I wondered if he had not ever wished to marry again, but when I mentioned it he laughed, and said, 'Who would have had me?' I truly think that my mother was the only love of his life and he wanted no other. It is a very moving thought.

We talked on until the birds began to sing, but eventually sleep overtook us both. When Jane came in the morning to wake him, she found the wine all gone, the fire out and me, still wrapped in his gown, asleep upon the bed beside him.

That day we were both tired, but when awake he was lively and quick to laugh. We sat in the garden for a while and he took much pleasure in watching his grandson play. The only time I tried to speak of Turlough he dismissed any discussion of him, other than to commend him to me.

'Turlough will not mind me spending so many hours with you. Don't fret about him. It is of no consequence, but I am gladder than I can say that you have regard for him. He has been such a comfort.'

I do not think he misunderstood me purposely, but it was difficult to tell.

The sun had gone behind a cloud, and I was about to suggest we went indoors when he suddenly became deathly pale and slumped against me. I caught him in my arms. His eyes rolled up into his head and I feared his heart had stopped. I carried him indoors and laid him on a couch. We closed the curtains, kept him quiet and hoped. I put my ear to his chest and listened to the intermittent pulsing of his heart. His breath was very light, and it almost seemed as if he might float away, he was so slight of body.

I thought of all the remedies I had in my box back in London and sent urgently to Chineborough for what I needed, though doubting that there was much that could be done. I had satisfied myself that Jane's drink that he liked so much was full of good things. Eggs, sugar and some of the finest French brandy were in it. It would do him as well as any physic I could suggest. I could have bled him, but in truth I felt he was better left in peace. Care and rest was best, as Jane had always given him. He was not such a very old man, being no more than sixty, and he had all of our loves, but his heart was the engine of his body and I feared it was quite worn out.

That night I slept in the chair beside his bed and in the morning I was rewarded by a little colour returning to his cheeks. In a while his eyes opened. He knew me and managed a spoonful of broth, but he was quite unable to sit up. Jane brought more pillows and we propped him, so he would not gather liquid in his lungs and drown, as so often happens. We took our turns to sit with him, but his eyes were mostly closed and he said little, other than to ask a few times for Turlough. I said nothing to Jane, but that afternoon she brought him to the room. I did not intend to leave him with my father but stood to one side while he knelt at the bed and took his hand.

'Turlough?'

'I am here.'

'Abel?'

'Here I am, Father.'

'Ah.' There was a long pause before he could continue. 'I am pleased . . . you have met.' He smiled, closing his eyes again he slept.

It was night when he woke again. It distressed Jane that he would not take any nourishment, but I could see that he was beyond such things. When I bent over him it was clear that his sight had gone. He held my hand for a while and then something seemed to rouse him. He became restless and called out in distress. 'Margarita! Margarita!' Immediately afterwards he smiled. He tried to raise his other hand and Jane took it in hers 'That lace at your breast,' he said. Jane had none and to my knowledge she never did.

I thought he had drifted into sleep, but then he spoke again. 'Abraham.'

At first it was no more than a mumble, but then he said the name very clearly, twice more, as if speaking directly with delight to a very dear friend. 'Abraham. Abraham!'

It was then he slipped into a deep sleep, with the smile still on his lips.

His breathing became heavier and laboured, with the loud rattle that presages death. Then, by the afternoon of the following day, his breaths changed again. They were now hardly discernible and I felt sure the end was near. For an instant a look of gentle surprise crossed his face. There were only a few silent breaths after that and then none. And so he died, peacefully, with the window to the garden open, the scent of his roses in the breeze and with the sound of birds singing.

Margarita had been my mother's name.

We all felt it miraculous that in addition to mentioning her, he had been called to God by Abraham.

Jane wiped her eyes and said, 'He often said he was not on good terms with God but see how the good Lord sent Abraham to fetch him to Him.'

William said, 'He was a good man.'

Turlough said little other than that he would miss him greatly. However, his distress was obvious and so I was content to include him with the household in prayers for my departed father.

Christophe held my hand throughout and wept much. I think he was also thinking of his mother.

I had been reunited with my father for such a little time. Now we were parted again. But I am a grown man of thirty years and it is in the nature of things for a son to bury his parent. Indeed, I think I had mourned him so long, my mourning was all but done by the time he came to die. I did shed some tears, but my sadness was mingled with gratitude for those few days we had together, when we learnt to love one another anew.

A death causes a hiatus in a family. While his coffin was being made and details of his interment decided, we lived as if the world had temporarily stopped. We were all, I am sure, thinking of the man who had died. I myself was regretting something I had not felt able to ask him, something he had chosen not to tell me. When one afternoon I came upon Jane picking some herbs in the garden, I decided to unburden myself to her.

'What do you know of my mother, Jane?'

'He seldom mentioned her. Just now and then.'

'He *never* spoke of her to me except to say that she was beautiful and dead. As a child I always longed to know more.'

'I will tell you all I know, if you like.' She stood upright and stretched her back. 'He said she was always laughing. He said that to me several times over the years. And she had blonde hair with little curls on her broad forehead and a straight nose. You know she was from Holland?'

I nodded.

'From the hints he gave I think she must have been quite wilful.' Jane smiled at me. 'She didn't like to obey her parents. And your father said he won her from a king! He could be very fanciful sometimes, that father of yours.' Her mouth trembled and she rubbed at her eyes. 'Lord, I miss him so.'

I patted her arm, but I would not be diverted. 'What more?'

'He said her mother was always telling her off for fiddling with the lace on her dress.'

'He mentioned lace while holding your hand.'

'Well, yes.' I had thought Jane too old for blushes, but she was not. 'It was not me he was thinking of, sir! It was your mother. Of that I am sure.'

We read the will, which was satisfactory, and indeed quite touching. It went a long way to remove the fears I had about Turlough, though I could not think that I would ever particularly approve of him and certainly would never call him 'brother'. However, he was most anxious to be allowed to make my father's memorial tablet. His work on the church seemed of fair enough quality and so I saw no harm in granting his desire. We buried my father with all the gravity he deserved and I told Turlough he could do the work. I wanted no mawkish poem on the tablet, simply the dates of his birth and death, and his name. I told Turlough to also carve the name and dates of my mother, as far as we knew them. As she had no known resting place, it would be fitting to remember her with him. Turlough wanted to pay for the stone but I overrode him in that. I did not wish to be obligated to that extent. It would be *my* memorial to *my* father, not his. He acquiesced with a good enough grace and so I shook his hand over the business and we parted in a proper manner.

IN MEDIAS RES

36

Back on the day Christopher and Abel were reunited, in the midst of that joyful time, the whiff of destruction had ridden by. And yet, almost at the point of death, both Christophe and Christopher were spared. But what of James Bramble, that man who knew how to gentle a horse, while having little mercy for his own kind? After a lifetime of meddling in the affairs of others, he was like a great, water-soaked tree, rolling half hidden in a swollen river, causing destruction to boats and bridges, while seeming impervious to hurt himself. And yet wood can be cut, and branches taken from the trunk.

When those two innocent boys, Christophe and his new friend Richard, son of Charlie the blacksmith, hurtled out of the alley and into the path of his horse, they were within a second of losing their lives. Having led Christophe past pigsties and wicket gates, chickens and washing lines, Richard's shortcut had cleverly brought them out directly opposite Rumfustian House. Like bullets they had exploded from the alley, careless in their enjoyment of the run. If their fond parents had known, both boys might have had a beating for it, but Richard would have borne the greater blame. For them, their escape was simple luck, but by fortune or whatever orders this world, that day innocence did evil to an evil man by setting his horse to bolt. He had known, this lover of horseflesh, that his life depended on him staying in his seat. The boys and village had vanished in a minute as the horse flew from the terror it felt. No man could have controlled it. Somewhere in that vast moor, nestling in a shallow valley, was the house that could have brought both horse and rider comfort, but the horse was too new to know his stable. He had no sense of direction, nor would he allow himself to be directed. He plunged into tangled gorse and heather, which slowed his pace. But each gorse slash at his belly maddened him more. He could not see where to put his feet and imagined that monsters assailed him on every side.

James Bramble considered that his life was now more in danger with the horse than without it. It was a gamble which course to take, and it grieved him sorely to abandon his fine horse, but off the hard road the heather would cushion him if he threw himself clear, and there was always a chance that, suddenly unladen, the horse might come to his senses. But the beast was heading for one of the small quarries that lay hidden in those parts. If he fell over the brink, James Bramble would have a much more dangerous landing, and would risk being trampled or rolled upon.

But to be free of the horse, he needed to reach the levers to release his metal fingers. Could his tired legs alone hold him in balance while his good hand did it? He had been meaning to oil the levers but had been too busy. There was a knack to releasing them, simple while still, impossible on the plunging horse. Leaning over its neck to keep his seat he reached instead under his coat, to the straps around his shoulder. Unfastening one was easy, but then his metal hand became unstable, his wrapped stump shifting in its metal arm. And then the worst happened. The horse stumbled. James Bramble fell and could not roll clear. He could not stand up, safe but bereft to watch his investment plunge on without him, for he was still attached by those metal fingers to the reins.

He had been in danger before, but of the swift, knifing kind or threat of poison, not the long, agonising journey to death by degrees, as this would be. So, having cheated death that day, Christophe and Christopher felt the joy of being alive, while James Bramble felt death stalking ever closer with his scythe to cut him down. He tried to keep pace with the horse, but the tangled roots and branches did not allow it. With one part of his mind he bitterly regretted the spoiling of his horse's mouth as the animal dragged him on, trying to rid himself of the weight on his jaw. It was a very slow progress. Both horse and man were in terrible pain. Both were lacerated by the golden gorse, and their legs were battered by hidden rocks. At length, exhausted, the animal stood at bay. Blood dripped from his mouth, onto the blood of the man. And then, as the horse trembled, James Bramble felt sure he could lose the remaining strap.

His legs would hardly hold him any more, but while the horse remained still he managed to free his shoulder of the second strap, speaking gently all the time to the ruined horse. When he gave one sharp tug the horse screamed in pain and reared, but James Bramble's stump was pulled free. He tried to roll clear, but the horse's hooves struck his shoulder before it cantered away, flecked with foam and blood, the metal hand still dragging at the rein.

If this had happened to another man, James Bramble would have found it funny. He would have been amused to think how some yeoman might have been terrified at seeing the riderless horse with fiendish, dangling arm, and it would have given him pleasure to think how the unlucky owner would never be reunited with either horse or limb. He might even have imagined the hand and hollow arm being given to the church or bought by some earl, to hang upon his wall as a curiosity. No doubt, the talk in the inns would have been of witches, demons and monsters, but none of this had been the misfortune of another man for him to enjoy. His two most treasured possessions were gone. The third, his life, was still his, but it dangled, like the metal limb.

And then, James Bramble, still living, was obliged to creep upon the ground like a beetle. How long could he survive? He was not so very far from his house, perhaps four miles, but how far could he go with his shoulder broken, his arm and hand in agony, while the other ended in a stump? His legs had been bruised black and one ankle was cracked.

The first day he was indomitable. Needing to crawl, not having a stick to lean upon, his rage carried him through his pain. The second, he sucked dew greedily from the purple moor, missing by half a mile the bog that would have answered his thirst, though it might also have drowned him in its peaty water. If he could only have reached the track that was but a few yards away a pedlar, or other travelling man might have come across him and seen it as his Christian duty to save him, little knowing who he was.

Perhaps, on the third day, while Christopher and Abel were happily getting used to being together again, James Bramble's legs might have held him up to look about him, although he was weak with thirst, and hunger and pain. If he could have stood, as a man should, he would have seen the track and the shallow valley where succour lay. Surely, even with his swollen tongue and fevered eyes, he would have been able to save himself? If he did send death away, he would have had to do it alone, for no one passed by for over a week. And if he did live, would he renounce all his evil past, dedicating himself to helping others in thanks for his deliverance? Only God knew. Only God would know if he lived or died and only God ever saw truly into the devil's heart.

ABEL MORGAN

37

After my father's funeral I collected all the documents I could find pertaining to my father's life. The journal I remembered him writing in was in his large travelling box, along with others I had not seen before. I added all the papers connected with his nursery business, which I would take to my lawyer in London. There was also a letter to me from my father, which his lawyer handed to me privately and which I was very glad to have. I packed everything into the box and the following day I took it and Christophe back to London.

There had been a little trouble over the will because I had changed my name in Jamaica and could not prove myself, but both William and Turlough vouched for me to my father's lawyer, allowing him to recognise me as the heir and allowing me to inherit. Back in London I spoke at length to my lawyer. I told him my change of name had been necessary in that lawless place, having been, against my will, surgeon on a privateer. I kept secret my life on board the *Revenge* and there were none to gainsay me. He drew up fresh documents restoring to me my proper name, which was a great relief. My friends found my story most diverting. Hans, once he knew my proper name, discovered that my father had been a member of the Royal Society, respected in past years for his experiments with plant breeding. It gave me much pleasure, as a member also, to know it.

I did not need to practise medicine for the sake of an income as I had more than enough without, so I chose to take very few patients, reserving most of my time for my friends at the Society, where we discussed all manner of interesting topics.

Christophe was soon at Oxford with his tutor and in his letters to me it sounded as if he was applying himself well. Letters from his tutor mentioned several exploits that Christophe had not, but I remained well pleased with him and amused at his small transgressions. However, in October, I learnt of the death of his mother and that grieved him badly. He came home for a while. I paid for prayers to be said and we went to church to hear them together. We also went to see the progress on the building of the new St Paul's. It had not yet been consecrated, but I promised my son that as soon as it was I would pay for prayers to be said there for his mother, every year, on the anniversary of her death.

Before he returned to his studies, he spent much time talking to me about our time in Jamaica and his love for his mother, as well as for the children who had been lost. I had not thought much about our island life since returning to England, but he needed to relive his childhood and I listened patiently.

The night after he had gone back to Oxford I had a terrible dream. I had, I thought, successfully buried the memory of the day when Rowan Mantle and Black Tom had died, but now out it came to haunt me anew. Again, I saw Rowan splayed on the ground, his sightless eyes an accusation. Again, I saw Tom step past me into oblivion; however, this time it was not Rowan's corpse he took with him, but me. I woke shuddering. I went to my father's box and took up the letter he had written to me. It gave me such comfort to read his wisdom within it. I thought of my own son and his sadness. He needed a mother and a house full of siblings to cheer him. Of course, I could never replace his lost playmates, but perhaps I should look about me for a new wife. I would do my best to choose wisely and try to be a more loving and understanding husband than I ever had before.

The year turned and spring came again. On a warm May afternoon, with bees busy in the apple blossom and lambs bleating in the pastures, Christophe and I travelled from London to Dario and went to church to say prayers for the soul of Christopher Morgan. It was our first visit since his death.

It is small, St Mary's, though charming and full of boyhood memories for me. Imagine my surprise when we went into the church to see a new tomb in the little side aisle where I had expected a tablet on the wall. Covering it was a cloth of dark velvet and next to it stood Turlough. I was confused and a little angry. He had not said he was building a tomb. Had he thought a simple tablet not good enough for the man he liked to call 'Father'? I felt bested by him in some competition, which was unworthy of me on this solemn day. I struggled hard to let the feeling go.

Prayers were said and then Turlough stood forward at the head of the tomb. He took one edge of the velvet in his stone-roughened hand and asked me to take the other. Together we pulled back the cloth to reveal his work.

My breath caught in my throat. This was most unexpected, and I was quite unmanned. Next to me, at the height of my shoulder as if on a bier lay the carved figure of my father. It was unmistakable.

He was dressed as he had been when we met in the arbour and his face was as recently remembered, with all its lines and creases. One hand held a single rose. The hand was on his heart, as so often it had been, and his eyes were closed. The stone was so beautifully carved he looked almost as if he might wake. It was the very image of my father at rest.

I looked across at Turlough to thank him. I wanted to compliment him, but I found I couldn't speak with my heart so full. I could see, in the delicate strokes of his chisel, how much love had guided his hand. It expressed a greater love for my father than I had felt for many years, thinking him already dead.

I looked again at the tomb through blurring eyes. It was broad, with room for another figure to lie beside him. I pushed my way around to the other side, so I could observe it. I cannot convey, even now, how much the sight affected me. She was beautiful, an exquisitely carved young woman in a delicate dress with embroidered roses at the hem, waist and sleeves, and lace at the top. Her hair fell in ringlets, with curls at her broad forehead. One elegant hand was at her breast, her long, graceful fingers entwined playfully in the marble lace. Her other hand was at her side, and when I stretched to look I could see that our father's hand was clasping hers.

I had dreamt so many dreams as a child of being rocked in my mother's arms. And now, for the first time since I had been a newborn babe, I saw her face. I felt a grief far greater than any I had felt at my father's death. Never had I sat on that lap, nor clung to her skirts as a little boy. She had never healed my hurts, nor had I ever slept with the scent of her near me. Seeing her marble image made me grateful to my foster brother for thinking of making it, and indeed I thanked him through my tears, but looking on her this way I seemed to feel the pain of her loss for the very first time, as if she had been taken from me only yesterday and I a helpless babe.

How curious are we humans and how wayward life can be. I had mourned my father years ago, when he was still alive. Seeing my mother over thirty years after her death, I only now was able to grieve instead of simply regretting her absence. And yet, looking on those images of my parents I felt a lifting of my heart. For they had both been lost to me and each other for so many years and now, at last, they were found.

APPENDIX

Letter found with the last will of
Sir Christopher Bardolph Morgan

My dearest boy Abel,
You will discover, if you ever return, that Rumfustian House,
along with my garden and the extensive nursery is yours. My will
specifies that Jane and William will remain there with enough
money to support them until such time as they die. After that, if
you are still not returned, the house will be let, the nursery sold and
the income invested in the upkeep of the house and outbuildings.
My lawyer in Chineborough, Mr Davies, insists I should enter
an end date to this curious arrangement and so I have set the last
day of December 1762, when you would have reached the age of
one hundred. In case fire or other disaster should befall the house
after my demise, I have directed that at my death various small
items should be lodged at Mr Davies' chambers for you. My books
and journals, my notes about my beloved roses and my old silk
dressing gown, along with the peacock feathers you so loved as a
child. They will all be there. Forgive the sentimentality of an old
man. I also leave you my pruning knife, which I had made to

my design and carry everywhere with me. It is a very useful little item. Who would have thought that I would finally become a gardener! I often think of our early endeavours with amusement, overlaid with much sadness.

I am investigating the purchase of a small house in Chineborough along with a workshop, which I will give to Turlough. He is already a promising stonemason and shows every sign of being a good businessman too. I hope you will learn to love him for my sake. Against all the odds, he found a place in my heart and has made it possible for me to live after losing you and, moreover, to continue to work and hope for your return, which I have steadfastly done.

The rest of my fortune I leave to you and Turlough equally. There will be enough for you both to live in a small way as gentlemen, if you so wish. If you have a profession or trade like Turlough it will ease your journey through life.

May God bless you, Abel, should He be in His heaven. It is my greatest wish to see you before I die. I cannot reconcile myself to your death. I simply cannot. But I have learnt to forgive myself for losing you. If I can offer you any advice, it is to look at your life squarely, at your achievements and failings. Be honest about them, resolve to put right what you can and do better in future. Above all, forgive yourself for anything that troubles your conscience. Don't allow guilt to damage your life, as I did for far too long.

If we do not meet again in this life I earnestly hope and pray we will be together in the next.

Your always loving father,
Sir Christopher Morgan

AUTHOR'S NOTE

On the theme of things not always being as they seem.

When I came across the word 'rumfustian' in the *Wordsworth Dictionary of Pirates*, which was first published in New York as *Pirates! Facts on File* it seemed perfect as a name for the inn in this story. It is described as a hot drink much enjoyed by pirates in the seventeenth and eighteenth centuries, containing not just alcohol, but also eggs and spices. However, on further investigation, there seems to be no earlier written use of the word than the early nineteenth century, which is much too late for my needs.

Maybe my choice was not in use during the seventeenth century, at least certainly not written down, but separately, both parts of the word certainly were. 'Rum', perhaps from the sixteenth century 'rumbullion' was in use for the drink distilled from sugar. 'Fustian' is much older, in use in the twelfth century for a type of cheap cloth. Dyed dark it could look good, but soon betrayed its lack of quality. It was often used for padding, hence the second meaning: pompous, overblown, cheap, pretentious.

Whoever invented this beverage, and there are various recipes online, the name whenever coined, must surely be a joke. For, in spite of it containing copious amounts of strong alcohol, in no recipe can I find any mention of rum.

ACKNOWLEDGEMENTS

Many thanks to my agent Jane Conway-Gordon for getting behind this book so enthusiastically, and to Jane Bailey, who read it and told me Jane would love it.

Thanks also to all the friends and family who read early versions and gave me feedback, or listened patiently while I rambled on about it. Helpful conversation came from writers Linda Newbery, Julia Jarman, Celia Rees and Adele Geras, as well as Jamila Gavin and Wendy Cooling. Thanks too to Rachel Hunt, until fairly recently House and Collections manager at Cotehele, National Trust, where I wrote some of this book, and took great delight in the metal hand and forearm which hangs in the great hall. A copy has now been made of that contraption and, if you are fortunate, you can handle it!

Some years ago, Mark Van Oss decided to hold his birthday dinner in Istanbul with friends and family. As well as having a hilarious time at dinner with Caroline, Mark and others, I so loved wandering about the old city that I was sure I would write about it.

It took a while, but *Outrageous Fortune* would be much the poorer if I hadn't gone on that trip, so thank you Mark for inviting me.

Some of the books I read were of particular help. The Cotswolds volume of the *Pevsner Architectural Guides* by David Verey and Alan Brooks, which spends much time in my car, introduced me to Stroud sculptor Samuel Baldwin, who inspired the ending of the book when I came across his exquisite work in Miserdon church. Many thanks to John Smith for giving me the book.

Other useful publications were *Postman's Horn*, an anthology of seventeenth-century letters collected by Arthur Bryant, Barry Coward's *Social Change and Continuity in Early Modern Britain*, Antonia Fraser's *Charles II*, Claire Tomlin's *Samuel Pepys, The Unequalled Self*, as well as several volumes of the Arthur Bryant biography of the same man. John Harvey's *Early Nurserymen*, from my late father's shelves, was also very helpful. On my Kindle is the fascinating and instructive *The Surgeon's Mate* by John Woodall, published in 1617.

Finally, many thanks must go to Susie, Kelly and all at Allison & Busby for making the journey from manuscript to printed book such a great delight.

CYNTHIA JEFFERIES is a long-established writer for children whose work has been translated into more than a dozen languages. She was born in Gloucestershire and her love of history was encouraged by regular family outings to anything of interest, from great cathedrals to small museums. Having moved to Scotland and back to Stroud, she has always made time to write and her abiding interest in Restoration England has never left her. *The Outrageous Fortune of Abel Morgan* is her first historical novel for adults.

cynthiajefferies.co.uk   *@cindyjefferies1*